Praise for

SCARS & STRIFE

"*Scars & Strife* is a gripping portrayal of the challenges faced by soldiers like Randy Andrews, echoing the struggles of many who served in combat. Randy's journey through the shadows of PTSD, his quest for redemption, and his unlikely bond with Matilda, the mountain lion, is truly captivating. This poignant narrative sheds light on the complexities of returning home from war and the power of resilience. A must-read for anyone seeking insight into the human spirit's capacity for healing and transformation."

—Melissa Melendez, California State Senator (Ret.), Navy Veteran

"In *Scars & Strife*, M. E. Johnson has produced a novel as indelible as Ben Fountain's *Billy Lynn's Long Halftime Walk* and just as powerful, but with a surprising and touching bit of weirdness that transcends the form. This is a work of violence, of grace, of compassion, and of the nature of the human spirit. I've not read a debut this confident in a long, long time."

—Tod Goldberg, *New York Times* Best-Selling Author of the *Gangsterland* Quartet

"M. E. (Mark) Johnson and I are both career military field-grade officers with advanced degrees, command experience, and combat deployments. I had a feeling that with all that training, education, and military experience, Mark could probably write a compelling, believable book. Boy was I right!"

—John McBrearty, Author

"A story of hell, redemption, and raging peace written by a veteran who has experienced all three."

—Aaron "the Hammer" Grant, US Marine Corps, Staff NCO, Author of *Taking Baghdad: Victory in Iraq with the US Marines*, Teacher, Master of Military History

"Colonel M. E. (Mark) Johnson delivers a bang-up story with a strong statement about the fine line between heroic and crazy. Retired Army Ranger Randy Andrews is a scarred hero, physically and emotionally, who rejects conventional PTSD treatment, and ultimately, with the help of a not-too-conventional therapy animal, finds his own peace. Johnson's frenetic pace and deft use of flashback enhance the sense of what Andrews experiences as his mind shifts between his violent past and his precarious present. Andrews is finally able to reconcile with his past, but his battle is never fully won. And neither are the battles of the far too many heroes that still carry their scars and have to fight every day."

—Brian Osterndorf, Colonel, US Army (Ret.), Author of *Finnegan Begins Again*

Scars & Strife
by M. E. Johnson
© Copyright 2024 M. E. Johnson

ISBN 979-8-88824-252-0

All rights reserved. No part of this publication may be reproduced, stored in a retrieval system, or transmitted in any form or by any means—electronic, mechanical, photocopy, recording, or any other—except for brief quotations in printed reviews, without the prior written permission of the author.

This is a work of fiction. All the characters in this book are fictitious, and any resemblance to actual persons, living or dead, is purely coincidental. The names, incidents, dialogue, and opinions expressed are products of the author's imagination and are not to be construed as real.

Published by

3705 Shore Drive
Virginia Beach, VA 23455
800-435-4811
www.koehlerbooks.com

SCARS & STRIFE

M. E. JOHNSON

VIRGINIA BEACH
CAPE CHARLES

THE RANGER CREED

Recognizing that I volunteered as a Ranger, fully knowing the hazards of my chosen profession.

I will always endeavor to uphold the prestige, honor, and high *esprit de corps* of the Rangers.

Acknowledging the fact that a Ranger is a more elite soldier who arrives at the cutting edge of battle by land, sea, or air, I accept the fact that, as a Ranger, my country expects me to move further, faster and fight harder than any other soldier.

Never shall I fail my comrades. I will always keep myself mentally alert, physically strong and morally straight and I will shoulder more than my share of the task whatever it may be, one hundred percent and then some.

Gallantly will I show the world that I am a specially selected and well-trained Soldier. My courtesy to superior officers, neatness of dress and care of equipment shall set the example for others to follow.

Energetically will I meet the enemies of my country. I shall defeat them on the field of battle for I am better trained and will fight with all my might. Surrender is not a Ranger word. I will never leave a fallen comrade to fall into the hands of the enemy and under no circumstances will I ever embarrass my country. Readily will I display the intestinal fortitude required to fight on to the Ranger objective and complete the mission though I be the lone survivor.

Rangers lead the way!

CHAPTER 1

Five minutes ago, I'd had it all figured out. But now Athena was gone, and the border, guarded by an agent I would have to talk to, was fifty meters away. Sweat beaded on my temples and trailed down the back of my neck.

It had been a while since I'd heard any sound from the truck bed, so I stuck my head out the driver's window, aiming my good ear at the cage. *Nothing.* She must have screamed herself out on the road north of Rosarito Beach.

I can fix this from the US side, I told myself. *She loves me. I can fix this. I can fix this.*

I tried to believe it.

That's when I saw the box. It taunted me, *"You think you got it figured out? Who the fuck are you kidding?"*

It was the size of a car tire, seventy-five meters ahead in a gutter just inside the US border. The flaps on top were interwoven. This was bad. Really bad.

A plastic bag floated in a light breeze down the gutter, brushing the cardboard. The box stayed, motionless. I began to see through its walls to the recesses within at wires, artillery rounds. I knew what it was capable of. I scanned the windows of the buildings on the hill to my right, looking for a killer on a cell phone.

Yes, Dr. Berlin, I know what triggers are.

I jammed on the brakes, my heart pounding hard, then harder still. My breathing turned to panting. I felt dizzy, the edges of my vision getting soft, the sense of losing it within a flashback.

No one cared. Cars drove by the box without slowing. Two cops walked on the sidewalk a few feet from it, laughing.

I looked in the rearview mirror, focusing on my face. Anything to keep moving, to force that fucking box out of my brain. *Focus Randy.*

Ruben and Athena were right. I did look like that sheriff in the old *Gunsmoke* series. I saw it then, for the first time. A bit more beat up, but not from age. Thirteen pain lines radiating from my eyes across to my temples, one for each tour. A jagged, tanned scar running down my left cheek, a remnant of that day I carried Tomlinson out of a kill zone in Fallujah, one of his legs gone, the other horribly shredded, a dead weight moaning in unconscious agony. Saving him to live in a wheelchair.

I was a hero, they said.

Better to die and avoid the pain of leaving soldiers behind. There was nothing from that day I wanted to remember, and so little to show for doing what I was ordered to do.

It was September 11, 2014. Thirteen years to the day after the merry-go-round began.

But the visions always came in waves. I looked away from the box to a Carta Blanca billboard that stood on the hill. The beer bottle glistened, becoming a metronome repeating words, telling me how fucking crazy all this was.

Turn back, Randy. This is sooo fuckin' stupid. I am everything you need.

That same voice once told me to run, and I did. Now what would I do?

A two-car-length space ahead of my truck now was empty, and horns sounded behind me. These weren't courtesy beeps. I tried to pull myself to the present. Sand, ashes, and three Pacifico beer caps were on the black rubber floor mat under my feet. The photo of my boys was smack dab in the center of my dash, torn and taped after seven tours. The dried blood on one edge was probably mine.

The voice of that billboard came from a neighborhood in my

head I would not visit anymore.

I smelled Athena's perfume and shampoo. "What's the most important thing?" she'd asked on our night at the beach. And I looked again in the mirror, seeing my son John's eyes in mine. Blue-green and piercing, letting me see so many things others missed.

Move it Randy, I told myself. *It's not an IED.*

I took my foot off the brake, letting the car idle forward a space. The honking stopped. A Buick with Iowa plates in front of me crossed into the US. I took a few deep breaths as I moved ahead, then stopped at the big white line across my lane. I handed my passport to the Border Patrol agent.

Black had no slimming effect on this guy. He had whitewalls, a hardcore military cut, but I knew this fat fuck never had served outside of a kiosk. The bulge under his lower lip said he was hiding a wad of gum, maybe dip. He took my passport but didn't open it.

Two chunky white hands, one holding my passport, appeared on the door, curling into my personal airspace in the cab. The gold ring on his left hand gleamed. That wouldn't come off without a hacksaw.

My ring finger had a deep empty groove.

I listened. Still no sounds from the bed. A snuffed-out joint was on the mat by the Pacifico caps. I kicked it out a rusty hole in the floorboard.

Then I heard a slight rattle from the lock on the crate.

"Something bothering you?" he asked, studying my face.

I was jumpy. This wasn't going as planned.

"No, I'm okay."

"So, what's in the back of the truck?" the agent said with a jerk of his head toward the XXXL dog crate under a blue tarp. He spoke with the authority of a man long accustomed to having his fat ass kissed. I envisioned him administering a full body cavity search—he looked like the type they gave that job to—and my rear end tensed.

Focus.

"I said, what's in the back of the truck?" He popped his gum twice, punctuating his words.

I took a deep breath.

Showtime.

"It's a cougar, a mountain lion." I added "Agent" as an afterthought—as much deference as I'd pay to a man with a gut stretching the buttons on an American uniform.

He studied my face like I was some freak, then moved his eyes to the bed of the truck. They went back and forth across the square bulk under the tarp. Then he angled his head sideways like a dog hearing a high-pitched noise. He let out a long, breathy sigh that said, *It's too early for this shit.*

I felt better, back on mission.

"A *live* ... mountain lion," I added.

He took his hands off the window, opened my passport and mouthed, "John Randall Andrews the third; birthdate, November 10, 1973. Age—" He paused, calculating. "Forty-two." Dumb fuck couldn't add. He held my passport, open to the photo page, by my face, jabbing it into my cheek.

"Really, mister, uh?"

"Andrews. John Randall Andrews. The third," I said.

He shut my passport with a snap.

"A lion? I don't hear a peep from whatever you got back there. You really want to play it this way? Mister—" He opened my passport again. "Andrews? You want to tell me what the hell's in the back of the truck?"

This motherfucker was really *that* dense? Then I saw the name on the tag pinned to his uniform and recognized the gene pool.

Clutterbuck? Could Captain Clutterbuck be related to this guy? Fuck me.

Seven years ago, Captain Clutterbuck got blown up by an artillery round shoved up the ass of a dead horse.

The day Clutterbuck hit ground in Tal Afar, two mortars dropped on the far side of the forward operating base, prompting him to suit up in full battle rattle and run to headquarters yelling, "We're under attack! Take cover! FOB Reasoner's under attack!" His face was flushed. He talked fast.

Those of us who had been there a while slept through impacts like these. They came all day, every day. When your time was up, it was up. So, we laughed at him. He was embarrassed. After that, he got dangerous, making a big show of being the badass. Clutterbuck was always trying to get the BC to sign off on some dangerous unnecessary mission. He got shot down every time.

"His men'll follow him anywhere," I said to the NCOs at our table in the chow hall, "but only for the fuckin' entertainment value." I got stuck following him that day in August 2005.

We were pulling a security mission to a refinery south of Tal Afar. Clutterbuck was the senior officer. The route we'd planned took us through the village ahead. From the lead vehicle, I saw the ass-end of the animal at two hundred meters. Eleven Humvees were behind mine.

"Slow down to walking speed," I told Espinosa, a scrawny Mexican PFC from El Paso with a ton of zits. He was getting a grip on a big one in the center of his forehead. "And leave that shit alone. Unless you want to die from some fuckin' haji infection."

I looked through binoculars. "A horse," I said to the air. "Camel, maybe." It was a hundred and sixteen degrees and the carcass was bloated. The stench must be unbelievable, yet the locals left it there? That was too much, even for these people.

I got on the radio.

"I'm calling a halt. Dead animal, two hundred meters. Possible IED. One o'clock. A horse, I think." I studied the map on the screen to my left. "That's Hami up there. We'll pick up that dirt road we passed a klick back. That'll skirt us around the village. It hits the forty-seven north of this shithole."

Clutterbuck was running drag two hundred meters back. Maybe I should have said, "Sir, recommend we call a halt." That would have let him pretend he was in charge. But I'd seen too many soldiers killed. Most officers had to be told what to do. Clutterbuck required spoon-feeding.

I expected, "Roger that, sergeant." Instead, his Humvee pulled to the left and moved up the line. As he passed the midpoint of the convoy, his voice came out of the radio. "Third platoon, fall in behind second. First, you're behind third." I was the first platoon sergeant. Eight Humvees were moving up on the left at five miles per hour, passing at low speed as if this was some fuckin' Sunday drive.

The air was dry and still; the only sounds were the hum of our engines and the tires moving on sand. Dust kicked up and hung. Clutterbuck's Humvee approached.

The fuck is he doin'?

"Hey. Espinosa. Open that fuckin' window." Clutterbuck's profile was in the front passenger window as he passed. I shouted at him. "What the fuck you doin', captain? Goddammit, stay back, we don't need to go there."

Clutterbuck must have heard, but he never looked. As his Humvee neared the bloated animal, he repeated his order. "First platoon, fall in . . . *the rear.*" His voice was metallic, staticky. It was deeper than usual, as if he was trying to sound important. I sensed his ego, another dumbshit officer who'd seen too many lead-from-the-front war movies.

His Humvee approached the animal. The blast was huge, probably three or four 155 mm rounds, rocking my Humvee. Clutterbuck's flew skyward at an angle, landing on its side twenty feet across the road. Then it was all one big fire, black smoke and dirt engulfing the town. Two of our SAWs, squad automatic weapons, opened up, but I couldn't see what they were firing at.

Half a horse leg dropped to the ground to the right of my Humvee. Bloody chunks of meat from the animal—and possibly Clutterbuck—spread over an area the size of a football field.

And, damn, the *stench*. That dead horse did smell to high heaven.

Something that looked like a ribeye steak cut by a hacksaw was hanging off the brush guard of my Humvee. It didn't smell, so I figured I was looking at a piece of the captain. Then it slid, hanging on until it dropped to the dirt, leaving a thin trail of bloody slime on the tan metal. It bubbled and dried as I watched.

Another dead hero. He took two GIs with him. They always do.

Clutterbuck's driver survived, but what's the fuckin' point? The kid lost his legs, right arm, dick and balls in that blast. And he had a TBI. I was told he wasn't right in the head when they shipped him home—a hero—to his family.

A horse's ass blown up by a bomb shoved up a horse's ass. Talk about poetic justice.

A few days later, Vince, Darnell and I were kicking it in Vince's trailer. They were my battle buddies, my best friends. We were drunk. I told them about that ribeye. Vince suggested I go back to Hami, find it and mail it to his parents.

"Whose parents?" I was laughing so goddamn hard I could barely make words. "Clutterfuck's? Or the motherfuckin' horse's?"

"Wait, wait, fuck, get this, fuckin' get this." Darnell paused, gathering air for something big. He held up his hand, palm facing me like a man taking the oath. "You think it would make it through customs? Or get seized for being a *fucking animal product* from an unapproved country?"

We spit beer in simultaneous explosions.

It all was so funny back then.

US Border Patrol Agent Clutterfuck was scowling. *Did I smile?*

Perhaps a deliberate tone would pierce his fog. I tried again.

"No, no, Agent Clutter... buck. There is a cage under the tarp, and inside that cage is a... fucking... mountain... lion. Like I said, the first time."

I said "fucking" rather than "fuckin," my customary shortened version of the word. I thought it made me sound dignified, more serious. I left out, *"you dumbshit."*

His mouth was open with the expression that of a man not quite ready to believe there's steaming dog shit on his manicured lawn. He exhaled a long, slow breath, then popped his gum again. He didn't know what the fuck to do but was trying to act like he did. He stepped into the kiosk, shut the door and spoke on a telephone. I couldn't hear what he said, but he walked out with a shit-eating grin that said, *"I'll show you."*

Clutterfuck, the name my mind had reassigned him, put his hands on the edge of my door again, then moved his face eight inches from mine. "One last time, Andrews. You want to tell me what's back there?"

I'd stared down far more dangerous assholes than this clown and wouldn't have flinched, but Clutterfuck's breath smelled like something crawled in his mouth and died. I pulled back. He nodded as if he'd scored a point.

I shook my head and spoke, facing the floor. "I told you. And don't stick your fingers near the crate during your inspection, agent. You'll lose them."

I held my breath.

Clutterfuck's expression said he wanted to beat my ass but could not spare the time. Important duties and so many more tourists to interrogate. It was almost nine in the morning, and a line of cars stretched a mile behind me.

"See that? That big sign over there? The one that says, *Secondary Inspection Area?* You see it?" It was bigger than a Greyhound bus with six-foot black letters on a white background.

His tone said I was a fool. Funny. Two men thinking the same thing, and only I was right.

He didn't wait for my answer.

"Pull into Lane Two." Then he barked. "Now!"

And then I was one hundred percent on United States soil, out of that goddamned line and downrange from Clutterfuck's breath. The Mexicans would have returned Matilda to the nightclub. Not now. Mexico could keep my baggage, but Matilda and I were home.

I drove by the box, still on the side of the road, and felt nauseous. I parked in Lane Two.

I kept scanning the people entering the US at the pedestrian crossing, hoping to see Athena, wanting the three of us to be together again, and finally safe.

The agent who came over after fifteen minutes was a short, wiry man with eyes that moved back and forth from the crate to me. "Good morning, Mr. Andrews. How are you today, sir?" Agent Dempsey spoke as if he really did give a shit about my day. He wore the Border Patrol version of fatigues, olive drab, complete with a vest with Kevlar plates. I could see his belt buckle.

"It's been reported you wouldn't tell the agent what's in the back of your truck. Then you told him you were hauling a lion. He said you were nervous and agitated."

"What?" I responded. "No, no, no, that's not true. I told Clutterbuck what I was hauling. Twice. No, three times."

"So. Tell me. What's in the back of the truck?"

I looked into his eyes.

"Agent Dempsey, on the bed there is a mountain lion. Not an African lion. A cougar, a big cat of about a hundred and twenty pounds in a locked dog crate. The key is taped to the lock. If you put your hands near the bars, you will lose them."

Dempsey nodded with an expression that said cougars routinely showed up at his secondary checkpoint. He moved outside my hearing, leaned his chin to his chest and spoke to a Motorola clipped to his shirt. He shook his head a few times and laughed as he discussed the wacko who said he was hauling a live mountain lion.

Three more Border Patrol agents, wearing the same olive drab uniforms as Dempsey, speed-walked from an office. They stopped near the front end of my truck and began shuffling their feet. None of them approached the bed. Their eyes darted from the bed to me, as if something dangerous was back there.

And I suppose that was not that far off.

"Get out of the vehicle. Stand here." Dempsey pointed to the ground by his feet. Five of us gathered at the front end of my truck. I watched the crate. They watched me. The only noise was a nervous scraping of rubber soles on concrete.

A fifth agent approached. He was leading a German shepherd wearing a vest that said *US Customs and Border Protection, EOD.* The pair began moving along my truck, the dog sniffing the front bumper, then the tires, then the doors. At the bed, the shepherd stood on his hind legs, bracing its front paws against the truck and trying to get his nose against the crate. He stretched tall, but four inches separated his nose from the tarp.

I'd watched bomb dogs. They alerted by sitting. But this shepherd lost all bomb-dog composure. He barked, then growled and lunged at the big blue cube on the bed. His teeth bared, he strained at the leash. His claws scratched the metal. I shuddered at the shrill sound.

Then the cage rustled.

Agent Dempsey walked with the handler as he hauled the shepherd away. They were talking, but the handler had trouble staying in the conversation. Seventy-five feet away the dog was still straining and lunging to get back to my truck.

Dempsey returned and stood before me. The three agents joined him, moving to a half circle. I was the center. Dempsey wasn't polite anymore.

"Okay Andrews. Let's talk turkey here. We *are* searching the bed of your truck. You're not moving a bomb and there are no drugs. You're *now* saying you have a mountain lion back there. Anything more you want to tell us about what's under that goddamned tarp?"

These guys were pumped, their upper bodies leaning forward. Unlike Clutterbuck, they looked as if they really might beat my ass.

"What? I've told you four *fuckin'* times there's a *live mountain lion* on the truck. You want me to take off the tarp? Fuckin' here. *I'll* do it."

I started to move, but Dempsey put his palm on my chest and shoved. "No way, Andrews. You stay here."

Dempsey tucked in his ass, puffed his chest and moved off. His light strut said, *I'll show you.* He took a knife from his utility belt and flicked it open with a fast wrist snap. Cutting the rope, he then grabbed a handful of tarp, yanking it into the air like a matador with a cape taunting a bull.

And Matilda saw sunlight for the first time in almost two years. She sat on her haunches, waiting, I think, for this moment.

Dempsey froze. Before him was an adult North American mountain lion, squinting in the bright light. The tendons of her front legs were tight and obvious under thick brown and tan fur.

Dempsey's mouth was open, his eyes bulging. He was staring directly at Matilda.

Big mistake, Dempsey, unless you want to throw down with a cougar.

Matilda screeched, her eyes locked on Dempsey's. It was a vicious cry that said, in cougar, *Don't fuck with me.* She jammed her right front paw against the metal bars of the crate. Four claws, each fully unsheathed and two inches in length, shot from the cage, aimed at where Dempsey's fingers had been a millisecond before. She jerked the paw side to side, hissing and snarling, claws clicking on metal. Then she pulled it back, once again ramming it into the bars and making the whole truck vibrate. I heard her water bowl hit the side of her crate.

Dempsey didn't strut anymore. He was no longer the boss. He stumbled backward toward his fellow agents. "Fuck!" he said, his feet not keeping pace with his momentum. He would have landed on his ass if two agents had not swooped in and caught his shoulders.

Well done, Matilda.

The agents stared, their faces frozen, palms on the butts of their firearms.

"Gentlemen," I said. "This is Matilda. She's American, and she's come home."

From behind came the sound of boots pounding on asphalt, getting louder. "That's him," somebody yelled.

I looked at Dempsey.

"Can you make sure she gets water? It's hot. Her bowl fell over."

Dempsey narrowed his eyes. I think he was trying to determine just how crazy I was. Then he nodded.

Four more Border Patrol agents arrived at my truck. Two of them grabbed my arms, digging their nails into my biceps as they pulled me away. Matilda watched, lowered her head, fixing her golden-brown eyes. The predator stare, sizing up kills. They saw it. We stopped.

I was not sure I'd see her again, so I looked into her eyes, a privilege she granted to only Athena and me. I felt her rhythm, understood her silent message. She would kill for me.

Then San Ysidro was gone. Instead, I saw Fallujah, that filthy square, Tomlinson screaming, Toney Bartlett's life running into a bloody pool of mud. This time I didn't leave anyone behind.

I understood this mission. Matilda stood, lifting her head, facing east where the morning sun was low in the sky. She screamed. It was long and loud, triumphant and almost human.

CHAPTER 2

Five months before, I was coming out of a flashback on the shoulder of the southbound San Diego Freeway. If the CHP officer hadn't stopped, I might still be there, staring at a box.

The cop was a big White guy with a sunburn and a deep voice who sauntered to my truck window with his hands on his hips. His hair, gray and cut short, said he was close to retirement. I saw my face in his shades. It was frozen, scared, like some fucked up death mask. I didn't recognize it.

"What are you doing here?" he asked. "I've driven by four times." He put his palm on the hood of my truck, impatient.

I told him.

His face changed from smug arrogance to bewilderment. "That's why? A bomb inside a box? That's why you're here?" I wanted to sink into the beat-up upholstery. Half-shaking his head, he asked for my license and registration. When I came back clear, he said, "Point it out to me. The box."

He couldn't see it at first. One hundred meters ahead, weeds covering most of it. "Is that it?" he asked, pointing in the general direction. He was smiling, then started chuckling. "I'll get that-there IED off the road, Marine."

Gallantly will I show the world that I am a specially selected and well-trained Soldier.

The Ranger Creed. How many times all of us had recited it on missions before going in to kill, or tackle anything big. *Rangers lead the way!* was tattooed on my arm.

But I looked away. Let him think I was a Marine.

He drove ahead and stopped, shaking his head as he picked up the box. He was laughing as he tossed it in his trunk.

I imagined him on a barstool after his shift, beer in hand, telling his fellow CHPs about the wack-job Marine who couldn't move because of a box. He was laughing, choking on his Budweiser.

"That goddamned Marine was sitting there for two hours. You get that? Two fucking hours, for a goddamned *box*. A box, a fuckin' box!" His buddies were howling, pounding their fists on the bar.

I watched him drive off. After ten minutes, I started the engine and continued south. I couldn't take him seeing me again.

Dr. Berlin didn't ask why I was two hours and ten minutes late, so I didn't have to lie. Other than a brief glance to see who answered to "John Andrews," she didn't look at me as we walked from the waiting room to her office. She waddled. I think her hips were bad.

"Good to see you again, John."

I had told her at our first and second sessions I went by Randy. The only reason I was meeting with this woman a third time was to prove to the judge I wasn't dangerous.

It was quiet, the only sound the ticking of an antique mantel clock on a credenza by her desk. "This is for you," Dr. Berlin said. The pamphlet made a whoosh as she slid it across the desk. It stopped in front of me in perfect reading position.

So you think you may have PTSD? The VA is here to help!

A nerdy-looking cartoon White guy at a desk had his hand on his chin. A big bubble connected to his head by smaller ones showed a younger version of him in fatigues, hands over his anguished face. He was looking down on a bloody body.

Dr. Berlin folded her hands into a prayer pose, and looked up with a patient smile. It was condescending, something adults save for little kids needing guidance. We were about the same age, but she had a good hundred pounds on me and was breathing heavily from the short walk to her office. Her face was round, pink-cheeked, and framed by red curly hair. Some would describe her looks as "pleasant." Not me. I only saw a bloated Raggedy Ann doll come to life.

How could this woman understand anything about me?

I think she was waiting for some spark of enlightenment, for me to hold up that pamphlet and say, "Ah, that explains the crazy shit." We just looked at each other. That pamphlet didn't tell me anything I didn't already know.

"John, I'm diagnosing you with post-traumatic stress disorder. PTSD. And survivor's guilt, though that's not a diagnosis, per se. Do you know what they are?"

She didn't wait for a spark this time. "John, post-traumatic stress disorder is a trauma- and stress-related disorder, a mental disease, if you will. It can be extraordinarily debilitating. Individuals with PTSD have trouble functioning in society. Their relationships, such as marriage, suffer. However, there are remedial options, regimens of palliative treatment such as prolonged exposure and cognitive processing therapy, CPT. Anti-depressants and anti-anxiety medications are often prescribed to suppress nightmares."

She paused.

"And, John, individuals with PTSD have triggers. Triggers," she paused again, looking at me briefly, "are otherwise benign events, things in our lives that *trigger* a traumatic reaction, called a flashback. Would you like me to explain them? Or to give you an example?"

Boxes? Thumbs-up? Dead animals? An engine backfiring? A girl with a heavy coat? Fresh concrete? Beach balls? Bridges? Where are the civilians; the street's too fuckin' quiet? The street's too loud? A HiLux? "Who Knew" by Pink? Whatever made me shove my wife's head through drywall?

Give me a sec, doc. I can come up with a dozen more.

"No, I know what they are."

"It happens like this, John. A soldier is sickened by witnessing a traumatic event, such as seeing someone killed. They may associate things they smell or see, *while the trauma is ongoing*, with the trauma itself. John, you've told me about a few traumatic incidents you have experienced. Though," and here she touched her pen to her lower lip as she rechecked her notes, "your descriptions are clinical, distant, as if you are reporting something that happened to someone else. Your brain has now attached sensory perceptions to those traumas."

Her hands were waving, punctuating. Raggedy Ann sure did like hearing herself talk.

"I worked with one veteran whose trigger, believe it or not, was a toilet. He was injured by a bomb hidden in a Western-style toilet on the road somewhere in Iraq. It caused him major adjustment problems in civilian life."

She smiled. I almost left.

A poor fuckin' GI is out there shitting on the floor because his trigger is a goddamned toilet. That is one sorry SOB.

My neck was tight. It hurt. I was shoving my head down into my chest, but it wasn't getting down far enough.

I half-listened.

" . . . become triggers . . . buttons that turn on your body's alarm system . . . one of them . . . pushed, your brain switches . . . danger modes . . . become frightened . . . heart to start racing . . . sights, sounds and feelings of the trauma rushing back . . . a flashback."

Who the fuck could live like this?

This doctor had a corner office. It was all windows. Outside it was bright, with the sun bouncing off the glass of the neighboring high-rises. San Diego Bay was shimmering blue. I saw cars, looking like a string of ants, moving across the bridge to Coronado Island. Maybe I'd get there one day.

"What's the treatment?"

She nodded, as if my question was a breakthrough. "The therapies, John, involve exposure, in a structured therapeutic setting, of course, to the traumatic incident. They are effective, meaning they have a high success rate, with individuals such as yourself afflicted with PTSD and PTSD-related social problems. Most people *do* get better." She fixed on my eyes briefly, impassive doll eyes staring out of her puffy face.

"Are they—the therapies—something you would be interested in?" She looked down and began writing in my file. In my left ear, I heard the tick of her clock. The ringing in my right ear kept getting louder like it did when my heart pounded. I was still shoving my head into my chest.

Dr. Berlin's words were rehearsed, as if she'd given these *options* to a long line of vets, including that fucked-up guy who flashed back when taking a shit.

"That is the recommended therapy, John. All the treatments involve facing your thoughts and feelings. Can we do that?"

We?

Exposure to the traumatic incident?

"No," I said.

I walked out of her office and never went back.

I stopped at the front desk of a Motel 6 in Fullerton, my home since I retired, to collect my mail. The clerk handed me two letters.

The first was from the Orange County Superior Court. Sitting on my bed, I poured a shot of Jack Daniels. Then another. Then a third. I would have kept going, but the pint was empty. I opened the letter.

I had been divorced for two days. The court limited my visitation with my boys: . . . *telephonic visitation every first and third Wednesday of each month from 6:30 to 7:30 p.m. Responsible party, either Petitioner or party designated by Petitioner, to monitor all calls. The Court will consider modifying this order to allow additional visitation only upon receipt of a letter from Respondent's therapist with the*

Veteran's Administration. Said letter must address Respondent's treatment and potential for violence against the minor children.

"Fucking dumbass," I said aloud. I don't know who I was most angry at. I handed that cheating bitch everything she needed to screw me.

I wished I could remember throwing Sara, *a.k.a. the Petitioner*, my now-ex-wife, into the kitchen wall. That was one flashback I wanted the satisfaction of reliving, of her head leaving a volleyball-sized dent in the drywall of the home she shared with my boys.

It was supposed to be *our home*. We would start over, be a family. How the fuck did she become the good guy in this?

"Randy's face was strange," she told the cop who arrested me. "He looked gone. He kept saying, 'Where's your helmet, corporal, where's your fuckin' helmet?'"

I *had* been gone. I was reliving nine years earlier on FOB Iron Horse in Sadr City, the huge Baghdad slum on the east side of the Tigris River.

Corporal Landin never had a chance to put his fucking helmet on. Right after I grabbed him the mortar hit, taking off the top three inches of his skull and knocking me on my ass. Landin's back absorbed the shrapnel, except for three metal shards that missed him and ripped into my right shoulder. It felt like a molten iron maggot crawling into my muscle. I wanted to scream but couldn't open my mouth. I saw tufts of black hair around the hole in Landin's head waving in the breeze. Then, nothing.

I had forgotten what I'd said to Landin until I read the police report.

The second letter was from John, my oldest.

He had stopped talking to me. He wouldn't answer my calls. I sent an email telling him how much I loved him, that, even though his mother and I no longer were together, the two of us would always be close. He had printed it off and written his answer in handwriting neater than I remembered.

No Randy you have no control in this relationship. You have no control over me. You are not my dad. You are my genetic father. So if you continue emailing me, I will find a new email address. I am not interested in your life. I am not interested in telling you about my life. I am not interested, nor legally required, to explain anything to you. The only reason I am contacting you is because you are my blood family. Do you understand? IF YOU WANT TO TALK TO ME, YOU NEED TO SEE A PSYCHOLOGIST.

He signed it, "John Kessler," using Sara's maiden name. I reached for the bottle of Jack, forgetting it was empty.

I left my room and came back with a fresh liter.

I woke up six hours later to shaggy bearded ISIS motherfuckers in HiLuxes waving AK-47s. I pointed the remote at the TV to change the channel when I saw the four smokestacks on the horizon. They were still pumping out that shit that made it so hard to breathe that day. Samarra.

I forgot a big one, Dr. Berlin. Smokestacks.

My vision blurred. It got so fuckin' hot that I coughed with every breath. It was August 2009 and Lieutenant Hamm was telling me I was always seeing fucking IEDs, and I was planning on getting that motherfucker back.

I woke up again. Morgan Freeman was on a beach in Zihuatanejo, Mexico. He looked happy and free. His friend Tim Robbins was smiling, working on a boat. *The Shawshank Redemption.* These men had suffered and were healing. I'd seen the movie at the theater with Sara when it first came out.

The next day, I left for Mexico.

I don't know where I was headed. Just south. I drove the beach road out of Tijuana, a Budweiser fresh from the ice chest wedged between my thighs. Seven empties rolled on the passenger floorboard.

Rosarito Beach was huge, just a mess of traffic and construction, not the quiet village Sara and I had visited in the '90s. Wall-to-wall bars. Ensenada was another thirty miles south. After that, the road opened up. I was headed down there, to a place where cell phones had no reception.

"Goodbye to You" sounded through the truck cab. Patty Smyth was as good as she'd been in 1983.

Ten miles outside of Rosarito, the engine clanked with the sound of a crowbar beating on metal. Then four more clanks, louder; now a sledgehammer bashing an engine block, followed by a grinding noise. Then the engine seized. The power steering died, and the wheel locked. I wrestled the steering wheel to the right, coasting the truck into a dirt parking lot outside a small motel. Smoke poured from under the hood. I stepped out. Oil was steaming on the engine. The inside of the hood was wet and greasy. *Fuck!*

I wasn't going anywhere, so I walked in the door under a red neon light that said, *Office,* and rented a room. The Motel Vista del Mar made the Motel 6 in Fullerton look like The Ritz.

It took three weeks and three hundred dollars for Jimenez Auto Repair to get my truck running. Its top speed was now fifty-one, and it smoked like a son of a bitch every time the gears changed.

My new home was a classic Baja dump with a million-dollar view of the ocean.

Three months passed.

CHAPTER 3

Lost, for the next ninety days—inside my head.
Those two little kids.

Charging in the front door, I kill the two jihadi motherfuckers with a burst from my M4. With a green light to take out anything that moves inside these walls, I'm running, kicking the door to the right at the top of the stairs, then seeing the AK barrel under the bed pointed at me. It's rising and I unload thirty rounds into that bed, reload, then pump another thirty, the dirty blankets turning into confetti, flying helter-skelter through the air.

I'm grabbing the bed, flipping it, seeing the two kids and the woman. They're all blood. Yelling and automatic fire from the other rooms. It's so fuckin' loud. But here it's silent. The woman's arm across the stock of the AK, her head pulp, the kids on their sides behind the woman, their arms covering their faces, trying to keep from getting shot. The little girl with the top of her head blown off, wearing no head covering, her long black hair lying in the bloody gray goo that had been her brain. The boy facing away from the door, his intestines curling out of his gut in every direction like those snakes Medusa has for hair. He's about two.

Then he raises his head and I see the big chunk missing out of it, and he asks why I killed him, his mom, and his sister. He has a high-pitched voice that sounds like John's at that age and, like always, I can't answer.

And there I was again.

Sitting up, screaming, my feet now off the side of the bed, awake and fucked up beyond all recognition, staring at an empty tequila bottle standing crooked on the lime green plastic chair I used as a nightstand.

My head was spinning. In the dark I could barely make out that chair. I was panting like an overheated dog. Sweat was making its way down my chest, heading to my crotch.

From outside came the sharp thump of a wave belting the sand, the tide incoming, drowning out my heartbeat and the ringing in my ears.

Everything started coming up. I reached for where the small trashcan was last time I'd used it. It wasn't there, so I moved fast to the bathroom, falling into the doorjamb while turning on the light. The trashcan was there, full of empty beer bottles topped with a film of vomit. I leaned over the toilet bowl. Just liquid. Small wonder I'd lost weight. I walked out and sat back down on the bed, then drank some more.

How did it get so fucked up?

Three-fifteen. Normal people are asleep, but I'd only been out fifty-two minutes. Once a pint bought me three, maybe four hours. Now I get a lousy fifty-two minutes?

Everything cost more these days.

Then it started: the room shrinking, stained cinderblock walls closing in with a high-pitched whine like the noise in your ears after a car bomb goes off really close. I tried to focus on listening to the radio I kept on 24/7 for white noise. But those walls got louder, drowning it out. I felt them the way you know something is close in the dark though you can't see it, some kind of primordial feelers that sense through air. Then those walls started broadcasting white noise on steroids, and I reached for an M4 that wasn't there to fight an imagined enemy.

Fight-or-flight kicked in. I flew to a standing crouch, waiting, my muscles tense and pumped. Sometimes when the walls closed in, I'd run outside to escape, then kept going to where the tide breaks.

This time I got lucky. The walls began to retreat. I heard the radio again. After a few minutes, I sat down.

There was some weed left, so I reached, feeling for the bong. I lit it, took a hit, then another, then a few more until there was only dead ash in the bowl. It didn't take long to kick in. I stared into darkness.

What is that?

My footlocker?

No. The footlocker is by the bed, pulling extra duty as the second nightstand. I shined the light from my cell phone. It was columns and rows of empty beer bottles. Four tall, constructed like some Lego masterpiece. Levels two, three, and four had cardboard floors. I counted ten bottles wide, twelve long. Eight tequila bottles were along the wall waiting to be added.

Who did that?

There weren't many options. It was either me, or me. I laughed. "Fuckin' me, or me," I said to the air. I was glad when the paroxysm of coughing started. I sounded crazy.

I turned on the light and sat on the linoleum before the temple I'd erected. The smell of old beer was strong, blending nicely into the room.

Where the hell did these empties come from?

The only waste can in the room was full of bottles and barf.

Then I saw the big trashcan by the door. It had been under the tree outside next to the other big trashcan, both cans filled the last I saw them. Now one was empty and blocking the door.

A car honked outside. I was the only long-term resident of the Motel Vista del Mar. Occasionally, a few surfers or some college students stayed for a night or two, but decent tourists saw the graffiti-riddled walls, the parking area strewn with used condoms and garbage, and moved on.

Two or three times a week I dumped the trashcan in my room

into one of the outside cans. That's as far as the empties went. The big cans never got dumped. I wouldn't look at them. Who wants evidence of every fuckin' thing they've had to drink for three months?

I multiplied four by ten by twelve, added in eight tequila bottles, then quickly made myself forget the total. I tried lying down but my head fell into the spins.

My black footlocker was along another wall. *Andrews, John R.* was painted in block yellow letters on the side. Written underneath was the last four of my Social and *A Co., 1st Ranger Bat.*

Twenty-one years of service was in there.

Purple Hearts, medical records, evaluation reports, promotion orders. My Silver Stars, including the two I wouldn't wear but couldn't throw out. The thank you notes for escorting my friends home in caskets under American flags.

Darnell's mother wrote how grateful she was that I was there when he died. I was the only White guy at his funeral. I don't remember much else. *I'm sorry we couldn't talk more and you had to leave right after we laid Darnell to rest. He was always talking about you, Randy, about how funny you were, about all the funny things you two young heroes did together. He loved you. You know that, don't you? Thank you for bringing my boy home. Maybe someday you can visit. We would be proud to have you.*

And the letter from Raquel, Vince's wife. I received it a year after his funeral. *When are you coming to visit us Randy? We're back living in Los Angeles. Please please please come see us. Vince thought the world of you, Randy. I know you know that. The kids want to see their uncle. And I am so sorry I forgot. I just remembered. I did not thank you—TOO BROKEN UP. Thank you, Randy. Thank you for all you did for us.*

I never visited.

Everything I received from John and Danny—drawings, Father's Day gifts made at school—was in that footlocker. After 9/11, I was never home. And photographs, including the one of John, Danny, and me on the couch at Fort Benning that made it through all those years. Sara took it in 2002 between my first and second tours to Afghanistan. John was my shadow back then, six years old, wearing the mini uniform I had bought him. We were so tight. Danny, the son I never got to know, was just a baby.

President Bush declared, "Mission Accomplished," but they kept sending me back.

The last thing was the receipt for my .45 and two 9mms from the gun dealer who agreed to store them while I was in Mexico.

I could dump that footlocker into the ocean, and nobody would care it was gone.

Cleaning always made me feel better.

I loaded the bottles into the trashcan, starting with the hard liquor empties, then working down from the top floor of my temple. I dragged the big can outside to its previous location by the other, where it would sit full for a long time, maybe forever. *You need to get out more, Randy.* The thought was so stupid I laughed.

The room looked like shit no matter how much I scrubbed it. I only puked one more time. I took a shower and got on the bed with one thought on my mind.

How do I unfuck my life?

I was ten.

I loved that basement. It smelled of gun oil and wood smoke and unfinished pine. Animal heads looked down with glass eyes that shone even in the dim light. There was a bull elk and a mountain caribou, their huge racks almost touching the ceiling. Two whitetail bucks and an antelope. The furniture was dated and beaten up, retired to the basement when something new and better replaced it upstairs. Country plaid was always in style down there.

My father kept the wood stove going 24/7 until my mother complained about rising heat making the house too hot. That was only in the summer months, though. It rarely got warm in Northern Idaho.

I was waiting for him.

"Well. Look what we have here. Happy birthday, Randy," my father said, walking down the wood stairs, his tone that of a man getting pleasantries out of the way. He never beat around the bush. He put a sheet of notebook paper on the table, then drew thick lines with a Marks-A-Lot. It was the silhouette of a fat bird.

"Okay. Let's talk about turkeys. You'll be hunting them with a .22. Not a shotgun. So let me explain something."

He was thirty-four then. In my memory he's older. And wiser. A big man, my dad was a mix of masculine and, with his wavy ash-brown hair and blue eyes, pretty. He just got off work and was still in his Forest Service uniform. It made him look bigger.

"You can shoot them in the body." He put an X inside the silhouette. "But you may find yourself chasing a turkey. If it flies, you'll never catch it. With body shots they only go down about half the time, maybe less."

Then he drew a small X over the eye. "Or you could shoot that bird in the head, and it will be waiting for you to pick up."

I was fidgeting from excitement and only half-listening. My parents hadn't given me a .22, yet.

"Of course, you would be aiming at a much smaller target. Your chance of missing your bird would be a lot higher." He had that *I want you to get this* look on his face, but I didn't understand what I was supposed to get.

"So where do I shoot?"

He paused and looked up at the caribou. "I'll get you within range. You're a good shot.

You *will* hit the bird if you aim for its body. But if you do not kill it outright, it'll take off and die somewhere. You won't find it." He paused. "You're the hunter, Randy. You have to make that call." He squeezed my shoulder, then walked to the stairs.

"We need to go join Becky and your mom. They've got your cake ready to go." On the third step he paused, looking back.

"It takes balls to go for the head shot, Randy. I won't fault you if you miss. Sometimes having the guts to make the tough call is what matters, not whether you hit your target."

CHAPTER 4

"Sir, *senor*, here. Look here." I had just left a bar and was already half in the bag. The kid held out a flier with a photo of a big cat.

He was maybe thirteen with a weaselly face. And dirty, like the crumbling sidewalk pockmarked with black gum under our feet. His forearm was one long bone with skin.

The boy's eyes darted like he expected to be smacked but didn't know where the blow would come from. He looked to be the type you watched because you knew he'd steal your shit. Like Iraqi kids. They'd rush our convoys as we'd pull up, cheering, wanting handouts. They'd pelt us with rocks as we drove off. *Little shits.* I studied the kid's pants, not liking how baggy they were, but only a bony ass was under the denim.

"Cougar! See the cougar, see the cougar!" His arm was still out there, like a pole with a banner.

In case I didn't know what a cougar was, the kid covered the bases.

"There's a puma at the Estrella, sir, a panther. The club has a real mountain lion. There, sir. Sir. There." He pointed three doors down at a big black double door under a green neon sign that read, *Nightclub Estrella.* It was sandwiched between the *Club Bambi with Live Nude Chicas Locas,* and a Mexican pharmacy staffed by people in clean white coats.

"Don't call me *sir.* I work for a living." I laughed fast, hard, and high-pitched, something I did when I was drunk. The kid's head jerked back. He moved a few steps away.

"Today's the Fourth of July, you know that?" I said, laughing harder, extending my hand to take the flier. He backpedaled a few more steps, letting it float to the ground. As he walked off, he took one last wide-eyed *what-a-cray-motherfucker* look at the laughing gringo.

Move on, you little shit.

I picked up the flier. The Nightclub Estrella advertised a cougar, a huge dance floor, nightly music and *live* nude girls.

The nice places like Papas & Beer and Carlos & Pepe's were across Juarez and another hundred meters down to the beach. They didn't need gimmicks. They had the ocean. When I was in town I drank on Avenida Juarez, home to the dive bars, the strip joints and the sleaze pits, all competing for the business of Americans under twenty-one wanting to get drunk. These clubs advertised naked girls, female mud wrestlers, dwarf bowling, and whatever else it took to get the business in.

But a *cougar*? I had to see this.

The Nightclub Estrella smelled of sweat, dried beer and cigarettes. And a faint undertone of piss. I stood just inside the door, waiting for my eyes to adjust. To the right was a long bar. To the left was a huge dance floor, a stage, and a runway. At the end of the runway was a stripper's pole for the *live nude girls*. The air was cool and still. It felt like those caves in Afghanistan. For a moment, I was there, clearing them again. I focused on the nightclub and got lucky. I was able to put that out of my head.

The place was the size of two basketball courts with a low ceiling and cement floor. What light there was came from a collection of bare fluorescent bulbs screwed overhead in no discernible pattern. Half were burned out or starting their death flicker. The walls alternated from black to maroon and were framed with gold molding and baseboards. Half of it had fallen off or never been put up.

Furniture was spread throughout the club. Most of it looked salvaged, and three or four mismatched chairs surrounded each table. But gathered near the door was a group of furniture painted maroon, black and gold to match the tattered décor. It all felt like somebody with bad taste tried to create a masterpiece, then quit halfway through the job.

Behind the long bar stood a paunchy middle-aged bartender with a Saddam Hussein mustache he kept smoothing down like he was checking to make sure it was there. His phony big toothy smile was plastered on. His hair appeared gray, but I wasn't sure in the lighting. Over the bar was a thirty-foot track of green neon. Dressed all in white, the bartender looked like an over-the-hill cabana boy gone radioactive.

Empty bottles and glasses were spread along the bar, evidence of customers long since departed. The bartender moved in slow motion, a man working hard avoiding work, acting busy for two customers. I was one of them.

He was fawning over the other, a woman with long wavy black hair down to her ass. I watched him replace the cocktail napkin under her drink, then lean in to chat her up like a guy on the make. She kept her barstool angled toward the door. I knew the posture. That's how I sat.

Most prostitutes in Rosarito and Tijuana, whether they were eighteen or sixty, dyed their hair hooker blonde, a slutty bleached shade. Not this lady. Hers was the color and sheen of obsidian. The green neon couldn't penetrate it. It was wavy, the type of hair men wanted to run their fingers through.

My eye was drawn from her to the one place in the club that was brightly lit. It was on the far right just past the bar, a fenced enclosure three times the size of a big dog run. The chain-link fencing went to the ceiling. With four floodlights, it was ridiculously bright. The concrete floor shined like it had been buffed. Surrounding the cage was a three-foot-high fence made of pipe. Two feet from the chain-link fence, it was designed to keep people away from the enclosure. Signs were posted on the chain links of the cage: *DANGEROUS ANIMAL! DO NOT CROSS OR APPROACH!*

But no cougar.

I was moving to ask the sluggish bartender, "Where's the animal?" when the big cat emerged from an area hidden behind the far end of the bar. I sucked in air.

I had expected an over-the-hill Mexican stripper stuffed into a cat suit. Saggy with fake tits, a fifty-five-year-old *cougar* on the prowl. Hey, motherfucker, the joke's on you. And this wasn't some grizzled zoo reject that had been sold because people wouldn't pay to look at it anymore.

This was a warrior.

Young, a female in her prime. A killing machine, the apex predator, top of the food chain. When she moved, her tan fur creased like the momentary ripples from a pebble thrown into still water. Then the lines vanished until she took another step. Powerful muscles, hard yet limber.

This animal could take down a bull elk.

She walked to the end of the cage, then made a U-turn. She walked to the other end of the cage. Another U-turn. Twenty feet, eleven steps each way. Pads on cement, claws retracted. I quit counting at twenty-one round trips. She kept going, always eleven steps until the turnaround.

I ordered a Pacifico from the bartender. I was pulling out my wallet when he put the beer and a bottle of vermouth side by side on the bar.

"You know what you call a Mexican with a bottle of this?" he said, lifting the vermouth to show me the label. "A dry Martinez." He stared, smiling, waiting for my burst of laughter.

I disappointed him. "Funny," I said walking away.

Leaning in by the cage, I felt the short fence pressing on my thighs. The cat stopped pacing and crouched in the far corner, her eyes fixed on mine. Muscles tense and visible, she was ready to fight or flee. Instincts honed sharp over thousands of years were kicking in, but she was caged. She could do nothing. So she stared, frozen.

I understood.

She had an earthy odor, a musky scent like old leaves and earth. I wouldn't look in her eyes.

"She thinks you're going to throw something."

It was the whore. Her voice was deep and sexy. She had an American accent with a hint of something else. I couldn't place it, but it wasn't Latin. She didn't turn to face me. In the dirty mirror behind the bar, her face was green, dim, and framed in bottles of tequila.

"She's preparing to dodge it," she said.

The muscles and bones of the woman's back and shoulders showed through her red satiny blouse, short-sleeved and well fitting. The material shined and looked expensive. She was lean, in shape. I got a side view of her tits. They were nice, pushing on the shiny fabric. She wore a black leather skirt that ended above her knees. I wanted to see her face.

"At night the music is very ... *very* ... loud. *Americans* get drunk and throw bottles at her. They break. Most of the glass is caught by the fence. Some of it hits the mountain lion." Her tone was clipped, accusatory, as if I'd been throwing things. She still hadn't turned, and I still hadn't said anything to her.

"The cat watches for danger always ... she never sleeps. See her? Look at her in the corner. She is making ready to defend herself, but there is no one for her to fight. *Do not* throw your bottle at her."

This woman must have eyes in the back of her head. Even when she told me to look at the cat she didn't turn. Her tone was just short of yelling. I didn't get it. Rosarito whores fawned over men until they emptied their wallets. Maybe she wasn't working. Or maybe she wasn't a whore. I took a swig from the bottle she told me not to throw.

"Where'd she come from?" I asked.

She swiveled to face me, her movement violent and fast. Her hair moved in an arc ahead of the rest of her. I sucked in air for the second time.

She was stunning, beautiful, her face chiseled like some goddess statue in a museum. Fair skinned, the contrast with her hair was striking. Actually, it was more than that. This lady was a major fucking turn-on. I felt like a little boy, staring.

She reminded me of someone.

The woman held her head high and proud. Her expression said I was a certifiable asshole. Her eyes were big like the cougar's—fierce, pissed off. About what? She looked in my direction but not at me. I still found myself not wanting to meet her gaze. She intimidated me.

She spoke, enunciating, pausing every few words as if I was a dumbass who could not comprehend any other way.

"Her mother was shot when she was a kitten in Northern Arizona. She's two years old now. The owner bought her, drove her here, and raised her in that cage. America sends its kids here to get drunk, its weapons and cash to our narcos.

"Nothing good comes here from your country... other than her." She turned with another fast jerk that said she would waste no more time on an American asshole like me.

I didn't let people talk to me like she had, particularly not a working woman. But I let it slide. It might have been because of her looks.

The door opened and a customer walked in. I felt a rush of air. It was bright outside. I sat in one of the mismatched chairs at the table nearest the cage. Two huge speakers stood a few feet away.

High on the fencing of the cage was a handwritten sign: "Do not throw things at the animal!" Glass pieces, some with partial beer labels, were piled three inches high around the base of the chain-link enclosure. A few half bottles rested on the shards. The mountain lion remained crouched in the farthest corner of the cage.

"Does she have a name?" I asked. The woman didn't answer.

"The mountain lion? Does she have a name?" I repeated, bracing for an insult.

This time, she looked at me when she turned. Her tone was soft, as if I was somebody she had decided she liked.

"Yes, she does... Matilda."

I looked in the woman's eyes until she turned away.

I sat in a chair near the end of the cage.

The cat made me feel good. She reminded me of my youth. But what was I was doing here? I looking for something but didn't know what it was.

I knew I was fucked up when I got back from all my tours. I wanted to to talk about it. I wouldn't open up to some doctor who couldn't get my name right. I wanted to tell only one person—Sara—the woman I had pressed my bare skin to and whispered to from inside that secret world of lovers, a place the nightmares could not enter. Even after I knew she'd cheated, I tried to get her back.

But it was too late. She wouldn't let me forgive her.

Sara was no longer my wife even though she carried my name. She was the petitioner in our divorce case. A week before I came home in October 2013, I was handed a petition for dissolution outside the personnel office at Fort Bragg. I had just signed my retirement paperwork. I was going home for the last time.

"You're served," said the process server, a pleasant-faced girl who walked up smiling. She moved off quickly.

I knew we had problems, but I was blindsided. I called Sara and tried to talk. She left me a voicemail. "Get a lawyer, Randy. Then talk to me through your lawyer," her message said to me. Sara's tone was hard, biting. She finished with, "Stop bothering me!"

Getting shrapnel blown into my shoulder did not hurt so much as those three words.

I lifted my arm and the cat's muscles tensed. She drew her head back, narrowing her eyes and fixing them on me. There was nothing in my hand.

So young. So damaged. Matilda had a teardrop-shaped scar just below her left eye. She returned to pacing. Back and forth, back and forth.

I watched her eyes from my side vision. They were gold with a dark center. She didn't blink. Once, on Caribou Ridge in Northern Idaho, I had looked into eyes like these through the scope of a .308. I was sixteen and my father didn't understand why I could not pull the trigger.

Matilda could live another dozen years. What would she become if she saw only the worst of humanity from inside that cage?

That cat probably took a healthy shit at least twice a day, yet the floor was spotless. There was a pressure washer behind the far side of the enclosure. Its handle was black, spongy and worn. Water dripped from the spout and moved in a thin stream to a drain in the floor. I watched it flow and my vision blurred.

The water turned red. *It's not real,* I told myself. *It's not red. There's no blood here.* I felt terror rising. *Please, God, not now.*

But, as always, I was just along for the ride.

It got so fucking hot. I smelled the sickly sweet, coppery smell of blood. I wasn't in a nightclub. Before me was a demolished Humvee, all jagged metal, scorched black with no tires.

It was August 2009 at Camp Speicher outside Tikrit, the end of my fourth and last tour to Iraq. I was holding the black spongy handle of a pressure washer, spray washing the Humvee my buddies died in. I was red and sticky and dripping. I had volunteered for this, believing it the honorable thing to do. No one else would do it. I was alone.

Water was blasting from the hose at the metal and canvas seats, washing away remains. There were gallons—literally fucking *gallons*—of undried human blood from five GIs on the floorboards, the seats, and the roof. Some of it had hardened in the heat and turned maroon and brown. That blood I had to spray twice—the first time, to soften it, the second, to blast it off.

With no fans and a corrugated metal roof, the inside of this building was suffocating. Heat pressed from all directions. Red mist floated in shafts of light from the roof.

Three streams of bloody water, each starting by a wheel axle, joined to form one large river two feet across and three inches deep. It started slowly but, as it neared the drain twenty feet away, it picked up speed, carrying with it dirt and cigarette butts and dead insects. Then it disappeared into the earth.

Blood splashed, hitting my face, washing off blood already there. There were red spots on my goggles. I tasted it, sick and sour. The paint mask got drenched, so I threw it away. Blood ran down my arms. My stomach jerked up to my throat, telling me how great puking would be.

But I kept spraying, kept pressing forward on my mission. The mission always came first. That's why I was so fuckin' deadly.

Half an hour and hundreds of gallons of water later, the river was still red. Another half hour went by. It still flowed red.

How much fucking blood is there?

Another fifteen minutes and the river finally—*finally*—went pink.

It took two hours for it to clear. Then, I saw everything.

Car bombs and body parts, men in my sights living on borrowed time, already in body bags as I started the slow trigger pull. Everything I would not think about. The water kept flowing and the visions kept coming.

I was supposed to see this.

Those two kids and that woman were thrusting their hands up and out of the water, wanting to know why I'd killed them. And a beach ball, back and forth, young hands catching and throwing it until all was gone in a blinding flash. Toney Bartlett was screaming from that liquid. "PLEASE, PLEASE, SERGEANT ANDREWS, DON'T FUCKING LEAVE ME. FUCKING GOD, SERGEANT, DON'T FUCKING LEAVE ME HERE TO DIE!" And I was again moving away down that alley, waves of guilt hitting the back of my head.

I saw that arm out the window of the Humvee, thumbs pointed skyward just before a blast meant for me vaporized all. Darnell and Vince should be spray washing *me* out of this Humvee. I killed them.

And Lieutenant Hamm's blood is in the mix, desecrating theirs.

I don't know how long I watched that water.

I don't know how long I watched it for the second time in the Nightclub Estrella.

I was looking in those damn mirrors, the ones that scared me as a boy.

Infinity terrified me as a boy. I'm not sure why, but I think it was because it was incomprehensible.

My little sister Becky and I shared a bathroom with mirrors—one over the sink, another on a medicine cabinet—facing each other from opposite walls. In them I saw myself in endless worlds, reflections of reflections of reflections, an infinity of reflections.

My mom once asked why I kept a towel hanging over the medicine cabinet and I lied, saying the mirrors made me dizzy when they faced each other. She nodded and left the towel where it was.

A flashback to my first flashback. I was stuck in hell, an infinity of flashbacks.

Then metal rustled. My vision cleared. I heard the sound again, chain links jangling, and I was back in the club staring into the eyes of a mountain lion.

Matilda was on her haunches, four feet from me, as close as she could get with the fencing between us. I punched my heels into the floor, jerking back and almost falling. If I'd been drinking from a can I'd have crushed it. A geyser shot from the bottle when I slammed it on the table.

Ears pointed to the ceiling, the cat's face was pressed into the metal links. Her eyes were huge laser beams boring into mine.

My instincts said *retreat, take cover*. She rubbed her face on the chain-link fence, marking it. Her muscles were loose. This cougar was acting like a housecat. She lay on her side, her body a semicircle.

I knew better than to look into her eyes.

But I did. These were not the eyes of prey, those dumb creatures living in a world of 360-degree views, seeing everything wide-screen, focusing on nothing. Hers were the eyes of a predator, seeing what is out of place, seeing weakness, with clarity. Forming a connection, if only to kill. Incapable of deceit.

I don't know how long we stared.

I sensed her thoughts. They weren't organized by time but more by the emotions she felt at a place. And this place was bad. I felt more—a distant memory, a good memory, of moving in the dark over vast lands. I felt her fear, the overwhelming futility of her existence and, again, I understood how she felt. Pacing was all she had.

Always watching for danger and never sleeping.

At least I could get fucked up.

But I felt something else, something bigger, something I couldn't quite accept. Then I could, even though I knew it wasn't possible.

The cat had seen all of it. The blood and what lie underneath the surface when the water cleared. I too had shared.

She focused on my eyes. I stayed in hers. Occasionally she would preen. My panic fell away and washed down the drain.

"Thanks," I said to Matilda. I stood up and headed to the door. As I passed the bar, the woman turned to face me. She looked like she had something to say. I kept walking.

When I got back to the motel, I dragged the fake red Adirondack chair from outside my room to the beach just above the high-water mark. There were black cigarette burns in the plastic. I decided to sit and watch the waves for the first time since coming here. I lit a cigarette.

I almost did not recognize how I felt. Unburdened, if just a bit.

The waves made a soft background noise. The day's beer had worn off and left me tired. I leaned back and quit fighting to be sane.

The hunt consumed me those two weeks before Thanksgiving 1983. It was my first mission; bag the turkey we would eat on Thanksgiving.

I lay awake in my bed wishing for my Henry Golden Boy lever action .22, secured in the gun safe in the basement. My father wouldn't let me sleep with it. I dreamed of campfire smoke and barbecued meat. I saw adventure and the rugged beauty of the mountains. My dad and I would camp, the silence broken only by the crackle of a huge fire and our laughter. Everything felt warm, exciting and perfect.

And I would hunt. I would shoot the turkey, hitting it with one long and impossible shot. Walking into our home in Bonners Ferry, I would hold up the bird, triumphant, then drop it on the kitchen floor with a *thump*. My mom and Becky would look with awe. On Thanksgiving, the smell of roasting turkey, *my* turkey, would fill the house.

That was my dream.

But my first hunt began with my father tearing me a new asshole while driving back down Border Mountain.

John Randall Andrews, II, told me several times to bring only what he told me to bring.

"Nothing else, Randy. Do . . . you . . . understand?"

And I had said, "Yes, Dad."

The makings of s'mores were not on his packing list. I brought them anyhow. It seemed a good idea at the time. At the turnout at the end of the Forest Service road my dad conducted a final inspection. I knew I was fucked when he stuck his hand in my pack and touched Hershey bars. "John Randall. What do we have here?"

We were probably the only humans for ten miles in any direction. It was so quiet I could hear misty rain landing on ferns. He upended my pack, dumping the contents onto the truck bed. The thunk of the graham crackers hitting the metal sounded like a gunshot. My feet made squishy sounds in the mud as I shifted my weight back and forth.

It was the Monday before Thanksgiving at 4:30 a.m.

"Put that junk food in the cab. Load up your pack. Shut the tailgate, then get in the truck." He waited in the driver's seat.

My dad took being in those mountains seriously.

We were headed to a dumpster. In the eleven miles it took to drive down the switchbacks, his verbal assault was relentless.

"Do you have a problem following simple instructions, Randy? Is there something wrong with your hearing? Is there? I think maybe there is. Why did you disobey me and hide junk food in your backpack?"

"I don't know." My stock answer in these situations.

"I don't believe that, Randy. I am sure you know why you did it, Randy. You rolled them in your underwear to hide the chocolate. You hid them, didn't you, Randy? I think you have a problem following simple instructions, Randy. I don't think I should trust you with that rifle. A man who cannot follow simple instructions cannot be trusted with firearms. We are now on a hike, Randy. This is no longer a hunt."

Our rifles hung in the rear window. I had been so proud putting my Henry on the rack over his. Now its shiny metal was a badge of dishonor and shame. I wouldn't look behind me.

He parked by a dumpster in the parking lot of the General Store in Good Grief.

"Throw that crap out. Then *get* in the truck."

Except for a few *hmms* from my dad, we drove up that mountain in silence. I wanted him to yell some more. He only made that *hmm* sound when he was disappointed. That was the worst.

I was sniffling. If I'd made any more noise he would have told me to shut up.

At the end of the road, he said, "Load up."

We backpacked seven miles uphill, stopping near the peak of Border Mountain. "We'll set up camp here." The fire of my dreams never got lit. "It scares the game, Randy."

The afternoon of the first day was work. We hiked miles. My father talked about the animals that lived in these mountains, how a human could survive up here. He carried my .22 and his Henry lever action .45-70. Hunting or not, he always carried that elephant gun.

I didn't talk. I shuffled. Shoulders slumped, the posture of a dumbass. My humiliation was boundless. The morning of the second day was even worse.

Late that afternoon, my father brought up the s'mores.

"Randy, of all animals in these woods, humans are the worst equipped. We have only our brains and judgment. Don't use both and you *will* end up dead. Every year, four or five people die up here. I pulled a tourist off Caribou Ridge just last week. He died a day later. Hypothermia. He got lost, then got too cold."

"The large predators would have smelled your sweets. I could not leave them in our truck. A bear would have taken off the door. We couldn't carry them. I didn't want that scent on us. A black bear *would* have smelled it and shown up. God help us if a grizzly was drawn to the smell."

He handed me my rifle. "Use your head, Randy. It'll keep you alive."

I awoke to the sound of the surf. My cigarette had left a shallow black trench, adding to the ones on the arm of the chair. I had slept for hours for the first time in what felt like forever.

CHAPTER 5

It was early afternoon, hours before the night crowds filled the streets and nightclubs of Rosarito Beach. The woman was again sitting at the bar. Four young guys in UCSD tees were playing pool. Other than them, the club was empty. The woman was watching television, her seat angled to the door though the TV was above the bar in front of her. The bartender was still bathed in green neon. I ordered a Diet Coke and sat in the chair by Matilda.

"What do you want?" I asked her in a loud whisper. Matilda watched me from the far corner, then her gaze moved to one of the college kids walking by her cage. The kid must have heard me talking to her because he studied me when he passed. He disappeared through a door with a blue triangle that said *Unisex Toilet*. He must be a regular. I hadn't noticed it behind Matilda's enclosure. The club's big bathroom, with its twelve-foot trough to pee in, was on the other side of the dance floor.

Matilda stood, focusing on me, her body relaxed as she edged closer along the chain-link walls of her cage. She was behaving like a housecat wanting her neck rubbed. But cougars weren't pets. They didn't act this way. In the wild, they were reclusive and wary. "It's okay, Matilda," I said.

I knew animals, but I didn't understand this. I wasn't sure everything happened yesterday the way I thought. But I knew I hadn't had a flashback for almost twenty-four hours.

Maybe she's lonely.

I made myself look at the pressure washer and heard my heart beating fast and loud in my right ear. My heartbeat was all I *could* hear out of that ear. I felt fear, but nothing more. My head stayed in the club.

I could provoke a flashback. Just had to think the wrong things.

Matilda now was sitting in the center of her cage, watching me. Her mouth was opening and closing. I thought she might be making soft noises. *Purring?* I couldn't tell. The scar on her left cheek looked like a bite. The pads of her back paws faced me. I saw they were cracked and dry.

I looked into her eyes. They were gold ringed with brown, beautiful. I saw the Idaho Rockies in them, a place where things made sense. I hadn't been back in twenty-five years.

I have to get better.

I thought of two boys throwing a beach ball, saw the red, yellow, green and white trying to blend into one color but not spinning fast enough to make it. Back and forth it passed. I heard them laughing. It sounded like it was in the club.

I knew what was coming. My mind pushed back, shouted, told me to avoid such a major trigger. Soon I would feel the hot rubber of the radio receiver and the heat of the explosion. I would smell it, too, then feel the horror at what I'd done.

As she had the previous day, Matilda lay down in a semicircle just on the other side of the chain-link wall of her cage. *Showtime. I can do this.* I thought of what I saw over that berm, thought of that day, and the air got hot and dry.

It was March 2003, the initial push to Baghdad. Our three Ranger platoons were forty miles north of the Regiment, moving in fifteen vehicles. It was another eight miles to Baghdad International Airport, BIAP, the staging area for the assault on the capital.

A KPV heavy machine gun opened up from the roof of a two-story building five hundred meters east of the road. I heard the *whap*

whap whap and the thudding clunks of the rounds hitting. An old Soviet weapon; its armor-piercing rounds could take out a tank or American aircraft. Or level a house with its 600-rpm assault.

We took cover behind a twenty-foot-high berm, one of the thousands of fortifications built by Saddam to fight the Americans that never got used. Until today.

The impacts left silver-dollar-sized holes in four of our Humvees. I was the senior NCO. "Any casualties?" I asked over the radio. None, but we would be towing two of the Humvees. It was the first of my four deployments to Iraq, my third combat tour since 9/11.

"We got no casualties, sir," I said to Second Lieutenant Dwight Roy, my platoon leader. Roy was a lanky kid fresh out of West Point. His soft round face made him look pleasant, friendly, and still in high school. One of the rounds missed his head by a few inches and blew up a water can. He looked as if he'd gone swimming in his uniform.

Roy wouldn't pull out his dick to piss without asking. "What's your recommendation, Sergeant Andrews?" Smart kid. And he wore Ranger tabs. He would have made a good officer, but I wasn't around three years later to recommend anything. In 2006, he was killed in an ambush in Tikrit.

Roy was talking with Carl Jenkins, another second lieutenant and every bit as green. Jenkins, a kid from some Midwest state, had straw-colored hair and a blistered complexion that always looked like shit in the desert sun. He'd slathered sunblock on his once-pale, now-red face. There were streaks of white goop on his cheeks he hadn't rubbed in all the way.

We'd been in several firefights the last six days. This was different. That KPV was just short of a cannon. Now two butter bars, with four weeks' field experience combined, were discussing how we would eliminate this static threat. They spoke fast, passing words back and forth and not listening to each other.

Their voices were high pitched. They both looked frantic, ready to lose it, like the authority the Army had given them weighed too much.

Jenkins suggested dividing into two columns and moving in on the house from "converging angles," whatever the fuck that meant. I didn't know what "static" meant either. What I did know was these lamebrains were suggesting we cross five hundred meters of open terrain with a heavy machine gun using us for target practice.

Roy, the senior officer by two weeks, began nodding.

"Fuck, this ain't good. Those LTs need NCO mentoring." I was talking to myself, out loud. I didn't want Roy giving a stupid order he would feel he had to enforce.

I walked over. "Sir . . . Lieutenant Jenkins. Can you let me in on this?"

"Yeah, yeah," Roy said. "It's all good, it's all good sergeant, no casualties, yeah, all good. The gun. What's your recommendation, Sergeant Andrews?"

"Look, sir. I want to keep it that way, no casualties," I said. Brief pause. "I don't think your plan's any good, gentlemen." Jenkins's eyes widened at a sergeant telling him his plan sucked. Roy didn't flinch. Both kept their mouths shut.

"Three options. Option one. We leave them out there for the next Americans to deal with. That's not an option. Option two. Your plan. We move across that open ground. Sirs, you are going to lose Rangers, maybe all of us. Why the fuck would we head out there anyhow? Let the Air Force light 'em up. That's option three."

They nodded. They liked it.

Now to keep them from calling in an airstrike on our heads. "With your permission, LT, I'll call it in." Asking was professional courtesy. They were the officers.

"You got this one, sergeant," Roy said.

Six minutes later the air controller in Kuwait said the impact would come in twenty seconds. We all were behind the berm. I sent word down the line.

I wished I hadn't looked over the berm through those binoculars. Two boys ran from the side of the house and began throwing a big plastic beach ball. They both were around seven, John Junior's age. The ball flew back and forth, back and forth, boy to boy. Those colors were so vivid against the dingy backdrop, all gray, tan, and brown.

One boy had on a tee with white and black stripes, like a convict in an old movie. The other was wearing a gray-and-brown-checked long-sleeve shirt that looked like a Pendleton. I remember thinking, *The kid must be hot.* Then I remember hearing their laughter. But I couldn't have heard it. Those boys were too far off.

Then I understood what was going to happen.

There was the flash, and everything disappeared. The explosion was deafening. A moment later, I got hit by the air blast, hot and monstrous. Everything in a circle seventy-five feet from that house vaporized into fumes and ash. I watched the smoke cloud lazily heading skyward, as if it had all the time in the world.

Heads poked up to look at the smoking hole. I heard "Hooah!" and "Get some motherfuckers!" along with a few rare words of praise for the United States Air Force.

Lieutenant Roy walked up, shaking my hand with a double-handed clasp. I felt the metal of his wedding ring.

I never told anyone. Those boys were mine to carry, alone. That made it harder. I thought I'd put them behind me. There was always a new mission.

But I never wanted to think of beach balls.

After I came home, Sara once asked why I never wanted to go to the beach anymore. "You used to love the ocean, Randy," she said, and I wanted to tell her. If I had known then how sideways my head would go, I would have. "I've seen enough places with sand," I said, then looked away. Sara laughed, then stared at me with serious eyes like she knew I wasn't telling her something.

Matilda was at the chain-link fence. I'd been staring, trancelike, into her eyes. I saw pain and guilt. I never would have called in that airstrike if I'd known those boys were there. "It was the right call at the time," I said, half believing.

She sees what I see.

Also, *That is not possible.*

Then the guilt was gone. Sometimes shit bad shit— *Isn't it always bad shit?*—just happens. Maybe I could set this one down, let it go.

It was possible.

Those boys?

They were living on borrowed time. Another 135,000 troops would move up that route after us.

And this time I put it down.

Drinking beer with a cougar was not what Dr. Berlin meant in recommending *cognitive processing therapy*. But I felt like I'd unloaded something huge and hurtful. And there was something else, something more. In Matilda's eyes, I was one of the good guys again.

And that was enough of a visit to the inside of my head for one day.

"How's your day going, Matilda?"

She ignored me, licking her paws, intent on grooming. She yawned, looked in my general direction, then went back to running her rough tongue over her fur. *Therapy over*, her actions said.

I walked to the bar. The woman was three seats to my right and facing straight ahead, her face reflected behind the hard liquor bottles. A pair of oversized sunglasses lay upside-down on the bar next to her. In my side vision, I saw her looking at me.

The bartender was again in his cabana boy attire, smiling. Up close, I saw his hair was gray. He introduced himself. "Ruben." We shook hands. "You know," he said, forever smiling, "You look like that sheriff in *Gunsmoke*. Matt Dillon. You know him? I bet you've heard that."

I had.

"No. I haven't," I said.

"You really do look like him. Big. Strong." He clenched his fists, shaking them. This guy was such a blatant ass-kisser that I laughed.

"No. You're the first," I said, then turned to Matilda. "That cat's going crazy in there." Ruben unclenched his fists, then put his palms face down on the bar.

"There was a time," he said, "for a few months after the owner brought the mountain lion here, I could pet her. That was two years ago. She was a kitten. Maybe six months old . . . and then she got big. And mean. I can't get near her."

Matilda paced.

I looked at the glass fragments on the floor. "Why do you let people throw things at that animal?" Ruben drew his head back. "Not you," I said. "I mean the club. Why doesn't the owner stop it? She's such a beautiful animal."

"I *don't* allow it. But I only work here. I put up that sign to stop people." He waved his hand toward the cage but kept his eyes on me.

"At night there are four, five, sometimes seven hundred people here. It is very crowded. And loud. Most of the customers are drunk. It's impossible to watch them all."

"I don't get why the club lets that happen." I sounded harsh, not meaning to. Ruben acted as if he'd forgotten something and walked to the other end of the bar. He began washing glasses.

I heard a glass move on my right. Then I heard it again and felt the woman's eyes on my profile.

There was a cold beer in front of me. Life was a little better right then. The woman was beautiful, but I wasn't eager for another lecture on the sins of America. I watched the tequila bottles behind the bar.

When she spoke, her tone was gentle.

"I've never seen Matilda go to anyone like that."

She had swiveled in her barstool to face me. I angled my stool slightly.

In another life she could have been a model. Or a porn star. Her blouse was blue, tighter than the red one, and open one button too many. Her breasts strained against the fabric, nothing short of magnificent.

The woman studied my face. "Only me. She only comes to me." She flashed a wide smile. Her eyes weren't angry. Under the obnoxious green neon it was hard to tell their color, but they were dark with bright flecks. She was around my age—early forties. I saw slight lines, just short of wrinkles, at the edges of her eyes. Pain lines, my mother would call them.

She probably thought I'd moved to the bar to hit on her. I turned, looking her up and down, trying not to be obvious about it. I didn't fuck prostitutes. Sometimes I got shit for that.

I met one of my best friends, Vince Alvarado, in 1998 when we billeted together for thirty days in the Philippines training their commandos on how to better kill people. The last night in country, we were drinking with three other Rangers. "Time for Plan B," one of them said.

Plan B was a hooker bar. I looked inside the door and said, "I'm not into this." I started back for the base. "What the fuck, Randy," Vince said. "You see those girls?" The place was high end. The ladies were beautiful. "Where *you* going? I got money if you need to borrow."

Most of the guys I served with cheated. We were never home.

"No, not tonight," I said, implying on another day I would join in the fun.

But I never would. I would never allow myself to be vulnerable before a stranger. Even back then, I never dropped my guard. Vince and I became friends. Sometimes he went with prostitutes. He asked me to join him one more time, then never again.

I almost asked what this woman at the bar charged.

But then I saw her scar.

It started just below her jawline on the right and trailed into her blouse. It disappeared into her cleavage. It was old, pencil eraser width and not much darker than her skin. She wasn't trying to conceal it. It was the intentional flaw sewn into a Persian rug. It enhanced her beauty.

I still hadn't said anything. She was looking as if trying to take my measure, that big smile plastered on her face. "I wonder why she came to you." It was a comment to herself. Her eyes moved over my tattoos, then across the scars on my arms and neck. She nodded as if she had solved the mystery.

"Well, maybe misery loves company," I said, trying to be witty. "That animal shouldn't be here."

Out of the corner of my eye, I saw myself in the mirror. Then I saw my smile. It looked stiff. She nodded and smiled again. I tried again to smile but it seemed I'd forgotten how. I ordered a shot of tequila from Ruben.

"You want one? My name's Randy." I downed the shot like a man in a hurry to get drunk.

She laughed. "Randy. My name is Athena. And, yes, I would love a drink. Ruben. *Un trago de Jameson.*"

"I don't know why she came over to me," I said.

Athena made me nervous. Other than to my ex-wife, family, or waitresses, I had not talked to a woman for longer than thirty seconds in a dozen or so years. All those tours, surrounded almost completely by men. In my green reflection I looked so strained. I ordered another shot of tequila. Athena was sipping her Irish whiskey. She gave a half smile when I emptied the second shot, then quit sipping and downed hers.

"Did she purr?" she asked.

"I don't know. I wouldn't have heard it if she had. I have—" She didn't need to know I'd lost hearing in the same blast that vaporized my battle buddies.

"She purrs for me," she said. "I bet she purred for you." I quit trying to make a good smile. She looked in my eyes, as Matilda had. Why? I think she was flirting. *This is the same woman from yesterday?* I looked away. I didn't trust her. She made me feel great, but vulnerable. I wanted to run—and I wanted to touch her.

"You weren't—" I started to ask why she'd been an asshole the day before. "Never mind." I looked at the seat next to her. "Can I sit there?"

"Please, Randy."

I moved next to her. Ruben was filling an empty Patron Anejo bottle with a clear liquid poured from a big plastic jug. Then he added a powder that turned the clear color to a brownish gold. He put the bottle on the top shelf behind the bar. He kept looking at me as if I was moving in on his turf.

Athena was staring at my right bicep. *Death Before Dishonor* was tattooed above *US Army*. Her eyes stopped at the nasty scar underneath, a souvenir from a 7.62 round that took out "Andrews, John R." and "O Pos."

"You're a soldier Randy?"

"How'd you guess that?"

She took my sarcasm seriously. "Your haircut. How you walk, everything. I like soldiers. I was— once—married to one."

"My ex-wife married one too."

Ruben was near, running a feather duster over liquor bottles that weren't dusty. "Can we get another round?" I said to him. "Another whiskey for her. I'll take your bar tequila. I don't need that top shelf you're mixing, Ruben."

She smiled, then went back to staring at my scar.

"I don't serve anymore. I did for twenty-one years. I'm done, retired."

I didn't believe in *once a Ranger, always a Ranger*. Marines said shit like that, but I only heard it from guys who couldn't see their dicks looking down.

She touched my scar and traced it with her forefinger, then

pulled her hand away before I could tell her to.

"It's nice to meet you, Randy."

The shots were kicking in. "Athena. The Greek goddess of wisdom. It's pretty." I looked at her hair. "How'd you get it? Your name?"

"My father was a Greek diplomat. He worked at the embassy."

"Oh?"

Ruben was standing within earshot. She continued, speaking low, just for me. "He met my mother in Mexico City and married her. Then he was stationed in New York City. He left for Greece when I was four and left us in New York. I saw him only a few times after that."

"Do you speak Greek?"

"I did, once. I suppose it would come back to me if I spoke it again. Someday I will travel to Greece. I want to see the temples of the gods."

I turned, and Athena caught me looking at her profile. She put the tip of her finger on my scar again and started tracing its length. It was a woman's touch, slow and soft. I wanted it but felt she was trying to manipulate me. I knew nothing of this beautiful woman other than yesterday she'd been a bitch and she seemed to be a regular in a sleazy Rosarito nightclub.

"Can you please not do that," I started, then switched gears to demand, "Why were you bustin' my balls yesterday, all that bullshit about Americans?"

My ex-wife once said I'd never learned tact. She may have been right. When I was nervous, I always went on the attack.

Athena acted like she didn't hear me. In the neon lighting our reflections were surreal. She quit tracing the scar, but her finger stayed there. I looked at it. She pulled it away. My right thigh touched her left. I felt her heat.

"I'm sorry, Randy. It hurts?"

"No. It doesn't. I just don't like people touching it."

Such a strange woman.

"I'm happy it does not hurt, Randy. It must have hurt a great deal once."

It did.

I saw the HiLux. Then a second. Both were empty, parked behind a mud wall that lined the road through the center of the village. The doors were open on one. Taliban. "Showtime, gentlemen," I said to reconnaissance platoon.

It was my second tour to Afghanistan. We were patrolling a village in Helmand Province when the 7.62 round cut a four-inch gash across my right bicep, just above the elbow. It was a lucky shot from a hundred meters. I never met a Taliban that could hit shit, even in an outhouse.

I saw the guy and raised my rifle ready to nail his ass, but he ducked behind a wall.

There were goats passing through the village, bleating in that dry cool air. We dropped a few mortars over the wall and the Taliban ran out, a Rambo charge. "One dumb shit Taliban," I said over dinner that night, laughing, my arm stitched and hurting like a motherfucker because back then I wouldn't take painkillers. He rushed, firing and yelling, his headdress flapping in the wind. I shot him three times in the chest. He came to rest in the dirt after a ten-foot slide that kicked up a dust cloud that smelled of goat piss. We cleared another ten of his friends from behind that wall and stacked the bodies like artillery rounds against that wall of mud.

Athena still looked familiar, but I could not make the connection.

"You're handsome, you know that? Ruben's right. You do look like Matt Dillon, or that actor who played him on television."

We were looking in the mirror. Both of us saw the strain in my face.

My fight-or-flight reflex was kicking in. I didn't believe her. Too many women with suicide vests snuck by our checkpoints, knowing

Americans didn't want to search females. Or they fucked other men while you were overseas getting your ass shot off.

But did I really feel that way about all women? And why was I so quick to think she was a whore?

"Do you work here?" I asked.

Whiskey flowed across Athena's lips. She was staring, trying I think to understand me. Then she looked away to the door like she wanted to leave.

"I'm a dancer here," she said.

"You're one of the live nude girls?"

She winced and nodded.

"Sorry. I sound like an asshole. You said you were married once. What happened?"

"He died" is all she said.

"Pain hurts, Randy. That's why we avoid it. That's why Matilda stays in the corner when people are in the bar. Except she does not hide from you."

"No shit," I replied. "Why you talking to me anyhow? You seemed mad the other day. Like you didn't like Americans."

"You sound like you want to argue. I don't. And you're right. I don't like most Americans. They give you a five-dollar tip and think they own you."

"So why *are you* talking to me?" I asked.

She turned to Matilda. "Because she came to you. She comes to the two of us. *Only* the two of us."

"That's why? Because the cat comes up? So, why'd she come to me?"

She spoke to her empty shot glass. "She knows you're wounded. That's why."

"I'm not wounded," I said.

Her face got serious and some of yesterday's bitch returned. "You're a soldier. Your type never admits it. Then you come home dead or fucked up.

"You always end up wounded," she added. "It's just a question of how much."

"Whoa," I said. "Where is this shit coming from?" My face was hot, and not from the alcohol. "Who the hell do you think you are, to say I'm wounded?" I was angry. I couldn't have said why.

"What about that?" She looked at my scar. "You may not admit it, but *Matilda knows*. She senses things like that."

"She's an animal. I'm not wounded." I punched the words and proved her point. I saw disbelief on her face. It pissed me off more.

"Why the hell does she look at you, then? You wounded too?"

She didn't answer.

I looked like a first-class asshole in the mirror. Jaw clenched, lips drawn back. Narrowed eyes. The green neon didn't help. An angry Shrek was looking at me from behind tequila bottles. Then I saw the pain lines along the sides of my eyes.

It was that fuckin' doctor again, the one who couldn't get my name right, speaking through a whore I almost believed was working as a spy for the VA. Every hair on the back of my neck stood. I called Ruben to pay the tab.

"You don't know me," I said, standing.

"You're leaving?" Her eyes locked on mine, pulling. "I'm sorry. I didn't mean—"

"I'm outta here."

"Why are you leaving?" she asked. We locked eyes. She was hurt. Sad. I felt it coming off of her in waves. This lady was as lonely and fucked up as me.

Part of me wanted to touch her, to say, "I know." Twenty-one years in the Army taught me to hide that side of me. Pride kept me moving. I began to feel like that fuckin' asshole looking back in the mirror.

"You're fine," I said. "I just have to go."

Ruben got a big tip because I wouldn't wait for change.

Headed to the door, I looked back at two females—one human, the other a cougar—watching.

What the fuck just happened back there?

It was a full moon. I could see miles over the water. The ocean was calm. I wasn't.

Why in hell had I run out?

I thought something was special about that cougar. Then the lady says what I'm thinking and I get pissed off.

Maybe I didn't run.

Yeah, I did.

She's a hooker. She was out to take me. That's why I ran.

That's not it. I don't even think she's a hooker.

I thought of Athena's face an inch from mine, her bare breasts against my chest. I saw myself running my tongue down that scar, following it to its climax. It was everything about that woman. Sometimes a bitch but, damn, I wanted to touch her.

Then I knew.

I was scared.

There. I said it.

Have to admit, it felt good. I'm not sure why. I laid my head against the plastic of the chair, then closed my eyes and listened to the water.

"Be quiet Randy."

I was shuffling my feet, hard snow crunching under my boots. My dad and I were in the Idaho Panhandle National Forest in a saddle just south of the crest of Border Mountain. I could see the cleared strip of land, the border, a mile to the north. Then, past that, the Kootenai River winding through the green plains of Canada like some huge snake.

My father had a big voice and had trouble talking quietly. He whispered, "Can you feel the rhythm of this place, Randy? It's in the air, in the sounds. The animals know the rhythm and they move to it. All things and all places have a rhythm."

I thought my ten-year-old ass would freeze and drop off. Cold was the only rhythm I felt. It was just before dawn and thirty degrees.

"No. I'm cold, Dad. I don't feel any rhythm. Can I put my jacket back on?"

My Henry was leaning against a tree.

"Quiet, Randy. Do you hear anything in these woods as loud as you?"

I longed for my sweater and heavy coat, hanging next to my father's coat on a cedar branch.

His whispers were sharp. "To understand the rhythm of a place, you must use all of your senses."

I backed into a tree that had split and fallen. The fiber of my T-shirt caught on the rough bark. A branch poked through my shirt, making a scraping sound. "Ow," I said, jerking away and taking several loud, snow-crunching steps trying to stay on my feet.

He looked at my face, his eyes stern.

"Randy. I told you to be quiet. A turkey's hearing is far better than ours. The birds will hear you a mile out. If you cannot be quiet, we will leave and buy a turkey on the way home. Do you understand?"

His eyes were boring holes into mine. He knew what would get my attention. The man never bluffed. He would pull the plug on this turkey hunt if I did not do what he said. I would suffer the disgrace of a store-bought turkey on our table tomorrow.

My breath turned to vapor in the cold air. I began shivering but I stopped moving, stopped making noise.

"Randy. Listen. Smell the cedars? What do you hear? What do you feel with your skin? Can you taste the air? Breath quieter."

I had an acidy taste in my mouth from the cold. But I began to smell fresh cedar boughs. And after a few minutes, the birds, pushed into silence by my shuffling and nonstop chatter, started making their bird sounds. I felt the rough bark of a cedar on my palm. I was cold, but not as cold as I had been.

We stood silently for another ten minutes. I began to hear something moving at the edge of a meadow a quarter mile away. The sounds were vivid, alive. My dad did not react.

I gestured with my head toward the noise. My father turned his head, left ear facing the meadow. Then he nodded and smiled.

It wasn't something. It was some *things*—the clucks and purrs and *kee-kees* of wild turkeys.

"Chamber a round, Randy."

I nodded and cocked my rifle.

"Leave it on safe."

I started to move to the coat. "Leave the jacket. Walk silently. Don't step on the snow."

Stepping on patches of grass, I went first up the ridge. We moved in small steps, each one considered before taken, and cut the distance in half. My dad stopped us just short of the meadow.

"Randy. Take your rifle off safe." His whispers were barely audible.

He looked through his binoculars, then handed them to me. He pointed to two large boulders two hundred yards away, and sixty yards from the birds. I moved in that direction. He did not follow me. This was my kill.

There was a light wind on my neck and face. The boulders were downwind from the birds. I looked back at my dad one more time. He nodded and I saw the tightness in his jaw. He wanted this one, for me.

It took me fifteen minutes to reach the boulders. The turkeys were still calling. There were eleven birds, all hens. I tried to feel the rhythm of this place. I put my bare elbows and forearms on the rock. The rough granite scraped my skin. I didn't feel it. I had goosebumps on my arms, but I no longer felt cold. The acid taste was gone. In that moment, I was a predator.

I smelled an earthy smell, different from the grass and the forest of cedars. Then I could taste it.

It's the hens!

I heard the soft crunches of their feet, saw their black leg spurs. I drew a bead just above the legs on one of the larger hens. I breathed in, held my breath, and started the gradual pull of the trigger, just as my dad had instructed. "A slow, steady pull, Randy. Don't jerk the trigger."

Then I remembered what else he said in our basement, and I lined up on the bird's head. Sixty yards with a .22 at a target smaller than a baseball? My mind started running over the effect of the wind and how many feet were in sixty yards.

Take the shot, Randy!

The lead bird moved toward the trees at the edge of the meadow. The other ten turned their heads to follow. The flock soon would melt into the woods.

The Henry fired.

It was clean and beautiful, the crack of a bullet in the silence of early winter in the Idaho Rockies. The sound traveled north into Canada and back south over Border Mountain. I heard it repeat two, then three times, echoing off the mountains of Washington to the west.

The turkeys panicked, a frenzied rustling and flapping as they fled to the woods. They were almost as loud as the gunshot. I tried to count them as they left the ground, hoping for only ten birds, but they bunched up and moved too fast.

Then it was silent, dead quiet, the only sound the shot ringing in my ears. I took off with my rifle across the meadow. I ran, heedless of the rocks and shrubs and torn-up ground left by bull elk in rut. Twice I stumbled and almost fell.

My father only let me have a single-shot rifle. I might have shot myself otherwise.

The turkey lay on the frosted grass, a white frame around the bird's black, brown and gray head feathers. A light breeze made the feathers dance.

She didn't look dead. There was a hole through her scaly head with only specks of blood along its edges. I stared, unbelieving, then I picked her up and held her over my head for my father to see, waving her like a cheerleader with a pom-pom. The hen's wings opened and she doubled in size.

I had the balls to take a head shot from sixty yards!

I'd smelled the same earthy smell I had at the boulders.

I really had smelled the flock!

I understood the rhythm of the place. I was a hunter.

My father, carrying his big .45-70, was running as carelessly as I had over the rough ground of the meadow—smiling.

"Dad, I did it. Dad, I got it! I got our turkey!" I kept yelling. It was all I could do.

He stopped fifteen feet from me, then walked the final steps. I handed him the turkey. He looked it over, then held it by his side.

"Helluva shot, Randy." He stood, nodding.

I saw a smile take over his face. He lifted the turkey and held it to the heavens. "*Yes!*" He yelled loud enough to be heard clean off the mountain. And I joined him, yelling, both of us dancing and passing a dead turkey.

"*Yesss!* I did it."

My father joined in and yelled, "You did it!"

And I realized it had been both of us who bagged the turkey, so I yelled, "*We did it!*"

I bet Becky and my mom heard us all the way back home to Bonners Ferry.

A big wave slapped the shore. I'd slept through the change of the tide.

I replayed that trigger pull in my head. Again and again. A good clean kill. Even after thirty-one years it still excited me.

CHAPTER 6

"She won't be in until tomorrow, Randy."

Ruben lifted his arm as if he was flinging something at the runway for the dancers. "Athena only comes in on the days she works. Wednesday, Thursday, Friday, and Saturday."

Ruben was devoting his time to looking busy, washing clean glasses in an empty club. He was curt and for once wasn't smiling. He didn't like me asking about Athena.

"How about a beer?" he asked.

"Not today. I'll be back."

I was talking to Matilda the next day when Athena walked in. She sat on a stool by the television, then took something from a bag and started eating. Ruben cruised right over to her with a Diet Coke before she ordered one, his big flirty operator's smile flipped on like high beams. Other than a casual glance, she ignored him. I walked over and stood beside her.

Athena turned her head to my reflection behind the bar. Ruben's eyes bored in as he walked off.

"May I get you a drink?" I asked.

She looked straight ahead.

"I'm surprised you're here," she said. "You left really fast the other day."

My left hand was tapping on the bar, moving on its own. I stuffed it in my pocket.

"Why?" she asked.

Her voice was serious but not angry. She turned and looked at me.

"You said something. You said . . . sometimes we need to look at our pain. You're right. Maybe I need to do that."

"It runs when we put the light on it," she said.

Like a cockroach.

"I've been here the last three days. I wanted to . . . I was looking for you."

"I know. Ruben told me."

My left hand was out of my pocket again tearing up a cocktail napkin. Athena saw the white pieces on the bar. I got the feeling she was enjoying this.

"Why? Why'd you come back?"

"Like I said. To see you. I like you. I'd like to talk to you more." I looked at Matilda moving back and forth. "And I wanted to see her. Can I stay around?"

She laughed and threw me a bone. "I would have come in if I'd known you'd been asking about me. Ruben only called me last night and said you'd been in. And . . . I'm glad you're here."

After a long ten seconds, she asked, "Something you want to say?" She gave me a smile, the big one that made me feel fantastic and nervous.

"I thought maybe we could do something together. Hang out."

Just like that, I was stuck at sixteen. I'd said those words twenty-five years ago to Sara the first time I called her. "And, I'd like to get to know you better."

I said that too.

Athena's face brightened and looked younger. The lines along her eyes softened. "Did I just fuckin' say that? Hang out? Lame," I said. "It's, uh, been a while."

She looked surprised. "No! Why would you say that? It's not lame." Ruben was edging closer, trying to act like he wasn't eavesdropping. She looked at him, then back at me.

"You were sitting at my table the other day. Did you know that? If you're asking, I'd love to sit with you, Randy."

"Can we sit at your table, Athena?"

"Yes, Randy. We can sit at my table."

It sounded a bit like she was patronizing me. I didn't mind. I ordered two beers. Ruben put them down, saying nothing. His big ass-kissing smile morphed into an intense gaze. I had this guy's number. I motioned for Athena to go first.

Her movements were graceful. Her heels clicked on the cement. She had on the same black leather skirt. It ended just above her knees. Her legs were bare, and I could see that her calves had lines of muscle from behind her knees to just above her ankles.

I watched until she turned.

"You coming? Or you just going to stand there watchin' my ass?"

I thought of protesting, to say I'd been staring at her legs. That would have sounded asinine. My eyes would have gone to her butt soon enough. I caught up and pulled out the nicest of the mismatched chairs for Athena. I looked at Matilda and smiled. Then at Athena as I sat in the chair across from her.

At least this time I was fixed on a woman's legs and not some fuckin' box on the side of the freeway.

CHAPTER 7

Matilda trotted over. Athena spent a minute talking to her, asking how she was doing. "I'm on at seven tonight, Mattie."

"So, this is your table? Why don't you sit here when you come in?" I asked.

"It's easier at the bar. I don't get hit on up there. Ruben hovers around me. He can be a pest, but men don't approach when he's talking to me. Sit here and someone comes over. They're half my age most of the time. I can deal with Ruben easier than the kids."

"Why do you—" I was starting to ask why she came into the bar when she wasn't working and stopped. Instead, "How old are you?"

She didn't hesitate. "Forty."

Matilda was against the fence. She looked interested, as if she followed our words. I tried to pick up her scent, to feel what she was feeling.

"So why does she come to you?" I asked. "What's your . . . secret?"

In the bright light near the cage, Athena's eyes were deep brown with gold flecks. She looked into mine. "I'll tell you, maybe . . . sometime."

"That's fine. Can you smell her?" I asked.

Athena shook her head. "No. What's she smell like?"

"It's a cat smell, but stronger. Like wet dirt mixed with leaves. I lived with cougars up north. I've smelled 'em before. Hard to compare it to anything because nothing smells like it." I left out the piss odor I was also picking up.

"What do you like to do?" I asked.

"I love the beach. Not these beaches," she was quick to add. "These are dry and crowded and worn. Tropical beaches, down south, in the places where palm trees are on the sand. Costa Rica, maybe. I've seen pictures of places there I like. But I've never been there. I love to dance."

"What type of dancing?" I looked at the stage and wished I hadn't. No sane woman could enjoy stripping. Could they?

She winced. "That's not dancing. I mean ballet. I love ballet. It's been a long time." She looked at Matilda. "She's beautiful, isn't she?"

Matilda was acting the housecat again, rubbing her cheeks against the chain links, pushing her nose through the openings. "Have you ever pet her?" I asked.

She shook her head. "Just with my eyes." She put her palm on the three-foot fence. "Ruben will yell if you step over this. She knows how I feel, though. I know how she feels. I talk cougar, you know that?"

She wasn't kidding. This lady was a little crazy with a lot of pain. I liked her.

"When do you work here?" I asked.

"So, you want to *hang out*?" she asked.

"Yeah, I do. What nights do you work here? And, that's all you do here? Just dance?" *Fuck*. I regretted those last two words as soon as they escaped. I never had a filter.

Her nostrils flared. "What do you think I am? You think I'm a whore? I don't do that type of work. Why the hell did you ask that?"

She was again the woman from the first day.

"No, I don't . . . I don't think that."

She was trying to skewer me with her eyes.

I'm a fuckin' asshole.

"You were sittin' in here alone. This ain't the best bar," I said. "I was afraid you were . . . I like you. That's why I was worried."

We didn't say anything for a while. We watched Matilda sniff the air as I tried to come up with something to thaw ice. "I'm sorry," I said.

She broke the silence. "Are you still asking if I want to *hang out*?"

Her eyes were wide and questioning. Then she laughed.

This woman had me so off-kilter.

"Okay. Okay. Look," I said. "I'm not good at this. It's been a long time. Why is this so fuckin' difficult? Yes, I do. Fuck, can we go out to dinner, Athena, like maybe now? One of those places on the beach?"

I almost added, "Please, oh please," but didn't want to sound any needier.

She was back to being happy, enjoying how stupid I sounded.

For years, Sara put off a y*ou don't measure up* vibe. She had been cold so long I forgot why I married her. Athena could be a bitch, but somehow, I knew she was never cold.

Bitch I could live with.

"Yes, Randy. That sounds really nice. I would very much like to . . . *hang out.*"

I stood. "You ready to go?" Matilda and Ruben watched us as we stood. Both were still looking at us when I stopped at the door and did an about-face for one last look at Matilda. I wanted to bring her with us. I felt bad leaving her in this dump.

CHAPTER 8

For years, Sara rarely drank. Once I told her she needed to drink hard liquor to kill the bug that had crawled up her ass. Our marriage wasn't doing so hot then.

Athena drank like a guy. Or like a woman who knew how to drink.

She upended a tequila shot and sat the empty glass on the table with a crack, then shut her eyes and bit her lime. She chased it with a sip of her margarita, which was almost gone. We were on round three and feeling no pain.

"We ought to lay off the shots. I don't want to get too shitfaced," I said.

Did I just say that? I thought of empties spilling from the trashcans outside my room.

I ordered a margarita for Athena and a beer for me.

The Rosarito Beach Hotel had a tattered elegance. It had seen better days but was palatial next to the Estrella. Everywhere inside was bright red, yellow and green.

The ocean filled the big window of the hotel. The sand began fifty feet below, down wooden stairs. I didn't care for the beach in Rosarito. It looked dirty, as if cigarette ashes were mixed with the sand.

"Your English is so good," I said. "I know you lived in New York." Then I blurted, "Can I see your eyes?"

Athena wore black sunglasses with huge lenses and shiny fake gems on the temples. During a year deployment to Bosnia, I got down to the beaches of Croatia. Italian women filled the cafes. All were tall and lean and wore sunglasses like Athena's. I thought they were so classy and unattainable, like famous fashion models. I couldn't believe I was getting drunk with somebody who'd fit in there.

She removed her sunglasses.

"I lived in the States for eleven years with my mother," she said. "Queens, in New York City. We stayed long after my father left us. I took dance at a studio in New York. My father sent money for ten years. I auditioned and was accepted into Juilliard, their pre-college program. It would have been on a scholarship for ballet. I wanted to go there for college."

"Juilliard?" I said.

"You don't know it? It's American. In New York City."

"No. If it ain't a military base, I don't know it."

"It's famous, the college for the arts. Music, dance, painting, acting," she said.

"But you didn't go? Why not?"

"My father quit sending money. My mother got very sick and died. We'd overstayed our visas by years. I was deported and lived with my grandmother. I went to high school in Guadalajara. I spoke Spanish, but Mexico was a foreign country."

"Sorry," I said. I didn't know what else to say. "You have kids?"

"No," she said. "Do you?"

"Two sons. I don't see them."

"Why not?"

I thought about how much I missed my boys.

"My ex-wife told them I am first-class shit so many times that they believed it. This is them." I reached into my breast pocket. My clothing had changed, but the photo had stayed there for twelve years. I placed it on the table.

"You look younger," she said. "Different. You're smiling." Athena looked at me, then back to the photo. "Younger and—"

"Yeah." I didn't know what else to say and I wasn't sure I wanted to know what she was going to add.

"When did your husband die?" I asked.

"He was in the army, a lieutenant. He died in service. He was a good man who believed in Mexico. That was eighteen years ago," she said it without emotion.

I understood. In my therapy sessions, I'd summarized killing close to three hundred people using the words, "I saw some shit."

Athena's eyes were fixed on the scar under the tattoo on my arm.

"How'd you get that?" Her tongue tapped her upper teeth. They were white, perfect. I would think of them at night.

"The scar?"

She nodded.

"Afghanistan. 2002. A bullet."

She was not quite smiling. Her eyes got large. She waited, keeping them on mine.

"I got the tattoo before I left overseas. Pissed me off to see it ruined. Fuckin' beautiful, it was. Had my blood type and name. Then that fucker messed it up. We were patrolling some shitty village near Pakistan. I knew something was up when I saw the HiLuxes."

She cocked her head in question. "Toyota trucks," I explained. "The Taliban drove them. That's all they drove. We walked into eleven of them—Taliban, not HiLuxes. There were two HiLuxes."

Her expression was intense. I felt like the most fascinating person on earth right then.

"Then? What happened then?" she asked.

"I killed him."

I'd forgotten. Civilians don't talk about killing like I did. Just about everybody I'd been around for twenty years had been military.

"Sorry," I said. "You didn't need to know that."

She didn't blink. "No, Randy, I *asked* you." She put her hand on the scar the bullet left. Somehow she knew touching it this time would be okay. Her fingers were soft, moving its length, flickering over my skin as if trying to turn me on. It worked.

Her eyes moved from the scar to my face, then back. She smiled and I saw the flush in her cheeks.

Is she turned on?

Athena downed her margarita and put the glass down hard. "How about another round?" she said. "Let's get shitfaced."

I needed to spend more time with this lady.

Back in my room that night, I thought of Sara.

"You don't know how to flirt," she'd said. "Nothing is nuanced with you anymore, Randy. Nothing is tender or romantic."

I'd looked up the word. *Nuanced: Characterized by subtle shades of meaning or expression.*

That didn't help. I didn't understand why I would want to be nuanced. I doubt Sara knew the word before she had read it in one of her bullshit women's magazines, the source of her wisdom.

She began to say things like that around 2007. I was home most of that year, but it was hard. We didn't talk. She didn't want me around. Sara said all of that without speaking.

I still loved her then. I told her how much I did. One time I said she could teach me to be romantic. I was smiling, but she turned her head away and said nothing. That hurt.

Maybe if I had seen those subtle shades of meaning or expression, I would have seen what others did. It wasn't until three months after I was served with divorce papers in 2013 that I learned Sara had had at least four affairs. One during each of my last four overseas tours.

Maybe thirteen years of combat had sucked all the romance out of me. I tried but could not compete. My wife was fucking *nuanced* guys.

I started getting anxious. The walls were closing in again. I looked up to the ceiling at the bare lightbulb. The on/off chain was moving back and forth in a three-inch arc. There must be a breeze up there.

I thought of how Athena's hair contrasted with her skin. Then I heard her laughing. I replayed her saying, *"Let's get shitfaced,"* and I smiled. I thought of calling her. Then I remembered she was working.

The walls stopped moving and I fell asleep.

For a ten-year-old, it didn't get any better. My turkey was resting on the floorboard between my dad and me.

At the truck, my father threw my turkey in the bed. "I won't lose your bird, Randy. Promise. We'll tie her down." Still, I was afraid our Thanksgiving dinner would bounce out of the truck on the drive home. I protested. He relented, letting it ride up front in the cab.

The general store in Good Grief was open when we came off the mountain.

"Just got to make a quick pit stop, Randy." I started to get out. "Wait here." I started to get out anyhow. "Randy come on. I said wait in the truck."

He came out with a six-pack of Coke and a handful of beef sticks. He broke off two Cokes, handing one to me, then placed the rest on the seat between us and gave me a beef stick.

"Randy, there's something you need to know about." His can hissed as he popped the tab. He took a gulp. "Ahh," he said. We were still in the parking lot.

"There are other women in my life. Patty and Laura. I love both of them. I would be happy if you did not mention this to your mother. And do not tell Becky. She'll tattle to your mom."

Since I'd shot the bird my father was treating me like I was grown up. Like a friend, almost. But this news was a gut punch. My dad loved my mom. He was always touching her, pulling her to dance through the house. One time Mom told me he would die to protect her. I saw it in his eyes when he looked at her. I felt happy when I saw him look at her like that.

I wanted to protest, but didn't know what to say.

He studied me, then laughed and squeezed my shoulder. "Hey, I'm teasing, Randy. There's only your mom." He opened the glove box, took out two cassettes, and handed them to me; Patty Smyth and Laura Branigan. Both had dark hair and were fair skinned like Mom. But it was Laura Branigan who knocked me back in my seat. She wore a red blouse and shiny black leather pants. At ten all I could think of was *so amazingly*.

"I think we'll start with some Scandal."

That 1950 Ford F1 was my dad's pride. An American heavy-metal masterpiece fully restored. He did a lot of the work himself. And he loved his music. The Bose speaker system was the best on the market in 1983.

He pulled onto Interstate 95 toward Bonners Ferry. He hit play, and then spun the volume knob. I felt the cab fill with "Goodbye to You" by Patty Smyth and Scandal.

Most of the cars heading south on 95 had Alberta license plates. "Randy, let's show these Canadians how we do things in Idaho."

He punched the accelerator, taking that old Ford to eighty-five miles an hour. Then eighty-eight. The windows were open, and the volume cranked as high as that cassette player could go. We drank Cokes, ate beef sticks, and sang loudly and off-key with Patty.

Cold, dry air blasted our hair. I had never seen my dad like this. I'd entered his world.

"Can we listen to her?" I gave my dad the cassette with Laura Branigan in the red blouse.

"You like Laura Branigan? She's my favorite, second only to your mother in beauty."

We listened to Laura, screaming with her to "Gloria" and "Spanish Eddie," laughing and bobbing our heads in time to the beat. We thought we were punk rockers. He kept his foot on the accelerator and got the truck up to ninety. Then ninety-one. We topped out at ninety-two, flying by the Canadian tourists heading south. Some of them looked at us open-mouthed and caught our eyes as we blew by them on the left. They probably thought we were crazy.

We were just happy.

My father pulled up to our home as Laura wrapped up, "How Am I Supposed to Live Without You."

"Laura brings me home with that song—it's slower, helps me regain my composure before I go in to see your mother."

I walked into our kitchen and threw that turkey on the kitchen floor at my mother's feet. It made a loud thump, just like in my dreams. The conquering hero returns.

My mom acted mad, but I knew she wasn't. She was tall and moved fast through the house. I never could get anything past her.

"Randy, that bird is not allowed in this kitchen until it's plucked. Pick it up. Give it to Becky." A few stray feathers fluttered off my turkey to the linoleum, along with some mud.

My dad put his hands on my mom's waist. He kissed the back of her neck.

"Randy, the ladies can relax. You and I are plucking this bird."

My mom ran the house. "No, John. That boy is not plucking that bird. Becky, take it out to the porch. We are plucking that bird. You men go down to your basement and do whatever it is you do down there."

Becky was eight and lanky from growing too fast. She was missing two front teeth. Hearing her groans as I handed her that dead bird was sweet music.

Late that night I took a flashlight and went out to the truck to look again at Laura Branigan.

I found the cassette. Her hair was black, long, wavy and tousled. I could only stare and think how much I wanted to touch her.

CHAPTER 9

"Do you have children?" Ruben asked as he was opening a Pacifico and placing it in front of me.

"I do. Two boys. John's eighteen, starting college next month. Danny's twelve and lives with his mom."

I *thought* John was starting college. I didn't know where. My bottle was sweating. I made lines in the condensation with my finger.

"What about you?" I asked.

"Eleven, soon twelve." He held his lips shut, nodded and patted his hips twice. "My wife's due in November." He kept nodding, a man satisfied with how life has played out for him.

"Whoa! Twelve. You're a fuckin' stud, man."

Ruben ran down his offspring, beginning with the oldest, Ruben, Jr., twenty-seven, and working his way down to Tino, who was three and lived with Ruben and his "young" sixth wife. They resided in the hills east of town. For each child, he told an anecdote. By the time he on Anna, the fourth eldest at twenty, my eyes were glazing over. He thought she was married and living somewhere near Mexico City. Other than Tino, Ruben didn't really know what any of his kids were doing.

He smiled grandly, proud of his fertility. I was envious, wishing for the careless ease he exhibited in discussing his offspring.

"How fuckin' old are you?" I asked.

"Fifty-two. My wife's twenty-nine." He sucked in his gut.

He launched into another long-winded speech, this one on why men should seek out younger women, extolling his wife's virtues over those of the five greedy bitches he'd so foolishly committed to in 1981, 1990, 1997, 2001 and 2005. "It can be tough at times, keeping Roberta happy." He winked as he smoothed his mustache. I looked at that wild gray line of hair on his lip and his big gut and wondered what *young* wife would find this guy attractive enough to marry.

"You must pay a ton of child support," I said. He didn't answer. There were six pesos, a couple of quarters and a lone buck in his tip jar.

I told him of the fishing trip I took with my boys out of Pensacola in 2007. "We caught two blue marlin. One of them was 350 pounds. We worked shifts dragging in that monster. Took us two hours. John and Danny thought their arms would fall off. Hell, I did too. We still talk about that fish."

Except Danny wasn't on the boat, and John, then nine, didn't help me bring it in. And the one marlin we caught was closer to a hundred pounds. That was our last family vacation.

For Ruben, siring a kid seemed to be enough. I hated that I had no contact with mine.

He began wiping the bar while I watched a soccer game on the television. Starting at the end nearest the front door, he worked his way to me. I picked up my bottle so he could clean beneath it. He put down the rag and put his palms on the bar, facing me. His face had a concerned look.

"How's my good friend Athena?" he asked.

He wasn't smiling.

"I saw you two walking out. She is a great woman, Randy. Really pretty. Great lady. She's funny, too. Can be. Maybe you haven't seen that side of her. How'd it go yesterday?"

Ruben rarely looked at you when he spoke. This time, however, he studied my face. My bullshit flag started rising.

"Good," I said.

He walked from behind the bar and began cleaning a table on the far side of the dance floor. Ruben cleaned like a Roomba. When his ass bumped a table he turned to clean it. I could discern no organization in his cleaning efforts. His voice was loud when he spoke.

"She's on tonight. You planning on comin' to watch her?"

I didn't answer. I wasn't planning on ever coming here at night.

He walked back to behind the bar, leaving two-thirds of the tables unwiped. "Do you know much about her?" he asked.

"I know enough to know I like her. What's your point, Ruben?"

He was again in front of me. I looked in his eyes until he looked away. He kept looking at me out of the side of his eye.

"Nothing. No point. She came to work here a year ago. She used to sit in that table over there, the one you two were in yesterday. Didn't talk to nobody then. Except that cat. Then she got *friendly*. She started sitting at the bar more."

"Yeah."

"Just wondering," he said, making an exaggerated show of touching his chin to appear thoughtful. "You seem like a nice guy. That's all. It's just . . . where'd she come from? What does she do for money? I'd want to know more if I were you."

"*You're* looking out for *me*. Why are you so interested? I don't know much about you either, other than you have a bunch of fuckin' kids all over Mexico. You mind cutting to the chase, man?"

Ruben held his hands up, showing me his palms. "Randy, Randy. Relax. No offense. She's a friend. It's just . . . she's just . . . not what she seems. There's . . . other parts to her job."

I stared. "What the hell's *that* supposed to mean? You talking lap dances, shit like that?"

He raised his eyebrows, a man offended. "No. We do not allow those things in here."

"So, make your fuckin' point."

"Okay," he said. "I hear she leaves with customers. Not a lot, though." He spoke like a man objectively presenting the mitigating facts, as if Athena fucking men for money wasn't bad so long as she didn't do it every day.

"You've seen this?"

"Well, no. I don't work nights. One of the night bartenders told me. He spoke to me in confidence." He gazed at the ceiling with a noble expression. "I will not give out his name."

"Why are you telling me this? I thought she was your friend."

"She is. I . . . I just don't want to see you get burned."

He looked down. This is friendship in the civilian world? No wonder I was having trouble outside the Army.

"So, why are you hitting on her?" I asked. I wasn't sure if he was. I just wanted to piss him off.

Ruben's head raised with a speedy jerk. His mustache vibrated in the green neon. He spoke loudly.

"What? What are you saying?" He stared, the perpetual smile gone, innocence on his face. "Randy, please. I'm a married man, *happily* married, with a *young* wife. Don't say that about Roberta."

"I said it about *you*," I shot back. "You know what, Ruben? You're full of shit. Just give me another beer and close me out."

I took my beer, sat by Matilda and tried to forget what that fuckin' asshole said.

"What do you want from me now, Randy?" Sara was breathing fast and loud on her cell phone. It was early January 2014.

I was at the Motel 6. She was four miles away from the home we were supposed to live in together when I retired. In my mind, I could see her—lean and in shape from spending half her life on a treadmill, her blonde hair cut short on the sides in that butch cut I never liked, makeup perfect. There were slight tremors on her jaw line as she grinded her teeth. Her mouth was tight, opening only to lay into me.

"I just want to talk."

Three months before, I came home to a court order giving Sara the home "during the pendency of the dissolution proceedings." My boys were to live with her. I was supposed to keep paying and see them two weekends a month and one night a week.

In those three months, Sara and I communicated by leaving messages. I would go to the house. She'd slam the door. I'd call. She wouldn't answer. This time, she actually did. I thought there was an opportunity.

I heard more breathing.

"Sara. Can't we talk? In person. You know, meet somewhere? Doesn't need to be at the house. A restaurant?"

"You can talk now, Randy . . . *right* now. Go 'head. What is it you want to say? Say it. I'm listening." *Let's get this over with,* her tone said.

I tried to stay cool. I'd rehearsed, but now that the time had come, I didn't know what to say.

"We've been together a long time."

"We've been *married* a long time," she said. "We haven't been together. You've been gone."

"I know. But I'm back."

I didn't know what I was guilty of. I was scared and lonely and had no one to talk to. The night before, I'd woken up screaming.

"You never came back, Randy. Not all the way. You come home, but you're still over there."

"I'm home now. Promise. No more tours."

We both breathed. "Anything else?" She asked.

I suspected she'd had an affair. One of her early messages said she had met someone. "He's there for me," it said. "He supports and nourishes my independence."

"Sara, look. I know it wasn't easy. I was gone for years. But I'm out. Retired." More breathing.

"You already said that."

I thought she was feeling guilty and that was keeping her from reconciling. "Sara. I know. I was gone so much. It was so hard for you and our boys. I know you may have done something you regret while I was gone. I do not care. You hear me? I don't care. I love you. We'll move forward from here. And we can—"

"That's what you think? You think I had an affair? *An* affair?"

Maybe she hadn't cheated.

"Let me make this clear. I quit waiting for you to come home four deployments ago. You got that? Four tours ago."

"What? What the—"

"You're such a goddamned fool. Such an idiot. So damned blind. You didn't see anything, did you? With me? With our boys? You're running around over there playing soldier while we wait for you to grow up. What'd it get you, Randy? Two boys who don't know who the hell you are. I moved on. We *all* moved on." Her breathing sounded like a bull readying for a charge.

"Sar—"

"Don't interrupt me. Shut up. This is our last conversation. Our *last!* Listen. Listen, Randy. Listen. I had four affairs, not one. You hear that? *Four.* I quit waiting for you to come home in 2008. In fact, I met someone. He's nice and respectful and kind. He listens. He doesn't kill people for a living. He's coming over in ten minutes. We're having dinner and playing Scrabble. Us and the boys."

She hung up.

And I went to her home to kick the living shit out of the asshole fucking my wife.

The places I'd fought were nothing like the sanitized suburban neighborhoods of Fullerton, California. But that didn't matter. I was in Sadr City, the slum of two million people on the east side of Baghdad. Corporal Landin wasn't wearing his helmet and I was tearing him a new one.

The war came home.

And then I went further back to November 2004, a time Sara and I had been getting along.

"You're home early," she said as I walked in at two. She smiled and looked perfect—her hair up and skin tanned even in dead winter, via a local tanning salon. She always looked that way. "Cool. We can do something. I wanted to go out and get pizza tonight. I know you hate Chuck E. Cheese. John's been wanting to go. Can you handle it?" She smiled, then winked. "We'll get a liter of wine and watch the boys."

I'd been home from Iraq for five months.

She began looking hard at my face. "You've been drinking. Haven't you?"

Drunk was a better description. Vince's wife Raquel had driven me home. Vince, Darnell and I had been celebrating at the NCO Club.

We got the alert that morning. Colonel Garrett Cox, the regimental commander, stood before 3,700 Rangers to deliver the good news. Another year in the sandbox. And the entire 75th was deploying, which meant I would be serving with my people—Rangers and Special Ops — and not a bunch of half-trained grunts. Cox sent us home for the day.

"When?" She asked.

"Six weeks."

Her mouth dropped. A blonde lock fell across her left eye. I'd come home wanting to have sex. That wasn't happening.

After an hour of fighting, Sara's tan looked like a bad sunburn.

"Just admit it, Randy. Do us all a goddamned favor and admit it."

She was trying to get me to say I loved it when the towers went down because I loved going to war. I shook my head and thought how fuckin' crazy my wife was getting. She walked out of the kitchen and into our bedroom, slamming the door, then came back a third time to beat me up more. She did that routine—leave, come back, leave, come back—when she was mega-pissed. This was maybe the third time I'd heard her cuss in fifteen years.

"That's fuckin crazy" I said. "I don't even get what you're saying. *You* don't know what the hell you're saying."

John, then nine, came home from school and began watching us from the kitchen. "Go to your room, sweetheart," Sara said. John and I were tight. He was a soldier too. We dressed alike. John hated when we argued. Sara enunciated her words. He walked out. I heard the door shut.

We kept at it for another hour. She was raising our kids alone. She needed me and I was always gone. I was insensitive to her needs. It sounded like bullshit she'd picked up from *Cosmopolitan*.

I thought she was selfish. I didn't hear what she said. "I'm in the military, Sara. You understand what orders are? Fucking orders?" I slowed my speech, pretending to be the voice of some higher authority, but we were no longer simply arguing. We were trying to hurt each other. "There's a war. I goddamn serve our country. You fuckin' *understand* that, don't you?"

"What are you saying Randy? That I don't understand some noble *call of duty* you have? This will be your eighth deployment. *Eighth*. One two three four five six seven . . . eight." She looked at me with that red face, pleading, but I would not see.

After my first deployment to Somalia, her face looked like that, but for a different reason. Red, tear stained. She was so happy when I walked off the plane. We went back to our small house on base and made love. That was fourteen years earlier.

Sara grabbed her car keys and walked out the front door. When we got on the buses six weeks later, Sara and my boys did not see me off.

I searched Matilda's eyes.
Sara was right. I loved it when those towers went down.

CHAPTER 10

"There, look!"

I used a knife, extending the reach of my arm. It was two days later. Athena and I were again at the Rosarito Beach Hotel. I saw whale spouts a quarter mile out.

"Sorry, Randy, I don't see them. I'm sorry."

Just then, one of the whales breached, shooting straight up and landing with a house-sized splash. "Fuckin' look at that! Look. Holy shit. I've never seen that."

"No, I don't see them."

I looked at her in disbelief. She started laughing.

"You're fuckin' with me. Aren't you? You saw them."

"Yes, Randy. I'm fucking with you. They're beautiful."

We laughed together. These were deep fuck-it laughs, the kind that help you forget things.

Nobody said *fuck* better than Athena. It was so sexy hearing that word come from her mouth.

"I was wondering," she said. "Why are you here in Rosarito?"

I knew what I'd say. "You ever seen *The Shawshank Redemption* with Morgan Freeman, Tim Robbins?"

"No. No, wait. Yes, I think so," she said. "I can't remember it."

I told her the plot. How a man unjustly accused of murder, played by Tim Robbins, serves twenty years in prison. Then he escapes to Mexico. In the last scene, Robbins is on the beach in Zihuatanejo. Morgan Freeman, his buddy from prison, approaches on the sand. They both look happy.

"I didn't have anything definite. I was going another three, four hundred miles south, maybe Bahia de Tortugas, or south of that. Just down there." I pointed to my left, down the coast to the south. "I thought my problems would go away if I came here." I started to add more, then stopped.

"But you're in Rosarito? What do you mean, problems?"

"I got divorced. My truck broke down. It's fixed, kind of. I stayed here." She was studying my face like I was full of shit. I didn't know her well enough to borrow a line from another movie and tell her I see dead people.

"I have a place I want to go," she said. "Costa Rica."

"You been there?" I asked.

"No."

"I don't know that place. Why do you want to go there?"

"It is so different, and better, than everywhere I have been. I'm from Mexico but there is much not to like about my country. America—New York—was ugly and gray. At least where we lived, it was." She paused, flicking an errant strand of black silken hair behind one ear. "I read travel magazines about Mexico and Central America. Then I saw Costa Rica. I saw a place I liked. Quepos. The water on the beaches is so blue and beautiful. Palm trees move in the rhythm of that beauty. It's so free. No drug cartels."

She showed me internet photographs of Quepos on her phone. It looked warm, slow and quiet. So green and tropical. "It's beautiful and it's not Mexico," she said.

I looked at her scar. "How did your husband die?"

"I was twenty-two."

"What happened?" I asked.

In my head, I heard Ruben telling me about Athena with other men. I gulped my beer to shut him up.

"I told you. He died in service. Things have only gotten worse."

I wasn't sure what she meant. I stared into her eyes, but she wouldn't meet my gaze. She looked at the ocean. The whales were gone. I wished I hadn't asked. She'd been laughing.

"That's tough," I said. "I spent twenty-one years in uniform." To fill the quiet, I added, "I'm in a motel ten miles south. You know the Vista del Mar? It's on the ocean. There's a sewage plant just up the beach."

"Filth and beauty, side by side," she said, still looking at the water. "Like everything here."

"I look at the view and don't touch the water. It's not what I pictured driving south," I said.

"Nothing in life ever works out like we plan."

"Yeah, but we can make it what we want."

I was surprised those words came from me. Once, I believed if I was smart enough and worked hard enough, I could get anything I wanted. Then my life became a bumper-car ride, ramming into problems I never saw coming. I'd quit believing.

I was starting to have faith again.

"I don't believe that," she said. "Tell that to the person dying of cancer."

"We have to believe it," I said. Her face was red, and she was hitting me with her angry stare again. "You're mad at me. Why?"

"Alberto, my husband, said things like that. It was always, 'We can build the country we want, a great Mexico.'"

I didn't know what to say.

She stood.

"I can walk myself back to the club."

I stood. "What are you doing? I don't get why you're pissed off."

"You are one super-dense *pendejo*, Randy." She paused, her eyes on mine. "I'm not mad at you. I'm mad at me. "You know why? Because I like you, Randy, and I don't want to like you. I don't need another soldier."

She walked off. I followed her for twenty feet, then stopped.

Athena and I spent the next afternoon together. She never mentioned what she'd said the day before.

We went to the shops on the north side of town. Normally, tourists packed these places, but it was a weekday and crowds were light. I didn't come here when it was busy. Too many triggers in crowds.

I liked watching her shop for things she wasn't going to buy. The stores were crammed floor to ceiling, front to back, with coats, belts, brightly colored piñatas, pottery—everything, as if the shop owners got awards for packing the most items on their shelves and display hooks.

It was so colorful and alive and noisy. Music blared from open-air bars. There was a wild, anything-goes vibe—a swap meet where most everyone was drunk. So different than shopping in the US. I bought a few onyx statues and two hats.

"That for you?" Athena asked.

"No. My boys."

"How old are they now?"

"John'll be eighteen in a month. Danny's thirteen . . . no. Twelve."

She was studying my profile as we walked. "It bothers you, doesn't it? Not seeing them?" I pretended I didn't hear her questions.

We went to a restaurant. She asked about them. I thought of Ruben taking the credit for the accomplishments of offspring he didn't know. "I don't see them," I said, then changed the subject.

I walked Athena to the club. She was starting her shift in half an hour. I told her I was going to my motel.

I stayed in town.

I didn't think she had lied when she said, "I don't do that," meaning she didn't have sex for money.

But once I would have said that Sara wouldn't be unfaithful, either.

Five hours later, just after midnight, I watched her leave the club. I was across the street, in shadows. Athena started up a street that intersected Juarez, heading east toward the poorer areas of Rosarito. She was carrying a bag, wearing jeans, sneakers and a windbreaker.

She walked fast, looking over her shoulder like she was trying to shake a pursuer. First left, then right. Then straight, then left again. I stayed a block behind her, almost lost her, then saw her cross a street ahead.

I didn't like her walking alone at this hour, but I kept my distance.

Her hands were in the pockets of her jacket. She stopped at a wooden door on the sidewalk. It was the entry point in a dirty white stucco wall about eight feet tall, topped with red brick. She opened it, shutting it behind her. An hour later she came out and turned left, up the hill and away from the beach.

She kept on up the hill, then opened a door to an apartment building. I milled about down the street for two hours. This time she didn't come out.

I got back to my room at four that morning.

I felt like I'd done something nasty.

We were at an early dinner on Saturday. In another two hours her shift would start. I tried not to think about it.

"You're so pretty. You're hard for me to look at," I said to Athena.

"Hard to look at? I don't know what you mean."

"Yeah, you do. My delivery may suck, but you know what I mean." Still no filter.

"I do. I think you meant it as a compliment. Thank you, Randy, for telling me I'm hard to look at."

Athena wore her black leather skirt with a red blouse. This one was long-sleeved. It hit me why I thought she'd looked familiar.

"You look like Laura Branigan. You know that? I was in love with her when I was ten. She didn't give me the time of day."

She laughed mid-swallow and spit beer, some of which hit my hand. I didn't wipe it off. The liquid was cool, running down my wrist and onto my forearm, heading toward my regimental tattoo.

"You know Laura Branigan?"

"Uh-huh. I do. I look like her?"

"Yeah, you do. When she was young, in her twenties."

Both ladies had the same hair, though Athena's was a deeper black. Same fair skin, same lips. But Branigan was cute and soft-looking. Athena's features were sharp, her gaze strong and sometimes so intimidating I would look away. She could play the warrior princess. Athena had Branigan's sexiness on steroids.

"I'd stare at her picture on the cover of the cassettes my dad had when I was a boy," I said. "I was getting ready to come home from Iraq when I read that she died. There should have been a worldwide day of mourning."

I thought of Branigan in that red, long-sleeved blouse and black leather pants. "You know what? You're a lot better-looking than her. Yeah. You are. Maybe we can go out tomorrow? You're off. We can take a drive south. Grab a six-pack. Sit on a beach."

Athena jerked her head back and raised her eyebrows. She may have been half-Greek, but her exaggerated gestures were pure Latina. Her eyebrows were almost hitting her hairline. I loved her expressions and I think she knew I did.

She gave a thumbs-up. I half smiled, then looked away, hiding a stab of nausea. "I'd love to do that," she said.

We'd been 'going out' for three weeks. We'd spent so much time together, yet I didn't know much about her. We'd barely kissed.

"Tomorrow?" I asked. "Two in the afternoon? Where do you live? I can pick you up. Maybe you can tell me a little more about yourself."

She shook her head. "I'll meet you somewhere." She spoke fast and clipped.

The nightclub was as far as she would let me walk her. "You don't need to come any farther," she said as she turned and walked up the street.

I set the alarm on my phone. At 12:05 a.m., I was across the street as Athena walked out of the club. Alone. She started up the street to the east, walking fast along a circuitous route. She took a different path this time, but again went through the door on the long stucco wall. I took up a position across the street. Again, she stayed an hour. I saw her emerge, once again walking up the hill to the same apartment building.

On Wednesday of the next week, the same routine. And again on Thursday, then Friday, then Saturday.

Why didn't I open that door on the stucco wall? What did I think was behind it? A whorehouse? But she was only in there for an hour.

That's enough time.

For what?

I didn't want the answer.

The more I liked Athena, the more I felt like shit following her. On Wednesday, as she was working, I walked the path she took home every night, passing the stucco wall, not stopping until I came to the apartment building she entered. The building sat right on the sidewalk. The window blinds were open on one of the bottom-floor apartments.

Inside was a woman of at least eighty watching television. I could hear it from the sidewalk through closed windows. I headed back in the direction of the club, stopping at the wooden door.

It was heavy, mahogany-stained wood with black wrought-iron hinges. It once had been nice. Now it was dusty and beat-up, like everything in this neighborhood.

I hesitated.

The door opened with a creak.

Inside was a well-lit brick courtyard and a dry fountain containing dirt and cigarette butts. Across the courtyard was another door along a long stucco wall. A couch was by the door. A man sat there, smoking and staring at the sky. He was about thirty, dressed in a dirty blue work outfit. I walked closer, planning on speaking with him. Then he smiled and gestured to the door, inviting me to open it.

I didn't ask what this place was. A dog barked somewhere far off.

The room was dark and lit by candles on the walls. It was a long room with four rows of wooden benches, then another six rows of white plastic chairs. To my left as I entered was an altar, a plastic table covered with white and green cloth.

The stations of the cross were on the walls. *Catholic.* I had entered to one side of the altar along rows of candles. Poor people worshipped here. I was alone.

To my right were rows and rows of candles. Several were lit. Before them was a short wooden bench on which to kneel. To the side was a red coffee can that had *Donacion* printed in large letters.

I almost left. Then I saw the photograph behind two candles in the top row. It was small, credit-card sized. I turned on the flashlight on my cell phone and leaned in to look. I knew what it was and didn't think I should touch it.

It was Athena holding a little boy. A man stood next to her. She wasn't the sophisticated warrior princess I knew. She was in her early twenties. Her face was softer, like Laura Branigan's. The man was around her age, maybe a little older. They were dressed in the light cotton clothing people wear to restaurants on the beach. She was holding the boy. All three were smiling. Behind was the ocean.

Her face was different, not etched with pain. For a moment, I felt my chest tighten. *She's beautiful. She would have other men in her life.* Above the candles on the wall was a sign that read, *Por los amado muertos. For the beloved dead.* I looked at the little boy Athena held. I could tell it was her son.

I shouldn't be here. I hadn't been in a church since I got married at eighteen. I walked out the door by the altar. The man was gone. I left the grounds through the door to the sidewalk.

Someday I would have to kick Ruben's ass for turning me into a stalker.

The next day, on the dirty sidewalk outside the club, I hugged Athena and kissed her cheek. I kept hugging her.

"What got into you?" she said.

"Just nice to see you."

"What's Randy been up to?"

"Not much," I said. "Randy's just really happy to go somewhere with you." I still held her. "I like you, Athena. Very much."

We got in my shit-box truck to drive south of Ensenada. Our favorite pastime was hiking to the deserted beaches down there and drinking beer. I didn't have the money to do much else. I could talk about anything with this woman.

CHAPTER 11

Matilda came right over when I sat down. Athena hadn't arrived yet.

"How did I wind up with you as a therapist?"

Her nose was pressed through the chain links. She made loud sniffing sounds like a hunting dog. It was quiet in the club. "You're the only reason I come into this dump. You know that? *Doctor Matilda, cat therapist*? Sounds like some dumb reality show."

Athena and I had been together almost every day for six weeks, half of that time at this table with Matilda. I still hadn't been to Athena's home. "And I like dark bars, Matilda. I wouldn't be sitting in this bright light if not for you."

I got CPT, *cougar processing therapy,* from Matilda. We talked. We understood each other. I showed her my wounds. She listened without judgment. She didn't have to review notes to know who I was. She never fucked up my name. We had a bond I felt through the chain links of her cage.

And I saw her wounds. Her eyes were more than their colors. They were expressive. Describing them as gold and brown was like saying the sun is yellow.

Athena was late. Her face was tight as she entered. She sat close to me. She wore jeans, a pink blouse, and tennis shoes like some preppy college girl.

"Something bothering you?" I asked.

She shook her head too fast.

I was working on a graph as she sat by me. "What's that," she asked. "Global warming?"

It was a handwritten chart titled *Flashbacks*. We used charts like these in the Army. They measured success and were usually just fluff designed to impress generals. This wasn't one of those. I started work on it in my motel room. The bright light by Matilda's cage was perfect for this task. A twelve-inch wooden ruler and pen were on the table next to my chart.

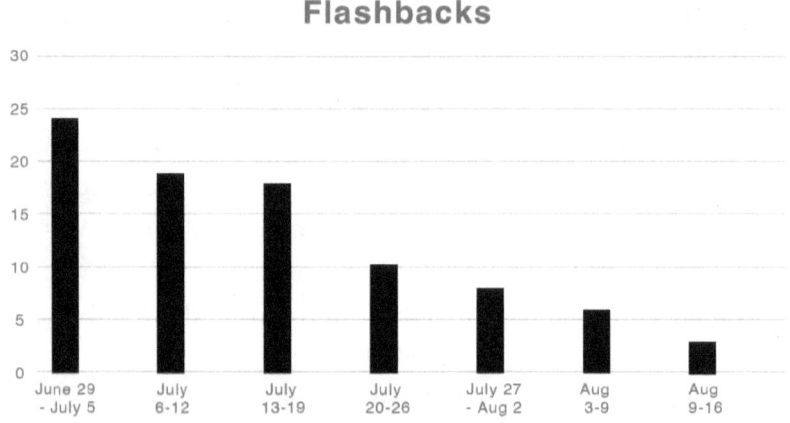

"No. They're metrics. It'd be going the other way for global warming. It's me, my problems, the flashbacks." She scooted her chair over and pushed it next to mine, then leaned her head over the table.

"Something's helping me. Look at this." I traced the point of the pen from the top left to the lower right of the graph. "I was having three, maybe four, flashbacks a day when I met you. Twenty-four the week of July 4th. That's an estimate. I wasn't keeping count, but that's pretty close. Look. Twenty-four. Nineteen. Eighteen. The week of July 20 to 26, I had ten. Last week it was down to three. I haven't had one in three days."

Matilda was still up at the chain link fence. "I think I'm getting better. I needed to see it, on paper."

Matilda's eyes followed, fixed on our movements. Athena was

pushing her shoulder against mine as she studied my chart. We looked like an old married couple going over monthly bills with their oversized pet cat.

Once I had said, "Misery loves company."

Mountain lions are solitary animals; yet somehow in this dingy club, one had packed up with two humans. Or maybe it was the other way around.

Athena looked in my face, then put her hand on my neck and pulled my head. She kissed me, kept our lips together.

"Can I have this?" she said.

I didn't ask why. "Sure. Yeah, you can have it." My face was still close to hers. "I like your name. Athena. I like you."

"I know that. I need to tell you something," she said. Athena kept looking at me until we heard a low growl.

Matilda extended her front legs. It was a growl of contentment, the type a dog makes stretching out on a bed next to a heater.

"It all got better the Fourth of July when I met you," I said. "And her. I'm not as fucked up as I was. I really *am* getting better." Just saying the words made me *feel* better. I felt like drinking, wanted to go somewhere nice and not stay in this shithole. Except Matilda kept us here.

I saw the three of us sitting on the beach, doing things couples do with their dogs. I know it was stupid to think that. Matilda was stuck. I walked to the bar and came back with two beers and two tequila shots, ready to celebrate with my pack.

Two college guys ordered beers and headed to the pool tables across the bar. "You mind taking our picture?" I asked one of them.

"Can we use yours?" I asked Athena. "My phone's cracked."

I put my arm around her and the kid took the photo. "That's good," he said, handing the phone back to Athena.

She looked at the screen. "It is. Thank you." He walked off. We went back to studying a chart that told me I wasn't so crazy anymore.

CHAPTER 12

Athena's thigh was pushed against mine. I don't know why I hadn't tried to make love to her. I would kiss her but could go no further. Sometimes I thought she studied me and was confused. I saw a small dark freckle on her arm and felt her heat. I wanted to put my hand on her thigh but couldn't.

It was Monday and Athena wasn't working. It was seven in the evening. I'd never been here later than five thirty. Crowds, triggers. Around a hundred people were in the nightclub and the door was opening and closing, nonstop. The DJ did not start for another hour and a half. The jukebox on the far wall was getting a workout. An overhead light illuminated the line of men standing before it, waiting to pay the machine. They looked like they were lined up to receive communion.

A college kid in a pink-and-red-striped shirt, lime green shorts, and flip-flops was walking back to the bar from the jukebox. "He'd get the shit beat out of him for wearing that getup in most of the bars I hung out in," I said.

I meant it as a joke. Athena laughed, but I think she was being nice. She had a *you're a hard man to figure out* expression. I had told her things I hadn't told Vince and Darnell, things I probably should have told Sara.

Athena was like Matilda. She didn't judge. She listened. Then she would say she understood, even if I told her really bad shit.

Except the time I told her I'd thrown Sara into the wall. She shook her head.

"You beat yourself up over that. How many times did she cheat on you? Four times, I think you said?"

"That I know of."

"You're a hero. In some Middle East country fighting a war. She's having sex with other men. A lot of other men."

It didn't matter what Athena said. I felt shame. For hurting Sara and for being so naïve.

"I don't know why you think I'm a hero. I'm not. Wasn't."

Once, I'd wanted to be a hero. Now I didn't know what one was.

"I've known men who would have killed her for that," Athena said.

"Yeah. They're called murderers. Dump her, yeah. Kill her? . . . Oh, come on."

"I didn't mean you. Take it easy on yourself. You're human." She gently squeezed my knee. She'd never touched me there. She left her hand. I felt another squeeze and electricity traveling up my leg.

"You hear me? Take it easy on yourself, Randy. You are a good guy, one of the good ones. I'm not sure you know that."

She paused.

"I need to tell you something," she said. I listened until the edges of her face blurred.

She moved closer, looked at me straight on, and touched my chest with the tips of her fingers. This was not a gentle, sexy touch. She pushed slightly, moved her head back to get a better view. I did not understand, and then I felt dizzy.

"What's wrong? What is it, Randy? *Randy . . . you . . .*" She was fading.

And I heard it. "Who Knew," played by that fuckin' college kid with the pink shirt who should have the shit beat out of him just for wearing it. Someone turned up the volume to blasting, or maybe I just thought so. The last thing I saw was Athena's wide eyes fixed on mine. She was saying something, but I could not hear any more. I felt my nails digging into the wood of the table, a soft hand on my forearm.

Pink's voice changed. She was shrieking, losing it on the treble notes. No, no, it's the loudspeaker, a tinny sound of blown speakers. I tasted dirt, oily dirt, like a car that had emptied out fluids onto soil that dried and got swept up by the wind. I took a deep breath and coughed. The air was so fuckin' bad here, the sky tan from pollution. I didn't remember it being this bad. I saw the brown-gray smoke pouring into the sky from the four smokestacks in the distance. I wanted to yell, "Pink, shut up, shut the fuck up!" My heart was pounding, trying to bust a hole through my chest wall.

Wind blows across the streets, north, moving paper and that fine dust that gets into everything over here. I'm scared. Not just scared, terrified. I don't know why. Nothing has happened, but I know something horrible will. I felt the press of my M-4 across my chest, barrel out the window, off safe, but it won't help. I can do nothing. The Humvees and the SUVs moving ahead, walking into it. Walking into what? I would not follow them. Fuck you, Hamm. I'm disobeying that order. I don't know how I know that. All of this has already happened.

The song kept on, the words on repeat. This was not the first time. Pink would sing over and over until . . . until what?

Then I did know. My heart beat even harder, thumping, blasting because I knew, fucking knew. *They are going to die.*

How do you know that? You can't know that. *The curb, the fucking curb, can't they see?*

Their Humvee is a hundred meters ahead, kicking up dust for the three Humvees and two SUVs following, each vehicle sucking exhaust from the rear end of the one in front of it. The lead Humvee, Hamm's, moving to the north side of the road, the driver pulling next to the curb, his left tires brushing crumbling cement. Except in one place it wasn't falling apart.

I'm not in that Humvee. First platoon is at a dead stop, *Fuck this shit*. We're not falling in.

Pink sang on, *"sad dreams about a lover who was gone but came in dreams . . . but I keep your memory. You visit me in my sleep . . ."*

Then I saw that arm jutting out the window and knew who was in that Humvee with Hamm. His thumb raised to the sky, a "fuck you" meant for me alone.

Then I knew it all, knew this was no dream, that this was fucking real. Everything disappeared in the explosion. My cheek burned, hot and fiery. I felt my right eardrum burst, felt the blood leaking down to my jawline. I felt the scream.

"It's okay, it's okay. Randy. Randy. Randy, Randy, it's okay. There. There. There. It's okay." Athena's face was an inch away, her forehead pressed to mine. "Sweetheart, it's okay. Sweetheart. I'm here."

Pink was still singing "Who Knew." Time had crawled. Only a woman could feel like this, on my face, rubbing my neck, my shoulders, the scar on my arm. I started to lift myself from the chair, the wood legs making a squeaking sound on the concrete floor, but she held my face, wouldn't let me go. It was a lover's touch, soothing and strong and compassionate.

"There, there, there, darling, there. There, Randy. There, that's okay. Randy. Randy." I settled my weight back into the chair.

I felt her arm muscles. Ariana Grande was now coming out of the jukebox.

People at nearby tables were staring, mouths open. "He's okay," I heard Athena say.

"You screamed," she said.

"I'm okay." I wasn't. My heart was racing. I looked at nearby tables and people looked away. Matilda was sitting up, her hackles raised in a long stripe from her neck to her tail, eyes boring holes into me. Her tail was smacking the floor in a huge wag. "It's okay," I said.

I thought of running out. Athena's hands were pushing on my thighs. I let her keep me in my chair.

"What was it? You were somewhere else." I thought of Sara saying I'd been "gone."

"It's one of those bad dreams, isn't it?"

I wish it was a dream.

I needed something to do. I took swigs of my beer. Matilda stared at both of us, looking from one to the other, then fixed on me. Hackles still raised, her brow furrowed into a human expression of worry, an emotion the cat could not feel.

Athena's head was by my shoulder. "She's worried," she said, as if everyone knew cougars worried. "I was, too. Did you *know* you screamed?"

I know the ending but, during the flashback, I don't. Never. Every time is the first. Except for the fear, the knowing something horrible is going to happen. I start the flashback in that place, then it only gets worse.

"Let's go," I said. I began to stand.

She shook her head, then pointed to my chart. "No," she said. "You should stay. We're here. I'm here. You *need* to stay." I didn't know what she meant.

"You need to think about it. Make yourself think about it. I'm here. Look at me. I'm here, Randy. She's here," she said. Matilda was tense, on her haunches, staring at me, at my face.

That cougar *did* look worried.

I did not know what I wanted. I looked down at a chart that now meant nothing.

"Randy, I'm serious. Go with it. You told me it helps you to think about these things. There will never be a better time."

I didn't answer.

"I understand," Athena said. "You think you have to run. I know what that feels like. I know. It happened to me. Unspeakable. It was so fucking terrible. But you always run to darker places. You think I liked living like I was? Always on the move? Always afraid? But I came here and told myself that you *have* to do it, unless you want to spend your life in hell."

Wasn't this why I sat in this dingy and special place, to think about these things?

Just not this one.

"They were my friends. Darnell. Vince. More than friends. I served six tours with Darnell, four with Vince." I looked at Athena again, felt her genuine concern. "I'll try."

I heard my dad. *"Trying means nothing. Steers try, Randy."*

"I'll do it." I looked in Matilda's eyes and took myself there.

We were assigned to a Stryker infantry brigade from the Pennsylvania National Guard, their first deployment since the Civil War. The Army had plussed them up with experienced combat vets, which is how Darnell, Vince and I got stuck with a bunch of guardsmen.

The night before that convoy, we were celebrating in the trailer Darnell and I shared. I'd been selected for promotion to first sergeant. It was August 2009, and we were going home in two months. The war was winding down. This time they said it was for real.

I would have taken a bullet for those two. We were always together, sergeants over three platoons of Charlie Company. The kids, junior enlisted guys, called us the "three amigos." I was the "White amigo," though they never said it to my face. I would have dropped anybody for fifty if they said that shit around me. Vince would have done the same.

The name didn't bother Darnell, though. Soldiers loved the "Black amigo." He was the guy they went to with problems. Everything was funny to Darnell Bradford. A guy with so much energy, he was in perpetual motion—always talking, watching, and gauging how others were doing. He wanted everyone to be happy. Even here. That was something I never gave a shit about.

"How you doing, soldier? Donovan, how's that good-looking wife of yours? Tony, you work that out with that car dealership? You need me to make another call, get that squared away?" People felt better when Darnell was around. He worked things out. His desire was to be a team-builder, to make everybody happy. I think it killed him.

His face was bold, chiseled, almost pretty, like one of those male models you see in magazines. Six-foot-one with two percent body fat. Women, even the ones wearing burkas, turned their heads for a second look when he walked by. He had never married and had no kids.

The "Brown amigo," Vince, was by Darnell on the floor. He was short, with a bodybuilder's huge biceps and a head that rose from his torso without a neck. There were folds of skin lined up on the back of his head. *Tough* came to mind when you saw him. He never said much unless he was drinking with Darnell and me. Then we couldn't shut him up.

They were both from LA, Vince from the east side and Darnell south central.

Vince lived three trailers from us, but he was always in ours, always a part of the laughs and the bleak humor that came from all the dying. The trailer was simple, about two-thirds the size of Matilda's cage with two twin beds. Darnell had secured a case of Heineken in sixteen-ounce cans and four bags of Doritos for the promotion celebration. We were all shitfaced.

Vince and I were tired of listening to Darnell's music. I handed Darnell my iPod. He began going through it, looking for a song to keep us happy.

"You got anything on this iPod from the last thirty years?" he jabbed. "Wait. Otis Redding, 'Dock of the Bay.' Good but too slo*www*."

His eyes were on the small screen. He laughed in bursts, like a dog's quick bark. "The fuck. Vince, Vince. Look at this. Look at this, shit." Darnell was spitting out words fast, his arms and hands shaking like a kid reeling in his first fish. He held the iPod out to show Vince. Their shoulders were touching, their backs against Darnell's flawlessly made bed. "The soundtrack from *Saturday Night Fever?* Journey. Scandal. Holy mother of Jesus, Randy. When the fuck you gonna learn what good music is?"

Their eyes were glued on that iPod screen. They laughed even harder. A set of rules for sharing emerged. Darnell found a bad song to announce, then he passed it to Vince. Vince found one, then passed it back.

"Mike and the Mechanics," Vince said, passing it to Darnell. When it came back to him, Vince said, "Night Ranger. Goddammit, Randy. Fucking Night Ranger?"

I didn't think this shit was funny.

The two of them were leaning on their sides, angling to get more air to fuel laughs. Then Darnell held up his hand, wide-eyed, the expression that of a man who has either thrown down a Royal Flush or found Jesus.

"REO Speedwagon! 'Keep on Lovin' You!' REO fucking Speedwagon? Randy, man, you listen to this shit? No, no, no, you know what? Let's play some REO fuckin' Speedwagon. I want that song in my head when I meet the goddamn Almighty."

Sara and I loved "Keep on Lovin' You." We would dance to it in the living room of our quarters at Fort Bragg. I was a private first class. She cried that night in 1991 I told her the 75th was deploying to Somalia. Sara wrote to me, said she played the song every night sitting on the couch with Zoey, our dog. We were so fuckin' young, both nineteen. I came home with three confirmed kills and knew I was a career soldier.

Vince and Darnell had lost the power of speech. Darnell began hyperventilating, only coming up for air to say, "Look at this shit." My neck was hot.

I spoke in the voice I used when laying into some private. "Give me that fuckin' iPod. Bring your own goddamm music next time, you fuckin' assholes. That's some good shit on there." They watched silently for a long four seconds. Then they laughed harder.

Darnell wouldn't give it back. His eyes widened. He held the iPod high in his fist, pumping it a few times, then showed it to Vince. He deepened his voice and sounded like a Southern preacher.

"Pink. 'I'm Not Dead' is on here. Stop it. Randy, Randy man. You bought Pink? Vince, Randy here has been redeemed. There is redemption for the White amigo."

I was not a Pink fan, but Darnell loved her. I loaded it a few days earlier for Darnell's birthday, still a week off. Pink's framed photograph was on his footlocker, facing him in bed like he actually knew the woman.

"I got that for you. Happy birthday, you fuckin' asswipe."

They stopped laughing. "Thank you, Top," Darnell said, using the informal address for first sergeant, even though I wouldn't pin the rank on for another week.

He hooked that iPod to his system, and we sang, yelling along with Pink. Vince brought his heavy-duty speakers, and the music was loud. The song was "Who Knew" and we stood, drunk dancing, three guys in their late thirties acting crazy like kids. We were swinging our arms in exaggerated movements, banging and ramming into each other to Pink's beat, yelling the words and fucking up most of them because we either didn't know them or were too drunk to remember. I fell onto my bed a few times, then got right back up.

Vince got shoved sideways, one of his shoulders slamming into the door. It gave way with a big crack as the metal and the wood of the doorjamb fractured.

Darnell paused the music.

"Fuuuck," Vince said.

A piece of cracked wood that had been under metal was now sticking out from the door at a ninety-degree angle. The deadbolt was bent at a downward angle. We stared, three inebriated brains trying to figure out how we could avoid paying for this.

"Sorry," Vince added.

"What the fuck you say sorry for?" I said. "That shit happened last night. I fell into it when that mortar hit."

I pulled the wood piece from the door. "That's a fuckin' NCO safety hazard," I said.

We got hit by mortars three or four times a night. The night before, one had landed close, rocking our trailer.

"Yeah, I remember that," Darnell said. "Randy here was standing up, goin' out to take a piss, and fell into the doorway. You know, Andrews, we need to report that shit, complain."

Darnell turned the music back on. The door was hanging open.

When the song ended, Darnell was saying he was going to hit on Pink and she was going to be his wife or at least maybe his girlfriend.

"The fuck is it with you Black dudes?" I said in my best Darnell imitation. "You always be looking for blond White women." I nodded at Pink's photo on the footlocker.

"No, that's where you're wrong, Randy. That is where you are fuckin' wrong, man. Those White women you're talkin' about? They are always looking for Black men. I just keep 'em happy." Vince had shifted sides and was on the floor next to me, leaning against my bed.

"The lesser races. White, Brown—you motherfuckers," Darnell nodded to us, "struggle to do a job that comes naturally to me."

I spit beer, laughing. "Fuck you," Vince said. Everything was funny again. That was the last time I was happy.

The Army recognized me. I would be a first sergeant, the NCO big leagues. The three of us were headed to Fort Bragg, the 82nd Airborne Division, in a month. We were blowing off steam. It didn't get better. Our families could never be a part of this. This was for us.

I was breathing hard from the exertion. "Maybe we could all go somewhere after this tour," I said. "The Smoky Mountains. Get some cabins on a lake. It's not that far from Bragg."

"Except your family's in California," Vince said. "You're sure

Sara'll come out?" Vince had four kids. His family lived on base.

The song ended. It was quiet. I heard our breathing. Sara sucked the air out of the room from 10,000 miles away. She and the boys had moved in with her mom and stepdad while I was overseas.

"They're going to move when I get back. To Bragg."

I hadn't talked this over with Sara, but what the fuck is the point of a marriage if you're not together? She had married a soldier.

My boys loved Darnell with his endless stream of bad jokes. Vince didn't entertain them so much. He tried, but his stories inevitably included waxing some Arab motherfucker. Vince, Raquel, and their four kids had been to our home for barbecues.

Vince looked away, reaching for a beer. Then he looked back, ready to tell me something.

"You're sure?" he said. "The minute you deploy, she moves. What, Anaheim? California? Her mom's there, right? She's left the base your last three deployments."

I turned to my left, looked at Vince's big head. "What the fuck's that mean?" I asked. "They're living with her parents. Yeah, I'm sure."

Vince started to say something. Then he glanced at Darnell. Darnell shook his head. It was almost unnoticeable. We were battle buddies, but this one time they were not making me a part of something.

I was opening my mouth to ask, "What the fuck is going on?" Darnell looked at Vince then raised his hands, open palms. "Let the man celebrate his well-deserved promotion, brother. I am sure we can set up that mountain trip. Count me in, Randy."

I never got a chance to ask them what just happened.

Then it was the next morning, August 13, 2009, Darnell and I in the motor pool next to the line of eight Humvees and two SUVs. We were watching the two lieutenants, Stan Hamm and Matt Pearce.

They were looking at a map spread on the hood of the last Humvee.

"That's fuckin' scary," Darnell said. I lit a cigarette, then handed one to Darnell. I lit his.

Vince walked up, ready to go, full battle rattle, an M203 grenade launcher mounted on his M-4. He only carried the launcher when he thought shit would hit the fan.

"Good morning, Top."

Four Humvees from first platoon were in the lead positions today. We'd be followed by two SUVs each carrying six million in cash. Second platoon's four vehicles would bring up the last four positions. As the first platoon sergeant, I would be in the lead vehicle. My officer would be in the fourth. Darnell, the second platoon sergeant, would be in the back seat of Hamm's Humvee in tenth position.

"The fuck you doing here?" I said to Vince. He was third platoon. "This ain't your mission, brother."

"Thought you could use another gun," he said. He patted the tube of the M203 below the barrel of his rifle. "Shit area you're going to. Bad vibes, man." Our convoys were always being hit outside Samarra, usually by IEDs, sometimes by ambush. Two platoons—instead of the usual one—were providing security.

I would have done the same for Vince.

We were headed to the oil refinery in Samarra with the twelve million, money to keep it operating for another month. The four contractors were laughing and smoking. They were thick, out of shape, wearing red caps and loafers and pulling down almost a quarter million tax-free dollars a year. They looked ready for eighteen holes and only left the wire with a military escort.

The privates protecting their lazy asses were bringing home fifteen hundred a month.

This was a three-hour movement through Sunni land infested with diehard Ba'athists three years after Saddam was executed.

My officer and platoon commander, First Lieutenant Matt Pearce, was tall, with Nordic good looks, everyone's idea of the handsome small-town high school football star in uniform. The kid was scared about being in Iraq his first year out of ROTC, but he was smart enough to listen.

Sometimes I was an asshole to Matt; he was green and needed it. But he kept coming back so I could tell him what to do. One time a bomb went off in a crowd during the grand opening of an American-financed water treatment plant. We were pulling security. He'd seen his first body parts, including the bottom half of a little girl in a yellow dress. A three-foot concrete barrier protected her legs up to her waist from the bomb. The top half of her was gone, vaporized into red mist.

"She was six. My daughter's that age." His voice and hands were shaking. He started crying. Then he threw up. I started to ask how the hell he could know she was six looking at her legs, then saw him trying to hide his tears. I grabbed his arm and squeezed it, then patted his shoulder.

"That's okay, LT. Try not to think about it, Lieutenant Pearce? Look at me, LT. We ain't getting killed over here. I'm not letting that happen."

Sometimes I didn't have it in me to be an asshole.

But Matt wasn't leading today. First Lieutenant Stan Hamm, with his ROTC commission from a small college in Pennsylvania, had three months of rank on him.

I had bad vibes, but not because of where we were headed.

Hamm was noisy and full of opinions he spewed forth in a high-pitched, whiny voice. He never came up for air to listen, particularly not to NCOs. A shameless ass-kisser to anyone senior to him, Hamm was an abusive prick to everyone else. He was tall with a brawny build, but he looked soft. He charged ahead when he didn't know what the fuck he was doing. I think that was his definition of *bravery*. Darnell was his platoon sergeant.

"I'm working with him," Darnell said. "We'll get him there."

But he couldn't have believed that. Hamm was an NCO's nightmare. God only knows what kind of fuck up he'd been as a civilian.

I told Captain Rose, the company commander, that Hamm needed to be moved somewhere he couldn't get people killed. I suggested Hamm check out basketballs and towels at the FOB gym. It was a closed-door meeting. I gave several examples of Hamm's incompetence during the three months he'd been in country. First Sergeant Maywood, an aging guardsman who never left the wire, leaned against the wall. The man smoked three packs of cigarettes a day, converted oxygen to carbon dioxide, and counted the days until he went home. Maywood came from the same small town in western Pennsylvania as Hamm.

Captain Rose's face seemed molded from pale clay but never finished. The only thing memorable were his thick, black Army-issue glasses. He was competent, had been brought in from the 82nd and didn't do stupid things, but I needed decisive. That, he wasn't.

"Lieutenant Hamm couldn't figure out how to take a piss if the directions were written on his dick, sir. He's gonna get soldiers killed."

Rose looked up fast. "Don't talk that way about an officer." But he didn't meet my eyes. *He knows I'm right.* "This stays in here. Let me talk to first sergeant, Randy." Maywood was against the wall studying the nicotine under his fingernails. "I'll get back to you," Rose said.

He never did and, a week later, my complaint didn't matter anymore.

"Saddle up, gentlemen. Saddle up." Hamm yelled. He was standing by the front passenger door of his Humvee at the end of the line. He made his voice deep. I almost didn't recognize it without the whine. Hamm was swinging his helmet in circles above his head. "Rally round," the movement said, though he wanted us to load up. Darnell and Vince were getting in the back seats of Hamm's Humvee. His gunner was already up top on the 240.

Who the fuck does he think he is? John Wayne?

I looked for an NCO. I needed to vent, but only three junior enlisted soldiers were around.

"Move out," I told Specialist John Franks, a skinny kid from

Philadelphia. He always looked serious and inquisitive, as if Iraq was some book he was studying.

The village was a kilometer ahead. The refinery on the west side of Samarra was another four beyond that. Heat was rising from the ground, rippling the horizon and the buildings of the village. A spinning dust devil rising hundreds of feet into the air traveled through the center of the road ahead. I smelled and tasted the dirt of the road. Then more, coming from a refinery ahead.

When I breathed, it felt like a cactus had been shoved down my throat. The four stacks of the refinery were pumping out smoke and God knows what else. The air was so thick and bad here, and the four of us in my Humvee were coughing. "You'll get used to it after a few minutes," I said. I'd been in a firefight here, had walked this village a few times in weapons searches. We always came up with a lot. They hated us.

Today, we were only passing through. The wind had picked up, blowing dirt through the streets. There were about fifty buildings, mostly cement and cinder block, all covered with dust. A small earthquake would level this place. There were a few two- and three-story buildings in the village center. The spire of a mosque stood tall.

We came to edge of the village when I heard the music. It was Pink, singing, "Who Knew," blasting from a loudspeaker. *Radio America.* The treble on the speakers was blown, giving Pink's voice a harsh bite. I couldn't tell where the sound came from.

Pink was big in 2009. She was singing about her emptiness when someone she loved disappeared. And I remember in that moment feeling the hairs on my arm standing on end, anxious, thinking the lyrics were stupid. Don't they always die or disappear? That's life, lady.

"Hey Randy. You hear that shit?"

It was Darnell on the radio. Hamm should have had told him to quit fuckin' around.

"Andrews, my man." His voice cracked with radio static. "Listen to that, Randy. It's my lady." And Pink sang on about how she had believed.

"Clear the radio," I said.

We could shoot our way through any threat. To do that we had to mass our firepower. The radio kept us linked and was all-important.

Where are the kids?

Something was wrong. The uneasy feeling always came first. "John. Slow down. Walking speed."

"We're slowing," I said on the radio. "Keep the gaps. I'm checking this out."

Music? No kids?

"What the hell is the holdup? What the fuck is up?" Hamm was back in whine mode.

I couldn't have answered because I didn't know.

"Pick up the pace . . . Andrews."

"No," I said into the mic. "I'm calling a halt."

I turned off the mic. *"Stop!"* Franks hit the brakes too hard and we jerked. His jaw was tight, teeth clenched as he studied the town. He was feeling it too. Hot dirt plumed. And still Pink sang.

Hamm kept Darnell with him. Not for advice. I think he wanted Darnell under wraps so he couldn't run off and think independently or call halts. But Vince was there too. Maybe they could keep Hamm from stepping on his dick.

"What the fuck is it?" Hamm again.

Fucking shut up.

I opened the mic. "Something's off. Talk to him, gentlemen."

I knew Hamm despised me. "*Sergeant* Andr—" Pearce cut him off.

"Hold on, Stan. Andrews has got something."

I heard a *"harrumph"* over the radio as I looked through my binoculars.

Then I saw it. A curb lined each side of the dirt road through town. Two hundred meters painted with white and yellow stripes and lining dirt, the start of another of Saddam's improvements. The road never got built. The cement was crumbling.

Except in one place. A twenty-foot portion was new, freshly painted, with dirt scattered on it. I fixed on it, the way a wolf sees the one limping caribou in a herd of thousands. And the music? It wasn't unusual to hear Western music in Iraq but in this shit-fuck village? Who's listening to Pink?

I felt the adrenaline hit, my mind seeing it all in full focus. Nerve endings hot, hairs on my neck straight and stiff.

Pearce spoke again. "Andrews called a halt. Possible IED, Stan." Pearce and I were thinking alike, working together. I took the mic. "IED one hundred fifty meters in the concrete curb, north side of road. We're going around this town. The dirt's packed along the south side of town."

"*Sergeant* Andrews called a halt? This is *Lieutenant* Hamm, the *mission commander*. Keep moving, Matt."

"No way, Stan. Sergeant Andrews says there's an IED. We're not moving."

The detour would have added a minute. The song was now close to over. Hamm must have been gripping the talk button of the radio handset. I heard arguing. Darnell's voice, then Vince saying, "What the fuck's our hurry, LT?" Finally, Hamm, almost screaming. "Goddammit, who's the fuckin' commanding officer?"

And "Who Knew" started over, crackling sounds through those staticky speakers. This wasn't Radio America. Someone was playing this music.

I heard Hamm yell. "What the hell is it? Another IED, Andrews? You're always seeing fucking IEDs, Andrews!"

Two weeks before, I had called a halt on a road outside Tikrit. Pearce backed me and Hamm ordered second platoon to lead. Nothing blew up. We got lucky. That night, Hamm, at dinner in the chow hall with the company grade officers, was bullshitting loud enough for me to hear. He had "pressed on, took charge," when Andrews wanted to stop. "Nothing wrong with that road," I heard him say, then he laughed too loud and too hard.

And I thought I'd make that motherfucker pay for that remark. Somehow, somewhere, someday.

And at that moment, Pink said, "That's right."

"Stan, look, look," Pearce said. "I see it, what Andrews is talking about. Eleven o'clock. See it. The curb. Let's get out, talk." I opened my door, was ready to walk down to have a conversation with my motherfuckin' commanding officer. Pearce knew me. "Sergeant Andrews, stay with your vehicle," he said.

I stepped out and stood behind the armored door of my Humvee. Pearce was walking down the row of vehicles toward Hamm's Humvee.

Hamm must have taken his hand off his mic.

Vince, Darnell, and Hamm were out of the Humvee by the rear bumper. Pearce walked up.

Another minute went by. Then another. The lieutenants were arguing. Then they were yelling. Darnell, palms out, stepped up to them, trying to work shit out that shouldn't need to be worked out. Only one call was right. Pearce turned, began walking to his Humvee. Hamm yelled at his back.

"Matt, goddammit, I am ordering you to fuckin' move out, push through the village. We are to maintain a presence in this village. How is it going to look to these motherfuckin' hajis if we take a detour."

"That's not happening, Stan." Pearce didn't look over his shoulder. Maybe I taught that kid something. Lyrics spun through my head as Pink said it was all so wrong.

Then Hamm gave the order.

"My Humvee will take the lead, through this village. Everyone got that? Second platoon fall in behind me. SUVs after us. First platoon, you're *now* in the *rear*. Fall in. Five-meter intervals. Lieutenant Pearce, we'll take this up with the BC. Tonight." It was the arrogance of a fool.

Second platoon moved out to the left.

Five-meter gaps? Is he fucking kidding?

Their vehicles were bunched, perfect IED targets.

I wasn't going over the radio with what I was about to do. Bunching our Humvees was stupid even for Hamm. I stepped behind our Humvee, waiting for Hamm to approach.

"What the fuck you doin', Lieutenant? You see that curb ahead? Look at the streets.

"Deserted. We don't need to do this. Fucking veer off, take us around this town." His Humvee hit the brakes and his window opened.

"Fall in, *Sergeant* Andrews. That's an order, a fuckin' order. You hear that? You get that? You understand the order. *Sergeant*?"

I knew two things from his red-faced screams. He wasn't backing down and I wasn't following his order. He slammed his window shut.

My stomach heaved. This was Clutterfuck all over again. And that fuckin' song. It just played, and played, beating my head with its tinny rhythm, talking about how everything was wrong. I wanted to vomit.

I stooped and looked in the backseat window. Vince looked away, his jaw clenched, right palm on the butt of his M4. Darnell leaned from the far seat, held out his open palms, then gave me the first thumbs-up of the day. He smiled and nodded. His lip twitched.

The two SUVs didn't move. Hamm came over the radio and told them to, "Fucking fall in." They moved, hugging the bumper of the fourth vehicle of Hamm's platoon.

"Fall in," I told Franks. "Slow. Fifty-meter gaps." I went over the radio. "First platoon. Fall in . . . as I do." The three Humvees spaced out, fifty meters between bumpers.

Hamm's Humvee was coming into the center of town. Crumbling lengths of curb were on each side of sixty-five feet of dirt. Hamm's Humvee was moving on down the center of the road.

"John," I said. "Slow up." I would disobey an order and direct Franks to veer to the right and take an alternate route through the south side of town.

Through my binoculars, Hamm's Humvee was a hundred meters

ahead, picking up speed and kicking up dirt.

I want to think I didn't see what I did, that Hamm wasn't more stupid and dangerous than I thought. His Humvee began angling north as it approached the fifteen feet of new curb, the left tires hugging it. The three second-platoon Humvees followed his, angling north.

Just before the blast, Hamm's arm shot from his window, straight out, his stubby thumb pointed to the sky. It was moving up and down, a *fuck you* wave to me. Right then I understood just how much hate that motherfucker had in him—and most was for me.

CHAPTER 13

"That's enough," I said.

Athena stroked my hair. I wanted her to stop. My mother used to stroke my hair as a kid when I was upset or crying.

Her face was a foot from mine. I pulled her to me, kissed her. Matilda was checking me out, that concerned look on her face. She began grooming, licking her big right paw, then rubbing it on her neck and chest.

"I don't want to think of the rest. Not today."

I thought she would argue. "Okay." She stroked my hair again, then put her palm over my cheek. "It's okay."

I was quiet for a while.

"Well, I thought things were getting better for me," I said. Matilda was watching. Her hackles were down.

I touched Athena's scar and moved my hand down her neck, following the line. I stopped above her breast. She would have let me go further.

"You're going to get better, Randy. I see it happening. I know you're starting to believe that."

"Thanks," I said.

I looked at the runway with its stripper's pole.

"This place is a fucking pit. I don't want you working here anymore."

"I need the money," she said.

"I know. But I don't like it." I looked at Matilda. "I don't want her in here. That's bad what they're doing to her."

Athena gave me a look. We all deserved better.

I touched her hair. "You think I'm special? I don't. But you're special. I know that."

"You don't talk about your boys much," she said.

"What's there to talk about? They don't talk to *me*. It fuckin' hurts," I said, then turned to look at her again. "You know, I tell you *plenty* about me. You don't tell me much of anything about you. It doesn't always have to be *me* doing the telling. I got no shortage of shit to talk about."

The three of us sat there, silent. I watched as Athena focused her eyes on something beyond the walls of the nightclub, far off.

"Like, where you live? Or how your mom died. Or you getting deported. Or what you've been doing the last 15 years. Or—"

I knew what I was trying to say, just not how. The music had stopped, and I looked at Matilda. "What did you show her?" I asked.

"What?" she said.

"What did Matilda see when she looked in your eyes?" Athena looked away. I was quiet. I would wait for her.

"My mother killed herself," she said finally. "She had bad depression. I knew something was wrong. She'd been slipping away for years. But I was a kid. I didn't know what to do.

"I wanted to dance. Remember, I told you that. I studied ballet for three years. Do you know what my instructors said to my mother? I was there. I memorized it. They said many people can perform ballet well. But a great dancer is someone who dances from their heart. A great dancer is great because of the light in their eyes and the sincerity of their approach to the art and the story they convey with their soul. They said it gave them chills. They said they saw it in me."

She cleared her throat. "I auditioned for Juilliard's pre-college dance program when I was twelve. I danced to "Total Eclipse of the Heart." Remember that song? I told my story. The most important person in my life was dying. I was coming apart in the audition because I knew nothing would get better for my mom. We suit up in armor to protect ourselves. The older we get, the more we wear.

That day, mine was off. It was only me, my real self. The audition ended and I was crying and embarrassed and scared I'd blown it. It had all been too painful.

"One day, three months later, I came home from school. My mother didn't answer the door, so I let myself in. She was in bed covered in puke and urine. She was dead. She took an overdose." Athena took a deep breath, as if steeling herself. "Three letters were with her on the bed, opened. One said we were evicted. The second said we were deported. The third was to me. 'Congratulations. You've been accepted to Juilliard's pre-college program.'"

"A week later, I was shipped back to Mexico. I knew nothing of this country. I spoke Spanish but I was the whitest kid in school. The kids were mean. They called me *La blanca.* They didn't mean it nice."

I tried again. "Why do you come here when you're not working?"

I thought she wasn't going to answer. Again.

"I don't like being alone," she said.

I didn't know what to say.

After a bit, she nodded. "I'll show you where I live," she said.

Matilda followed us with her eyes as we stood and walked to the door. More and more people were coming in. Ruben watched us walk to the street.

Athena led. She took a direct route, walking toward the hills east of town with their mansions on one ridge and shacks with no plumbing on the next. Her face said this was unpleasant but had to be done.

"How far is it?" I asked. She didn't answer. I didn't want her to know I'd followed her.

We passed the stucco wall of the church. Athena turned to the door, paused, then continued for another five minutes uphill to her building and let us in. At the top of the stairs, she put her key in the lock of a door with a number *3*.

It opened to a narrow, one-room apartment. Cheap studios like this were all over Rosarito for workers at the hundreds of bars and resort hotels. She flicked on the lamp on a nightstand. A crucifix hung on the wall over the head of the single bed.

The room had the sparse feel of the home of someone who wasn't planning on staying long. There was a small window with no screen. A horn honked on the street below. Along one wall was a refrigerator, a microwave and the door to a bathroom. Along the other wall was a beat-up, ornate armoire; next to her bed, a nightstand on one side, a shelf loaded with books on the other. All classics: *Pride and Prejudice, Wuthering Heights, War and Peace, Othello*. No fluff on the shelves. Other than the crucifix, the walls were bare.

It was sterile, like a hospital. No dust. In Rosarito, that took regular cleaning. With nonstop construction, silt got into everything.

She opened the drawer on the nightstand and found matches. Then she lit two candles on a small table with two framed photographs. She took my hand.

I'd seen photos of these people at the church.

The young man wore a Mexican Army uniform. His expression said he knew the photographer. He was smiling, caught mid-laugh walking out the doorway of a home. Maybe twenty-five, a lieutenant. He wore his uniform with pride. In the other photograph was a boy of about three, dressed in a green and red jumper, smiling. His expression was self-satisfied as if he had accomplished something important, like putting on shoes.

Four other photos on the table were unframed. In one, a young woman was with the man and the boy. It looked like Athena, but I would have to look closer. A set of rosary beads connected the candles in a wavy line.

"Your husband?"

She nodded.

"That's your son? What was his name?"

She didn't answer.

"Did your boy die?"

She adjusted the rosary beads, straightening the line they formed.

"My son was Alberto. He was Alberto the third. Like you, Randy. They died in 1996."

Athena was close, looking at my face, her expression hopeful. She was quiet. She wanted something. It wasn't sex.

I had asked to come here. Now I didn't understand why she brought me.

I looked around the room. I could not imagine living here.

This is fucking creepy, Athena. They've been dead for eighteen years.

Yeah, and aren't you the guy who sees shit that isn't there?

She was not the tall, beautiful woman who drank like a man and said "fuck" so beautifully. She'd shrunk. I wanted her to say more.

"Athena." I put my arms around her back, pulling her to me—soft, then hard, gripping her so she knew I wouldn't bail on her.

"I used to have those flashbacks, like you," she said. "Almost twenty years I had them. I drank like you said you did to make them go away. Matilda helped me. Just like she did for you."

I reached down and picked up the photograph of Athena with her family. She was young, beautiful and smiling. Different. The pain lines weren't there. She didn't have a scar. I put it back in its place. Everything had a place.

"You're young," I said.

"I was twenty-two," she said. "We were in Cancun on a vacation. I've never been that happy."

"Who did it?" I asked.

She started to speak, twice, then closed her mouth.

She turned to the window. "It was the Gulf Cartel. They were big, dangerous. We lived in Villa Hermosa, near Brownsville, in Texas. He was a lieutenant. Alberto led raids against the cartel. One night, the men came to our home. I saw them die. I could do nothing.

"Tell me?" I asked.

She didn't want to. "Tell me," I said.

"It happened in our home. The men came in the night."

Athena looked away to the crucifix above her bed. She was silent for a long span. When she spoke, her eyes were focused somewhere outside this room.

That night was twenty years ago. Her husband heard a noise, and she saw him standing, then she saw the silhouette of Alberto's rifle and she became frightened. And then there was an explosion, and she found herself on the floor, stunned, barely able to take a breath.

Alberto yelled for her to run. Men were yelling, rough voices, cussing. They shouted, "*La madre que te parió!*" Your mother is a whore! Alberto was screaming. She had never heard him scream.

The big one came into the bedroom. He grabbed her by the hair and dragged her into the living room. His wrists brushed her cheek. They were hairy and wet and disgusting. She saw Alberto on the floor, face down, his hands zip-tied behind his back. She tried to stand, to run to her son, but the big one hit her in the face, over and over, breaking her nose and teeth. All she could do was scream, and he hit her again and again until she was quiet.

Another man was holding little Alberto in the air by his jumper. She saw the purple smiling Barney face on his chest. He was screaming. "Mama, Mama, Mama!" She begged, «Please, Please, Please, Dios!" The big one said, «*Me cago en Dios*," I shit on God.

Athena paused and was still for moment.

This was unspeakable. Be careful what you wish for. *Why did I push her to tell me this?*

She continued. The big one said to the man holding Alberto Jr., "Shut that fuckin' kid up. Here. Fuckin' give him to me. Take her." Another man grabbed her. The big man took her son, then swung little Alberto by the feet, cracking his head into the plaster walls. He did it again and again. Then he held out their son's limp body by the feet, like a hunter holding a pheasant. Then he threw little Alberto's body so it landed by his father's head.

The big man tore open her T-shirt, telling her what great tits she had, saying she wanted it. And he taunted Alberto, turning her to face him, wanting Alberto to see.

She paused again. I felt sick. This was a trigger beyond all triggers. *Not now. I need to be here, for her.*

The big one tore her underwear off and pulled her to the floor by her hair. He began spreading her legs but she fought, screaming at the nightmare, and he hit her seven or eight times more, calling her *"puta," "perra."* She lay there as he entered her. *Destroyer, invader,* she thought. Alberto was crying and he kept saying, *"Te quiero, Sofia,"* and *"Lo siento, lo siento, lo siento."* Ashamed, she looked away from him.

Turning from her husband's gaze had haunted her for years. "I should have looked at him," she said. "I loved him."

And then the big man cut her so she could remember the best dick she'd ever had. She screamed, then she heard the gunshots. The last thing she remembered was feeling blood and brains spraying her face and hearing the laughter of the men.

Athena was silent, staring at me. "In my dreams, my family was alive," she said. "I would hear my boy laugh and call to me, 'I love you, Mama.' I didn't want to wake up."

While some questions lingered—like *Who is Sofia*—I understood why I was here.

She is showing me her wounds, her pain. Just like I showed mine to a cougar, because I was afraid to show them to a human. Until Athena.

"Athena, do you know what? I love you, lady. I love you. You must know that. I am in love with you. I fuckin' *love* you."

I was whispering, my mouth pressed to her ear.

"I love you so much."

Someone else was talking. This was the me who hadn't killed so many goddamned people, who hadn't cleaned up body parts left after car bombs. This guy was romantic, maybe even fucking nuanced.

She cried and looked at me. Her emotions were raw and strong. She loved me. I was aroused, wanting to kiss down her neck and feel her skin. I wanted her here, naked, now.

At that moment, I knew that would be wrong.

"They left me alive. I don't know why," she said.

Leave one maimed. It's the worldwide MO for thugs.

I touched her scar.

Cartels didn't divide the battlefield into combatants and noncombatants. They murdered innocent Mexicans by the truckload while Americans kept buying their drugs and giving them guns.

We should be killing them, not a bunch of Arabs.

Lines of tears moved down her cheeks. This was so fucking horrible. I wanted to kill somebody, to take it all away. I wanted the right words, then I heard my mom, something she told me at the funeral for my best friend's little brother. I was twelve. I had avoided my friend because I didn't know what I could say.

"He needs you. Just listen, Randy. Sometimes silence is best. The best friend." I'm sure she quoted scripture. Athena straightened the rosary beads by the candle lit for her dead son.

Where the fuck *was* God? I believed in Him but had no faith.

So, I just held her. Her lips were moving but silent. I think she was praying.

"Thank you for this. Let's walk to the beach, sit on the sand and listen to the ocean," I said.

Athena briskly nodded like she was shaking something off.

"I love you," she said.

It sounded easy when she said it.

CHAPTER 14

I still hadn't tried to make love to Athena. We'd kiss, then I'd hit a wall and wouldn't know what to do. Sometimes she looked at me and I could tell she was wondering what was holding me back, what more was wrong with me.

Maybe if we went somewhere? A week later I talked her into a vacation, or at least thought I had. We would drive four hundred miles south to Bajia Tortugas. "It's so cheap down there even I can afford it," I told her. "Quiet, really great beaches."

"You look like a little kid, you know that?" Athena said. "The way you're bouncing around." We were standing by Matilda's cage. I looked down. My weight moved from my right foot to my left. It had been years since something excited me. "Randy, that's far. I *do* want to go somewhere. That would be so much fun. Anywhere. Maybe something closer?"

It was Sunday, September 7. She had traded shifts and would work Sunday and Monday instead of her usual Wednesday, Thursday, and Friday. I didn't hear what she said. I just wanted to go somewhere far. We would leave Tuesday just after midnight and drive all night, then into the day.

We sat at Athena's table. A few times she started to speak then stopped. Her lips were pressed together. Something was bothering her. She would not say what. I thought it was concern for my shit-box of a truck and the hundreds of miles of desolate roads south of Ensenada.

I showed her the internet photographs of deserted beaches in southern Baja lighting up my phone. "Beautiful, aren't they?"

I kissed her. She was staring at something on the other side of the room. "What is it?"

"Randy, I need to tell you something. I know how Matilda got that scar on her face."

I quit thinking of Bahia Tortugas. "You said you didn't know."

"I didn't when you asked. Ruben told me yesterday." I hated that Ruben talked to her. But I knew it was stupid. I mean, did Athena even talk to anyone in town besides Ruben, and now me?

"So, how'd she get the scar?" I asked.

"The owner fights her, puts dogs, big dogs in with her. They bet on how long she takes to kill them. She always kills them, but one of them bit her on the face."

I stared at Matilda's scar, letting this sink in.

"How do . . . no, that's not right. Ruben. That fucker. He knew this."

Three times I'd seen the owner in the nightclub. He'd walk in the back door behind Matilda's cage like a man in a hurry. His shirt was always open two buttons too many, and a gold medallion the size of a Krugerrand floated a half-inch over his skin on a bed of gray chest hair. His black head of hair had to be a rug. He was sixty trying to look forty.

At the bar, he'd knock back three shots of the real Patron Ruben kept in a cabinet beneath the sink. One time a sleazy-looking woman half his age was on his arm. Each time he chewed out Ruben for something, then left as fast as he walked in.

I pictured him and his asshole buddies. Drunk, laughing and cheering while Matilda killed a dog.

"Once they let in two dogs and she killed them," Athena said. "On Thursday they're putting three dogs in with her. Three pit bulls. Some man is bringing them from Ensenada."

For one beat, I didn't know what to say.

"What time is this going down on Thursday?" I asked.

"Eleven in the morning. The man is bringing the dogs at ten-thirty. He wants them to smell their prey."

Pit bulls are fast, and they grab the throat and hold on. One pit bull was no match for a mountain lion. Two probably weren't either. But three? Three's a pack. Working together, they could kill Matilda, particularly in an enclosed space where she couldn't maneuver. No matter who won, Matilda would be hurt, and badly. So would the dogs.

Matilda was licking her right foreleg. Her eyes went to mine. They were soft, and I felt her feelings. She had been waiting for this, wanting to show me something. What she wanted from me.

I saw an animal confined when she was young, vague memories of openness and dark quiet. Home. Now, there was only this bad place. She ate what was thrown. Attacked without warning, forced to fight beasts who charged while humans jeered. No sun. A world of artificial bright light then darkness, concrete and chain-link fencing. Terrible smells.

Soon another mob would gather, loudness erasing all thought. Lights and walls alive, dodging beer bottles and other things thrown. A dangerous place without rhythm.

She was comfortable with me. No. *With us.* For the first time, I heard her purring. She had helped me.

Matilda wants to be free.

I wasn't making her life better by watching her while I drank a beer. It was time to return her favor. I just needed to know how.

She'll be dead in a year, and they'll stuff her and let drunks take selfies with her.

"That shit ain't happening," I said. "I'm not letting it."

"How? Randy, there's nothing you can do."

"There's always something you can do." I believed that, now.

"We call the police," Athena said.

I scoffed.

"And tell them fuckin' *what*? They drink in here. The cops all know she's here. Don't they pull security at night?" Athena looked away. Matilda was watching two humans stress out. "It sucks. It's all so fuckin' corrupt here. Sorry to say that about your country. But it is."

I took a deep breath, laying out the facts in my head as if planning a military operation. "She has to be out of here before Thursday. That doesn't leave a lot of options. I take her out and figure out what to do with her."

Athena shook her head, her expression resembling one that sane people reserve for lunatics. "You're *serious*?"

"You're goddamn right I'm serious. Why the hell didn't you tell me this shit before?"

"I only just found out." She looked ready to cry.

"No, no, no. That's right, you did. I'm sorry. I'm not mad at you."

"How are you going to get her out? And what'll you do with her when you take her?" She was listing all the reasons why what I was suggesting was a bad idea. "Why is this so important to you?"

"It is to you too. I have to. It's called *loyalty*. Helping a buddy." Even as I said the words, I knew that wasn't all of it. I just didn't know what the *all of it* was. "I have to get her out of here. We're not going on that trip south. You know that."

"I didn't want to go down south," she said. "It's really hot down there now. You could pick me up after work tomorrow night. We can be together. For a few days."

All that macho shit about taking Matilda from the club? That's all it was. Back at my room, I didn't know what the fuck to do.

I thought of that last hunting trip with my dad.

He had heard the screeching up Caribou Ridge two days before. This was my dad's turf. The poachers and out-of-season deer hunters considered it theirs as well, so every day he was up here.

It was May 27, 1990. I was sixteen, and my junior year of high school would be over in five days.

We had been tracking the cougar the better part of a day. "I think it's a female," he whispered. "From the tracks, about a hundred pounds. Looking for a mate." We moved silently through the low brush. We came to a log with claw marks. It smelled like piss.

"That nose of yours, Randy. I don't smell it."

I was not the same kid I had been on my tenth birthday. If it moved on four legs or flew, I killed it. Two mounted heads in the basement, an eight-point buck and a bighorn sheep, were mine. The only animals I hadn't killed were a grizzly and a mountain lion. I carried a Winchester .308 semi-automatic and loved to hunt.

A partial lion print near the log pointed to a jumble of huge boulders a hundred meters up the ridge. The wind was blowing from the rocks. The musky smell of old leaves and urine hit me. Again, my dad couldn't smell it.

"We'll set up here," he said.

My father and I lay behind a fallen log, our bodies pressed together, our heads inches apart. Ferns from the rotten wood brushed my cheek.

"Cougars see the world differently than the animals you've hunted," he whispered. "Think of a huge field of yellow wheat? What do you focus on?"

"I don't know," I said. "The wheat? Nothing?"

"You're right. Nothing. Now suppose there is an area where the wheat is sick, brown in color. What does your eye go to?"

"The sick part."

"Right. Or how about this. Suppose a tiny piece of silver foil is slowly blowing over the wheat. What do you see?"

"The foil," I said.

"Right again, Randy. We humans focus on what's different, out of place. Cougars see the world like we do. They see flaws, weaknesses. It's called predator vision. So, if you want to take one, we blend in."

A cougar's scream came from the rocks.

It was long, raspy, and high-pitched. We heard another. This one went up and down in waves. We lay behind a fallen tree, grass growing up its length, my rifle aimed in the direction of the racket. "That cat's in heat," my dad said. Safety off, my finger was on the trigger.

She walked from behind some rocks and began scratching at the bark of a tree.

The stars could not be better aligned. We were downwind, faces painted, indistinguishable from the brush. I sighted behind her shoulder, centered on her heart. I started a slow trigger pull.

I was probably a hundredth of an inch from firing when she turned and looked in my direction.

She could not see us, but she looked directly at me.

It was the first time I had looked into the eyes of a predator. These eyes were different from other animals I'd shot. They were focused beams that bore into the soul. Prey animals, with eyes to the sides of their heads, couldn't do that. Deer and rabbits saw everything and focused on nothing.

My father was starting to whisper. "Ran—" I took my finger off the trigger and raised my rifle. "I can't do it." My dad didn't take the shot. This was my kill to give up.

We talked about it driving home. "Why didn't you fire?" I began wishing I'd fired a foot over the cougar's head. I never missed, but a miss would have been easier to explain.

"I looked in her eyes. She was looking at me, too." He wasn't angry, but I could tell he did not understand. So, we talked about other things as we drove home.

I never hunted with my dad again.

CHAPTER 15

At noon on Monday, I sat with Matilda. Just the two of us. In another twelve hours Athena and I would meet and spend three days together. I tried not to think about her. Walking around with a hard-on would fuck up my plans.

Today Matilda trotted from the far corner as if expecting me. She pushed her face into the chain links. "Help me, girl. I need to figure out what to do."

I had to touch her. A Tecate beer truck was parked out back. Ruben was outside supervising the delivery. Two men were wheeling in cases of beer stacked on dollies.

I stepped over the railing of the short fence. The fur of her cheek was pushing out from the chain links of her cage. I moved my hand slowly, watching her body language, particularly her ears and tail. Relaxed. I touched her fur, rubbing my fingers on her face through the links. She didn't move or back off, just kept pushing her face into that chain-link fence.

It was thick, deep and soft. Oily, it felt waterproof. I heard the back door slam and footsteps and stepped back over the railing.

I sat. "How the fuck do I help you, Matilda?" Waiting for an answer, I found the gold in her eyes and went to Fallujah.

Toney Bartlett was screaming when I left him.

It was Operation Vigilant Resolve. We were rooting out extremists in Fallujah, going house to house. All civilians had been ordered to evacuate. We were clearing houses, six an hour, a hellaciously dangerous pace. It was over 110 degrees and hard to see with the smoke from all the blasts and fires hanging just above the ground. We'd been at it for nine hours. The sewer lines were blown, brown streams running through the dirt streets. Smoke, shit, and piss were all I smelled through the two rags over my face.

Loudspeakers were blaring Arabic. It wasn't the call to prayer. This voice was male, angry, never coming up for air. Spit must have been flying into his mic. The Marines blared back through huge speakers mounted on Humvees, drowning out the screaming with AC/DC and Guns N' Roses.

Our personnel carriers and trucks were moving down the streets. I could taste the filth they kicked up. I saw my face in a mirror of one of the homes. Mud had formed the shape of lips on the outside of the rags. I looked like an eerie Halloween mask.

House to house. Quiet, then mortars and 7.62 rounds would hit, unreinforced concrete walls lighting up and exploding. Falling, sometimes on us. We would return fire, then the helicopters would buzz over and I'd pray I'd called in the coordinates right. Everything was so tight here. No room for error. A building would get lit up and collapse. The shooting would stop, and we would move to the next house. Until the next mortars and 7.62 rounds hit.

"Welcome to the Jungle" was the last song I remember hearing that day.

Last house. We were wrapping up the day after this. Tomlinson and Bartlett were ahead of me out the door. Blind bad luck for them. I was fourth, pushing a zip-tied prisoner with a bag over his head. We found a cache of AK-47s and RPGs under the floor of the man's kitchen.

The prisoner saved me. The mortar landed in a deafening blast thirty feet into the square. Shrapnel shredded him and I found myself holding a bloody mess, dead weight, a wet and red shield. Intestines dropped, hitting the ground just before I let go. Only one scratch on me. Maybe more than a scratch. My left cheek was sliced open from shrapnel.

Bartlett and Tomlinson were lying side-by-side fifteen feet into the open square. I didn't order suppressive fire at the rooftops. I didn't think, just ran into the kill zone. An AK opened up. I heard the impacts hitting the dirt and the wall behind me as I moved from cover into the open square. I felt the bullets passing, concrete chips from the walls hitting my arms and neck.

Fucking blind luck. I don't know how I didn't get killed.

Bartlett was moving his mouth, but only blood and dirt came out. Tomlinson was screaming, wordless, guttural yells.

Toney Bartlett was from some bad area of South Chicago, raised in a walk-up tenement building. He enlisted to get out. Toney always had a wide toothy smile. He talked fast, like some carnival huckster, and told jokes, making himself the brunt of them. We liked him from day one.

Toney lay in that dirt, his dark skin ashen, the smell of the blast heavy in the air. I don't know where his helmet was; he must have left the strap undone and it blew to God knows where. Most of his hair and a piece of his skull the size of a cocktail napkin was gone. There were red lines of blood running through the gray dirt on his face. His face looked like a high-altitude photo of Arizona or New Mexico, somewhere dry and dusty, only the rivers were red. His abdomen was open. He couldn't breathe. I didn't think anyone that fucked up could be alive, but he was.

One of Eric Tomlinson's legs was shredded like ground meat. The other blown off. Eric was from Seattle, a rich kid, blonde. He wore a slight cocky smile and looked like a model in a Sears catalog. He also enlisted to get away, but he was escaping his parents' demands he attend an Ivy League school. His hair was always too long, with enough to comb over and back. It was his Declaration of Independence from the Army.

These two kids with nothing in common were inseparable. Neither was old enough to drink. They were going to Disney World together when the regiment came home. I heard them making plans at the chow hall, down to which rides they would go on first.

Good soldiers. It was their first combat tour. They thought I was King Shit. I promised I would get them home safe. The song was still blaring.

Tomlinson looked like he'd make it if he got to the hospital alive. I put a tourniquet on each of his legs. I wrote off Bartlett. He was trying to talk. His guts were leaking out. I plugged a sucking chest wound. I almost wish I hadn't. It gave him his voice again. He grabbed me, digging his fingernails into my wrist as he looked at me through that mask.

"Please, God, Sergeant, don't leave me here!" he rasped. "PLEASE, GOD, DON'T FUCKING LEAVE ME HERE TO DIE SERGEANT ANDREWS!"

His mouth shot red spray.

"I got you, Toney." I squeezed his bicep, feeling warm wetness on my palm. "I'll be back, just a few seconds. Promise, brother. I promise." He couldn't hear me. "WHY ARE YOU . . . FUCK, IT HURTS, WHY ARE YOU FUCKIN' LEAVING ME HERE, SERGEANT ANDREWS? SERGEANT ANDREWS?" I carried Tomlinson—a light weight with one leg gone—a hundred feet down a six-foot-wide corridor to the vehicles. Bartlett's screams followed me, the sounds reverberating off the plaster walls. He screamed faster and faster, as if he knew he had to.

I heard "WHY THE FUCK ARE YOU LEAVING," then nothing. I was running back when his body started arching and jerking as bullets hit. I hoped he was dead. Then his face disappeared.

God forgive me. I felt relief when I saw Bartlett's face explode. I didn't want to go back out there.

I was awarded the Silver Star for saving Tomlinson's life. He lost his legs but made it home. The citation read, *"Sergeant First*

Class John Randall Andrews, III, moving under relentless enemy fire and with no regard for his own safety, demonstrated unparalleled courage and presence of mind in saving the life of Specialist Eric James Tomlinson. His actions reflect great credit on himself, the 75th Ranger Regiment and the United States Army."

A few years later, Tomlinson called me from Disney World. He was with his parents. Another hero out of service and completely disabled. He could walk again with artificial limbs. "Thank you, Sergeant," he said. Then he cried and couldn't talk.

I never wore the medal.

I wrote Toney off and left him to die. The medal, the thanks? None of it mattered. All I hear are his screams.

Was that really my call, triaging with Toney's life?

I looked in Matilda's eyes.

I only had seconds. I had to make a call.

"What choice did I have?" I asked myself. Matilda heard my voice and wrinkled her brow. She did look worried. This animal had faith in me. I continued to look, to dig deeper, and I got my answer.

"You'll die if I leave you here. Won't you?"

I stood and walked out.

CHAPTER 16

Athena and I would dine by the ocean at some fancy place. Then we'd sit on the beach, my arm around her, passing a bottle of wine. I didn't even like wine, but it was more romantic than a six-pack. Fuck nuance. I would tell her again I loved her, then ask her to marry me. She would flash her big smile, the one that made her young, and she would say, "I love you, Randy, and . . . yes. Yes, I'll marry you." And we'd walk hand in hand from the ocean to my room.

That was fantasy number one. In number two, we fucked. A lot.

We were by my bed and I was grinding my hips into hers, showing her how much I wanted her. I told her I had wanted to make love to her, to fuck her, that first time I met her in the bar. Even when I thought she was a bitch, I'd wanted her. I stared into her eyes and said what I wanted to do, raunchy things, tender things.

I smelled her perfume, the shampoo in her hair. I felt the muscles in her arm, saw the contrast of her black hair on that fair skin. I put my mouth on her neck and traced that scar with my tongue, then moved to between her legs. My arms were wrapped around her thighs, gripping them, feeling her muscles tense and release, hearing her make beautiful sounds. I smelled her, tasted her.

She whispered things only for me. I felt the muscles of her ass, felt how hard they were. We tried to make one body, moving closer until we got there. Every fantasy ended with us lying alongside each other and me saying I would take care of her, protect her always because I was in love with her.

We were supposed to meet at a restaurant after her shift was over.

I parked outside and walked two blocks to the Nightclub Estrella. I heard the music a block away.

Two men in shirts that said *Security* and two Rosarito Beach cops—all four burly —stood outside the door of the club, wearing *give-me-an-excuse-to-fuck-you-up* expressions. It was ten o'clock, two hours before I was to meet Athena, but I wouldn't wait. I had to see her dance.

Five hundred American college kids were in the club. I saw at least a hundred UCSD and San Diego State logos on shirts and caps. Almost everyone was drunk and under twenty-one. Men outnumbered women four to one.

Two waiters wearing multicolored sombreros and serapes moved through the crowd with bottles of tequila in leather holsters. One collected money. The other poured shots into mouths opened to the ceiling like baby birds. Once the amber liquid was poured, the money collector shook the drinker's head to the sound of a ringing bell. I saw many kids who were so drunk they were stumbling. The club kept on selling to them.

The music was so goddamned loud. Everyone was yelling. I felt anxious, my breath getting hard and strained. Crowds were ideal targets. Things started to get soft around the edges. *Don't flashback here.* For starters, those thugs guarding the door would beat the shit out of me and throw me to the sidewalk.

I leaned against the wall, closed my eyes, and saw Athena's breasts, tight in her shirt. My breathing slowed. The here and now returned.

I wonder what Dr. Berlin would think of my coping mechanism.

There were three bartenders, each half Ruben's age. I ordered from a young guy who moved back and forth behind the bar like a nervous chipmunk. I pointed to a Pacifico on the bar. Every chair and bar stool taken. Cigarette smoke hung in a solid cloud a foot deep along the ceiling. The dance floor was the only place with breathing room. By the stage and runway, it was all men.

The bright lights over Matilda's cage were on.

She was in the far corner of her enclosure in her fight-or-flight crouch, surrounded by humans with glasses and beer bottles. Some just looked. Others were trying to communicate with "meows" and "hey kitty," and other asinine bullshit. A few were taking selfies or having their friends photograph them standing with Matilda in the background. I watched one kid shake his beer bottle and spray beer on her. She hissed as he disappeared into the mob.

There were a few people whose faces said they were disgusted. They never approached Matilda's cage.

I was ready to have a talk with the guy who sprayed the beer when a huge beefy kid moved next to Athena's table. He was maybe twenty and bellowing like a fat seal, loud enough to be heard over the racket, putting on a show for his eight buddies. They were dressed alike in jeans and San Diego State tees.

He rushed Matilda's enclosure, his hands balled into fists at his sides, chest pumped and leaning forward, yelling. He grimaced and must have thought it would scare Matilda and get his buddies laughing. It only accomplished the latter.

"Hey, fucking cat! Hey mother-fucking, cock-sucking cat!" He looked at his friends with an exaggerated smile that said *watch me*. He threw his beer bottle at Matilda. It shattered on the chain-link fence. Liquid and shards of glass shot into the enclosure. Matilda hissed and jumped to the right as if the floor was electrified. Then he yelled again, adding "pussy-eating" to his epithets.

Beer was dripping from the *"Do not throw things at the puma* sign.

He announced, "I gotta take a fuckin piss," and strode to the small bathroom on the far side of Matilda's enclosure. I moved to where he'd been standing when he threw the bottle. Matilda faced my direction, but she couldn't see me. I don't think she could see anything. She stayed in her crouch in a far-off world, her eyes focused somewhere outside—anywhere but here.

I watched for a few minutes as more people stopped to look or take selfies. One kid yelled "hey" and ran his beer bottle on the chain links. Her eyes stayed wide, and she didn't flinch. As he moved off, two more drunks approached, asshole-walking attitudes indicating they were going to fuck with her.

Ruben was right. Stopping people from tormenting Matilda would be like trying to put out a wildfire with a squirt gun. I walked away.

Cheyenne, a mousy blonde with fake breasts that looked like a pair of softballs sewn under tight skin, was dancing. If you could call it dancing. She was skinny and spent most of her time on her knees with her bare ass facing anyone who would slip a buck into her butt crack.

A table ten feet from the stage emptied as Cheyenne was picking up the last of the few bills thrown on the stage. I ordered two beers from a waiter who showed up seconds after I'd sat. He was back in less than two minutes.

The curtains on the stage were faded gold, threadbare in spots. They parted as a fast-talking announcer said Brittany was up next.

Unlike the previous dancer, Brittany was a substantial woman. She sported a tramp stamp of an eagle above her ass, strutting in five-inch heels onto the stage and down the runway. Her face was tired. A drunk kid in a SDSU shirt was staring a hole through her one asset, a pair of massive watermelon-sized breasts. Brittany was a star among the fanatical tit men in the audience.

The stretch marks just below each of Brittany's underarms showed the strain of hefting that pair. She bent at the waist, allowing gravity to draw them toward earth, then shook them from side to side.

The big beefy kid was back. He leaned his palm on one end of the stage, yelling, "Hey hey, girl, over here!" holding a buck folded lengthwise. Brittany ambled over, pulled her arms together, bunching her tits, leaving a tight slit for him to deftly slide in a dollar bill. I got the feeling he'd practiced the move.

Brittany finished on her back, spreading her legs wide for bucks.

This is sexy? I wondered how the human species reached eight billion people. I supposed alcohol helped.

I wished I hadn't seen this.

What in hell are you doing here, Athena?

The DJ broke in on my thoughts. "Let's give a warm Club Estrella welcome to Chelsea, who wants to *show you some heaven.*"

From the speakers came the slow beat of "Show Me Heaven" recorded by Laura Branigan. I smiled. I didn't think I'd heard the song in twenty-five years. I knew who would come from behind the curtains.

Athena moved down the runway in black heels and a red bikini. She wore a red blouse, all the buttons opened. It was the one she wore the day we'd met.

She scanned the room, her eyes stopping on mine, moving to area of the runway nearest my table. She smiled, slight and knowing, as if she wasn't surprised I was here. I think only I saw it.

I wanted to see her. *Be careful what you wish for.* Hundreds of guys were also seeing her. Soon Athena would take off that blouse and bikini. I drank the first beer in gulps, not knowing it was empty until my lips hit the rim and nothing came out. I took gulps of the second. I felt like a twelve-year-old sneaking a look at the dirty magazine under the mattress. I thought of walking out.

Her face was serious but that slight smile stayed. The crowd didn't exist. Only me. Athena did not pretend to look at anyone else. Muscular, powerful. Lithe, moving like a gymnast, squatting, dropping to her knees, then pushing up as easily as she went down, all to the rhythm. My eyes traced the lines of her thigh muscles.

She was a dancer. It was in the ease and flexibility of her moves. Exquisite, she stood out in this shithole. A feral cat. Her movements were wild, sensual, a feline signaling her want. So beautiful, she didn't hide her scar. I saw its end, just above her waist.

I avoided her eyes. Not because I didn't want to look. I felt intimidated, afraid to look. Hers were primal, a stare that had signaled for millennia, "I want you to mate with me, make love, whatever you want to call it, just fuck me."

All that shit was going through my head.

She dropped the blouse and stood in her bikini. As the song neared its end, the crowd chanted, "Take it off, take it off, take it off!" I looked into her eyes. *You're not staying here.* I shook my head. Slight, like her smile. *Not for these assholes.*

I would step over ten Laura Branigans for this woman.

The beefy kid was on the edge of the runway, holding a folded buck for Athena. His voice was excited, as if he was offering something of great value. "Hey, lady, over here. Hey, ass first, lady. Fuckin' take it off. Take it off. Come on, lady."

I felt a jolt of adrenaline, my body hot. The kid was linebacker sized. Athena ignored him. He kept up his yelling.

I'd seen his type. College boys, big and soft because they drank and ate too much, bodies undefined like a sculpture half complete. Athena kept ignoring him. He got louder.

"Hey, Grandma. Get the fuck off the stage, Grandma! Can we get someone here who isn't a senior citizen? Hey, old woman. Get your fucking ass off the stage." He still held that bill in the air, as if Athena might change her mind when she saw it.

I still might have given this asshole a pass. After tonight, I wouldn't be back.

"And what's this shit?" He pointed to Athena's jaw, then traced his hand from his neck to his gut. "Somebody cut you, bitch?" He turned to the DJ. "Why don't you get this fucking old whore off the stage?"

Athena still ignored him.

I wouldn't.

He proclaimed, "I'm taking a fuckin' piss." He paused by Matilda's cage on the way to the small bathroom.

"Hey lion! Hey lion!"

Twice he rushed, fists again clenched. Then he stomped off after almost falling over the railing.

He entered the small bathroom behind Matilda's cage. I followed. He didn't see me lock the door behind us.

It was only us in that closet-sized room. It contained only a sink, urinal, and toilet and smelled like a stairwell where transients piss. The fluorescent lights were dim and flickering. My jogging shoes made squishing sounds in the liquid on the concrete floor.

I stared at his profile as he stood before the urinal. A red mole on the side of his cheek made shadows with every flicker of the bad light. My right hand rested, fist down, on the porcelain sink.

The kid turned and smirked. He had at least ninety pounds on me. I stared, reading him, seeing beneath his swagger. I knew this asshole. He bullied with his bulk and big mouth. Phony bravado, weak in the face of real challenge. The flickering light kept making mole shadows.

He looked down at his dick, then at me.

"You got some fuckin' problem?" he slurred.

His wince said he'd been drinking all day. His hands were moving, shaking off the last drops of piss. I was locked on his eyes. He flushed the urinal.

If he had picked up the rhythm, he would have charged then. In this crowded john, his bulk may have prevailed. But his type drove into ambushes. They were arrogant and undisciplined. Lieutenant Hamm lasted three months in a combat zone. I don't think this kid would have made half that.

Then it changed. It was Lieutenant Hamm stuffing his dick in his pants, forgetting to zip. Clutterfuck stood there in desert camo. He was that asshole fucking my wife who did not have the common decency to stay around long enough to let me kick his ass.

Then, they were all there—the dumbshits who got people killed or fucked up beyond all recognition. The goddamned politicians who talked tough and sent me to war for bullshit reasons that changed with every blow of the political wind. A commander-in-chief who declared, "mission accomplished," then sent me overseas for another ten years.

And, finally, he was the motherfucker who called Athena a whore.

The kid put his hands on his waist. "You mind getting out of the way, old man?" he said. He wasn't stopping at the sink on the way out. I was glad Athena hadn't touched his money.

I didn't move. He rolled his eyes. "What? Ah, fuck, not again. You some fuckin' faggot?"

My hand no longer rested on the porcelain of the sink. I moved closer, a foot and a half between us. His looked away, his eyes darting from my chin to the door behind me.

He'd lost his smirk. His eyes were confused. I watched him breathing, waited for the next time he exhaled.

"What the fuck do you—"

I buried my fist just below his sternum, feeling it sink into his gut, a blow designed to lay this motherfucker out. I heard a rush of air, felt it hit my abdomen through the cloth of my T-shirt as his head and upper body fell forward. I grabbed the back of his head and kneed him in the face, then belted him with my fist, then my elbows, until he went down. His cheek was in the liquid making sucky, splashy sounds.

He was on his side, hands over his face, bellowing. "Waa the fuccck! Awww, Awww, Whaaa, Whaa!" I kicked him eight, ten times; heard a rib cracking, then another. He kept wailing. He lifted his head once, piss dripping from his cheek. Then he laid it back on the floor.

"She's not a whore, you fuckin' piece of shit." Twenty-one years went into that.

I was spent. I leaned my ass against the sink, taking deep breaths. Then I washed my hands and walked out. I made my way through the crowd and left. I didn't look at Matilda.

The cool air hit me in a breeze coming off the ocean. I smelled salt and seaweed. It was so fresh. The blues, reds, greens and yellows of neon lights up and down Juarez were brighter than I had remembered. My aches and pains were gone. I couldn't remember feeling so light.

Athena wouldn't be off work for another forty-five minutes. I waited for her in a restaurant.

CHAPTER 17

Just after midnight, Athena walked in and scanned the tables. When she found me she smiled, and I got happy. It was just after midnight.

She was wearing jeans and a light sweater. She kissed me on the cheek, then my lips for a long five seconds. "I'm so happy to see you. You okay?" she asked, hugging me. She looked in my face, smiling like she loved me.

It had been so long since anyone had looked at me like that.

We didn't stay at the restaurant. The coastal road south was quiet, almost deserted. My left hand was on the steering wheel. She was holding my right on her lap.

"Randy, may I ask you something?" She paused. "A man was beaten up in the club. Bad. He was found in the bathroom. His nose was broken. The bouncers thought he had three or four broken ribs."

I looked ahead to the road and the occasional palm tree that showed up in my headlights. The fronds waved in the light wind.

"He was the young man who called me a whore. His friends took him to the border so he could go to a doctor."

It was dark in the truck. I felt Athena's body close, felt her pulse where her fingers touched mine. "Did you do that to him?"

I didn't answer.

"Don't do that again, Randy. I know why you did it. Please. Don't."

Light from a luxury hotel lit the interior of the cab. There were shadows under Athena's cheekbones. Her hair glistened. I would do anything for her. We needed each other. I was afraid it would end soon and I would lose her.

"I can't promise that. Nobody calls you a whore. Ever!"

"He was hurt."

"Do you really think I give a shit about that son of a bitch? He threw bottles at Matilda. Do you really care about him?"

"No. I don't. I care about *you*. I don't want to see *you* get arrested."

"I won't get in trouble." I laughed. *Says the guy who's going to steal a cougar.*

"I don't want you to get in trouble," she said.

I felt her staring at my profile. She didn't say anything. How often would I have to drop some big blowhard?

"Okay. I won't do it again."

She smiled. "Good," she said. I felt her hand tighten over mine, squeezing. "Now. Why'd you do it?"

"What?" I looked at her. She was serious.

"I told you . . . *nobody* calls you a whore. I love you. And—" I didn't finish. I considered her mine, but it was too soon to say that. "I'd step in front of a bullet for you. You must know that."

She leaned into me and touched the scar on my right arm. Smiling, her eyes were misty. "Thank you," she said. "Thank you, Randy."

"Hey. What's this Chelsea shit? You're not a fuckin' Chelsea. Aren't all Chelseas nineteen and blond? Then they die off at twenty."

She laughed. "My stage name used to be Minerva. The owner said it was an old-lady name, told me to get rid of it. He said my stage name had to be Chelsea."

"*Minerva* . . . Roman for Athena."

"You know that?"

"I read Greek mythology as a kid. I loved the stories about their heroes. I agree with that asshole. Just on that. Minerva's an old-lady name. But Chelsea? No, no, you don't need any more names. You don't need to be doing that shit up there anymore."

After I parked at my motel, we walked to the beach. We sat in the sand, our shoes off. I had my arm around her. Each of us held an open beer. The sea was rough. I blew out a small mushroom cloud, then passed the joint to Athena.

"I used to be really against this shit." I took another hit. "Rangers do not smoke weed. I said shit like that, and I fuckin' meant it." I held the smoke to get maximum THC. "But I went down to the front desk to complain about the trash piling up outside my room. They never dumped it. He gave me a few joints instead, like he thought the trash wouldn't bother me if I stayed high." I laughed. It seemed really funny. "So I thought, 'Hey, this shit ain't bad.'"

My voice was high-pitched, like I'd inhaled helium. I sent another cloud into Mexican air and we laughed. "Now I view it as a necessary part of my PTSD therapy. Really, though, it's you. And Matilda. I'm functioning. Maybe not great, but I wasn't at all before. You should have seen me three months ago."

"Beautiful here, isn't it," she said. The full moon lighted our faces. We were a few hundred yards down the beach from my motel. This was one of the few areas of undeveloped coastline between Rosarito Beach and Ensenada. I loved the buildup of the water getting sucked out and the slaps of waves bashing the sand, the crescendo.

"Yeah, it is. I thought I'd be watching waves, getting better. That didn't work. I'm glad I went out on the Fourth of July."

"I'm glad you did, too. Why'd you come tonight?"

I tried to think of a non-X-rated reason but drew a blank. "I wanted to see you." I was forty-one and acting like a sixteen-year-old boy working up the nerve for a kiss. That bullshit fantasy about grinding my hips into her while she moaned with pleasure was just that—a fantasy. I was scared to touch her. She smiled, looked in my eyes, and I felt like I was caught watching internet porn.

Athena wasn't letting me off easy. After another hit, she started up again.

"Why the club? You knew I'd be on the stage. Why'd you come to the club?"

"You're too good for that dump," I said. "You don't have to be alone. You can be with me." The moon made a line in the water all the way to an island miles offshore. For some reason it made me think about how little I knew of her. "Why do you like me?" I asked.

"I love you," she said.

"But why? Really. I don't get it. You knew how fucked up I was from day one."

"You're not fucked up."

My eyes rolled.

"Maybe a little," she said. "I'm a little fucked up, too, you know. We can be fucked up together."

She studied my face like it was a map. "I saw what Matilda saw. She saw your pain. But she saw more. You don't even know how special you are. There aren't many guys—people—like you. Brave. Honest. You'd march into hell for something you believed in. Actually, I think you did just that too many times."

"I don't know. Look where it got me," I said.

I dug my heels into the sand then, literally and figuratively. Fuck, this seemed as good a time as any.

"Listen. I have a plan. I want you to come with me."

I told her how I would steal Matilda and we would marry and live somewhere down south. Maybe Bahia de Tortugas, my original goal. I would build a big enclosure for Matilda. In two, three months, I would go home, fix things with my sons. Then I would come back and eventually we'd buy a place, a restaurant, and Matilda would have a huge enclosure with trees and things to play with. No one would get hurt. No battles to fight. No one to kill. No more loud music or bad dreams. My boys would visit. I would be a father again.

I finished and looked at her. Her laughter started slow. It built until she was howling.

She choked out, "God, I love you, Randy."

I was getting angry. Confused and hurt. "I'm asking you to marry me, Athena. I want that. Why the hell are you laughing?"

She stopped sputtering. "Randy, you're talking about us running away, an American soldier with PTSD and his stripper wife, living with their pet cougar, hiding from the *Federales*." She exhaled slowly, shaking her head. "You know that can't work."

I had this all planned.

"You're *not* a fuckin' stripper! Why the hell do you do it, anyhow?"

She kept stifling laughter. "And what about your sons?" she asked. "You wouldn't see them much from down there."

She was right. "Well, yeah. Maybe somewhere in the US, then. But I can't leave you in that club, Athena . . . and I won't leave that cat there. You need to hang on for a few more days. Thursday morning, Matilda will be out. We could work. *Us.* You, me, somehow it can work. Somewhere. It can work."

My voice was raised, my neck hairs on end. "Don't laugh. This shit ain't funny." I put my hand on hers. "I'll bring Matilda here. Then we'll head—" But I didn't know where we'd go.

"Your manager won't let you keep a cougar in your room." Athena laughed even harder.

"That's pretty dumb, isn't it?" I asked. "Sharing a room with a cougar? We'll forget I said that."

"I'm sorry I laughed, Randy." Then she laughed harder. This time I laughed, too.

"Dumb's all we got," I said. "There aren't a lot of options with Matilda. Maybe she won't die Thursday. But she'll die, soon. I can't sneak her into the US through the back country. Can't release her. She won't survive."

I remembered something. "You have a passport, and a border crossing card, don't you?" I asked Athena. "That lets you into the US."

"You mean drive north. The two of us. Without Matilda?" She acted surprised. "Randy, you could drive over that border right now, show your passport, and you're in. Home."

"I'm not leaving her behind. I won't leave you, either. We, the two of us, take her across the border Thursday morning."

Athena's laugh said she thought I was joking. She studied my face.

"You're not kidding," she realized, sobering. "You know that's crazy talk, Randy. You'll get arrested."

I wasn't laughing. I'd do the right thing for the right reason. Fuck the consequences. Take out the motherfuckers. Thinking of it made me feel the way I did when I wore a uniform.

Neither of us spoke for a few minutes.

"What's the most important thing for you, Randy?"

"You're one of them," I said.

"You've got me. So, what is *the* most important thing? Really?"

She was right. It wasn't her. I had to be a dad again. The absence of my sons was a hole in my gut. My PTSD had been so consuming I did not know how big it was. Now I felt the depth of what I'd lost.

"My boys are north. I'll take her north. I'm just giving you a ride. If we get caught, I'll tell them you don't know what's in the truck. What'll I be looking at? A month? I've done that. She'll be out of Mexico, and we can find her a place. You'll be out of that club." I crossed my arms like a man who had figured it all out. "I can't leave you behind. And you didn't answer my question. Will you marry me?"

She just smiled. "Let's talk about something else," she said.

We were quiet. She rubbed my thigh as I tried to figure out what to do next.

"Do you want to make love here or in your room?" she asked, her tone nonchalant. It made her sexier and me more nervous.

"Can I tell you something?" I said.

I was digging my heels into the sand again, feeling the dampness just under the surface.

"I've only been with one woman."

It took her a moment to turn. At first she had a dull look, then her eyes narrowed.

"No, come on . . . really?"

"Really. I've only made love to one woman. I got married at eighteen. I didn't cheat. I hung on even after it was all gone. She didn't feel the same." I shook my head. "I was such a fool."

Athena started to say something, then closed her mouth. We watched the waves as they hit the sand. I felt small.

"Maybe you just married the wrong woman."

"My father was so gentle with my mom, worshipped her. I threw everything he taught me away when I threw Sara into that wall."

"Did you hear me, Randy? Maybe you married the wrong woman."

"She was so California, with that blond hair and blue eyes. Maybe I was different. I came from Idaho. Nobody at Santiago High School joined the military back then. I never made enough money. I know she wasn't happy with me for years. Or with anything about me, for that matter."

"You're still blaming yourself for shoving her?"

"I wasn't raised like that."

"You shoved her. It happened."

I kept my eyes on the waves but felt her studying my profile.

"Are you listening?" It was her bitchy tone, the one from the day we met. "I've said you made a mistake. You married the wrong woman. Get over it." I kept looking over the ocean.

"Remember you told me you like it when I say 'fuck,' Randy?" She put her hand on mine. It was gentle, unlike her tone. "Okay. Why the fuck do you think right here, right now, I want to talk about your ex-wife? I love you, but you can be fuckin' dense sometimes. I don't understand why you can't forgive yourself for hurting her. She deserved it."

She put her fingers on my cheek.

"Well, Randy? It's *showtime*, Ranger."

Athena took off her sweater, then her undershirt, then her bra. Her movements were those of a woman changing into sweats after work. She shone in the dark. I'd once thought she could be the model for a Greek statue. The sculptor would have made her breasts smaller. They were a size too large, which made them fucking perfect. Her nipples were dark. She reached and grabbed my shoulders, pulling my shirt over my head as casually as she had removed her own.

"You liked looking at me, didn't you? You were thinking of me, weren't you? Thinking of making love to me, weren't you?"

My shirt was off.

"I have a lot of scars," I said. She took in the bullet scars on my arm and side, the shrapnel scars on my shoulder and neck, the tattoos about honor and death. Twenty-one years of eating shit and asking for more. I laughed a nervous laugh.

"Yeah, you do," she said. "What are these?" She touched the nasty patch of scar on my right shoulder. "That must've hurt."

"Naaah. Didn't hurt at all—just like a motherfucker." She laughed. "I still got some metal in that shoulder."

My mouth was dry from the pot. I took a sip of beer, then three swigs in quick succession.

"That's okay." She whispered, "I like them."

I was no value added right then. We both knew she had to take the lead.

Athena lay in the sand, her scar visible in the dim light. She was looking up at me as she undid her pants and slipped them off. She pulled my hand and put it on her scar, and I felt it for the first time, moved my hand along to where it ended.

"Only one woman? Really. You're not bullshitting me?"

I couldn't think of anything to say.

"No. You're not a bullshitter." She looked up to the stars, then into my eyes. "Let's make that two."

She pulled me down to her.

We were on our backs, looking at the stars. Though I was dressed again, I still felt naked, like everything I'd built in my head to protect me was gone.

I felt it rising in my gut, then up to my chest. Then my face. I began sobbing. I tried to choke it off, then I turned away from her.

"Why are you crying?" she asked. "What's wrong? Randy. What's wrong?"

I hadn't cried since my father died.

"Nothing. Nothing's wrong. I'm not sure why. I don't know why. I don't know."

But I knew. It had been so long since I'd felt like this.

Athena hugged me, kissed my cheek. We lay there quietly, lips a centimeter apart but not touching. I felt her breath.

I quit crying, but my tears were still rolling off my cheeks into the sand. I stayed quiet. I ran my hand from her shoulders, down her side, feeling the curve of her waist. I fell asleep looking at her, like she'd evaporate if I didn't keep my eyes on her.

CHAPTER 18

"You really have to do this?" she asked. "You'll get arrested. They'll put you in jail."

"You told me that. I know."

We were on the dirt lot outside my room. It was littered with cigarette butts and used condoms. One rubber sheath had been on the ground so long it was beginning to biodegrade. The Motel Vista del Mar had a timeless quality. Nothing ever got thrown out.

I was breathing hard from wrestling the crate onto the truck bed. We found it in a department store in Tijuana. XXXL sized. According to the box, it was: "Suitable for canines of the Newfoundland, Saint Bernard and English Mastiff breeds." It had thick plastic handles for a human to carry his Newfoundland like a suitcase.

Seeing the loaded truck gave me fresh confidence. "Maybe I won't. Maybe the Border Patrol won't check. They're just a bunch of wannabe cops."

It was close to midnight. Neither of us wanted to sleep. Every minute or two, headlights on the Rosarito-Ensenada highway lit us up.

The crate filled the bed from the toolbox to the tailgate and stood three feet taller than the cab.

Athena shook her head, her eyes shifting from the truck to me with an are-you-fucking-kidding-me? look. "You think they won't check?"

The headlights of a southbound bus lit up the lot. We began shaking our heads in unison. This was all about as inconspicuous as a Rose Parade float.

"Yeah," I added. "And maybe monkeys will fly out my ass too."

Our laughs turned to coughing. Then we laughed some more, until we walked back into the room.

Even with all the beer and pot, I was too wired to sleep. We whispered in the twin bed, faces an inch apart, too dark to see each other.

"You want to marry me. You don't know much about me."

"I know enough to want to marry you."

"That's silly, Randy." I loved it when she said my name.

"I don't think so."

"You got your boys to worry about. Get them back in your life and then it might be the right time for us. You don't need me in your life right now."

"You are in my life right now." I couldn't hear waves. Must be low tide. "You could tell me some things. Then I would know more."

She'd lived in Guadalajara after she lost her family. Two years later, she left for the West Coast. She'd been dancing in clubs for fourteen years.

"How'd you end up in Rosarito?" I asked. "And why's your place so small? You don't have the money for anything bigger?"

"I do. I have money in the bank. I kept moving west. First to Cabo San Lucas, then north. Someday I'll make it to a good place to live."

"I can give you a good place." I saw something for us better than strip clubs and cheap motels. "I'll go back to work."

Doing what? I could make a ton of tax-free money with one of those private mercenary companies like Blackwater. Then, in a few years, I would have a new set of terrifying visions, and maybe more shrapnel in my body.

Outside of that, I was qualified for nothing.

"I've wanted to go to Costa Rica. Quepos, somewhere around there. I wanted to go years ago."

I listened to her tone more than her words. I felt her body. *She's not telling me something.*

"Randy. You asked why I started talking to you. I said it was because Matilda came to you."

"Okay."

"That was true. But I also needed to talk to somebody."

I touched her scar. I'd had the impression she'd lived a fast life. Now, I wasn't sure.

"What are you saying? You were lonely?"

I felt her nod.

"Tell me the rest." I felt her breaths.

There was more. I just knew it.

She nodded.

"They left me alive. A few years later the dreams started. I saw the man over me, sweating, straining. Felt his palm on my mouth, murdering my husband and son. Everything reminded me of that night. I still have the nightmares. But they only come in my dreams. Before, it was all the time. Everywhere. And—"

I wanted to protect her. Hard waves were now slapping the beach.

"My name's not Athena."

At first, I didn't understand. I sat up.

"What'd you say?"

"My name's Sofia."

I had suspected she had changed her name.

"And Athena?"

"No. My name is Sofia Maria Calderon Katsaros.

"Why'd you change it?"

"I need to tell you something else. The big man who hurt me?"

I nodded.

"I killed him."

Athena sat up next to me, her back against the cinder blocks. She looked like a woman expecting to get hit. I reached over her and turned on the light.

"You still want to marry me?" she said.

"I don't know what to think. You just hit me with this. I'm not ... I've got to hear this."

She stared, silent.

"Tell me." She didn't say anything.

"No, no, no. Don't do this," I said. "You gotta tell me."

"You've got your boys. You don't need a woman who's killed a hitman for the cartels."

"Let me hear it."

She stared.

"Please, Athena. You brought it up. You let me in. Tell me."

She looked away as she spoke.

Sofia drove eleven hours to Saltillo to Cesar's Rock Bar, the place Carlos, a Navy commando she had befriended, said she would find the man who killed her husband and son.

She rented a room at a hotel across the street. The occupants were prostitutes and drug addicts. "No guests for more than two hours," the manager told her, staring at her breasts.

At eight, Jorge Ramirez Contrar, *El Perro,* pulled his car in front of Cesar's Rock Bar. This was the place Carlos said he drank. She recognized him and peed herself. Her chest tightened. She had trouble breathing. The Dog lit a cigarette and walked into the bar.

The Dog left with a women three hours later, walking across the street to Sofia's hotel. An hour passed, and the two went back into the bar. An hour and a half later he walked out, alone. He had trouble starting his car. Sofia saw him drop the keys and lean forward to pick them up. After a few minutes, she heard the engine start. He drove away.

She watched him for three weeks. For an assassin, he was remarkably predictable. Every Monday, Tuesday, Thursday and

Saturday he was at the Rock Bar. He arrived around eight, left around eleven with a prostitute, then returned to the bar an hour later.

"You cannot just walk in and shoot El Perro," said Carlos. He got her the gun but she could tell he did not believe she could kill El Perro. "You may kill him, but you will be killed. Everyone in that bar will be armed. You need to lure him somewhere to be alone with him. To do that, you need to become a part of that bar."

There was only one way a woman could do that.

Sofia talked to the manager. He looked her over. "You're hired. You want business, you need to show more of your tits," he said. "Who wears a turtleneck? Fifty percent goes to the bar. Ten percent to the bartender."

"Forty percent to me? That's it?" Sofia said.

But the manager had moved on. And that night, she sat in the corner with the other women, waiting for the bartender's signal. Three times he waved her over to meet men. Three times she left the bar and had sex with them.

The Dog came in the next night. She saw him looking at her and she felt a sudden need to urinate. She was terrified he would recognize her or that she would do something to give herself away. But his look was not knowing. *He doesn't recognize me and he wants to fuck me.* Then El Perro turned to the bartender, and the bartender called Sofia over.

She sat on the barstool next to the man who destroyed her life. His shirt was open almost to his navel, and the hair on his chest shined with sweat though it was cool in the bar. She drank with him, her turtleneck covering her scar. She was relaxed. That surprised her. How many had he killed? How many women had he mounted, as he did Sofia, forcing them to take his dick, sweating and saying horrible things? She let him touch her. "I'm Jorge," he said. Then he moved his hand up her thigh to her vagina, feeling her, rubbing his hands over her.

"Not here," she told him.

He said what he would pay.

"I wanted to meet you when I saw you walk in," Sofia said. "My room is not nice."

"I don't care," he said.

"You will," she said. "I can make things really nice. I know a place. By a lake. You could make love to me there. I will masturbate for you. On my knees, nothing on. You need to trust me, Jorge. Did you see the moon tonight? Full." She reached and touched his crotch, feeling his erection. "You are, too. You want to fuck me, don't you?"

He would never comprehend what it took for her to smile at him.

"Why not let me show you my place by the lake? It will cost you more. We'll be gone longer, but I'm worth it. Or you could go with one of the other ladies." Sofia looked to the women in the corner. They were around her age, but tired and thin and not pretty. Drug addicts. "You know how I'm different. I don't fake it. I will suck your cock. Then I will fuck you and I will come. And so will you."

He was hooked. And somehow it felt good saying those things to a man who had raped her. She had purpose again. She was in control.

"I saw you drive up. Your car's out front. Are you ready?" She rubbed him again. "You are. Let me get my purse."

Sofia directed him to a quiet spot on the lake south of town.

And she was no longer afraid. This man saw women only as prey. He suspected nothing. He was so easy to lead.

"We will fuck here," she said as he stopped the car. "Over there," She pointed to a spot under a tree by the lake. "It's so pretty to make love by the water."

He opened the car door quickly. He walked over and began pulling at her turtleneck.

She pushed him off, gently, touching his crotch. His zipper was open and his dick pointed from his underwear. "Wait . . . be gentle." She patted his arm and walked to the tree.

He sat and began taking off his clothes.

Sofia took the Beretta from her purse. It felt heavy, black metal shining in the dim moonlight. He turned his head, his smile like the mouth of a jack-o'-lantern and his eyes widened as he saw the gun.

She knew he carried a gun and would reach for it, so she shot him twice in each shoulder, leaving his arms useless. Then she put a bullet into each of his kneecaps.

He screamed. First in Spanish, then in English, then in Spanish. She was a whore, a puta. She loved his rage and pain, his panic.

He needed to know.

She pulled off her turtleneck, revealing the scar. It was dark red on her skin. Time had not yet lightened it. She saw his eyes. At first, he didn't recognize her. He begged. *"Por favor. Por favor."* His eyes got wide. *He recognizes me.* "Tu. No. Tengo din—"

She lowered the barrel and shot him in the balls.

Was he going to say he had money for her?

She hadn't planned on shooting him *there.*

He screamed a suffering, animalistic cry. She had heard the sound in her home that day from her husband. *"Por favor,"* then she said, *"Dios, dios,"* and again she saw this man's face above her and felt the pain of him ramming into her and torturing her husband and laughing—*laughing* —as he destroyed them.

Sofia remembered his vile words and she caught his eye, and said, "*Me caguey en ti,* I shit on you, and she emptied the magazine, another eight bullets, into his face.

She felt good.

Vengeance was so liberating. She felt powerful.

She threw the gun into the lake and walked to her car, two hundred yards away, hidden behind a stand of trees.

She drove west.

"My name is Athena Perez," she told herself, over and over.

She was waiting for something from me, like a kid wondering if she was in trouble. "Now you are disgusted," Athena said. "What I told you? That's me."

I wasn't disgusted with her killing the man. But she had sex with other men. For money. She'd lied to me.

It was fifteen years ago. And she had to kill that man.

I thought of how she walked the times I followed her, zigzagging across and along streets to her apartment.

"Do you worry that they'll come after you?" I asked.

"I did," she said. "I did, for years. Then I read of the battles between the cartels over drug routes. The man I killed was listed among the names of men assassinated in cartel violence. It's been eighteen years. They would have found me by now, if they were looking. I never use my name."

"You really think what you did would bother me? Do you know how many men I've killed?"

"You killed in war, Randy. I just killed. And it didn't bother me. And *that* bothered me. It's not what I believed."

"You mean your religion? 'Thou shalt not kill' and all that crap? With *that* piece of shit? That was your war."

"That's not something to just ignore. *He's* not something you ignore. And the souls of the dead stick to you. Someone told me that—Carlos, the man who got the gun for me. He had also killed many men. He was right."

Once at dinner, probably around 2004, I said what I believed to Sara and the boys: "I'm protecting you guys. Protecting our freedoms." But I never protected shit within 8,000 miles of America. They ordered me, I would go. I got the green light, I went ahead.

Then Sara and the US didn't need me anymore, and they moved on.

The first man I killed stood before a building in Mogadishu. We were tearing through the streets. It seemed the whole city was shooting, trying to kill us. It was like a video game. I saw the man in sandals and gray clothing in front of a door with the AK, but he never raised it. That didn't matter. That AK made him a lawful target under a set of rules that we made up and he never read. He was smiling as I cut him in half with the SAW.

I always wondered if he really was a combatant, or just someone guarding a building in all of the chaos.

I thought it didn't bother me. But it would have been nice to know *why* I was killing. It would have been nice to waste some motherfucker who actually deserved it. I could kill the piece of shit that raped Athena a thousand times over and never have PTSD.

"You did what you had to do," I told her. "Probably saved hundreds of people taking that motherfucker out. Yes, I want to marry you. I'll never feel good without you."

She looked sad, the way she had that night in her apartment.

"I'll go with you," she said. "I don't want to stay in Rosarito Beach, alone. Not anymore."

We lay there in the quiet for a few hours. Neither of us slept.

"Should we swing by your apartment before we get Matilda so you can pack up?"

"Yes," she said.

It was time for us to leave Mexico.

CHAPTER 19

I jammed the claw of the crowbar into the doorjamb and pulled. Then I yanked. Three times, each yank harder than the last. The wood bent, then gave in a wrenching crack. The deadbolt fell from the door to the cement with a clang.

I opened the double door, and Athena and I walked into the Nightclub Estrella. The alarm started beeping and blinking. Athena punched in the code for the alarm, something she learned looking over Ruben's shoulder as he closed up.

"This should work," she said.

The alarm stopped beeping.

My truck was just outside the back door. We got lucky. The back entrance of the club was three steps higher than the asphalt parking lot, and the truck bed, with the tailgate open, was the exact height of the floor. I took this as an omen of success as I wheeled the crate off the truck bed onto a furniture dolly and into the club.

It was six o'clock. Rosarito was a party town and everyone, police included, drank until late at night. No one was on the streets early morning. In five hours, three pit bulls would show up to fight.

The club was dark, silent. Matilda's enclosure was just inside the back door. She was crouching, primed to spring, ready for an assault until she recognized us. Her muscles went from visible to hidden. She walked to the chain-link fence, yawned, then stretched, and started rubbing her neck against the links. I stepped over the short railing and rubbed my leg against her fur. Then I reached down and scratched her neck through the chain links.

Athena was staring at the crate. On a furniture roller, it was only half the height of the doorway into Matilda's cage.

"What if she won't get in?" Athena said. "She could jump on top of that crate and run out of the bar."

I pictured a hundred-and-twenty-pound cougar running down the main drag of Rosarito, or on the beach. The tourists would have a thrill until somebody, probably the Federales, would shoot her.

"We can work this out," I said. I was tired, but anxious. This operation had to go off—*now*. I'd planned for us to spend five minutes in the club.

Athena looked just as tired. "We should have gotten coffee," I said.

"Okay," I said. "We'll do *this*. Put a large thing—I don't know, a wooden box, something —over the crate. Something to the height of the doorway to cover the opening."

Back in the day, I'd have been righteously court-martialed for planning an operation this idiotic.

"Those speakers will work," I said. I picked up one by the DJ booth and put it on the crate, following with the second. "Look at that. Perfect." Once I opened her door, the two speakers would plug the gap.

Athena's eyes narrowed, then she smiled and said, "A perfect fit." My head pounded. I was still a little drunk and a lot hungover.

"How are you doing, girl?" I said. Matilda was alert and relaxed, nothing like that spaced-out cat of three nights before.

"We're good to go," I said. I put the crowbar in the box on the back of the truck, trading it for bolt cutters. "No *problemo*," I said. The lock was small and gave easily.

We opened her door. There was a three-second time gap when the door was open and not fully blocked. She stayed in a far corner. I pushed the crate forward to the opening. It was six inches wider than the doorway.

"Here goes." The door to the crate was open. I threw a raw chicken into the crate.

Matilda was staring at the chicken, then at me. "Do you want to stay in this shithole your whole life, girl? Or go for the head shot?"

Matilda walked to the door, looked at me one more time, then moved into the crate. I shut the door, locking it as she tore into the chicken. God only knows what kind of shit they'd been feeding her.

"Son-of-a-bitch. Look at *that*. Maybe this wasn't such a stupid plan after all."

Matilda gave her first screech as I moved the crate away from the open door.

"Hold on!" One more thing. I walked out to the toolbox on my truck and grabbed the stuffed animal I'd found at a shop in Tijuana. Nala, the lioness from *The Lion King*, could pass for a fat cougar. I sat her next to a fresh pile of shit, then shut the door to the enclosure.

I pushed her crate. "We don't need anyone showing up. Let's get this done," I said. Matilda was getting agitated, hissing and crying with the movement. Her tail slapped the inside of the crate.

I wheeled that cage to the open door, shoving it onboard my truck. Athena's two suitcases were jammed between the cage and the toolbox, which held the contents of my now-abandoned footlocker, which stayed at the Motel Vista del Mar. Time to let it go. I shut the tailgate and threw a blue tarp over the cage. Matilda kept screaming as I tied the tarp over the bars. Only the three of us were around to hear.

Athena was crying as I shut the tailgate.

"Why are you crying?" I asked. "It's okay, Athena. It's okay ... that's all right, sweetheart. I love you. Why are you crying? We're together. All of us. Well, we may be apart for a while. But we'll be together."

She just stood there, quiet, pulling away slightly as I hugged her. We were exposed. All it would take was an early-rising cop to fuck the whole operation up, but I kept hugging her. She looked up into my eyes. "You won't go unless I do, will you?"

"That's right," I said. "Take this before I forget." I slipped an envelope into her hand. Inside was $3,800, most of my savings. She opened it and looked at the stack of hundreds. "You'll need money if I get locked up for a while," I added.

"We gotta go, Athena. I want to cross the border before nine. The lines are really bad later. I don't do well with lines." We got in the truck.

The Nightclub Estrella grew smaller. We headed north, officially starting the most half-assed smuggling operation in Baja history.

As we drove, I started to think of my next steps. Maybe we could get Matilda to somewhere nice, like a cat sanctuary. Even better, a place we could live with her.

CHAPTER 20

I checked the rearview mirror. No one had followed us out of Rosarito.

Maybe what I said last night wasn't total bullshit. Maybe I wouldn't get arrested at the border.

Yeah. Keep dreaming, Randy.

We were on the coast road north. I pushed the truck to fifty-one, top speed, and Matilda started going ballistic, ramming the bars and screeching to high heaven. I pulled over and talked to Matilda through the tarp, trying to calm her. She wouldn't shut up. So, I got back in and put on music, full-blast, and sang with Laura Branigan.

Athena's face was tight, the tendons in her neck taut. She kept her lips jammed shut, seemingly oblivious to the screeches coming from behind her head. She leaned forward, her eyes fixed straight ahead like someone driving in heavy fog. I quit singing. *She's scared.* "It's gonna be okay," I yelled, patting her thigh, then resuming my duet.

I passed a guy on the left chugging north in a beat-up sedan, worse than mine, a toothpick perched precariously on his lip. He stared, squinting, then began rubbing the gray stubble on his chin.

He saw a man in a Ford Ranger yelling to music, acting like a kid. He probably thought I was stone-cold crazy.

And he would be right. Who else but a crazy motherfucker drives a mountain lion to an international border?

We got to the lines early to beat the crowds, but 20,000 other drivers had the same idea. We inched along for over an hour. Move one car length, idle. Move another. Idle some more. Cars jumped between lanes, squeezing into faster-moving ones, then shoved their way back into the lane they came from. The entire world was pissed off and honking horns. Sort of like Twitter.

The border was three hundred meters ahead.

I took a deep breath, taking it all in. It was hot, already ninety degrees. The signature Tijuana smells of shit and exhaust filled the air. And there was something else I recognized but could not quite wrap my head around, a rhythm I was picking up. Chaos?

Something was calming that cat down. Perhaps Matilda found all this familiar and comforting. I did. It reminded me of the third-world shitholes I'd called home for the better part of the last twenty-one years.

Taking her from the club was fuckin' crazy. *Whiskey tango foxtrot.* I pondered my actions. I was saving her. I didn't fully understand why.

But I felt good, like I'd dropped a seventy-five-pound ruck I'd been humping for a day. Or years. I had a mission again. I was taking the head shot.

"Randy." Athena turned her head, the first she'd looked at me since leaving the club. She spoke in a monotone. "I'm not going with you."

I didn't look at her. We'd been over this.

"Yeah you are. It'll be fine. I'm takin' the rap. I'm just giving you a ride. You *don't know* what's in the back." I patted her thigh again, this time leaving my hand there.

"That's not it. You don't listen." She touched the photo taped to the dash. "These two are your priority. You're not ready for me, for us. And I'm not, either. Not now. Maybe someday."

"Come on," I said. "You know we need to do this, today."

"For her, yeah," she said, looking through the window in the back of the cab. "And *you* need to go home. I'm not coming with you."

"I'm not leaving you behind. I'm done with that."

I fixed my gaze on the bumper of the car ahead, as if that would get us back on track moving north.

"You don't have a choice," she insisted. "I thought it might work but I made up my mind on the drive. Right now? Today? It's a fantasy. I can't help you. Go fix your things up north."

We were moving just two miles per hour when she opened the door and swung her legs out.

I hit the brakes, jerking the truck. The crate screeched, metal on metal. I heard a second lone screech from Matilda. Athena went to the back and spoke to the tarp. "Bye, Mattie," she said. *"Que tú por ayudarme.* I love you." She took her suitcases from the bed and slammed the passenger door.

She looked in the open window, her eyes on mine, begging me, I think, to let her go. "I love you," she said. "I'm doing this for you. Here." She threw the envelope with the cash on the empty seat next to me.

"What the fuck are you doing? Why are you doing this? Get in the truck. Athena . . . goddammit, get in the fuckin' truck!"

We locked eyes for three seconds. I knew her face. She wasn't coming back. "That's yours," she said. "Take it, you'll need it. Get your boys back."

"No." I leaned and stretched my arm, putting the money in her hand, then rolled up the window.

She yelled through the glass, but I couldn't quite hear her. I think she said, "I'm sorry."

A car jumped into the fifty feet of open space ahead of me. Two cars honked, at first tapping on their horns, then laying on them. They were angry, get-your-fuckin'-ass-moving honks. "Hey, asshole," someone yelled. "What the hell you doin'?" Athena was weaving between cars, pulling her suitcases through the lanes. I thought of getting out and running to her.

She's really not coming back.

I opened my window and screamed, "Athena!" She made it to the crowded sidewalk shops selling all manner of cheap tourist junk, cutting through the line of pedestrians waiting to cross. She passed plaster of Paris statues of Bugs Bunny, Pokemon and the Virgin Mary, then I lost sight of her.

A world of horns opened up. I moved forward. I didn't know what else to do.

CHAPTER 21

I spent my first hours back on American soil in a holding tank where everyone, except me, had been caught sneaking over the border.

It was all gray cement walls and benches. Fifty or so Latino men were marched in. They spread out, filling the cement benches in the room. Three hours later, the door opened to the bright lights of the hallway. Somebody yelled something in Spanish, and the fifty filed out. For ten minutes, I had the tank to myself. Then fifty new tank mates filed in and spread out across the room. Three hours later, the process repeated.

The first time the call came to empty the room, I stood. "Not you, Andrews," somebody yelled. I sat back in my corner. I was now watching the fourth rotation file out. I imagined the US Border Patrol had no idea who would take the lead on my case, but that would just be a guess.

The tank smelled of the worst of humans—body odor, shit and piss. It was around ninety degrees and humid from evaporating sweat. The two ventilation fans in the ceiling just blew bad air around.

The light was dim, like in a nice restaurant, except in one area. Two spotlights illuminated a sign that read, Welcome to the United States of America, *Bienvenidos a Los Estados Unidos.* Beneath that were photographs of President Obama and Secretary of State Clinton. Both were smiling. Beneath stood the lone toilet.

It was white porcelain, with no seat, and shit stains on top of shit stains. Most were inside the bowl. Some ran down the outside. The parts not covered with shit glistened white in the light. Every rotation, I was treated to the sight—and smell—of six or seven tank mates squatting over the bowl.

I would have shit my pants before I used that thing.

God Bless the United States of America.

I sat on the concrete bench furthest from my smiling civilian leadership, my back leaning against the wall. Along another wall were cases of water bottles wrapped in plastic and stacked six feet high. Next to the cases was a trash can. Empty plastic bottles spilled from the can onto the floor.

The Army taught me to sleep anywhere, including on rock-hard benches in sweaty, shit-scented air. I dozed to pass time. Olfactory fatigue was kind enough to set in. I tried not to think of Athena. I thought of Vince and Darnell and what they'd say about this. For a moment, we were back in my trailer, bullshitting.

What the fuck'd you get yourself into now, Randy? Vince said as Darnell held up his beer, laughing. Just for a while, I forgot they were dead. I leaned back and laughed loudly with my friends.

I was the outsider. No one sat within a five-foot radius of my corner. No one said a word to me. I got an occasional nod, but only from somebody who'd just rotated in and didn't know better. They left me alone.

What the fuck *did* I get myself into?

I closed my eyes again and smelled cedar. I loved cedar.

The door opened and a bright light from outside the tank stabbed my eyes. "Andrews," a voice said.

"Yeah."

"Get over here."

I walked to the door, which opened next to the toilet. Three agents, none of whom I had met earlier, were waiting. They wore black uniforms and had the same attitude as Clutterfuck.

Wind rushed in from the hallway, causing some of the toilet paper lying around the floor to flutter. I stepped over it. The outside air had a faint hospital smell of ammonia. Any air outside this tank was fresh.

Spotlighted on the toilet was a fresh eighteen-inch shit streak.

"You see things, Randy, notice things other people don't," my father once said.

Right then, I wished my senses weren't so keen.

"Do you clean this place... *ever?*" I asked. These three didn't appear to notice the smell and the used toilet paper fluttering in the doorway.

"Hands out," one said.

One agent grabbed my shoulders. The prick who cuffed me in the front couldn't have known he did me a favor. With the shrapnel in my shoulder, I couldn't put my right arm behind my back.

"That way." One of them pointed down the long hallway.

I walked fast from long Army habit. Though the agents had to hustle to stay with me, I was shoved three times in the minute it took to walk straight down the hallway, turn right and arrive at a door labeled *438*.

One of them opened the door. "Inside, Andrews. Sit down." he said, and I walked in. The room was small, with just enough space for two chairs and a table. I took the seat facing the door.

"No. There."

He pointed to the chair just inside the door. As I sat, he put his hands on my shoulders and pushed. He walked out, shutting the door behind them. The lock on the door clicked, then silence.

Fingerprints covered the silver metal table. There was a mirror along an entire wall. I breathed in, relishing the air conditioning. The handcuffs made a sharp metal-on-metal sound when I moved them across the table.

The door opened. Two men entered. First in was a Border Patrol agent with an eagle on his black shirt collar. He leaned against the wall, arms crossed, looking every bit the asshole town sheriff in an old western. He glared, unblinking.

The other guy wore the patch of the United States Fish and Wildlife Department. He took the open chair. His arms were spindly, like the legs of a beach bird. His dirty blond hair was combed extravagantly in an attempt to conceal a bald spot the size of a salad plate. He put a clipboard on the table between us, pushed his glasses up, then spoke.

"Mr. Andrews, I am Investigator Howard Clifford. I work for the United States Fish and Wildlife Department. Our job, one of them, is to protect the United States from the importation of hazardous wildlife. That is why I am here. And this. This is the supervising chief of the San Ysidro Border Patrol Station, Chief Hector Rosales." Rosales's stare said, *I want to fuck you up.*

"Chief Rosales's job is to supervise border activities for this entire sector, which extends from just east of here to the ocean. Chief Rosales is here representing the United States Border Patrol."

Clifford paused and picked up a pencil attached to the clipboard by a dirty string. I read upside-down. He printed in neat block letters, *Introduction. Explained roles of B.P. and F.W. Dept.* His pencil was dull and made scratching noises when he pressed it hard to the paper.

Clifford kept shifting in his metal chair. Each move made high-pitched screeches on the cement floor. I cringed. He didn't seem to notice.

He made small talk.

Did he really give a shit how my day was going?

Then he wrote, *Put interviewee at ease.*

"Mr. Andrews, you are under arrest, so I am going to inform you of your rights. Okay."

Clifford took a card from his shirt pocket. It was laminated and looked as if it had never been used.

I began feeling uneasy, and not from PTSD. This might be more serious than I'd thought.

"You have the right to remain silent. Anything you say can and will be used against you in a court of law . . . do you understand these rights?"

I nodded.

"Okay. Having these rights in mind, are you willing to voluntarily talk with us?"

Again, I nodded.

"I need an audible response, Mr. Andrews."

"What happened, happened," I said. "Yeah. I'll talk to you."

"Okay. Let's go."

"Let me summarize why we are here, Mr. Andrews."

Clutterbuck reported that I claimed to be hauling an African lion then refused to allow inspection of the cargo. All agents said I was "evasive."

"Hell. That's not true," I argued. "*How* was I evasive? I told Clutterbuck, then Dempsey, a cougar was in the cage."

"That's not the issue, Mr. Andrews. How did you come into possession of the mountain lion?"

"How's Matilda?'

Rosales's jaw moved slightly, a man trying to conceal the gum he is chewing. Gum must be standard issue for the Border Patrol.

Clifford pushed his bifocals higher on his nose.

"Matilda?"

"The mountain lion. On my truck."

"So, you acknowledge you had a mountain lion on the back of your truck."

That was fuckin' dumb. I didn't answer.

Clifford had a self-satisfied expression, the one detectives in old movies get upon discovering the smoking gun. "She's fine. She is in an animal shelter in San Diego. I was there earlier. They don't get many mountain lions at that animal shelter. She certainly gave animal control a scare."

Clifford didn't look at me. He stared at his clipboard and wrote things. He must have seen me reading his notes. He tilted his clipboard so I couldn't see.

He chuckled and pushed his glasses higher on his nose. He was enjoying this, a man obviously cut loose from analyzing the statistics on endangered smelt or something just as boring. This was probably the biggest case of his career.

Chief Rosales narrowed his eyes and shook his head.

"I took her from the Nightclub Estrella in Rosarito Beach. It's on Boulevard Juarez, one of the clubs on the main drag. The owner bought her in the US and smuggled her into Mexico. She was in a cage."

"You mean you stole her?"

"No. No. I *took* her. That mountain lion shouldn't have been there, in that club. She was dying. They were fighting her, putting dogs in her cage, then betting on who won."

Rosales stifled a yawn.

What did I expect? That these two would think I was *justified*? Clifford wrote quickly. I wanted to tell him to sharpen his fuckin' pencil. The scratching sounds were making me nervous. That sick feeling got worse.

"You must have known you'd be arrested coming over the border."

I did not answer.

"Then why did you do it?"

"I wouldn't leave her in that place."

Rosales leaned in and put his fists, knuckles down, on the table. When he spoke, his tone said he would wrench a confession out of me.

"So that's why you wouldn't tell our agent what you had on your truck? Or why you said that you had *a lion—not a cougar, a lion*—one of the big ones from Africa?

These two never would understand. Let them think I was crazy.

The three of us stared at each other.

"You're accused of smuggling a dangerous animal into the United States," Clifford said. "Do you know that's a violation of 18 United States Code, Section 42?"

"I couldn't leave her there."

He wrote some more. Rosales's breathing got louder.

Clifford pushed his bifocals into place, then looked up again.

"Animal smuggling carries time in a federal prison and a fine."

"You keep telling me I smuggled her into the United States. I drove Matilda on the bed of my truck to the border and told six US Border Patrol agents she was in the crate. I call that returning an American to her homeland."

Rosales moved in closer and now was almost on top of me. He shifted his weight back and forth from foot to foot. He huffed, then yelled.

"Six Border Patrol agents could have been killed by that animal, Mr. Andrews! Or seriously injured. Do you give a shit about that?"

"She wasn't going anywhere. She was locked in a heavy-duty metal dog crate."

"All of the agents say you were lying, that you were evasive. Agent Clutterbuck also said you wouldn't tell him what you had on that truck."

I now officially *hated* the US Border Patrol. All their gum-popping, shoves in the back, sarcasm and lying bad breath.

I spent years getting my ass shot at while these pricks were rousting illegals.

My jaw was tight. I found Rosales's eyes, ready to get under that motherfucker's skin. I no longer felt nauseated.

"Your agents are a pack of fuckin' liars, Chief."

Rosales's dark complexion went darker.

"You can just shut the fuck up! Right now!" He began to move on me, then looked in the mirror and backed off.

Rosales turned to Clifford. "You question this fucking asshole," he said. He straightened his uniform and walked out of the room, slamming the door. The mirror rippled like a pebble thrown in still water.

Clifford winced. He put his dull pencil down. His tone was soft.

"I am sorry about that, John. Chief Rosales is upset. He feels his agents could have been hurt. He cares about them."

I understood that. I'd cared for scores of men, many of whom weren't alive. I couldn't believe anybody, however, could feel that way about Clutterfuck.

"This was a large and dangerous animal, an apex predator, Mr. Andrews. Mountain lions are extremely powerful and can be unpredictable. They can—"

I tuned him out. We sat without talking, the only sound coming from Clifford's squeaky pencil.

The door opened and Rosales walked in with a piece of paper. He took his earlier spot against the wall. His grimace was gone.

He almost looked friendly.

"Sergeant Andrews. We searched that tool locker on your truck. We found your military awards." He looked at the paper. "Three Silver Stars, seven Purple Hearts, eleven Bronze Stars with valor?"

Clifford turned his head from Rosales to me. "Were you in the military?"

No, dumbshit. Silver Stars and Purple Hearts come in cereal boxes. Is there one goddamned person in this whole fucking place who understands?

Rosales glared, but this time it was at Clifford.

"I was. Twenty-one years. I'm retired."

"You have three awards of the Silver Star?" If there had been an available chair, I think Rosales would have sat.

I didn't answer. Rosales looked at Clifford. "Nobody has three Silver Stars, Howard . . . *Nobody.*"

"Aren't you supposed to get a search warrant before going through my shit?" I asked.

"We don't need one, Sergeant. You were crossing a US border," Rosales said. His expression was soft, the face people show to friends or family. I thought it was condescending. I may have been wrong.

"Your background could help you," Rosales said. "Anything you want to say about your military experience? Any issues dealing with your service?"

I didn't answer. I heard the ringing in my right ear. We were going down that crazy vet path again. Americans waved flags and thanked you for your service, but they didn't want you around.

Rosales continued. "Sergeant Andrews. I was in the Army, 1976 to 1980. Fort Sill. Artillery."

He probably said that to make me trust him.

I trusted only one person. Everyone else was dead.

Just being a vet didn't cut it. Tell me you've served under fire, and maybe I'll listen. Service like his—a few years in the States—wasn't worth shit. My belief in that was something I'd earned from thirteen combat tours.

"Someone must have helped you," Clifford said.

Rosales looked at Clifford, shaking his head.

Clifford said the usual bullshit. "It would go easier" if I named people.

My hands were on my lap. I lifted my arms and put my elbows on the table. The handcuffs kept my wrists together.

I looked like a man praying. I wasn't. The sleeves of my black T-shirt pulled up, revealing *75th Ranger Regiment* on my left bicep over a skull in a black beret. Beneath were the words *Rangers Lead The Way.* My right bicep read *United States Army* and *Death Before Dishonor.* The rest was the scar Athena traced with her finger.

Clifford followed my gaze.

"You want me to rat out people? You're talking to the wrong guy, investigator."

I'd had it with the sound of his pencil.

"Why don't you take that fuckin' clipboard and that motherfuckin' dull pencil and shove it up your ass, Clifford?"

Clifford's eyes widened. I watched his face go red.

Rosales acted as if he didn't want this to end. "Sergeant. Can't you give us a little more before we close this out?"

This time, Clifford shook his head. "No, no. We're not talking any more to this guy. We'll just turn it over to the US Attorney."

"I want a lawyer," I said. "I'm not saying any more."

Rosales frowned. Clifford secured his dull pencil under the metal clip at the top of his clipboard. Rosales started to say something, but didn't, then they walked out.

A single Border Patrol agent walked me back to the holding tank, where I sat for another hour. I heard my name called again, and I was handcuffed and walked to a van that drove north to the federal jail in downtown San Diego.

CHAPTER 22

A federal marshal opened the thick metal door and walked to the center of my new tank. His eyes were on the sheet of paper he was holding.

"We're pulling bodies for court. Listen up for your name. Andrews. You're first. Get your ass over here."

He read another ten names after mine, ending with Santiago.

My ankles were chained. I was at the head of a line and told to walk through an open door, then a hallway, then down another long hall with dim lights every fifteen feet or so. The air was cool and still.

There was rumbling, loud and powerful, coming from the ceiling. It was cars and buses above. This was a place of vulnerability and danger. We were walking under the street and I was leading a group of ten criminals, none of whom would be worth a shit in an ambush.

With my ankles chained, I could not run. I felt panic rising, starting in my crotch and shrinking my testicles, then working up to my abdomen and chest. I was weak. That was something I never could allow myself to be.

Freaking out could get me killed.

I put my legs on autopilot, walking one step, then another.

"United States versus John Andrews. Where's Mr. Andrews?'

The federal judge sat twelve feet above us. I was to his left in one of a dozen chairs inside a jury box. All of us were in yellow, except for one guy in a red jumpsuit. I figured he was a child molester or a snitch.

This place was cold, humorless. And quiet. Sounds echoed off the high ceilings. The floor had the level of shine that comes from daily buffing by people with expensive equipment and tons of free time.

From the chin up, the judge was an older version of God. His hair was pure white.

"I'm here, Your Honor."

"Do you have a lawyer, Mr. Andrews?"

The cheapest quote I got from three lawyers was $7,500, paid up front. That didn't include going to trial. A trial would cost another $12,500.

My assets were that envelope of cash I gave to Athena, a 2005 Ford Ranger with 167,000 miles and a top speed of fifty-one, and a bank account with less than a grand until my retirement check deposited in nine days. None of the lawyers trusted me to make payments.

"No, Your Honor. I don't."

"You're charged with violations of two sections of the United States Code. One of Title 18 and one of Title 16. The smuggling charge carries up to twenty years in a federal prison. The other carries five years consecutive to that. Do you understand that?"

I think I quit breathing.

"Mr. Andrews."

The judge's tone said I wasn't answering fast enough.

"Do you have the funds to hire an attorney?"

"No."

"Court appoints Federal Defenders to represent this accused. Mr. Maxwell? Mr. Maxwell?"

An old, red-faced guy who hadn't combed his gray hair sat at one of the tables. He wore a gray suit with a vest and seemed tired. The papers in front of him looked like they'd been scooped off the floorboard of his car. Everything about him was a major malfunction. *Please, God, don't let this be my lawyer.*

He stood.

"Your Honor, yes, we accept appointment. Ron Maxwell on behalf of Mister... I'm sorry, Your Honor, this is for which accused?"

"Andrews. Are you ready to arraign, counsel?"

"No, Your Honor. Can the Court recall the case after the break?"

The judge called the cases of the other inmates in the box. During the break, Maxwell read for five minutes and then walked over to the prosecutor, a woman of about sixty who acted like an uptight version of Marcia Clark. Her black business suit was a tad too tight, the hem of her skirt too high. She looked at me, then turned back to Maxwell, and laughed. It was loud and forced, the type made by people who don't know how to laugh honestly anymore. They spoke for less than a minute and Maxwell walked over.

"Mr. Andrews, I'm Ron Maxwell. You're set for arraignment today."

Maxwell's hands were wrinkly, the color of a catfish belly with light brown cigarette stains. He coughed, a raspy phlegm-filled choke, then covered his mouth with his right hand. He never put out his hand to shake, thank God.

The short walk across the courtroom had him wheezing. Maxwell wore an expensive suit, or at least it had been at one time; but, taken in consideration with his weathered red face, he looked more like the town drunk cleaned up for church than a man with a law degree. I smelled cigarettes five feet out as he approached. He had a clipboard.

"There is an early disposition offer I think you should consider," he said, smiling.

"What's that?"

"An offer of settlement. A plea bargain."

I stared.

"Do you want to hear what it is?"

Not really.

"Okay. What is it?" I said.

"The US Attorney will drop the Title 18 charge that carries 20 years and let you plead to count 2, the violation of the Lacey Act, importing a mountain lion without a permit."

He paused, then flashed a stiff smile.

"That only carries up to five years. *Five years.* I think you should accept their offer."

His face said he was pleased with the good news. If I hadn't been handcuffed, I might have grabbed his tie and yanked his head into the wooden railing between us. This was just another officer with a good idea that would get me killed.

"You're fucking kidding me," I said. "You're kidding me, right?" I looked in his eyes. He *wasn't* fucking kidding me.

Maxwell sighed a tired sigh, the type adults reserve for frustrating children.

"Mister . . . " He looked at his clipboard. "Andrews. I've read the reports. The prosecution can prove the smuggling charge. That carries twenty years. They will let you plead to something with a maximum of *five* years.

"Do the math," he said. He held out his right hand, palm up.

"You could get less time. That's what we'll work on." He mustered up another stiff smile and nodded. "Together."

I didn't say anything. Maxwell seemed pleased, like he was making progress converting a nonbeliever. I knew I had no bargaining power, nothing, so I tried to keep my mouth shut. I studied him as he checked his watch.

That did it.

"You didn't even know who the fuck I was ten minutes ago," I blurted. "Now you want me to bite off on five years after talking to me for all of thirty seconds? Where the hell do you come off thinking you can do that?"

Maxwell gasped, then went from zero to asshole.

"Oh! Okay, that's it. So you think you've got a really strong case, Andrews? You think you can get a jury to believe there wasn't a cougar in the back of *your* truck? Or that you weren't driving *your* truck? Or how about it jumped into the cage, which, by the way, was empty and already on your truck, and you didn't know it? Good fucking luck with that."

This was the real him. He didn't give a rat's ass about me. Or his job. He coughed another phlegmy throat spasm that made me want to lose the bologna sandwich delivered to my cell at five in the morning. He spit into a handkerchief he took from his left pants pocket, then crumpled it up and shoved it back where it came from. He wore a wedding ring.

I imagined his wife going through his pants pockets and finding *that* surprise.

"Get the fuck out of here, Maxwell," I said.

He rolled his eyes and walked off, shaking his head. He sat by the prosecutor. They talked like old friends. Marcia Clark looked at me and bellowed one of her phony laughs. She leaned in close to whisper something to Maxwell. She must be a smoker too.

When the judge called my case again, Maxwell asked to move my arraignment three days later. "Mr. Andrews, Your Honor, needs a little time to *consider* the US Attorney's offer." He looked over to the prosecutor. "Ms. Feuerstein is *graciously* agreeing to keep the offer—a plea to count 2—open until the next hearing, Your Honor."

"On the issue of bail, counsel?"

"Mr. Andrews is a flight risk," Ms. Feuerstein said. "Mr. Andrews was living in Mexico, Your Honor. And his crime, smuggling a mountain lion over an international border, is, to say the least, *bizarre*. Bail should be set high. We recommend $375,000."

A flight risk? She flashed me a shit-assed smirk, then smiled at the judge.

The judge smiled back.

I was looking in the window of a club I never would be invited to join.

I waited for Maxwell to say something. He didn't. He just coughed into his palm, stuffing his hand into the pocket with the crumpled handkerchief.

"The court sets—"

"Your Honor, I'd like to say something." I sat up higher so I could see another inch of the judge's face.

The American flag on the wall above the judge was huge, larger than the judge and the bench on which he sat. I saw one that big in Firdos Square, the day we felt like heroes. *Heroes.*

"Quiet!" The judge's palm was up. "You interrupted me, Mr. Andrews. Bail is set at $375,000. Get him out of here." The judge looked to a deputy marshal, who gave me a hand signal to stand and follow him.

He walked me back to jail under the street, alone.

Just before we reached the jail, he said, "Hold up."

I turned. We faced each other.

"Great opening day, Andrews. You're making friends. You tell your attorney to fuck off and the judge boots you out of court for interrupting him. You need to chill, my friend, or you're going to find yourself doing twenty years in a federal prison."

His tag said *Coker.* I think he was trying to help, but I felt worse.

He walked fast under the street. His head was shaved on the sides, short on top.

"Army? Marines?" I asked.

"Marine Corps. Sixteen years. I got shot in the chest. They put me out on a disability."

"Army. Ranger, Retired. Twenty-one years. I got shot a few times. Where'd you serve?"

Both of us were in Fallujah in 2004. We'd chewed a lot of the same turf.

"Well, Andrews, can I give you a piece of advice over and above what I've already said?" His tone was soft. "You need to lose Ron Maxwell as your lawyer. He's a dump truck. You know what a dump truck is?"

"I can figure it out," I said.

"Ask your buddies in the tank about him."

"How do I lose him?"

"Talk to the judge, tell him Maxwell isn't doing his job."

My face must have dropped.

"Not fuckin' Hancock, man. That was him today. He's a mean old SOB. He won't do shit for you. Once you enter a not-guilty plea you go to a new court, get a new judge."

We were at the big iron door to the tank. Coker reached out, patting my shoulder.

"Good luck, Ranger," he said.

Those three days felt like an eternity, lying on my bunk waiting for nothing to happen, years hanging over my head. Dead time. Forty-four other guys in my tank waited for nothing to happen.

I was facing the possibility of spending more time in prison time than I'd served my country in uniform. My lawyer was a dump truck. I would lose my retirement. I would lose my boys. Athena was gone. Matilda, too. I'd been a fool, again, obsessed with not leaving anybody behind.

Yet Athena had *wanted* to be left behind.

"Things have a way of turning out okay if you do the right thing, Randy," my mother always would say.

But I saw that for what it was. Bullshit. I'd spend years locked up, for what? Saving a goddamned animal? Always going ahead, being first, doing the right thing, fuck the consequences. I'd always been so smart in the field, so savvy—so good when shit hit the fan, relying on instinct and wits to stay alive.

Not back home, though. I didn't know what the fuck I was doing anymore. I was looking at losing *everything* over a fuckin' cougar.

Athena warned me. I should have listened. I missed her.

Sara wouldn't stay out of my head, either. I saw her smile when she learned of all this; saw her sitting on a loveseat, talking to my boys on the couch across the coffee table, dropping her voice low like she did when she was full of shit and wanted to sound wise.

"Your father. Something went wrong when he came back from the wars. Probably best if you forget about him. For good."

I saw myself talking to John and Danny through thick glass.

Scratch that. They'd *never* come to see me.

I was such a fuckin' fool.

My mother said to think of something good when times were bad.

I ended up thinking of those two days that ended at Firdos Square.

CHAPTER 23

I got our orders.

We were at the International Airport, ten miles west of Baghdad, the staging area for the assault on the capital. The 75th Ranger Regiment was attached to a task force operating ahead of the 1st Marine Division. Our mission was to secure key infrastructure and kill high-value targets before they disappeared.

My platoon would be transported by choppers across the Tigris, well beyond the real estate owned by the 1st Marines and the 3rd Infantry Division. Some might have called this a suicide mission.

"Secure Abu Nuwas Street. That's your target. Captain Hank Franklin, my company commander, was pointing at a location on the map. "This is an electrical relay station. And, here. That's a radio station. This is the Sheraton Hotel. The Baghdad Hotel. Along here, these are all jewelry stores. Nothing is taken out of those jewelry stores on penalty of death, Andrews. None of these hajis fucks with anything on that street. You got that, Ranger?"

Franklin was giving a final pep talk, his voice rising and lowering for effect. We knew each other from Afghanistan. The special-ops community was small.

He was energized, but he wasn't going on this mission. The leadership was staying at the staging area to coordinate the teams spreading out across the city.

Franklin's face was lean, with prominent cheekbones that gave him a skull-like appearance. He spoke with the exaggerated flourish I saw in officers on a fast track through the ranks. If he hadn't been killed four years later in some fucked-up black-ops mission in

Djibouti, he would have made colonel, maybe even picked up a star.

"You are to hold that street until the Fifth Regiment of the 1st Marines arrives," Franklin continued, warming to his military sermon. "You will hold it, Andrews, as if it is a part of our beloved United States of America, then turn that chunk of real estate over to those jarheads. You will have Republican Guard visitors. That is a no-shit, drop-dead fact of life, Staff Sergeant Andrews. Someone fucks with that relay station, waste him. If a rat walks out with a cracker from one of those jewelry stores, you are to terminate him. With extreme prejudice. If you see anyone in a uniform that is not American, you are to annihilate them. You got all that, Staff Sergeant Andrews?"

He liked to hear himself talk.

"Yes, sir."

Franklin's expression was stern, then he broke into a smile. He gave me a slap on the shoulder with one of his long arms. He had the wiry muscles of farmers and men who work at physical labor, day in, day out.

"You will be ahead of the front for hours, maybe two, three days, Sergeant. Your relief, again, is the 5th Marine Regiment."

"Hooah, sir," I said. "Rangers lead the way!"

We would show those jarheads how much fucking better Rangers were, give them a taste of real class. We were set to launch.

"Got it, sir," I said. "A rat takes a shit on that street and we drop him."

Franklin laughed, gave me another slap across my shoulder, harder this time. We were in our headquarters tent. On the boards he was using as a desk, there was a photo of him with a smiling wife and four kids.

As I was lifting the tent flap, he yelled, "Bring my Rangers back in one piece, Sergeant Andrews. You're the best NCO I've got. You got this."

Time to rock and roll.

I spoke to the nineteen standing before me, all graduates of the toughest training in the military, explaining the mission. Two Blackhawks were warming up, loud, their blades whizzing and kicking up dust. We were waiting for the signal to board.

I yelled, in my best Tom Cruise imitation. "I feel a need, a need to make some haji motherfuckers bleed!"

That shit always got a laugh. I was acting platoon leader, a lieutenant for this mission. Lieutenant Roy was out with a foot injury he got jumping off the back of a truck onto a nail. I had what I always wanted—no officer interference.

I thought of Sara's blond hair and how beautiful she was, what a sexy smile she had. She had always wanted me to be an officer, and today I was one, albeit only an acting officer.

Sergeant stripes never were good enough for her.

How easily I moved then; how well my joints worked. This was before mortars and bullets and years of humping heavy shit tore me up. I was twelve years in uniform, already on my seventh combat tour at thirty-one years old.

"You sure you're up for this, old man?" Sergeant Jim Lane yelled over the noise.

He was from San Diego, tall, muscled like a bodybuilder, and strong like a draft horse. He always had attitude. His hair was too long, but I never gave a shit. The kid was a squad leader and a fuckin' rock star when shit hit the fan. Lane was twenty-two, the second oldest soldier in the platoon with one tour to Afghanistan.

We were being cut loose to do what Rangers do best—blow shit up and kill people. We were fired on adrenaline, laughing. My experience and age gave me near-to-godlike status among the other eighteen. Except for Lane, they were all kids on their first combat tour.

"You just make sure your shit's locked down tight, Jim. And the rest of you. This is what you trained for, ladies. Let's hear it."

"Rangers lead the way!" we yelled, trying to drown out the helicopter blades. I got the signal to move out to the Blackhawks. We each were carrying sixty pounds of gear. Our helmets and the

Kevlar plates in our vests added another thirty.

The flight run was eight minutes skimming over the tops of buildings at a hundred and thirty miles per hour. Baghdad was burning. Two hundred plumes of smoke rose in puffy lines, most of them in the center of town. The Blackhawks dropped us in the open area between the Baghdad Hotel and the Tigris River. We set up in front of one of the jewelry stores.

Abu Nuwas Street was Baghdad's Rodeo Drive on the Tigris. A few scattered civilians scurried like rats into doorways. With the exception of a couple of mangy dogs digging through trash, the street was deserted as the helicopters moved out to return to the airport.

Baghdad was imploding, screaming, a mass of explosions and gunshots and crowds and looters running crazy in the streets.

But not here.

Civilians should be cleaning out these shops. The hairs on the back of my neck were on end. The rhythm was off. I lived for this, fucking loved it, because we were the twenty baddest motherfuckers in Iraq.

Then even the dogs hid. I looked to the rooftops, three stories up, the green potted plants with palm fronds hanging over the edges, a few bright pastel umbrellas that looked out of place. Abu Nuwas was a dead-end street. The threat would come from the north. I left Lane with four Rangers and a SAW, squad automatic weapon, and told them to set up behind two trucks on the street.

"What the fuck, Randy? You're splitting us? Why?"

I couldn't say. I just knew.

"Just fuckin' do it, Jim. You are to let them see you, but you are not to engage. Until I give the order, you are not to fire. Do you understand that? Keep that radio open and, again, make sure your shit is locked down tight, you got that? Can you repeat that back to me, Jim?"

"Yes, sir," he said. "Until you give the order, we are not to fire."

He looked unconvinced. "And I'm a sergeant. Remember? I actually get shit done."

I took fifteen of us, two SAWs and all of the grenades. We flew up the stairs onto the roof, began moving along the rooftop, parallel to the street. The buildings were interconnected and the first stairway we found was unlocked. We spread over the roofs of two buildings, a hundred-foot line of Rangers behind a four-foot concrete wall that looked over the streets. Fucking perfect.

"No one sticks his head over the wall, understood?"

These kids were scared and confused. Their faces said so. Nothing was happening, but I was acting like something was going down.

This was a lost cause for the Republican Guard. Their asses would soon be kicked, but they could walk out of this rich. All they had to do was visit this street. They'd come. I knew it. The civilians knew it, too.

It wasn't long, maybe fifteen minutes, when I heard the engines—soft at first, then louder and louder. I put a mirror over the edge. Four SUVs and two trucks, crammed with Republican Guard, were a half-kilometer up the street and moving our way.

At a hundred meters, they opened up on the five Rangers below. Maybe fifteen AKs.

"How many are there? Do not fire, Jim."

He screamed over the fire.

"Seventy, maybe seventy-five. They're moving slow, walking speed. Lead vehicle now fifty meters. No gaps. They're on each other's asses. Last SUV thirty meters back of that," he said.

Using the mirror, I looked over the wall again.

Then I heard more, maybe thirty, then forty, AKs, Lane still narrating. "Thirty meters. Twenty-five." The Republican Guard were out of their vehicles, firing. My Rangers were looking, their wide eyes saying, "Why aren't we helping them?" The AK-47s were now a serenade of maybe fifty. I heard screams and yells in Arabic.

But I was the boss.

"Jim, the last SUV, how far?"

"The SUVs pulled next to the trucks. They're within sixty, maybe seventy feet. All of them." Lane began to narrate without me asking.

Just a little longer, Randy.

This was so fucking hard. I walked away from the edge because I knew it was only another two, three seconds.

These Republican Guard motherfuckers thought they were going to bag five Rangers, then live as rich civilians.

Not on my watch.

"Fire," I yelled loud enough to be heard over the gunfire and down the line. "Hit 'em. Waste those fuckin' assholes."

From thirty feet above, we were firing from the rooftops—dropping grenades, dumping everything we had. The Iraqis didn't know where the bullets were coming from. They saw their comrades dropping like dominoes and they intensified their fire on Lane, who was making good use of the SAW.

One of them looked up, raised his AK, but I made his face disappear.

Shooting fish in a barrel. I wanted to scream. *We are the best, the absolute stone-cold toughest motherfuckers on the planet!* The firefight lasted forty-five seconds. All but four Republican Guard were dead. Those few still alive were moaning in their blood, cut to pieces. They died within minutes.

Not even a scratch on my Rangers.

We searched the dead, taking anything that looked military and loaded their personal belongings—family photos, prayer beads—into plastic bags pinned to their shirts. Then we stacked them, thirteen towers of six dead Iraqis each. We piled their weapons, mostly AKs, along a wall. Then we smoked their cigarettes and spent all night on that street, bullshitting, wired and wanting more. No one could sleep.

In the center of the street, we stood up a ten-foot-wide slab of plywood spray painted with *3rd Platoon, B Company, 75th Ranger Regiment.* Underneath read, *Rangers Lead The Way.*

This was our turf.

"Good job, Headlock," I said to Specialist Williams. He painted the words in old English script, gang graffiti. Headlock, from Detroit, was actually "Little" Headlock. He enlisted when his older brother, Headlock, was shot by a rival gang.

Headlock had good combat instincts, courtesy of the lessons he picked up on the streets back in the Motor City.

I pissed on the edge of the sign. "This is third-platoon real estate, gentlemen. We fucking earned it. Feel free to mark our territory. Just don't take a shit, got it?" They all laughed. Everything was funny.

Some twenty hours later, 5th Regiment, 1st Marine Division began crawling across the Yafa Bridge. Most of their vehicles split off to the right and began heading along Abu Nuwas.

"Let 'em pass," I said to Sergeant Lane. He was a quarter mile off, radio in his hand, blocking an armored personnel carrier.

The Marines moved up the street at walking speed, armored vehicle after armored vehicle, more fifty cals and heavy weapons than I'd seen in one place, ever. Moving up the street was enough firepower to take over a third-world country.

I held my fist up and said "Halt" to the gunner on the APC. "Which unit?"

I could see the 5 painted on the bumper, but I was following protocol. The Marine was starting to answer when an open-air Humvee pulled up on his right.

A Marine colonel was sitting in the front passenger seat. He was a big guy, square-jawed, a poster boy for the Corps. He was smoking a cigar, blowing smoke out to the sky.

If I had ten bucks for every Marine colonel who smoked a cigar on a battlefield after the fighting was over, I'd be a rich man. Only the tip was burned.

Nine Rangers stood in a semicircle behind me.

"Which unit, Colonel?" I yelled.

He needed to say two words, "Fifth Regiment," and I would hand over the con.

But his command sergeant major, a sour, bookish type sitting in one of the back seats and wearing a uniform that looked like he had just picked it up from the cleaners, said, "Stand down, Army."

I knew this guy, a buzzcut shithead constantly on the hunt for haircut and uniform violations. They were always sergeants major. *Where do I start?* was written on his face as he studied me. I hadn't shaved in a week. My DCUs were all dirt and blood.

I ignored him.

"Your unit, sir?" The sergeant major was poised to tear me a new asshole until the colonel held up his palm. Buzzcut gave both of us a look that would have cracked Kevlar.

"I'm Colonel Downing, commander, 5th Regiment, 1st Marine Division. And you are, Staff Sergeant—"

"Andrews, sir." I went to attention and saluted.

To the right of my boot were three teeth lying in piss.

"You're our relief, sir. You mind stepping into my office so we can discuss the handoff?" The colonel stepped off his Humvee and strode ahead.

"What took you guys, Sergeant Major?" Over my shoulder, I gave Buzzcut a shit-eating grin, then walked into the jewelry store before he could say anything.

I briefed the colonel on the AO. "Where are you from, Sergeant Andrews?"

"Idaho, sir."

"Beautiful country, Idaho. I've been there. Elk hunting. I'm from New Mexico."

We walked outside to the bodies. My Rangers were bullshitting with the Marines. The colonel was looking over the stacks of Republican Guard. "Your men did all this, Sergeant Andrews? With no support?"

"That's right, sir."

The street was painted with coagulating blood. We moved next to the pile of bodies. An Iraqi with the top of his head blown off was stacked by my feet, his brains mixing with the red asphalt. I was standing on something gray.

"The street's secure, nobody looted these stores?" he asked. "The radio station, the electrical relay station? They're good? And there were no casualties to your soldiers?"

"Yes, yes, and yes. No casualties, no looting. My men are all good. We're *Rangers*, sir. Rangers lead the way."

The colonel looked at me, nodded with a coy smile. He looked at the piles of dead Iraqis. "No shit. Well done, Idaho." Nineteen Rangers were now behind me. "Well done, Rangers."

The colonel turned to Headlock's sign. "Is that piss down there?"

"Yes, sir."

He turned to a tall, lanky Marine wearing a major's leaf. "We'll set up here. And, major, after that sign dries, you make sure it is carried with respect back to the 75th Ranger Regiment at Camp Victory."

The colonel looked back to me as we moved up the street. He was again studying the stack of bodies.

"Andrews! If we cross paths at home, Ranger, the beer's on me."

Six weeks later, I was awarded the Silver Star.

The citation read, *"With uncanny situational awareness and unflagging courage in the face of relentless enemy assaults, Staff Sergeant John Randall Andrews, III, B Company, 75th Ranger Regiment, led his platoon in eliminating an entire Republican Guard Company. Facing overwhelming odds, SSG Andrews demonstrated unparalleled composure under fire. His actions reflect great credit on himself, the 75th Ranger Regiment, and the United States Army."*

Our pickup would come as soon as I called for it. I started to get on the radio, then we heard the cheers coming from Firdos Square. It was only two blocks away, so we moved in that direction, our mission accomplished. There was no threat here. We bullshitted with Iraqi civilians, Christian women hugging us, the Muslim ladies staring but not walking over, kids laughing and running up to touch us, men shaking our hands. The 1st Marine Division arrived after fifteen minutes.

A huge statue of Saddam looked down from the center of the square. It was a big party. We felt like famous actors. We were all Vin Diesel, Tom Cruise or The Rock.

I was smoking a cigar a shop owner had given me, even though I don't like cigars. I watched the crowd growing larger and larger, and then one of the Marines draped an American flag over Saddam's face. I hugged every Marine I met, giving them shit. "What took you motherfuckers so long?" This time I was speaking to brothers in arms and meant no offense.

Saddam's statue was pulled down. American Psyops was driving this; it was made to look like the Iraqis rose up and tore it down when it really was a publicity stunt put on by us.

Liberators. We'd saved the Iraqis. I thought the war was over.

Three days later, I got phone time to call Sara and the boys.
"I'll be home soon."
John was on the line and he was nine. He didn't hate me—yet. He looked like me, had my features. He was my shadow. We were so tight then. Sara said he would not take off the military uniform I'd sent him for Christmas.

Danny was two, good-looking, with blond hair and blue eyes like his mother, a happy boy I never got to know because he was born just before 9/11.

"Do you know how much I love you?" I said those words in so

many ways to my two boys and they said, "I love you Dad, we love you Dad." Over and over, back and forth we passed it. They had been afraid I was dead. I hadn't called home in three weeks.

And I told Sara how much I loved her three times, yelled it into the phone, told her how wonderful she was and how we would take the kids and our dog, and we would go to the Smoky Mountains as soon as I got home. I would make it all up to them, catch up on what we had lost.

But Sara never said she loved me. "I know, Randy," was all she kept saying. She laughed and I was so happy and pumped I thought she had said it.

I didn't go home. I did not return to American soil for another 14 months and, during those four-hundred-twenty-nine days, I had forty-seven more confirmed kills. That's counting only direct fire. I have no idea how many died from artillery fire or airstrikes I called in.

And when I did go home in July 2004, I only stayed five months. I was deployed again to Iraq a few days before Christmas in 2004. I was promoted to Sergeant First Class during that year in Tikrit. After that, I deployed five more times to Iraq, Afghanistan, the Philippines and the Horn of Africa.

When I told the story of the best two days of my life, wiping out that Republican Guard unit, normal people looked at me like there was something wrong. It was a look of disgust mixed with pity. And fear. Sara was the first.

It was all downhill after that day. I quit telling the story. Nobody who hadn't been there understood.

I wished I'd died at Firdos Square.

CHAPTER 24

"Where's your lawyer, Mr. Andrews?" The asshole judge's tone implied I was responsible for Maxwell not being in court and he was seeing through my game.

It was 8:45 a.m. Court had started fifteen minutes before. Maxwell hadn't come by the jail to talk about my case, either. Not that I had expected him to. Maybe he took me seriously when I told him to "get the fuck out of here."

"I don't know, Your Honor."

"Well, we will take this up after the recess." The judge called the cases of ten more defendants. Maxwell represented six of them.

The defense table sat empty until a woman in her twenties walked in and sat in Maxwell's chair. She had one file that she put on the table. She opened it, read for a while, then stood and looked over the eleven of us in the box.

A paralegal, I thought. Maxwell's assistant. Young strawberry blond hair in a tight bun. She was cute and moved with an air of efficiency, a woman on a mission. My mom would have called her pert.

I was the only guy in the box who wasn't leering. She spoke to Coker. He nodded at me. She walked over.

"Mr. Andrews. Nice to meet you. I'm Jenny. Jenny Bayless." She thrust her hand, pointing it like a spear at my gut. At first it didn't dawn on me why she held it out. I hadn't slept much in three days.

It felt small when I shook it.

She leaned on the walnut railing between us. "Where's Ron Maxwell?"

"Ron is out. Health reasons. I've been assigned to represent you."

She was smiling, nodding, waiting for me to say something. This girl didn't look old enough to be a lawyer.

"I *am* a lawyer, Mr. Andrews."

"What happened to Maxwell? He was a real charmer, by the way. Wanted me to sign for five years after talking for about as long as we just have."

I thought of Maxwell's slimy handkerchief and the cigarette odor heralding his arrival. "What? He die of a heart attack?" I thought I was funny.

She stared, mouth agape. "Yes, Ron had a heart attack. A bad one." She paused. "He's dead."

I never celebrated anyone's death, even those of humans I'd escorted to the afterlife. Ron Maxwell was different.

I stifled a laugh. I wouldn't have to ask for a new lawyer.

"Jenny? You're my lawyer?"

She looked like a high school cheerleader. I shook my head, said "Jesus" not quite under my breath. She smiled, but I saw her jaw tighten.

"There is no need to be rude, Mr. Andrews. Why don't we have a meeting? See if you like me." She flashed another big, kill-him-with-kindness smile. "I'll come by and visit you this afternoon. Three o'clock? Will that work?"

Her tone suggested I might need to check my busy social calendar.

"Three o'clock works."

She can't be worse than Maxwell.

"Okay. And as for that five-year offer, I agree with you, Mr. Andrews. I think that is ridiculous, absolutely ridiculous. I'd like the judge to arraign you. I will enter a not guilty plea on your behalf, and we will set a settlement conference. May I do that when the judge takes the bench again, Mr. Andrews?"

I looked at her, puzzled. I didn't know what the fuck was going on.

"I'll explain things when we meet," she said patiently. "You don't want to take that deal. So we plead *not guilty*."

"You'll be by to talk with me?" I didn't like the whiny sound I heard in my voice.

"I promise."

Mine was the first case called after the break. Jenny spoke.

"Mr. Andrews would like to enter a not guilty plea to each of the charges, Your Honor. And we would like a hearing to reduce bail. The amount, as set, is excessive."

Just before I was walked out, she came over again.

"I'll see you at three. Maybe you can tell me what you were thinking when you drove a mountain lion into the US."

"Andrews," the marshal said. "Attorney visit."

At a minute to three, I was sitting in front of her in the interview booth. I liked her punctuality. My elbows were leaning on the metal shelf on my side of the thick glass separating us. She picked up her telephone.

"So." Jenny put her hand flat on the shelf. "How are you today, Mr. Andrews?"

She had the same patient, condescending smile as Dr. Berlin. Her voice had a metallic sound over the telephone.

"I'm doing great. Four walls and a jumpsuit. The bologna sandwiches are amazing. Good group of guys. I get to march in formation again."

How the fuck do you think I'm doing?

Her smile stretched. "Ah, you're funny, Mr. Andrews. You must have been in the military. My boyfriend's a Marine at Camp Pendleton."

"Army. I thought about the Marines at one time, almost enlisted in the Corps. That was just after Desert Storm. What's your boyfriend? A second lieutenant?"

"How'd you know?"

"By your age. And you're a lawyer. Wouldn't date an enlisted guy."

She winced.

"You know, you can bail on this Marine now. Things keep going the way they are and he'll be gone. A lot."

Jenny lost her smile. "I'm just *dating* him, Mr. Andrews."

I was tired of "Mr. Andrews."

"Randy."

"Randy, okay. So, Randy, how old are you?"

"Forty-one. How old are you?"

"Twenty-six."

"How long you been a lawyer?" I asked.

Jenny shifted in her seat. "I was sworn in last June."

"Four months? You've been a lawyer four months?"

She added, "I'm volunteering at Federal Defenders, trying to get a job with them."

I stared a long seven or eight seconds at the concrete blocks on the wall to my left. A gangbanger had scratched *East Side Crips* into the paint. "What the fuck?" came from my lips. "A fucking *volunteer*?" I stared at her face. It was flushed. Her top lip was twitching. "I'm looking at twenty-five years. You know that, don't you? And they give me some kid who's a goddamn volunteer?"

Her lip kept twitching.

My dad taught me to always respect women. He wouldn't have approved of my behavior right then. But he'd never dealt with shit like this.

I sat there, quiet and frowning.

Jenny must have known her lip twitched when she was upset. She pursed her lips, took a deep breath loud enough for me to hear then looked into my eyes.

"Mr. Andrews. Randy. If I go back to the office and I tell my boss that you are unhappy with me representing you, he will replace me. He'll do that because I am an unpaid volunteer. And then he will assign another attorney as your lawyer. All of the other attorneys in the office are—*were*—Ron Maxwell's friends.

"Remember him, that guy who died, the guy who wanted you to plead guilty and take five years?" She raised her eyebrows, lifted one hand in a there-you-have-it gesture. "One of Ron's friends will represent you. Ron's probably already talked about you over smokes on the back patio."

I saw it. Legal burnouts bullshitting about the nut job who drove a cougar over the border.

Jenny took another deep breath, letting it out slowly. Her voice got louder and sharper the more she spoke.

"But — and you need to know this — my boss won't assign you a new attorney a second time. Most of our cases involve smuggling drugs or people or guns. Your case sounded interesting, so I asked to represent you. I wanted to understand why someone would do what you did. So, I would suggest we talk now."

Jenny opened the tablet on the metal shelf in front of her, took her pen in her hand. Her movements were jerky, those of someone who was upset and trying to keep it together.

"We will talk as long as we have to, as many times as we have to, for me to do a good job of representing you. We will work together on strategy. If you don't want me as your attorney, I will go back and tell my boss we are not working out. I will wish you luck and he will assign you a new attorney—one of Ron's friends."

She wrote *John R. Andrews* on the top of the pad, then added *"Randy"* in quotation marks. "But if you do want me, *Randy, don't* talk to me like that. I get enough of that *shit* from those asshole US Attorneys and the old men at my office.

She looked briefly at the wall on her left, then back to me. "You know what? I really don't give a rat's ass anymore, after how you just talked to me."

She was staring, not blinking. The redness in her cheeks had spread to her chin and was working up her forehead to her hairline.

I was starting to trust people again. Even women. I thought of Athena, then tried to understand why Jenny was willing to help me. This was my life, *everything.*

Jenny waited, still looking at me.

Is she sincere?

She was. It was on her face. She wanted me to want her as my lawyer. What's it like to be a young and quite hot woman surrounded by asshole men who would love to fuck you but treat you as less?

Whiskey tango foxtrot. Lawyers weren't lining up for this mission.

"I would like you to represent me, and," I paused, "I give a rat's ass."

She stared, focusing on me, then laughed.

"I'm sorry I talked to you like I did," I said.

She nodded, her eyes wet. They were big, Disney character eyes. She would never be a good poker player. "Of course I will," she said. "Represent you, that is."

"You go by Jenny. Not Jennifer? It's uh . . . wholesome. I like it."

"I'm named after Jennifer Grey. My mom was a big fan of *Dirty Dancing*. The star in that movie. Remember her? I'll probably start using Jennifer one of these days. Sounds more lawyer-like."

CHAPTER 25

She wrote slowly in tight cursive, intent on getting everything down. She didn't look up, just asked questions. Then she asked if I'd been arrested.

"Yeah. I was arrested. And convicted."

"When was that? And where?"

"A year ago. I was convicted of misdemeanor vandalism. In Orange County court."

Her eyes narrowed. "Vandalism? You've been convicted of a vandalism?" She paused, processing. "That doesn't seem like your type of crime, I mean. Not that . . . not that any type of crime is your type."

"No spray paint, no graffiti. I shoved my ex into a wall, left a dent in the drywall shaped like the back of her head."

She drew her head back, eyes wide. It was a definite flinch. I saw something in her eyes. Fear? Disgust? I wasn't sure.

When I was nine, I walked into my room and found Becky going through my drawers. Becky wasn't allowed—my rule—so I smacked her on the shoulder. It was light, but her wails sounded as if she was being burned at the stake. She ran to Dad. He sat me down. To compound the offense, I lied, said I hadn't touched her. After wrenching a confession, he grabbed me, squeezing my biceps, standing me up.

"John Randall." I was *John Randall* only in times of severe wrongdoing. "Never harm a woman. *Ever!*" He was pissed, something I rarely saw. "We always treat ladies with respect in this family."

I had difficulty viewing my little sister, who bugged the crap out of me and always was getting into my stuff, as a *lady*. However, she was born a girl. That was enough to qualify her for special treatment in my dad's book. Becky could rub shit in my face and I would be wrong to smack her hand.

My father used *gentleman* and *man* interchangeably. To him, the two were the same. "Only bad men hurt women, Randy." After marching me to Becky's room to choke out an apology, he had me pulling weeds in the side yard the rest of the day.

I was glad he wasn't alive to know what I'd done.

"Where's the vandalism?" Jenny asked.

"The DA dropped the felony assault and let me plea bargain for vandalism, a misdemeanor. I used my wife's head to vandalize? I don't know what he was thinking. I couldn't have a felony or domestic-violence conviction. I would have lost my gun rights."

Before I could say anything, Jenny asked, "So you're not married. Do you have kids?"

"Two boys. Twelve and nineteen."

"How about other family? Parents? Siblings?"

"My father's dead. My mom lives seventy-five miles north of here. I have a sister in Orange County."

"Have they visited you in jail?"

"No. Last time I saw them was about nine months ago. Then I went to Mexico."

I'd been such a shit down south, only telephoning my mother twice during five months in Mexico. I never called my sister.

"I don't want them visiting me in jail, especially not my mom. I talk to them on the phone. My mom, every few days. She wants me to call. My sister, every other week.

"I'll see them when I get this behind me," I told her. "They don't need to see me in court."

More gang graffiti, in Spanish, was scratched into the metal near my left elbow. *Flaco-Surenos 13—Chinga tu madre*. "Do you want to know why I went to Mexico?"

"No. Not yet. We'll get there. I want to know why you shoved your wife into a wall."

I was looking at her shoulder. "Now my ex-wife. I don't know why I did it."

She cocked her head.

"I don't remember much of that day. Other than the guy my ex was fuc ... having an affair with was there. That was supposed to be my home, *our* home, but my ex filed for divorce before I retired from the Army. She got an order for me to move out. I'd never moved in. My kids were in the home and the guy she was having an affair with was there, sitting on my fuc ... couch. I was going to kick his ass, but he ran out the back door.

"I don't remember shoving her."

I paused, then went on. "I didn't want a divorce. People in my family don't get divorced. But—" I stopped. She didn't need to know of Sara's indiscretions.

"How do you know you shoved her if you don't remember it?"

"Sara said I did. I remember going to the home. I remember being there right after, seeing her close up with my hand on her mouth, then sitting on the couch till the police came. I saw the dent in the wall and heard her crying and tell the police, 'He did that,' as I was being hooked up."

Jenny's expression was intense, unreadable.

"I read the police report later. I kept saying, 'Where's your helmet, Corporal?' I'd said that in 2005 to some kid just before he got his head blown off. I'd never told her what happened to that kid. Or what I said. *I'd forgotten.* Till then."

Jenny's eyes had changed. They were soft.

"Screwed up, isn't it?" I added.

She feels sorry for me.

"Look, I did it." My voice was too loud. Jenny winced, then went back to studying me.

"I still don't understand how it is you don't remember actually assaulting her? A blackout? Were you drinking?"

I was antsy, feeling confined. I shook my head. "You can't make shit like that up."

Jenny nodded and put her pen down and smiled big. I didn't smile back. "That's enough. I'll be back tomorrow. Hang in there, soldier." She stood and knocked on the door behind her.

"Ranger," I said. "I'm a Ranger."

The door opened and she walked out.

The lights went out on the attorney half of the booth. My reflection in the glass mirrored my shame.

"You're in no hurry to get out of here," my public defender had said to me a few weeks before I took the plea bargain in Orange County for the vandalism.

He was right. The DA had offered the same deal three weeks before. I wouldn't take it and I wouldn't tell him why.

Inside, I knew the threats, understood what had to be done. There was structure. I had a mission to survive. Things made sense in jail.

It was everything that was missing on the outside.

I only took the deal to see my sons and then I ran to Mexico anyway.

Ten minutes after Jenny left, the deputy walked me back to the tank.

I was watching television in the day room when a short Mexican kid ambled over with his hands in the pockets of his jumpsuit. "Andrews, hey . . . fuck, man, you got that hot lady lawyer. Jenny, what a *fuckin' babe,* man. Fuckin' lucky, dude. I got some really *nasty* shit I'd like to do to her."

He said *nasty* with five syllables, relishing every one like an orgasm. He ended with a trio of Michael Jackson humping motions, his hands gripping a pair of imaginary ass cheeks.

The scrawny little fucker wasn't over nineteen. He looked inbred. His eyes were wide and staring at something only he saw on the beige wall. I watched him salivating.

"Get the fuck out of here, you little creep, before I kick your ass."

"Hey fuck you," he said over his shoulder as he walked off.

I was the one who needed to get the fuck out of here. Nothing made sense in this place.

CHAPTER 26

Jenny organized papers into stacks on the metal shelf before her, then picked up the receiver.

"Have you been diagnosed with PTSD?" she asked.

I'd only had one flashback in jail. The woman and those kids again. Always the woman and the kids, reaching. Thankfully, my cellmate was out to court. "Yeah. A doctor at the VA said I have it." She kept looking at me, wanting more. "Your turn," I said.

"This isn't a back and forth. I can't help you if I don't hear from you. Have you been to a doctor for it?"

"I went to a VA doctor. That was after I got released from jail. I was trying to get visits with my boys."

I remember the disappointment on my divorce lawyer's face when I got arrested for assaulting Sara. "Why don't you just hand your kids over to her, Randy? Permanently."

Jenny had that *I feel sorry for you* expression again.

"How many years were you in the Army?"

"Twenty-one. I retired as an E-8, came home to be with my family."

"An E-8?"

"A senior noncommissioned officer, a senior sergeant. I was a first sergeant. We run everything, NCOs do, in the Army," I explained. "I was going to stay in, be a sergeant major, but everything went to shit. I lost my family. You're looking at the only guy who didn't see it coming."

Suddenly, I thought of the pain in Athena's distant eyes.

Jenny's were different. She hadn't been fucked over nonstop by life yet.

"How many times have you been sent into war, Randy?"

"How many combat tours, you mean? Thirteen."

"Thirteen?" She snapped. "You've been to combat *thirteen times*?"

"Thirteen *years*. And thirteen times." I recited the list, "Somalia, 1991. Blackhawk down, you know. I was in Mogadishu, Bosnia, Kosovo—easy tour, even with people shooting at us. Four tours in Iraq. Horn of Africa twice. Afghanistan three times, and the Philippines once."

She wrote it all down. It was all the shitty wars and things they called police actions in the years since Desert Storm. She got to the end and shook her head.

Jenny was looking at me like those Border Patrol agents looked at Matilda. *Fear.* Was it also a look of sympathy? That unspoken message of *I feel sorry for you but stay away*?

I'd seen it before, always from people who knew nothing of service.

"Anything you want me to know?" she asked.

"Why are you looking at me like that?" I stopped myself, afraid I might say something I would regret. I sounded harsh.

Her chin dropped and her mouth opened. "No, I was just thinking how long that is, how many years."

"I wasn't one of those fuckin' Blackwater assholes, mercenaries making a ton of money. I wore a uniform, you know. Everywhere I went, I was ordered to go. I didn't volunteer for shit."

A deputy marshal looked in the glass on the door behind Jenny. "You okay?" he asked.

I didn't realize how loud I'd been.

She looked back, gave him the thumbs up. I looked away.

"Randy, I wasn't looking at you like you think I was. I'm not afraid of you. Do you understand that?"

I looked at the shiny steel shelf under my arms. I thought of why I ran to Mexico, why I ran out of the nightclub when Athena said I should look at my pain.

This time, I wasn't going anywhere.

"I'm here because I want to help you," she said.

What I thought I saw on Jenny's face—pity—wasn't there. I don't think it ever was. It was something else. *Empathy?*

"Get me out of here. Please. I hate it. I'm sick of this shit. I don't want PTSD, the guilt, any of it, anymore."

I wanted to say how disappointed I'd become in everything and everyone, but mainly me. I didn't. I couldn't understand how it all went so sideways.

And I thought of the four smokestacks.

"My buddies died protecting real estate that got handed to thugs. I believed in it, all the God, country and family horseshit. Then I come back messed up and nobody wants me around."

I brought my hands to my face briefly, running my fingers through my hair and taking a deep breath as I tried to pull myself together. "I got fucked and never saw it coming. I'm sorry to be so rough."

Jenny's eyes drooped. I imagine that's how mine looked. "I wanna help you," she said. "I'm just not sure how. *Yet*. The US Attorney is stuck on that five-year offer."

She hung up the receiver then looked down and to her side. Her lips were moving. She was talking to herself. I couldn't hear her through the glass. We sat like that for a minute as she talked to the floor. I wanted to go back to my cell and crash on my bunk.

Then she looked up with a different face, one that kept smiling bigger and bigger. She picked up the receiver. "That's it! Simple," she said. "I have an idea. I need to think on it. I'm gonna walk you out of here. And you, Sergeant, I mean *First Sergeant* Randy Andrews, are going to help me get my job at Federal Defenders."

I wasn't ready to join in her sudden high spirits.

Jenny was loading her briefcase, the receiver still to her ear. "I'll be back in two days.

"You'll get some writing paper delivered to your cell today. *Use it.* Explain everything that happened from the time you first saw the mountain lion until you got arrested. And your background. I really want to know about your time in the military. All the awards, everything you did for twenty-one years.

"Write a lot. None of your quick, soldierly, straight-to-the-point answers. Get me your story, all of it, and I'll get you out of here. Promise."

Two hours later, I was sitting at one of the metal tables in the dayroom with a legal-sized tablet and a stubby pencil, the only writing implement allowed. I wrote until lights out at ten, then started again the next morning and wrote the whole day.

I guess there was a lot to tell.

CHAPTER 27

Jenny was reading what I titled, *Background*. She made notations on some of the pages, highlighted other parts in yellow. She looked up when she reached THE END on Page 37.

"Your awards? What about those?"

"Back of that page."

She scanned the list, then talked without looking up. "Is this all of them? Even the ones you said you won't wear?"

"Yeah."

Someone had cleaned the interview room. I smelled bleach. "Thank you," she said. "Thank you for this."

"Lot of shit to write about."

"Randy. This is *good*. I didn't peg you as a good writer."

"A writer? That's a fuckin' first. Hmm. Well. I got shit to write about."

She opened to a random page. "I like this: 'The jihadi M F hid behind a HiLux (a truck), so I waxed him with a 203 round. We found most of him behind what used to be the front end. One of his hands landed in the town well, contaminating the water supply. They never shot at us again in that village.'"

She stifled a laugh. "Sorry," she said.

"You think it's funny? That shit's *funny*?" She was in good spirits. It was rubbing off.

"How about *this*?" she asked, reading another excerpt aloud. "The LT was such a fucking dumbass we made him a strip map to the shitter. Somehow he managed to make it through the whole tour and not get himself killed. But he did catch a piece of shrapnel in his ass. I'm told he had to stand taking a shit for six months."

She didn't stifle her laughter this time. "It's not funny, the *topic* I mean. It's not funny. How you write it is. It's colorful. Vivid. Has a brutal, casual honesty to it. It's like you don't know . . . I don't know how to describe it."

"Like I write about really bad shit like it's a trip to the office?" I offered. "It was. For me."

"That's it," she said. "But it is funny. Maybe I got a weird sense of humor. It's good. You're an honest guy." I half expected her to draw a happy face on page one.

"Well. There *is* humor in uniform."

Once upon a time, I laughed a lot. Even in horrible places. I wasn't as honest as she gave me credit for, though. I left out the worst and put a soft spin on other parts.

"And, I have an idea," Jenny said. "To get you out of here. It's good."

Her hands fidgeted, her nails tapping the metal on her half of the shelf. I could hear the taps over the phone line. "You gonna let me in on it?"

"It's a good idea."

"I know, you told me that. Twice."

"I'll tell you again. It's good."

"Jesus Christ. You're fuckin' with me. You're as crazy as I am, lady!"

"Hey. I'm kidding you, just teasing you. That was a joke."

This was a new her. Her face was flushed, excited.

"Okay. Okay. Okay," she said. "I'll tell you."

She acted like an adrenaline-pumped lieutenant with a *good idea*, but I'd been fucked too many times by green officers who'd been visited by the Good Idea Fairy to take her seriously. Not yet.

"This is it," she said. "We go to the media. You talk to a newspaper reporter. We get your story out."

"That's it? I talk to the press?"

"Your story deserves to be told, Randy. *Needs* to be heard. What about your military record? Does that mean nothing? Matilda's story *needs* to be heard. What was that mountain lion doing in that bar in the first place?"

She might just as well have told me to dig up Ron Maxwell and tell my story to him too. "I'm not talking to the media." My stock comment to the media overseas was, "Get the fuck outta my way."

"You don't see it, do you?" she said. "You're not a criminal, Randy. You are a hero—*an American hero*—who served this country bravely and saved a cougar—*an American cougar*—from a horrible fate. You're a take-charge, kickin'-ass-and-takin'-names kind of guy. Do the right thing, to hell with the consequences. The public loves guys like you."

The yellow jumpsuit I wore made it hard to share her enthusiasm. "I managed twenty-one years in the Army without talking to the media."

"This time, I'm asking you to *please* talk to the reporter. This is my idea. You want out of here or not?"

I shook my head. "What part of it aren't you getting? I'm not talking to a reporter."

It seems she'd lost her hearing.

"A reporter from the *San Diego Union-Tribune* is coming by this morning at eleven," she said, looking at me brightly. "That's an hour from now. I'll be here for the interview."

She hung up the receiver and knocked on the door. As she walked out with those thirty-seven pages of my life, she pretended she didn't hear me banging on the glass.

They left me in the interview room for that hour.

At ten past eleven, a kid in a green bow tie came in the door to the attorney side of the booth. Standing against the wall, he made a big show of smiling and waving—as if I wouldn't see him otherwise. Jenny walked in and sat in front of me.

"Don't be mad," she said.

"I told you I wasn't doing this."

The college kid leaned in, trying to hear. He wore a gray suit with a folded green handkerchief to match his bowtie. There were a few greased, combed brown hairs over his pale upper lip.

Give it up, kid. That mustache ain't happening. He looked barely old enough to drink.

Jenny spoke fast, not leaving time for me to repeat what I'd told her twice. Or to get a word in edgewise.

"Just be you Randy. I think he'll ask you a lot of questions about your military background and don't be modest tell him *why* you rescued that cougar remember Matilda's an American cougar and talk about all your medals and leave out that stuff about you not wearing some of them." She paused for an oxygen reload. "Got it?"

Jenny started to get up, then sat. "And, Randy? You can't make your case any worse, so tell him *everything*." She paused once more, looking at me meaningfully. "I asked if you wanted me as your lawyer. You said, yes. This is *my call* as the lawyer. You got that?"

Her big, Disney eyes were drilling into mine.

"Fine. Tell him I'll talk," I said.

She'd worn me down with her enthusiasm. Besides, what else did I have to lose?

Jenny smiled. She lay the receiver on the metal shelf, stood and said something to the kid in the bowtie. Then she leaned against the wall with her arms crossed.

It took him awhile to get the hang of talking to a prisoner. His mouth was moving in silence until Jenny handed him the telephone receiver.

"My name is Kyle Rowe. I'm with the *Union-Tribune*. It is a pleasure to meet you, Sergeant Andrews. Jenny's told me a lot about you, about what happened. I hope you feel you can be candid with me because frankly, sir, I think you are a hero."

He made a fist and put his knuckles on the glass between us.

They hung there.

Some gesture of brotherhood? I wasn't sure what the fuck was going on. His knuckles were clean and soft, a writer's hand. It got awkward after ten seconds, so I put mine against his. He nodded like we'd crossed a milestone.

"All right," he said, then pulled his hand off the glass and picked up a pen. Jenny winked.

"I can be *really fuckin' candid*, Mr. Rowe," I said loud enough for Jenny to hear through the receiver on Rowe's ear. She rolled her eyes.

"Kyle," he said.

"Kyle. Okay. What do you want to know?"

"Can I call you Randy?"

"Yeah."

"Randy, I've read what you wrote. I am here to introduce Sergeant John Randall Andrews III to the world. We can start with your military background. Like I said, you're a hero. Then we will work to what I've been calling the Rosarito Beach cougar heist. It was gutsy, Randy. *Gutsy* to say the least."

He chuckled. Kyle spoke with a flourish, a young guy full of himself. He was peddling what I knew was bullshit, but I enjoyed hearing it anyhow. He'd be a good officer. I was actually starting to like him.

He picked up a small recorder and held it in his hand along with the telephone receiver. "I'm going to record this, if you don't mind. Keeps me from having to make notes as we go along."

I told him almost everything. Twenty-one years, but only the good times. I told him of Somalia, Bosnia, Iraq and all the other places. Firdos Square. I didn't tell him the things I shared with Matilda, or that I shared with Matilda at all. I said I learned of the three pit bulls from an employee of the Nightclub Estrella. I'd forgotten his name.

Five times, Kyle changed those one-hour tapes. Twice, I had to be let out to take a piss. Jenny stood there for all of it.

Kyle had visited Matilda at the animal shelter.

"How's she doing?"

"Okay. She looks well fed. Didn't seem too happy about the cage she's in. They're still not sure where she's going."

"Anything's better than that nightclub."

"Randy. One last question. Why was it so important to get her out of that nightclub?"

I didn't answer right away.

"I'm done leaving people behind."

At four-thirty the next afternoon, a deputy set four copies of the morning edition of the *San Diego Union-Tribune* on the metal tables. Not a word about me.

In the tank, I was the only White guy. The rest were Latinos. Unlike the little creep who wanted to do nasty things to my lawyer, most did not speak English.

At seven, the metal door opened, clanking, and three tatted White dudes were walked in. They laughed, loud, like men in a hotel bar on vacation. Two of them were about my size, six feet. The big one, the guy in charge, was hairy and huge, six-five and probably three hundred pounds with a crazy, unblinking stare. He looked like a gorilla, only bigger. His eyes scanned the tank, like a man looking for an ass to kick.

I stood out. He rolled up his sleeves and I saw the winged death's head on his bicep. *Hells Angels.* It was only a matter of time.

All three kept their eyes on me as they went to their assigned cells. I stayed where I was. I didn't go to my cell. I didn't want any shit, but I'd take a beating before I ran.

Two hours later, I was still reading the *Union-Tribune* at one of the tables. I'd been tuning out the televisions but looked up when I heard Anderson Cooper.

Cooper said, "Good evening. Thank you for joining us."

What the fuck?

My face was on both screens over. *John Randall Andrews, Combat Veteran.* Then the caption: *"War Hero Charged with Cougar Smuggling."*

The cougar in the photo didn't have a scar. It wasn't Matilda.

"Breaking news from San Diego, California. John Randall Andrews, a highly decorated combat veteran, is in federal custody in San Diego. Andrews was arrested smuggling a caged mountain lion across the San Ysidro International Border Crossing in Tijuana, Mexico. He faces up to twenty-five years in a federal penitentiary..."

Cooper talked while photographs and video showed the border crossing, the strip of bars along Rosarito Beach, the Nightclub Estrella, then the San Diego Federal Correctional Facility.

"Andrews is accused of breaking into the Nightclub Estrella in Rosarito Beach, Mexico, to steal the animal. The mountain lion, named Matilda, was on display in the loud and crowded nightclub to draw business."

The hairy biker and I were the only two watching. Everybody else was talking. If the closed captioning hadn't been running across the bottom of the screen, I would have missed my fifteen minutes of fame.

The biker was staring a hole through me. Then he looked back to the television. Then back to me. He laughed a big *I don't give a fuck* laugh, then pointed at me.

"Hey look! Look! It's him. Andrews! The guy on the television. Fuckin' quiet!" Three Mexican guys at a table kept talking in Spanish, then burst into laughter. The biker walked to them. "Hey! Shut the fuck up!"

The tank went to as close to absolute silence as possible on this planet. This guy could run troops. He moved to a table near one of the televisions, leaned his knuckles on the metal and watched.

"Rosarito Beach lies twenty miles south of the California border. Its primary draws are miles of open beach and wall-to-wall nightclubs and beach bars, all competing for the business of a crowd of largely American college students. They come to take advantage of the drinking age of eighteen and the late-night partying. Kept within a cage in one of the spots frequented by partygoers, the Nightclub Estrella, was Matilda, a mountain lion. Matilda was on display for the entertainment of the patrons in the establishment.

"Ironically, the big cat was smuggled as a kitten from her birthplace in Arizona across the Mexican border to spend her life in a cage.

"Angel Ramirez, a college student at San Diego State University and a frequent patron of the nightclub, describes the big cat's living conditions."

Angel looked like a frat boy who'd just smoked a joint. He wore a blue cap with the letters *SDSU* in yellow.

"It was horrible man, just horrible," Ramirez said. "The music was super loud, and people drank and threw things at that poor animal. I cannot believe how that cat was treated. I'm glad somebody finally did something."

"Outside the federal courthouse in San Diego is Kyle Rowe with *San Diego Union-Tribune*. He is joined by Andrews's attorney, Jennifer Bayless."

Jenny spoke. "First Sergeant Andrews and I are not disputing the facts. What we are disputing is whether he committed a crime. Matilda was stolen from the United States, and the owner of the Nightclub Estrella is the very person who stole her. He, the nightclub owner, smuggled this *American* cougar into Mexico. An *American* war hero, who seven times was wounded fighting for our freedoms, rescued her, bringing her home. "What the US Attorney is doing is so very wrong," she added. "If a thief stole a car, would they prosecute the rightful owner for taking it back? That's what's happening here."

"Kyle," Anderson Cooper said, "you spoke with Sergeant Andrews. Did he tell you why he took the cougar?"

Kyle nodded. "I asked Sergeant Andrews that very question. I sensed this was important to him. He said, 'I'm done leaving Americans behind.'"

"Live from the Pentagon is Major General Garrett Cox, Andrews's former commander."

I'd known Cox since he was a captain. He commanded the 75th Ranger Regiment as a colonel. He looked every inch the warrior, with his sharp, lean features—an officer the Army loves putting before a news camera.

"I know Randy Andrews well. This man served thirteen combat tours, multiple tours in Iraq and Afghanistan. He'd already served six times in combat *before* 9-11. He was the best I served with—brave, professional, a very decent man. I assigned him as the platoon sergeant to my new lieutenants so they could learn. I never lost *one* of Randy's lieutenants."

"You know," and here Cox paused deliberately, "he has several Purple Hearts and *three* awards of the Silver Star. I don't know if your audience knows the significance of that. I will repeat: The Silver Star is one of the highest military honors. Three is unheard of."

I was momentarily grateful to the big, hairy biker for scaring everyone into silence, as I was trying to catch every word. It appeared Cox wasn't finished yet. "And you know what? Randy Andrews won't wear two of those Silver Stars and three of his Purple Hearts," the major general informed Cooper and his viewing audience. "Once, I asked him why. He didn't think he deserved the awards, didn't feel he had done enough to prevent his friends from being killed. I can tell you he did. I put him in for two of those Silver Stars."

Anderson's face was sympathetic. He was nodding. "What do you think is going on with this veteran, general?"

Cox paused, cleared his throat. I thought he was looking for the right words until I saw his eyes were wet.

"I don't think most Americans understand how much we ask of our service men and women. Twenty-one years, thirteen tours, wounded multiple times? That takes a toll on the best of us. I've been told by his friends his service killed his marriage."

That, and Sara fucking other guys.

"All I can say is, if Randy Andrews took a cougar from a bar in Rosarito Beach and brought it across the border into the US, he had a damn good reason for doing so."

Anderson shook his head. His lips were tight. "Ryan Clarkson, director of the American Mountain Lion Foundation, is with us from Sacramento."

Clarkson spoke like a man who believed his foundation was finally getting the attention it so richly deserved. He would not squander this opportunity.

"This Sergeant Andrews is a hero in my book," Clarkson said fervently. "The mountain lion, cougar, catamount, panther—this animal goes by many names—is a part of our American heritage. Yet they are being pushed to the brink of extinction, rapidly, due to hunting and habitat destruction.

"Mountain lions need a lot of territory to roam and hunt. Some states still place a bounty on these animals. A hunter can get paid for killing one, no questions asked." Clarkson looked straight into the lens. "Imagine an America without mountain lions.

"Big cats are exploited worldwide," he continued. "And this animal was kept in a cage to draw revelers into a nightclub. They were fighting this animal . . . *for sport*. This cougar was horribly abused simply to make money, and this happens all over Mexico. Their authorities do nothing, absolutely *nothing*, to stop it." Clarkson shook his head, genuine dismay and disappointment on his face. "I frankly do not understand why the US Attorney is prosecuting this man and not the bar owner who stole the animal from the US."

Anderson was back. "Matilda is currently housed in an animal shelter in San Diego." The video paused on a sign that said, *County of San Diego Animal Shelter*, then switched to Matilda. I saw her scar. She was in a large cage, hissing at the camera. Agitated, her tail was whipping.

"We reached out to Jorge Rangel, owner of the nightclub. He declined CNN's request for an interview. The United States Attorney for San Diego has also declined comment, stating this is a pending case. We will continue following the case of Sergeant Andrews. All I can say is "Good luck, sergeant.""

The segment ended with a close-up of Matilda screeching.

"Just ahead, I'll speak with Congressman—"

The big biker started clapping. He looked around the tank and the jumpsuit-clad audience clapped, even the three guys he'd told to "shut the fuck up." I'm not sure most knew why they were applauding.

The biker and the other two guys walked over. I stood, not wanting to be on my ass.

"Andrews, Ralph Barton. Bear. This is Frank. This is Lewis. Yeah, that's his fuckin' name." Frank was a scroungy, smaller version of Ralph. Lewis was clean-cut but, with his wall-to-wall tattoos, he looked like a college kid gone bad.

Ralph and I shook hands. "Thanks for your service, brother," he said.

"You a vet, Ralph?" I asked.

"Bear. I go by Bear. Fuckin' A, yeah. Desert Storm. First Marine Division. Ooo-rah. I got an honorable discharge. Believe it or not, the only fuckin' thing, according to my ex-wives—actually, only one of them—I done right. A Bronze Star and a Purple Heart, too."

"Where'd you get hit?" I asked. In answer, he opened his jumpsuit to show a nasty gunshot wound to his left shoulder. He sized me up.

"Stealing a cougar and bringing it across the border in broad daylight. I thought I was psycho," he laughed, "but you must be fuckin' crazier than I am, bro."

Right then, in this tank, crazy was good.

I relaxed. Ralph Barton was one of the good guys. He gave me a hug. I felt the thick padding of chest hair under the cloth of his jumpsuit.

"So, what the fuck were you thinking bringing a mountain lion across the border?" he asked. "I got busted with coke. That makes sense. I got to hear your shit."

Jenny told me to not talk with anyone, but that was before I discussed my case with the world.

"Grab a seat, Bear."

"Fuckin' A," he said.

Frank and Lewis moved off to their bunks after twenty minutes. They weren't vets.

Ralph got caught with six kilos of cocaine he was running to San Bernardino. He was offered two years but was holding out for a better deal.

We bullshitted for three hours, mostly about the fucked-up shit officers asked us—the enlisted—to do. I hadn't laughed like that in years.

"You're gonna be out of here soon," he said.

All I could say was, "Huh."

"After that shit I watched? You'll be fuckin' out of here. You watch what happens. You'll get a good offer. Trust me."

A few minutes before lights out at ten, I heard the clank of the metal door.

"Andrews." It was Coker, the deputy who told me my first lawyer was a dump truck.

"Yeah."

"Grab your shit. You're out of here."

I walked over. "I'm out of here?"

"Yeah. You're out of here. Bailed."

"*Bailed?*"

"Is there an echo in here, first sergeant?" He was laughing. "You're goddamn right. Some wildlife group posted your bail. Now, grab your shit."

Bear came over. "What'd I tell you?" He gave me another hug, then said if I was ever near San Bernardino, I was to swing by The Roadhouse on Fifth. "Just ask for Bear. I got the beers. We'll pick up where we left off."

Coker walked me to the front office. "Hey, Randy," he said as he passed me off to another deputy. "I watched that CNN broadcast. Nice. Good luck, brother."

The out-processing deputy had the no-nonsense demeanor of a man coming to the end of a long shift. He gave me a clear plastic bag with my clothing, wallet, keys and a receipt for the storage of my truck. A small print contract said I was paying forty dollars per day for the service.

He handed me a second bag. "These are from your lawyer."

The bag contained a sky-blue polo shirt, khaki pants, belt, socks, and loafers. Preppy, college-boy crap. A Post-it note on the shirt said, *Wear these. You'll look good!!! Jenny.*

The deputy watched my face. "Just put the shit on, Andrews. We don't take clothing just so somebody can look good walking outta here, but your lawyer was in here bugging the shit out of the associate warden. She said no way we were putting a war hero on the street dressed in a T-shirt and jeans."

Jenny met me in the lobby.

"Well, there he is. Would you look at that. Doesn't somebody look handsome?" She circled me, studying. "I did a good job with sizing. Randy, you look great."

"What the hell's going on?"

"You're out. The World Wildlife Federation posted your bail. They've even gotten you a room at the US Grant Hotel just down the street. You're a hero, did you know that? For a lot of reasons."

She was jumpy, her hands moving quickly.

"You need to brace yourself," she said, looking at me again. "The media's out front. They're not allowed in the lobby. I suggest you get ready."

I just about shit my pants when I looked out to the street. I could see eleven media vans, each with a huge antenna heading into the sky. ABC, NBC, Fox, CBS, CNN, Telemundo, and Univision. A few others I didn't recognize.

"Just answer the questions like you did for Kyle. Stress the horrible conditions Matilda was in. She was in a cage—a *cage*, not an enclosure. You saved her. They were fighting her. You didn't steal her. You—"

"Twenty-one years, I don't talk to the media," I told her. "What's this, payback? Why not *no comment*? Let's just walk by them."

"What?" she breathed incredulously. "You *got* to be kidding. No, no, no, Randy. *No.* You don't do that. You *can't* do that. Just suck it up, Ranger. They're going to ask you . . . you know the story. Tell it." She shook her head and stepped in front of me, reaching up to position her hands on my forearms as if to steel me. I might have laughed at the absurdity of the situation if it hadn't felt so good to really have someone in my corner. "Just be yourself," she told me, face flushed and Disney eyes earnest. "Let's get this over with. Everybody knows your story."

We went outside and stopped at the top of the stairs. Tactically, it was a great choice. We looked down on the media. The more I told myself to relax, the bigger my eyes felt in their sockets. I was a raccoon in a spotlight.

Jenny spoke. "Sergeant Andrews has been jailed unnecessarily. This has been a difficult ordeal for him. But he will answer a few questions."

I didn't see who asked what. The crowd was a blur.

"Why did you steal the cougar?"

"I saved her."

"How are you feeling now?"

"Good."

"Are you happy to be out?"

"Yes."

My face felt like a death mask. The questions were softballs. Jenny leaned up and whispered in my ear. "Loosen up Randy. Remember. Be yourself."

Then the reporter for Univision, a pint-sized Latino with thick glasses and an officious attitude that said he wasn't allowing his native land to be slandered, read from an index card. "Why didn't you notify the local authorities, the Rosarito Beach Police, rather than stealing the animal, Mr. Andrews? The police would have acted. And why did you break into the nightclub under cover of darkness if you were truly, as you say, saving her, Mr. Andrews? I am very curious if you would have taken the same action in America?"

"That's *bullshit*," I stated. "The Rosarito Police drank in that nightclub. They pulled security there. I saw them. *A lot* of times. Everybody in Rosarito Beach knew Matilda was in that club. And people knew the owner was fighting her for money. And you say I should have asked the police to take her out of there? No sir! No sir! And you ask, 'Would I do it here?'"

I had to think on that. I was surprised he didn't interrupt.

"You're goddammed right I would!" I said. "And that's *First* Sergeant Andrews, by the way."

People clapped. I didn't wait for questions anymore. I told the story. The Univision reporter tried to interrupt a few times, but I talked over him. I got the feeling his fellow reporters didn't like him. This crowd was on my side.

"Sergeant, thank you for your service. I think you're a hero, Sergeant Andrews. Do you?"

It was the lady from Fox. She was knockout-gorgeous, with a face that said she could tear anyone a new asshole.

"I don't know," I said. "I just did what I was ordered to do."

She asked another. "Did your taking of the cougar have anything to do with your service?"

"I wasn't leaving anyone else behind."

CHAPTER 28

I watched myself saying "bullshit" to that Univision reporter a dozen times. Most of the broadcasts bleeped out the obscenity. *The New York Post*, however, wasn't concerned with offending its readers. My photograph was on the front page under the caption, THAT'S BULLSHIT!

I was interviewed by the media eight times over the next week. A campaign began on GoFundMe to pay for a home for Matilda. Someone created the hashtags #FreeSergeantAndrews and #FreeMatilda.

We were trending on Twitter.

I became the face of PTSD. People wanted my opinion—a big turnaround for a guy who once was stuck staring at a box on the side of the freeway. Talking heads discussed PTSD and me. They disagreed on every possible thing, except one; the Veterans Administration wasn't doing enough to help our veterans.

I thought the slams on the VA were unfair. They tried to treat me, and I walked out.

The Grant Hotel was beautiful, elegant, and way above my pay grade. The World Wildlife Federation even gave me seventy-five dollars a day for meals.

The night I was released, I went to the hotel business center to check my email. Athena hadn't written. And nothing from my sons, though I hadn't expected anything from them. I sent short *How are you doing?* emails to John and Danny.

I typed out a message to Athena, then deleted it. Then typed out a second and deleted that, too. Over the course of the next hour, my email to her went from nothing to a sentence to two pages, then back to one sentence. Finally, I typed, *Where are you? Can we talk?* and hit send.

I waited around the computer for an hour, then went to bed.

I got my truck back. The storage company gave me a break on the fees. Ten bucks a day.

Looking at that piece of crap, it didn't seem worth paying the money. But my awards and photos were locked in the toolbox on the bed. I wanted most of the awards and all of the photos.

I walked an hour—no destination in mind—and found myself in the Gaslamp District. I saw a girl of about eight in a yellow dress. Her father was grabbing her hands and swinging her.

I once swung John that way.

The weather was so perfect. I thought of Lieutenant Pearce and that car bomb.

Nausea hit hard and fast. That little girl cut in half bothered me. I thought I'd vomit. Then I heard someone behind me say. "Hey, Sergeant Andrews. You're Sergeant Andrews, aren't you?"

It was a young couple with a boy and a girl. I think they were twins, toddlers. They had a golden Labrador retriever that looked like Zoey, a dog Sara and I once had. The father had the pale complexion I saw on White guys who'd been in jail for a while. He wore lavender shorts, tall white socks and sandals. "I can't believe what you did." The father put his hand out. "We were hoping to run into an actor out here. You're even better."

We shook. "Where you folks from?" I asked. "Nebraska," he said. I agreed to a picture. I kept staring at their two kids. "Jimmy, Tabitha, this is Sergeant Andrews. He's a real-live American hero," the dad said.

"Sorry," I said. "I can't do this." I walked off fast, leaving a puzzled dad still readying his kids for the photo. I bought a Pepsi to settle my stomach and walked back to the hotel.

Every day, two or three people would recognize me. They all wanted pictures with the war hero. Sometimes they wanted my autograph, too.

I tried to be polite.

An old guy stumbled over as I was walking through the lobby of the hotel. I'd seen him. He was a fixture in the bar. "Hey. You're Andrews. Hey, you're fuckin' Andrews," he said, slurring. "You're a fuckin' hero. You know that? You're a fuckin' hero, bro. Not for taking that cougar. That was stupid, Andrews. Risk it all for an animal. Risk it all? What were you thinking? You should have left that fuckin' cat in there. No . . . no . . . no. For killing all those fuckin' Arabs. Over two hundred and fifty kills. Wow. That's what I saw on the news. You're a hero. We ought to fuckin' level that fuckin' place over there."

I hadn't known my confirmed kills had been put out there. I'd quit watching the news. Two sixty-one was the number.

He had his hand out to shake. I walked off. I wouldn't touch that prick.

Sometimes the nightmares came. They were bad, but they didn't have the punch they once did. I could make most of them go away. Sometimes I couldn't and I would feel the walls of my room closing in. I would pace in the lobby, always at strange hours. The desk clerk eyed me, wary. I said I was worried about my case.

And I was. People may have thought I was a hero, but I was a hero facing years in prison.

Every day I called my sons. I learned John had me blocked. Sometimes Danny would answer. We'd talk, but it was always short answers from a boy in a hurry to get off the phone.

I never knew what to say. Hell, I didn't even know him.

Every day I sent them emails. John never answered. Danny sometimes did. He said he was happy I took Matilda from the place that was keeping her.

And I sent another email to Athena. I told her what was happening on my case. Then finished with, *Things will settle down here. Do you have a phone number? Where are you? Please contact me. I love you and miss you. Randy.*

She didn't answer. My plan was to keep emailing her. Eventually she would have to respond.

Wouldn't she?

I called my mother a few times a week. And my sister every other week. Becky had two children. Both were doing well.

I had given Athena my mother's address.

"Who is this Athena lady, Randy?" my mom asked. "She must be special. I'm sorry. I haven't received any letters from her."

The last few years had been tough on my mom. My boys hadn't spoken to her since the divorce. She wanted to visit and attend court, but I asked her not to. She didn't need to see her son facing serious prison time.

I was walking to the beach, something I did seven or eight times a day. Beach balls didn't bother me anymore.

Jenny called, as she did every day. Today she asked, "You want to see something amazing? Come over to the office."

I made a U-turn and headed toward Federal Defenders.

Jenny met me in the conference room. On the table were three file boxes marked *Andrews*. They were filled with letters addressed to me, *Care of Attorney Jenny Bayless*. Thousands of letters — they came from all over the world, but mostly from Americans. I read most of them while Jenny was in court.

Six women, five Americans and one Brit, wanted to marry me. One of them, a nurse in her mid-thirties from Butte, Montana, was damn good-looking. Her husband, a Navy corpsman, had been killed in Afghanistan seven years before.

"You were raised in Idaho. That's near to Butte. I think we might have much in common," she wrote. She seemed like a normal person, a good woman.

But I was in love with someone else.

The day before my court appearance, Jenny called.

She was talking before I had the phone to my ear.

"Come by my office. The US Attorney is offering to settle your case. I think you *will* like this."

"What is it, what's the offer?"

"No, no, no. Let's wait until we talk. You get over here," Jenny insisted. "Walk down here. I'll see you in a—"

"Come on, what is it? It's good. You're talking fast. That means you're happy, which means it must be good. What is it?"

"I'd rather we go over it in person."

I heard filing cabinets opening and closing. She was breathing like she'd just finished a workout.

"Okay," she said. "You plead guilty to a new charge—failure to declare an item. A misdemeanor—no time, no probation. There'd be a two-hundred-fifty-dollar fine deemed time served by the nineteen days you served in jail.

"Your case is over Randy."

I never expected to walk out of this with nothing.

"I thought you said I wasn't pleading guilty. I saw you say that on TV. Like, I just stole my property back from a thief. Remember?"

I was fuckin' with her. There was an extended sigh on her side of the line.

"I did say that. Randy, Randy, Randy . . . just *get to my office* so we can talk."

I heard a harrumph, then she hung up.

Jenny was standing in the waiting room. Radiant and smiling, her cheeks were puffed like a chipmunk's. I had a bag with me, a gift for her I bought on the walk over.

"Hi. Follow me." She walked fast. We didn't turn at the door to the conference room. She looked back. "Keep going. Sorry if I was short on the phone."

She walked into a small office, then sat behind a desk. It was a clear fall day. I saw the gray ships of San Diego Naval Base four miles to the south. The air stayed clear until the border, then it got hazy. I almost smelled Tijuana.

"Nice view. This yours?"

"It is. This is my office."

"Pretty nice, lady." I knocked on the wooden desk. "You got the job?"

She smiled, her pride evident. "You are looking at a deputy federal public defender."

"Wow. I'm happy . . . I'm really happy. Can I give you a hug?"

I stood and put my arms around her. "Congratulations," I said. "There's a lot of good news today."

A photo of Jenny and her boyfriend in his Marine Corps dress uniform was on one side of the desk. A second lieutenant, he was a good-looking kid with no hair on the sides of his head. He had that clear white skin and the optimistic, slightly cocky smile of someone his age. Jenny stood pressed into him in a turquoise strapless dress, showing a lot of skin and a tight figure. Her smile was huge, a loving smile. She fit with that Marine.

I was thinking she looked good when she broke in on my thoughts.

"Randy, my advice to you is to take the offer. Yes, I did say you were innocent. I was talking to the media. Go ahead, ask your questions. Do you want me to tell you all the hundreds of reasons you'd be an absolute fool to turn down this offer?"

I grinned at her.

"I was just fucking with you. I'm not an absolute fool. I want this done. I'm taking it."

Tomorrow in court would be our last time together. I would miss her. She was such a cool person. She saw things as they ought to be and tried to make them that way. I went overseas trying to do that. It was a privilege of youth.

Except she might actually pull it off. She would be defending people, not killing them. She saved my ass.

I was looking at a photograph on her credenza. "Where's that?"

Jenny's hiking outfit was cute and coordinated, the type worn by women who don't like to hike but want to look good doing it. Behind her was a beautiful lake with a city along one shore. There were high peaks in the distance.

The lake was shaped like an arrowhead.

"That's Coeur d'Alene," I said.

"John took that. We were on a driving trip through the Rockies, up into Canada."

"You're on Caribou Ridge."

"How'd you know?"

"My dad and I hunted up there. I loved to look down on Lake Coeur d'Alene. Our last hunting trip was up on that ridge. He died three days later."

I wished I hadn't said that.

"I'm sorry."

"You don't need to say you're sorry. It was a long time ago. I hadn't thought of it for a long time."

His dying still hurt, but I acted like it didn't. I changed the subject.

Jenny had written notes on the pad in front of her. "Why take the offer," the heading read.

"I see your notes. Hey, this wasn't Ron Maxwell's office, was it?"

"It was. You're sitting in his chair," she said.

I thought I smelled cigarette smoke.

"I'm just fuckin' with you, Randy." She laughed.

"That is funny. Hey, I have something for you. A gift for all your help."

I put the cougar statue on her desk. The cat was sitting on its haunches, like Matilda did. It was as tall as her desk lamp.

"It's a thank you gift. You need some stuff for your new office. And—"

Jenny's eyes were red and wet. She was turning the statue on her desk. "I *love* —"

"Let me finish. Just give me a moment," I said. "I want to say this right. You made me feel like what I did was important. I didn't feel like that a month ago."

She came around her desk, bouncing her head up and down as she walked, tears on her cheeks. I stood.

"I will treasure my cougar, First Sergeant Andrews. Well," she sniffed, trying to regain composure. "Randy, let's continue." She laughed, enjoying this as much as me.

"This is *my* gift to you." She slid the guilty plea across the desk. I signed it.

"Thanks for letting me be your lawyer. And, can I add one thing? Some advice? I want you to hear the end of my closing argument."

"What?"

"I did not like you when I first met you. But now? I like you very much. And you know what? It took *balls* to drive that cougar over the border. You *are* a hero. So, listen to me. Move on with your life. Get your sons back in your life. Aren't they the most important thing right now?"

CHAPTER 29

It was eight-thirty in the morning.

"United States versus John Randall Andrews." This was a different judge than that first asshole. He was around my age but looked more like a college kid turned forty-five.

I was found guilty of failing to declare an item at an international border. The prosecutor dismissed the smuggling charges and recommended the fine. The judge sentenced me to pay the fine, then ruled I had served it off in jail.

Everything seemed scripted, except the judge's last words to me.

"Mr. Andrews, I read the report of the probation department as well as the materials Ms. Bayless submitted," he said, his eyes meeting mine. "I reviewed your record of military service to this country. Three awards of the Silver Star for bravery under fire. Seven times wounded in battle.

"I was impressed, to say the least. Thank you for your service. I wish you luck, and . . . I hope things go well for you in the future, Sergeant."

My case was over.

Though it was broad daylight and well into the beginning of the workday, the crowd of reporters waiting outside was a third of what it had been when my bail had been posted.

The Fox News reporter asked the easiest questions. "What are your plans, Mr. Andrews?"

I mumbled something about taking time off and getting on with my life. But, other than reconnecting with my sons and sending emails to Athena, I had no plans.

"Would you do it again? another asked.

"I plead the Fifth," I said, and the crowd laughed.

Walking back to my hotel, though, I knew the answer.

Fuck 'em. I would steal her again.

I went to the hotel and emailed Athena.

I wish I hadn't watched the news that night.

I was lying on my bed with a beer. Life was starting to make sense. Then I saw Sara's lawyer on the television. KESD was a local television station in Orange County. I was their top story. My photo, taken on the steps of the courthouse, was under the caption, *War Hero Assaults Local Woman*. The photo caught me in a scowl.

Grant Byers's lead off with "Sergeant John Randall Andrews's current legal dilemma for stealing a cougar did not come as a surprise for family law attorney Madeline Gore of Fullerton, California. Gore represented Sara Andrews, former wife of John Randall Andrews. The couple divorced in early April of this year."

Byers looked like a lean, gray-haired Cary Grant. He didn't have the actor Grant's sense of humor, though. He had the gaze of a hawk looking for something to kill.

"Gore describes a night in January 2014 when Andrews, enraged because Ms. Andrews was dating another man, bust into her home in a jealous rage to attack her."

Gore was a big woman all the way around, late thirties with a nightmarish, thrift-shop wardrobe and stringy hair. Twice she ran her fingers through her hair as she spoke. "Andrews shoved his way in through the front door of the home his now ex-wife, Sara Andrews, shared with the couple's two boys. A family friend was visiting. When her visitor wisely retreated to the backyard, he turned his rage on Sara. He shoved her head into the wall hard enough to leave a dent."

Byers's voice narrated as the camera showed closeups of my divorce judgment. "The court denied Andrews any visitation with his sons, fearing for their safety."

Gore was back. She shook her head. "The assault was just another in a long line of mistreatments suffered by Sara. The Orange County judge, thank God, saw through Andrews's *hero* façade."

"Thank you, Ms. Gore," Byers said.

"We contacted Sara Andrews at her home in Fullerton."

The door opened. Sara stood wide-eyed. It looked as if there was a bright light shining on her face. Byers shoved a mic into the doorway.

"Ms. Andrews," he said. "We have some questions about your ex-husband. We realize they may be painful. About the assaults documented in court papers."

"Assaults?" she asked. "There was the one."

"So, your ex-husband John Andrews *did* harm you. I know this is hard for you. Was Randy's abuse the reason for the divorce?"

"No," she said. "I don't want to talk to you."

"We just want to make sure the public knows about Mr. Andrews," Byers insisted. "You know he's being depicted as a hero."

"Talk to the *Army* about him," Sara said. "Overseas, he was." She slammed the door.

Byers looked at the camera and nodded as if the sound of the slamming door told the viewing public everything it needed to know.

He then introduced two talking heads. Dr. Helen Mellor was a gynecologist/woman's advocate at UCLA Medical Center. Dr. Helen Gorsuch was a clinical therapist specializing in the "healing of abused women."

"Sara Andrews has the classic symptoms of a woman who has undergone long term physical and emotional abuse," Mellor said. "PTSD is no excuse for this barbaric behavior. Abusers abuse. It's generally caused by their upbringing. As boys, they see their fathers assault their mothers. They learn violence is an appropriate response to being challenged by a woman."

Byers asked, "But you heard Sara say this was a one-time occurrence?"

Gorsuch answered. "I agree with Helen. Her denial is actually the strongest evidence that the prior abuse happened. Victims will protect their abusers, even after a divorce."

I tuned them out, hearing only occasional words. "Power dynamics ... cycle of violence ... tension ... control."

"Dr. Mellor. Dr. Gorsuch," Byers interjected. "Do you have recommendations for Sara for healing?"

I shut the television off and went down to the bar. The drunk was in his regular barstool. I sat in a booth at the other end.

What if my sons saw that? After five Jack and Cokes, I hadn't calmed down. Somehow, it seemed a good time to email Athena.

Athena:

Let me start by saying what a shitty thing you did to me. You split at the border. Now you ignore everything I send to you. Did you need a ride? Was that it? Or money? I believe now that you were only fucking with me down in Rosarito, that you never really liked me.

You used me.

Randy.

Even as I hit *send*, I knew what I wrote wasn't true. I ordered another drink.

Sara actually surprised me. I would have expected her to invite Grant Byers in, offer him a cold beer, then tell all.

"You're stark-raving madly in love with me, aren't you?" Sara touched my shoulder. "Tell me how much you love me, Randy? I love *you.*" It was October 1995.

I was sitting in a half chair, watching the waves off Panama City Beach in Florida. Zoey, our golden retriever, was a few feet away kicking up sand. Sara found her three years before hanging around the military housing area, filthy and starving. Zoey was her constant companion when I was deployed.

Some of the sand hit me in the face. "I like you more than that fuckin' dog, I'll tell you that." She made an exaggerated sad face.

God, she was so fucking cute.

"Come on, Randy, say it."

"I love you more than the earth and the sky, Sara."

I'd been home from Bosnia for three months. We'd left for the beach right after the awards ceremony. I'd received a Bronze Star for valor. "You looked so handsome in your dress uniform," Sara said. "I'm so proud of you."

She was happy. My enlistment was over in four months, and I'd promised her I wouldn't re-up.

"Coors or Bud?" I asked, opening the ice chest.

"Just a Coke," she said.

"A Coke? You're kidding?"

Panama City Beach was our fun spot. It was 191 miles from Fort Benning. We came down every six months. We'd get drunk watching the waves, then go back to our cabin and make love. Then back to the beach. Then back to the cabin.

There was a town somewhere around here, but we never saw it.

"You're not drinking beer?" I was disappointed. Who gets ripped alone?

"I can't," she said.

"Yeah, you can." I cracked a Coors and handed it to her. She left my arm hanging in the air. "Okay, I'll drink it," I said.

"The doctor said I shouldn't drink."

"What's wrong?" I got worried. "You're sick?"

Sara's face was flushed. Her eyes got wet. "No. No, Randy."

"What's wrong?" I touched her leg.

"Nothing's wrong. I'm just pregnant, that's all. We're having a baby."

"What?" I didn't know what to say, just looked at her with my mouth open. "If we, like, do it, will that—"

Her face drooped and she started crying. Then I knew.

"Yes, Sara Christine, I'm stark-raving madly in love with you," and I hugged her.

My cell phone rang. It was Jenny. I was staring at an empty glass.

"I'm so sorry, Randy. I saw the broadcast. All those things they said. I know it's not true. That's not you."

"I got out of jail because of the media. I guess you take the good with the bad."

"I still believe you're a hero, Randy."

"So does my ex-wife," I said. "I don't know *what* that means."

The next morning, I sent an email to Athena.

Sorry, it said. *I love you and was mad because you're not answering. Things are weird here. Are you getting these?*

Later that day on the boardwalk along the beach, two short, mousy women were staring at me. They both were around my age.

"Are you proud of what you did?" one asked. "Beating that woman? You're a predator. You beat women."

They began to walk next to me. "Now the big war hero just wants to walk away." I turned to cross the street.

I was beginning to understand the media. If I said anything, I'd be watching these two on the news tonight. One of the women kept trying to get in my way, so I walked faster.

She erupted. "Look at me when I'm talking to you. You think assault doesn't matter?"

They followed me for two blocks. "Coward!" one yelled as I walked into the hotel lobby.

In the morning, I checked out of the US Grant and into something cheaper. With my case over, the World Wildlife Foundation wasn't paying for my room.

With my fifteen minutes spinning out, the media went in search of another hero to rip to shreds.

CHAPTER 30

Two days later, I visited my mother for the first time in almost a year.

Elizabeth Andrews lived in a senior community in Temecula, seventy-five miles north of San Diego. You had to be fifty-five to live there, but at sixty-nine she was a youngster in this place.

She still had the black hair and fair skin my dad loved. But she seemed so settled, like she spent most of her time in the chair she now occupied across from me.

"Have you talked to John and Danny?" was her first question. I was still adjusting my butt on her couch. She always went straight to the point.

"They won't talk to me," I said. "Danny will, a little. But nothing from John, not for six months."

"You two were so close. Once."

Sometimes I thought John was lost to me, that maybe I should focus on keeping some connection to Danny. Cut my losses. But this wasn't a military operation. There were no tactics. I couldn't cut my losses.

Somehow, their rejection of me turned into a dismissal of my entire half of the family. John and Danny had been close to my mom. She'd filled in during the frequent absences of their father. I imagine she missed them, since they quit talking to her when Sara filed for divorce.

My mother made tea, Earl Grey laced with cinnamon. It smelled like our home in Idaho. My cup had a ton of sugar.

We talked about all the television and newspaper articles and what it was like being on the news. And Matilda.

"What does she eat?" Mom asked.

"She ate junk down there. Now, I don't know what they're feeding her. Chicken, maybe? I got her into the crate with that."

Her home was so quiet and boring, an old person's home. The ringing in my right ear was loud in the silence.

"Elizabeth and Cory are doing well. Liz was by last week. Cory is now a senior." They were my sister Becky's kids, both students at a high school ten miles away. "You need to get over there and visit them, Randy. Becky would like to see you.

"And John?" she added. "He must be in college."

"I think he's going to Arizona State," I said. "Danny let that slip."

My mom hadn't remarried. I don't think she'd dated. I never asked her why.

"You know, Randy, your boys love you. You know that, don't you? Johnny used to dress like you as a little kid. Remember that uniform you bought him? He wore it all the time around you. When you were away, he wouldn't take it off."

"Yeah. And? What's your point?" My tone was disrespectful. "Sorry, Mom. Not my favorite topic of conversation."

"I know. They need you, Randy."

We had plowed this ground on the phone.

"I write them. I call them," I said. "I don't even know where John's living."

"You're still their father." She studied me. "You don't sound like that guy I listened to on the news, that one with all the medals and Silver Stars and Purple Hearts, the guy who told off that Mexican reporter."

"His question *was* bullshit."

She raised her eyebrows.

"Right, you said that word on national television. I gave up trying to teach you not to cuss when you joined the Army." She shook her head resignedly. "Are you the same man who brought a cougar home to the US, Randy? Do you know what? I was so happy you did. It's horrible to treat an animal that way.

"Your dad was like that. Always stepping up to the plate to do the tough things that needed done. He would have saved that cougar. I don't know if he would have smuggled it, though."

Her eyes were wet. "And you know what? I was proud seeing you on the news. Why are you giving up on your boys?"

"Did you see the local news two nights ago?"

"No," she said. "Are you going to answer my question?"

Through a ripple in time, I could see her young; her hair raven black, long and wavy, her eyes a blue found only in gemstones. They were still as radiant as in her youth.

"Here we go," I said.

"Yes. *Here we go.* Why are you giving up on your boys?"

I was ten again. She sounded like my dad.

"Randy?"

"Sorry, Mom." For a moment, it seemed like we were in our old family room in Bonners Ferry. "I'm not."

"Good. Enough on that. You'll do the right thing. You always do."

Abruptly, as mothers do, she changed direction. "So, who's this woman? You must like her."

"Athena. I do. She works at one of the resorts in Rosarito." I gave an abbreviated version of our relationship. My mother would have told me if a letter arrived.

She nodded. She knew I was leaving out most of the story.

Mom made an exaggerated show of remembering something, putting her open palm to her face. "Oh, Randy. I forgot something."

"No you didn't. You've always been a bad actress."

"I have something for you. I'm not sure why I didn't give it to you years ago. Just never seemed the right time. Come. Follow me. Take a look."

She walked me out to the garage.

Fire engine-red paint gleamed under fluorescent lighting. "This has been at Becky's house for fifteen years. Beautiful, isn't she?"

She was. It was my dad's Ford F-1, built in 1950, the best truck ever made. I thought it was gone, long sold. I moved my fingers across the hood, felt the metal, smooth and waxed, warm in the hot garage. I'd been so out of touch.

New whitewall tires. Dad never liked whitewalls on his F-1, but they looked good.

Twenty-five years had passed since I'd sat in this truck. The leather of the seat was cracked. Two rifles hung in the gun rack in the rear window, my father's Henry .45-70 and my old Henry Golden Boy lever action .22. I took the .22 down and sighted on an imaginary turkey far beyond the garage.

"Randy. It's yours. The truck. The guns. They're yours."

It didn't register. I started to ask if I could borrow it for a drive.

"Did you hear me?" my mom said.

Then I did. I couldn't say anything. I just smiled and tried to take it all in.

Mom looked back from the door to the house. "Think about what I said. Now I'll leave you out here to look over your new truck. Maybe we can get a picture of you in the driver's seat before you leave."

She walked back and kissed my forehead. "Things'll get better, Randy. I know."

I sat in the front seat, put my hands where my dad's had been and looked at the indentation in the leather on the passenger side. The rifles were wrong. The .45-70 was on the top rack. I switched them. The window our dog slobbered on had long since been cleaned.

The glove box was still crammed with cassettes and truck registrations. I placed the cassettes on the seat.

Patti Smyth and Scandal. Then I found the one I was looking for. Laura Branigan. On the cover, she was wearing that red silk blouse and those black leather pants. Her hair was long and perfectly messy.

I always thought her hair was black. It actually was dark brown.

June 3, 1989. High school had just let out on the last day of my junior year. I ran the half-mile home from the bus stop because walking couldn't get me home fast enough. That evening my dad and I were leaving for four nights of camping and hunting.

I turned the bend and saw the two sheriffs' cars with flashing red and yellow lights in front of our home. A Fish and Wildlife Service truck was parked next to them, but it wasn't my dad's.

Everyone was in the living room. Four sheriff's deputies were standing along one wall, their arms crossed. Their faces said something bad had happened. My mother was on the loveseat. Her face was red and tear streaked. Becky was sitting against her making a weird sobbing sound like she was having trouble breathing. My mom was rubbing her neck and shoulders.

"Come here, Randy, sit next to me." My mother moved and pulled Becky to her, clearing space on the loveseat. I wouldn't sit there. I sat alone on the couch. I looked at the four cops and they looked away. I felt nauseous.

"What is it?"

My mom started to answer, then began to cry. Her face answered, though. I was afraid to speak. Time went so slow. I sat there looking at those cops. They wouldn't look back.

Chad Garrison walked over. He was a Fish and Wildlife deputy and my dad's best friend. He'd been to the house a lot. I remember his curly red hair. He lowered himself like the couch was a bed of nails.

"Randy, there's been an—"

He rubbed his eyes. "Your father was shot . . . hunter thought he was a deer."

Nothing registered. I only knew my dad was hurt. He would walk in with a bandage on his arm. Garrison closed his mouth tight. His lips quivered. He opened his mouth but didn't talk. I didn't want to hear what he couldn't say.

"My dad. But he's, but he's—"

Garrison put his arm around me.

"Your father's dead, Randy."

I do not exaggerate when I say my first sixteen years were perfect. Perfection ended that day.

A hunter shot my father as he stood by his Forest Service truck. The 30-06 round went through the center of his chest, killing him instantly. "He didn't suffer, Randy."

Garrison, I think, thought my father's instant death comforting. I didn't. I wished he'd lived long enough for me to talk to him. There were things I would have said.

That was the only time I cried for my father.

Three months later, the day before we left for Southern California, I saw the man who killed him. Leonard Graham's skin color was pale, a man who spent his life indoors. He was a big CPA in Denver, and he had a lot of money to hire an expensive lawyer who flew in with him. Graham had a wide face and a bald spot he tried to hide with a combover.

He entered a guilty plea to involuntary manslaughter, a misdemeanor. It was a plea bargain. Today, he would be sentenced.

Becky stayed home with my mom's parents. They had flown in from Orange County.

Driving to the courthouse, my mom said she wanted Graham to come to us before court and say, "I'm sorry." He never did.

"The Lord says we should forgive, Randy. An apology would have made it easier." She wanted to forgive the man. "It was an accident, a bad accident." She was crying.

Graham's family was in court, and they were crying, too. He would have to go to jail.

I wasn't crying.

My mother and I were in the first row of the audience seats.

I heard him speak. Graham, through tears, vowed to never hunt again, to never pick up a firearm so long as he lived. He was "so sorry, so sorry," he said to the judge. He wished he could trade his life for my father's, that good man with such a fine family. He never looked at us.

How could you think my dad was a deer?

I never got an answer. He was just sorry, over and over. My mom was nodding, her eyes glistening. She had on the print dress she wore on Easter Sunday.

Then the judge began to sentence Graham to what he'd bargained for—sixty days in jail.

"My client is a working man, Your Honor," his lawyer said. "He has a wife and two children. He respectfully requests to serve the time on home detention. He would be confined to his home except when he is at work. This would allow him to provide for his family."

Who was providing for us? We were leaving Idaho the next day to move in with my grandparents.

"Your client is from Colorado, counsel. How are we going to ensure he'll actually do the time?"

"As an officer of the court, I will provide the proof, Your Honor."

The judge shook his head. I looked from the judge to the lawyer to the man who killed my dad.

"No, the court—"

Graham started wailing.

"I can't do time in jail."

As the bailiff put handcuffs on him, he sobbed. "My family, my family. Please, Your Honor. Please."

He cried like a baby as he was being led out. He caught my eye. "Please," he said. "Please."

In my dreams I scream, call him the coward he is. In others, I kill him and it feels good.

But I did nothing that day. I just looked at him.

That piece of shit served a lousy thirty days for killing my dad.

The next day we drove to Southern California to live with my mom's parents.

I have never been back to Bonners Ferry. My dad is buried there.

I remembered something else about that first turkey hunt.

My father came out of the general store in Good Grief with those Cokes and beef sticks. And he had a bag. He handed it to me.

Inside were graham crackers, Hershey bars and marshmallows. "I thought some s'mores would be nice tonight," he told me. "Your grandparents will be here."

Dad always knew the right thing. So many times, I've wished I could sit with him again in that F-1 and ask how to fix what went wrong with my boys.

But that day, the day I shot my first hen in the woods, I didn't say anything. I just held onto that bag and smiled.

Sitting in his truck, I thought of those doctors on KESD who told the world my dad taught me to abuse women. But they were wrong. He would never have done that. I had dishonored his name.

Some fuckin' war hero.

CHAPTER 31

I had no job and no place to live.
But I had my dad's truck and my first email from Athena.

> *Randy:*
> *I am so happy you have been released from jail and your case is over. I was so worried. I watched all of the news coverage. I watched the night when you were released from jail. And I watched the news on the day your case was over.*
> *Tell me how Matilda is.*
> *I know you don't understand why I did what I did.*
> *I was planning on going with you. And trust me, I want what you want. But I know you as well as anyone, I think. Until you have your sons in your life, you won't be ready for us. And until you are ready for us, I can't be ready for you. You know what is most important. Please, please. You deserve those two in your life again.*
> *Remember the things I told you in my apartment and your room at the motel? I have never told anyone those things. Know I love you. And please think about what I am saying before you send a response. Sleep on it, maybe?*
> *Athena*
> *Plus! I want to send you the money you gave me. You shouldn't have done that. Give me an address.*

In the seventeen emails I sent to her, I hadn't mentioned my legal troubles.

Of course, I didn't take her advice. I fired off a response.

Athena:
You didn't answer my questions. Where are you? Did you ever stop to think I wouldn't have kept going if I knew you would run off at the border? You left me in that line, looking like an idiot, holding the bag.
Randy

Her response came in less than a minute.

Randy:
You're right. You wouldn't have kept going. You and Mattie needed to keep going. No, I didn't leave you holding any bag, whatever that means. And no, I am not telling you where I am or my phone number. You know why? Because you will come. You will leave right now to come here. You do nothing halfway. And part of me wants you to. But this time you need to listen to what I am saying.
Athena

Fuck.

I spent the next half hour typing responses, then erasing them. Finally, I sent *I'm not taking the money back*, and went to bed.

Matilda was leaving for her new home at Big Cat Rescue in Northern Arizona. The $367,480 raised on gofundme.com — "to find Matilda a good home" —would go with her.

She didn't need the money. Ferd Garrett, director of Big Cat Rescue, accepted her before he knew she was rich. But it would find a good home for a lot of other big cats.

I wanted to see her.

Ferd's Rescue was north of Williams, Arizona. I'd spoken with him to set up a time to say goodbye.

On the phone he had the deep gravelly voice of an old smoker. We hadn't met in person, but he'd served three tours as an Airborne Ranger, boots on the ground, in Vietnam. We talked easily. Ferd took in the animals nobody wanted. His one hundred-acre property housed one hundred and seventeen large cats, most of them old zoo or circus animals. His passion started while working at the Phoenix Zoo in the '80s. He didn't like what happened to these animals when they were no longer young and pretty.

Matilda would be the only cat who came from a nightclub.

"Come down to the shelter this morning, Randy. Ten o'clock."

Ferd cleared his throat. "Randy, I don't know how the hell you got that animal into that dog crate. They can't move her without a stun rod. That cat is traumatized. Bad. She won't eat. She attacks the fence when we come close."

I waited.

"Randy, there are some animals that are so damaged that—" I heard breathing. "Randy, that mountain lion—"

She let me see her pain.

"I'll be there in twenty minutes."

It was Monday. The shelter was closed. Waiting out front was an animal control officer with an expression that said he didn't like working on his day off. "You Andrews?" He opened the door to the front lobby to let me in, then shuffled off to the vending machines along a far wall.

Ferd Garrett looked like a man who'd made a habit of plunging headlong into life's battles. His face was rough, with deep folds surrounded by mostly gray hair. The sun damage to his skin said he'd spent his life outdoors. He wore a cowboy hat with a snakeskin band and worn boots. He was a real cowboy, not somebody who dresses up that way on Saturday night.

"Randy. Good to meet you, brother. Ferd Garrett." I felt years of hard work as we shook hands. I didn't like the uptight look on his face. We walked through the next room.

Hundreds of dogs in small runs were barking frantically. It was energized in here—deafening, noise without rhythm. It smelled of shit and piss. Most of these dogs would be killed. Panic was moving through the building.

I heard Matilda's screams before Ferd opened the far door labeled *Large Animals.* The dogs heard her, too. They barked faster and louder to drown her out.

Inside, there was a cage about the size of the one at the Nightclub Estrella. Outside its sturdy fencing was a three-foot walkway along a wall. The racket in here was muffled but still loud. Matilda crouched near a four-foot door in the back corner open to a chain-link tunnel leading to a loading dock. Pressed against the dock was a cargo van, its back doors open. The van had a built-in cage.

"We need to get her out that door and into that van. The van's ready to go. We've tried everything. We can't move her. Sheila there almost lost a finger."

Sheila was about seventy, a skinny lady who obviously hadn't heard Woodstock had ended. Her hair was stringy and gray, stretching to her waist. Her earrings and necklace were peace symbols. She was close to tears and holding a buzzing cattle prod. Next to her at the fence was Kelsey, a college girl with attitude. She also held a cattle prod. Their khaki shirts read *Big Cat Rescue.* Both were looking wide-eyed at Matilda while their prods buzzed.

I wanted to nail each of them in the ass with ten thousand volts.

Matilda hissed, then launched, slamming into the chain links. The women fell back, their backs hitting the brick wall behind. Sheila's prod made an electrical clang when it hit the concrete floor.

"You see? See what I'm talking about?" Ferd's voice was higher and less gravelly.

Sheila picked up her prod. "Did you hit her with that?" I asked.

She looked away. "What the fuck?"

The air was musky with Matilda's scent glands, smells foreign to humans who spent no time in the wild. I looked in Matilda's eyes. She was terrified and still growling, but I could tell she knew it was me. Ignoring the racket, I looked at her. The muscles in her face relaxed. It was slight. Only I could see it.

All things on God's earth have a rhythm.

Ferd and his Big Cat Rescue women didn't know shit about these animals.

"I thought you guys were the fuckin' experts!" I said, shaking my head. "Don't you understand what is going on with this cat? You can't feel her fear? She feels *yours*. That's all she feels."

The entrance door to her cage had a heavy bolt. It wasn't locked.

I took a few deep breaths.

"I might be able to get her into the van. Can we try something? Be quiet. Don't look at her eyes. Everyone relax, try to hear her breathing. And turn off those damn prods."

Kelsey kept whispering. I glared, a look honed in the Army, and she shut up. It took seven minutes for Matilda's growls and snarls to fade, another three for them to end. The dogs had quieted to a rumble. Another few minutes and I began to hear Matilda breathe. Then her muscle tension eased. Her tendons were no longer obvious.

Am I really going to do this? I closed my eyes and kept them shut for two minutes. When I opened them, Matilda was lying in the middle of the enclosure, curled and facing me. I knew she'd be there. Her back left leg was extended, her paw pointed at me.

Her body language said, *It's time.*

Ferd and the women were silent.

I undid the bolt, opened the door and walked in. The door made a soft clank as I eased it shut behind me. I moved at quarter-speed into the enclosure. I glanced back. Ferd and the women stared with mouths agape, then shut them without saying words, as if talking would get me killed. Someone sucked in air. I watched Matilda's body language. Her tail was motionless, lying flat on the floor. Her eyes were interested, soft, her ears pointed up.

"What the—" Ferd said in a whisper. I didn't look at him. "Randy. Randy, that cat's dangerous. Trust me, she's been abused." He waved his head at the door.

I nodded to Ferd. "It's okay."

I kept watching Matilda. *Still relaxed.* Then she sat up on her haunches.

Relying on instinct, I sat next to her cross-legged on the cement, then lowered my head and rubbed it on her neck. She did the same, rubbing the top of her head on my neck. I pet her shoulders and heard her purring. It was loud, a steady beat, like a helicopter in the distance.

Even the dogs shut up.

I rubbed her big head, feeling the depth and thickness of her fur. Then her paws, feeling the cracked dry pads. I smelled her earthy cat smell. My voice was soft, whispering and quiet like my father had taught me.

Matilda's nose had a red slice. Blood was on her cheek by her scar. I saw some of it on her right paw. There was blood on my hand. I tensed, hating to see her hurt. I felt her neck tense and she looked in my eyes. Then I relaxed and wiped her blood on my jeans, and I felt her relax.

"We'll get this cleaned up before your big trip, girl."

I looked in her eyes. Always the same. Capable only of truth. I leaned in, half-hugging her. "Thank you for everything," I said. Matilda was pushing her nose into my neck.

It was time to let her go.

"You have to get into that van, Matilda. That means you have to walk through that door. Will you do that for me? No one'll hurt you. I'll go with you."

I stood and looked at Ferd, then stooped and moved through the short door out the back of the enclosure, then walked to the van.

Matilda followed. The musky fear smell was gone. I stepped into the van. She followed. I stepped out and shut the door behind me. I looked in the windows in the back of the van. She was crouched.

I looked in her eyes once more and said, "Goodbye, Mattie."

"Randy, can I talk to you for a minute?" Ferd was by the door where I'd entered the cage. He was shaking his head. "Let's go to the lobby. Ladies, would you mind waiting here? I want to talk to Randy alone."

In the lobby, he turned to me.

"*How* did you do that? Why? You didn't think she'd hurt you?" He spoke fast, shaking his head like he'd seen something miraculous. "How in hell did you do that?"

"No. I didn't think she'd hurt me. I feel her rhythm, Mr. Garrett."

"Have you touched that animal before?"

"No. Just a rub of her fur through a fence," I said. "I *owed* her. She un-fucked my head."

Ferd kept shaking his head. He looked at the ground and blew out air. I think he was trying to figure out how crazy I was. Me, too.

He held out his hand. We shook. He held on and pulled me closer.

"That was the goddammdest thing I've ever seen in my life." He let go, then put his hand on my shoulder.

"Randy, I think I know you. We're both Rangers. And, yes, I saw that crap on the news last Saturday. Your ex says you didn't abuse her, so that means you did? I didn't believe a fuckin' word of it.

"I saw what you did in there. How would you like to ride with Matilda and me to Williams? We're driving straight through, ten hours. Kelsey was going to drive the van, but, if you don't mind, she can drive that cherry F-1 of yours you drove up in. Give us a chance to talk. We'll pay you for this, of course.

"And, after we get there," he said, "you can look over our spread. Maybe I can interest you in something permanent. We need people like you."

He waited a beat, then added, "We *were* going to leave now and drive straight through, but we can give you a few hours to get packed."

Maybe Ferd Garrett *didn't* think I was crazy.

My head was spinning. "Everything's in that tool locker on the bed," I said slowly, looking at him. "I've never been to Arizona. Mind if I think about it for a minute?"

I looked outside. Kelsey drove up in the van and parked just outside the front door. "I am going to go look in on Matilda," I said to Ferd.

I walked outside and peered in the window in the back of the van. Matilda was sprawled out on a large dog bed. She saw me looking and stood up, putting her nose to the glass of the window.

For a minute, I couldn't say anything. I got the feeling she knew my answer before I did.

"Why not?" I said to her. I walked back into the shelter and up to Ferd.

"Okay. I'll do it. I don't need a few hours. We can leave now."

"That's great," Ferd said. "Hop on in and join your cougar, Randy."

"One thing, Mr. Garrett," I said. "You mind if we stop for some Cokes and beef sticks on our way out of town?"

"It's Ferd. Call me Ferd," he said.

Athena:
    Matilda is doing great. Right now I am riding with her to a cat sanctuary ten hours away. Things are looking up. Write me, please. And give me your contact information. I don't understand why you will not tell me where you are.
    I love you.
    Randy

CHAPTER 32

We made a strange parade, walking into the gymnasium at Evans Elementary School in Irvine, California.

Two local volunteers for Big Cat Rescue led my two dogs. Sheila, the old hippie from that day at the San Diego Animal Shelter, had Sandy the Labrador retriever. A boy about sixteen led Buddy, the pit bull, on a leash. "I'm Kevin," he said, putting out his hand. He was clean-cut, the type of kid who volunteers to be a police explorer. "I just started with Big Cat Rescue. Thank you for this opportunity, First Sergeant Andrews. I liked what you did for this mountain lion."

These days, my fame always seemed to precede me. "I'm Randy."

Cleopatra the raccoon was next, struggling to keep up, taking four steps for each one taken by the dogs.

Matilda and I came last. I led her on a chain.

I was back in Orange County for a combination educational and fundraising trip on behalf of Big Cat Rescue. Ferd loved sending my team on the road. "We're bringing in money hand over fist since you and that cougar came on board."

Matilda quickly became the face of Big Cat Rescue. Everybody wanted to meet the man who thought smuggling a cougar into the US was a good idea.

I lifted Cleopatra onto the table before me, then spun her around to face the kids.

"Good morning!"

The kids were always happy and loud. "Good morning!"

"My name is Randy, and I am here on behalf of The Big Cat

Rescue. This is Cleopatra the raccoon."

Cleopatra raised her paw in a half-assed wave.

It took me two months to teach her to do that. I slipped her a slice of apple.

"And these two are Sandy and Buddy."

On a snap of my finger, the dogs raised their paws and waved. It took me two days to teach them that trick.

"And *this*," I motioned with my head, knowing that hundreds of eyes followed mine. "This . . . is . . . the star of our show. Matilda, the mountain lion."

Matilda didn't wave. I had given up trying to teach her anything.

My shirt had *Big Cat Rescue* stitched below *Randy*. I wished my Ranger buddies could see this so they could give me shit.

"These animals were abused. They needed a lot of love to make them happy. They couldn't have come to your school like this when I first met them."

"Matilda is a North American mountain lion, also known as a cougar and a lot of other names. Matilda is three years old."

Matilda's shoulders were against my leg. Her muscles were tense. She was always uptight at the start. The room was filled with the sound of antsy kids whispering, shuffling their feet, moving metal chairs on the vinyl floor. An older teacher with gray hair and an anxious face was on my right, her eyes fixed on Matilda as she edged toward the stairs off the stage.

Matilda was watching her too, eyes wary.

Matilda moved her head from side to side, looking about, sniffing the air. She started to lower herself into a crouch, but I pulled her leash to keep her sitting. Her tail was slapping the floor in a rhythm.

"It's okay, girl. These are friends." I rubbed her neck.

Cleopatra was gnawing on her apple slice. That raccoon was happy anywhere, as long as she had fruit. "Cleopatra is one of Matilda's best friends. She was raised in a cage and had not seen the sun for three years."

Cleopatra came from a cramped dog crate in the garage of some asshole in Kingman, Arizona. During a police drug raid on the home, she was taken to the animal shelter. She was "too damaged" and was going to be put down.

It was the same old story, one I understood. I adopted her and she became friends with Matilda.

Raccoons were lunch for a mountain lion. I didn't think a mountain lion could be friends with one, but Matilda and Cleopatra hung out with each other for hours each day. A lot of things I never thought possible happened with that cat.

"Buddy is a pit bull and Sandy is a Labrador retriever. I rescued both of these dogs from the animal shelter. They are also Matilda's best friends. They are here because they wanted to come to California, and they keep Matilda happy."

Matilda's first few shows were a disaster. She was tense and looked ready to eat the front row of the audience. Then I got the two dogs on the day they were set to be euthanized. They kept her calm on stage. Both were about a year old.

"Do you see the way she is moving her head from side to side? See her tail, the way she is whipping it back and forth?" I asked the children." Matilda is telling us she is scared. There are a lot of you here and some of you are staring into her eyes. That makes her nervous. The noise makes her nervous, too. Do you want to make Matilda feel welcome?"

"*Yeeesss!*"

"Let me show you. Can we turn the lights down a bit?"

I whispered into the microphone on my shirt.

"You are all too loud. I need you to be quiet. Do not look into her eyes," I emphasized. "You are going to have to be quieter. I need you to be even quieter. Quieter. I still hear you. There's still noise in this room." Bear, my buddy from the jail, could quiet down these kids. Then every parent would file a complaint about his methods.

And then, magically, it was silent.

The kids always wanted Matilda to feel at home.

I whispered into the mic.

"I want you to feel the rhythm of this big cat. She has a rhythm. Did you know that? Where she comes from it is very quiet. She lives alone most of the time, except when she has kittens. She moves at night when other animals are asleep."

I held the microphone under Matilda's nose.

"Can you hear her breathing?"

It was rhythmic, the sound of light air puffs. One after another. I put my hand on her head then ran it down her back, feeling her muscles. She was relaxing.

"Let's see if we can get her to purr like your cat at home."

I scratched behind her ears, her favorite place. We all heard the helicopter sound.

"Mountain lions are the largest of the cat family who purr. Did you know that? The bigger cats like lions and tigers don't purr." I looked back at one of the school staff, respectfully watching from the farthest edge of the stage. "Can you turn the lights back on?" I asked him. "All of you please stay as quiet as you have been. For Matilda."

Matilda was sitting on her haunches. Then she lay on her side but kept her head up in alert watchfulness. She was guarding me. Only I could walk her on a leash.

I'd gotten better at this since I was hired by Big Cat Rescue six months ago. Ferd and I were friends. Two weeks after I started, he saw me practicing in Matilda's enclosure. "Jesus Christ, Randy. You're not talking to a bunch of soldiers. You're talking to kids. Remember? Don't start by announcing the learning objectives and telling them to keep their mouths shut. Make this fun. You need to relax. And, please," he added, "don't fuckin' *cuss* in front of the kids."

I talked about mountain lions and how they live and how they needed to be protected.

These were city kids. None grew up in homes with bear rugs and animal heads staring from the walls. Protecting cougars was an easy sell in Southern California.

"I used to kill a lot of animals," I shared with them. "I was raised in Northern Idaho and my father and I hunted together. I killed deer, elk, bear and turkey. Rabbit, quail, coyote. I never killed a mountain lion, but they were considered vermin back then. You could kill them all year long, as many as you wanted. Now we understand better how important they are to their ecosystem."

"Okay. Who has a question?" Several hands went up.

"You." I pointed to a boy of about seven in front.

"Can we pet Matilda?"

"No. You can't. You need to earn that privilege with an animal like this. She needs to trust you first. Humans hurt her really bad when she was younger, so she doesn't trust many people."

I looked over at Sheila and Kevin, still handling the dogs.

"But you can pet those dogs. They're Matilda's best friends. And you can hold Cleopatra."

"Can Matilda go back to the wild?" a girl asked.

They always wanted Matilda to be free.

"No. She doesn't have the skills to survive in the wild because she was put in a cage when she was six months old," I answered. "But, where we live, Matilda has a really nice home with trees to climb. It's about the size of this auditorium. And she lives with Buddy and Sandy and Cleopatra. And me. She travels three months a year to meet boys and girls like you. She likes to look out the window of the van. Matilda even has a swimming pool, and she swims with Sandy."

"The young person in back," I said, pointing.

"Can you stand up, so we can see you?" I asked.

The laughter started in back, working its way to the front. A boy in the first row said, "She *is* standing." The kids laughed harder.

"I thought it was nice . . . what you did," a girl said.

The anxious lady on stage helped.

"Cynthia, you talked to me before. Do you want to know why Randy took Matilda from that place in Mexico and brought her to America?"

Cynthia nodded.

I always got this question. I tried to tell the truth.

"Well," I said. "I do not recommend anybody do what I did. I was arrested and spent nineteen days in jail."

I looked like these kids once. Then I went to war.

Some of them would be shipped overseas to protect American freedoms from people who weren't trying to take them away. Some would come home fucked up. Some would not come home at all.

Cleopatra was still gnawing her apple slice, flipping it between her paws. She always made me laugh. I concentrated on her.

Then I was able to speak.

"Matilda was part of my therapy."

The adults laughed. They thought I was joking. I didn't laugh.

"I was sad. We talked to each other. She helped me. We were Americans living in Mexico. Both of us had to come home."

The teachers studied me, their eyes narrowed. *They just don't get it.*

The children did. They understood animals talked to us.

One of the adults cleared her throat. The auditorium was quiet.

"I *had* to save Matilda. I couldn't leave her behind to die. I never would have forgiven myself if I didn't get her out of that place and bring her home."

I visited three other schools in Orange County, then four in Los Angeles County. The *Los Angeles Times* covered one of the events. The newspaper took photographs and interviewed me. Like the other news outlets that sometimes covered my show, they didn't care about where mountain lions fit into the ecosystem. They wanted to talk about me smuggling Matilda over the border.

The next day an article appeared in *The Times* local section. That night, Athena wrote.

I love reading about your show, Randy. How did you teach those animals to do those things? I am so happy Matilda is doing so well. She looks so happy and healthy. You look good too. You don't even know how different you look. Relaxed. How are you doing? How is Arizona? Matilda came from there. I am glad you took her home.

How is it going with your sons?

I love you. Athena

I answered.

Athena. Thanks for writing. Matilda is doing well. I am doing pretty good. I love Arizona. It reminds me of where I was raised. I never told you much about Northern Idaho. That is where I am from.

The mountains there are so high and beautiful. Rocky. The taller ones always have snow on their peaks. Everything is clean up there. I remember when I was a boy. My father and I would camp up there. Sometimes it would snow. And the snow would cling to the cedars, and it would all smell so fresh, and whatever troubled me would be gone.

Still the same with John and Danny. I hope you are doing well, too. I take it you still want me to contact you by email. I can live with that for now.

Always, Randy.

CHAPTER 33

I wasn't driving my F1 into Mexico. I parked at the border and took a taxi to Rosarito Beach.

The Nightclub Estrella was still a dump, just now one without a cougar. I walked in about the same time I had on the Fourth of July ten months ago. It didn't smell like animal urine. The short fence was gone, leaving holes in the concrete. Matilda's enclosure now had a large opening in the fencing. A sign over the entrance read, *Former Home of Matilda, World Famous Cougar.* On the chain-link fencing were two boards with dozens of newspaper articles about the cougar theft.

The same two mismatched chairs were by Athena's table. I was standing by it when I heard a voice yelling from the bar.

"Randy, is that you?" I tightened up, thought of moving out quickly, and then relaxed when I saw it was Ruben. He was walking toward me alone, smiling.

"How are you doing?" I asked. "How's Roberta?"

"Excellent. Gloria was born in November." He looked up, lost in thought. "The sixteenth. November 16." I got the feeling he pulled the date from his rear end, that he couldn't remember the date.

He continued. "And guess what? I am again blessed. My Roberta is again with child. If our baby is a boy, there will be another Ruben Jr.

Deja vu.

"Congratulations," I said, without enthusiasm. We shook hands.

"I read about Matilda. I believe she has a nice home. Looks like she's doing well. All the Baja newspapers reported on her for a while. How is she?"

"Big Cat Rescue's good for her. It's quiet, near the Grand Canyon. Peaceful, too. Just what she needed. She's happy now, doing well. She's come home."

"She was from Arizona," he said.

"So what happened after I took her?"

He laughed. "The owner came in and found the empty cage. There was a stuffed cougar. He held it over his head, shaking it, yelling. 'How could this have happened? How could this have happened?' He threw the stuffed animal across the room onto the dance floor and Brittany—remember her, the stripper with the big boobs—laughed. 'You're fired,' he said. 'Get out.'"

Ruben continued. "The police came, but no one knew where Matilda was. We were all questioned. The police told us she had been freed. They said they looked for her in the hills, but I don't think that was true. You want a beer?"

I pulled out my wallet. He shook his head.

"This is on the Nightclub Estrella. As much as you want. Just don't tell the owner.

He returned from the bar with two Pacificos, handing me one.

"The owner and the police thought Athena stole Matilda. She never came back to work."

He answered my first question, so I asked my second. "Do you know where she went?

"No." He studied my face. "I don't. I'm sorry. She was so beautiful. Strange, too." We were both quiet.

"Anyway, I'm watching the television here one afternoon and I see your photograph. And then a photograph of Matilda. Our cougar was world famous. Much of the press was bad for the nightclub. But the crowds at night got larger from people hearing about our club and wanting a photograph in Matilda's cage. Everyone wants to dance in the cage."

We looked into the enclosure. It seemed longer than ten months since I'd been here. Another life. The power washer was gone.

"Randy. Did Athena help you take Matilda?"

I looked at the runway with its pole. Then Athena's table. "No, she didn't. I gave her some money a few days before I left. I think it was enough for her to get out of here."

I drank two more beers at the bar, making small talk with Ruben. He didn't have much more to say. Nothing much happened in this town. American kids still came to get drunk.

"Wait," Ruben said. "I have something, something Athena left. I found it where she kept her purse in the back room. You should have it."

He walked off, then returned with a photograph. It was the one the customer took just before "Who Knew" played, the day Athena took me to her apartment, the day we said we loved each other. She'd had it printed.

Athena and I were smiling. Matilda was in the enclosure behind us, pushing her nose into the chain links.

"Thanks." The green neon strip still lit up the bar. "I'll tell you what I should have done. I should have busted out that fuckin' green light." We both laughed.

It was time for me to leave.

"Randy." He shook my hand, clasping his left over our right hands. "I want to thank you for getting Matilda out of here. I know you went to jail. That was brave. I hated her in that cage. I hope things go well for you in the future, my friend. Come back anytime."

I wouldn't return.

I walked up the side street to Athena's apartment. I knocked on the door and a man answered. He was old and looked like he'd spent a lot of time working outdoors. *"Lo siento,"* I said.

Walking back to Juarez to catch a cab to the border, I stopped at the small church. It was empty. The photo of Athena and her two Albertos was gone. Only a few candles were lit.

I threw a five in the Donation can, then lit two.

On the cab ride north, I looked at the three of us in the photo.

Our smiles looked forced, like we didn't deserve to be happy.

There was a message on the back.

> *Randy. The hardest person to forgive is yourself. I hope you can do that someday. You deserve the best. I love you. Always know that. Athena.*

For a moment, I was angry. She left that there a few days before I took Matilda from the club. She planned to leave me.

But I knew that wasn't true. We both were flying by the seats of our pants back then.

During the forty-minute taxi ride to the border, I thought back to my two months in the Nightclub Estrella with an odd feeling of nostalgia. I thought of power washers and my first reaction to looking into Matilda's eyes. And Athena's hand on my face when I was hurting. And drinking beer and laughing. Man, was I fucked up.

As the taxi was nearing the border, I wrote to Athena from my phone.

> *Athena.*
>
> *Ruben gave me the photograph with your message. I agree. I do. And you also need to follow your own advice. I love you. Randy.*

She was right. I needed to forgive myself. I just didn't know how.

CHAPTER 34

"This reminds me of Idaho," I said. From Ferd's back porch I saw the snow clinging to Humphreys Peak to the east, more than twelve thousand feet above sea level.

His porch looked over an open area about ten football fields in size. The wind was blowing west, light on our faces. We were downwind, making it a good evening to see elk or deer. Right about now, they would come from the trees on the far side.

If the wind switched, the meadow would be deserted because it carried the scent of one hundred forty-nine predators, not including humans, on this property.

Ferd cracked a Budweiser and handed it to me, the first casualty of the second six-pack. The moon soon would rise over the trees on the ridge.

"You keep dancin' around your problem, Randy. When are you going to lean in, face it head on?" He paused, opened another beer for himself. "When it gets too big for you to handle?"

We drank beer in these chairs on Friday nights in the warm circle created by Ferd's propane heater. The cold stayed long at 5,500 feet. Ferd and his wife, Janet, lived in a three-bedroom cabin on Big Cat Rescue. I had a two-bedroom cabin. Two full-time employees and four volunteers lived in the third and fourth cabins.

The Rescue owned a hundred fifty acres donated by a rich hunter who'd once killed animals on this land, then swore off hunting as he got close to death. The cats here were injured or retired. The injured were almost all mountain lions and bobcats hit by cars or shot. The rest were circus and zoo castoffs, mostly lions and tigers that weren't pretty enough to make money anymore. We had one three-legged snow leopard.

All of them came here to finish their lives because no one else wanted them.

We were way out, twenty miles north of Williams, then thirty miles east along Highway 90A. The last mile was a packed-dirt road.

But we had top-of-the-line internet and telephone coverage. Ferd's idea. We had to stay connected to raise money to feed all these cats.

I wouldn't see people from off the property for days at a time. I loved it. I had run to Mexico looking for something I ended up finding here.

"You know I'm right," he added.

I heard growls and sighs and the occasional light roar from cats settling down for the night. Matilda lived in an enclosure next to my cabin.

"I talked to Janet about you. Want to know what she had to say?"

We had talked for hours on that ten-hour drive from San Diego. I had dinner with Ferd and Janet one night per week. He knew all my problems. In our early conversations, I shared haltingly, but I think knowing he understood the rigors of war, coupled with my growing experience in talking in front of groups of kids gave me what I needed to confide in him.

Ferd battled PTSD after Vietnam. "I was crazy," he said. "It ruined my first marriage, though. That union was probably best put down." He knew about my boys. He knew about Athena.

Ferd and Janet had two daughters around my age. They treated me like their son. Most of the time, I liked it.

I put up with Ferd's advice because he cared, but it was edging closer to nagging. For the past month, he'd been pushing me to make peace with Sara and to write off that "Greek chick."

"Look at that," I said. A buck and three does were moving at the edge of the trees. In my head, I lined up on the buck's heart. It was habit.

"You gonna answer? Or keep finding other things to talk about?"

"If I say no, you gonna talk about something else?"

"No. You want to hear what a woman said or not?"

To Ferd, any woman was an expert on anything involving women. I thought much the same way.

"Not really."

"I'll tell you. She thinks you should call Sara. Bury the hatchet."

I turned my head slowly, staring.

He leaned back, away from me. "You don't need to look at me like that. I'm not one of your privates, you know. We're friends, remember."

"Okay." I didn't know I had looked at him like he was a private.

"Have you had contact with your boys? Any contact at all? Have you talked to Sara?"

"Not really. Sara did a job on them," I said. "I call and ask her how they're doing. I talk to Danny sometimes. He's living with her."

It had been nine weeks since I'd talked to Danny, a year and a half with John.

"I know you think she's telling them shit about you. You know that for sure?"

"Yeah. The last time I talked to John, it was like talking to her. Sara's shit, but coming from his mouth. I'm a narcissist, it's always *all about me*. That crap. Now Danny called me a narcissist too, the last time we talked. What twelve-year-old uses words like that?"

Ferd cleared his throat, then shook his head.

"You know, you did put the woman's head through drywall."

I felt blood heating my face. I was tired of doing penance for something I couldn't remember.

Ferd was sixty-six. My dad would have turned sixty-six this year. He would have agreed with Ferd.

"What's your fuckin point?" He didn't answer so I turned in my chair, looked in his eyes.

"She was badmouthing me before that, you know. And... and... and I didn't tell her to fuck all those other guys. Dumbass here thinks she had one affair, on my last tour. Why can't we work this out, Sara? I forgive you. We have a family, our boys. I'm home for good. We'll make it up to each other. But no, no, no. She blows up, lets it all out, 'Fuck you, Randy, you want to know what?' She'd had affairs my last *four* tours. Different guys."

I leaned back in my chair, took a long draw on my bottle and waited for calm. "You haven't had to deal with *that* shit, Ferd. I don't need you to tell me what the fuck I'm doing wrong."

I don't know who I was mad at. Ferd was convenient. He puffed, and I felt air hit my arm. He leaned closer and made his face look stern.

"Don't talk to me like that. You get that tone, that you-are-a-fuckin'-asshole tone. I'm on your side, remember."

"You've been riding my ass for a month on this. I tell you I don't want to talk about it. You keep bringing it up," I looked over, could *see* his concern. "Okay. Sorry."

"That's okay. The drywall thing doesn't seem like you. I know that. Look, Randy, you're pissed at her, I get it. I'd feel like you do. The cheating? That's on her. I'm not asking you to forgive her for that. I want you to fix what *you* did wrong."

He reached over, gave my shoulder a squeeze. "Clean your side of the street."

"I send cards to my boys, call. I write them emails, messages."

His palm was on his forehead, his head shaking. *This guy's brainless*, his expression said.

"Randy. Listen. Let's take this slow. What's the source of the problem?" He took a swig of beer, then another. "It's your relationship with Sara. Sometimes negotiation, even surrender, are successful tactics. You don't need to take out every enemy. Sometimes a little diplomacy is best, even with guys like us. Make peace with Sara, man."

He was excited, his open hands in front of him.

"You look like you got your hands on a pair of tits," I said.

I laughed. Ferd gave a perfunctory laugh in return.

"Think about it," he said. "Talk it over with that therapist." I'd been going to PTSD therapy for six months at the VA in Williams.

He knew how far he could push. We talked about Matilda, Cleopatra, the dogs and next week's fundraising trip to Utah.

Crickets were starting up. Then frogs, then an owl. Then Ferd. He cleared his throat, something he did when he had a point to make. "You know my background," he said.

He came back from Vietnam screwed up. Two arrests for bar fights. One assault on his first wife. "Carole. She was my wife. We were always drinking and fighting and fucking. Then fucking some more. I was crazy about her, even after she walked out."

"You know what?" he said. "I was a broken record. At the American Legion, people avoided me, didn't want to hear about it again. Then it hit me. Sometimes things just don't work out. It doesn't matter who did what wrong, so quit looking at it that way. You need to bury your dead, Randy. They come back as ghosts if you don't. You know what I mean?"

I didn't. "Thanks for the beer." I stood. "I'm gonna go."

"Sara was your wife for a long time. I'm sure she loved you."

I winced.

She had loved me.

I fell in love with the Army in Somalia. After the Blackhawk went down, the Army put a halt to calls home. For ten days, I couldn't call Sara. We were both twenty.

The day the regiment returned to Fort Benning, she said, "Please get out of the Army. Don't go away anymore, Randy. Please don't re-enlist. I can't take it, the not knowing. I love you too much."

But I was doing God's work, serving our nation, killing people. Sometime over the next two decades, Sara quit loving me and I didn't even know it.

I'd missed the biggest, most vital rhythm of all.

"I'll think about it," I told Ferd, grabbing my half-finished Bud and walking back toward my cabin.

The air was so clean. I liked taking deep breaths. The air up here washed away all the bad shit I'd breathed.

Matilda rubbed her neck on the fence by my leg as I said goodnight. It was nine o'clock, the same time I came by each night. I scratched behind her ears, her favorite spot, through the links.

"What do I do, girl?" I asked. We looked at each other.

Bury my dead?

CHAPTER 35

The VA sent me to Dr. Patrick MacAfee for PTSD counseling. During our first session, MacAfee said he had cancer of the plasma cells in his blood. Multiple myeloma.

"We're gonna get you better. But if our therapy goes on for more than two years, I might not be around," he said.

"Why do you keep working?" I asked.

"I like working with vets."

In our third session, he told me he was gay.

"That bothers some people," he said.

Pat was in his mid-seventies. He was proud and always held his head erect as if he expected to be noticed. With his white hair and mustache, as long as he stayed in his seat, he looked regal. If he hadn't been just five feet three inches, he could play the role of King Lear.

"I don't give a fuck," I said. "It's none of my business. And you've helped me."

Six months before, we'd met every week. Back then he weighed twenty pounds more. After a few months, Pat didn't think I needed to see him as much, and our sessions went to every other week. It had been a month since I'd been in to see him.

"We just need to cover a little more ground, and I think we can cut you loose," he said.

His couch was big and fluffy, swallowing me like river mud. He always kept his office warm. I looked out his window at the forested hills north of Williams. "You keep your office so goddamned hot I'm always ready to fall asleep."

"You know, I was thinking about you. You have a bigger-than-life personality."

"Not sure what to do with that. That's good?"

"Just an observation."

We talked about the animals at Big Cat Rescue, his upcoming vacation to Palm Springs, and the cold weather. I ran Ferd's suggestion by him. "He says I should call Sara. She's screwed me every chance she could during our divorce. And our marriage. You know all that. Ferd won't let up."

No matter how much I slanted the facts, he didn't give me what I wanted. "I think Ferd's right," Pat said.

It took effort, but I sat higher in the couch.

Pat picked up his phone. "Darcy," he said. "Can you bring in Mr. Andrews's file from the VA."

Two minutes later, Darcy opened the door and walked to Pat. For Darcy, it was a tight fit between Pat's couch and his crammed bookshelf. She bumped the bookshelf, and Pat deftly reached up to save a teetering vase.

After Darcy left, I said, "Jesus," just loud enough for Pat to hear.

"What did you say?" Pat asked.

"Nothing important," I said.

"No. I think you said 'Jeez,' or 'Jesus.' Why?" Pat stared.

"If your secretary would lose that fat ass she's carting around, it might save some of your decorations."

"Randy," he shook his head, smiling almost to himself. "You have a problem with heavy people, don't you?"

"I wouldn't call it a problem," I said. "Think it shows a lot about a person, though. A lack of discipline."

Pat frowned. "Darcy has a thyroid problem. Her thyroid hormones are always all over the board. She has trouble with her weight. She was stationed with her husband in the '80s—with the Army—in Germany during the Chernobyl disaster. She thinks she got it there. Bavaria got hit really hard. Her husband died of thyroid cancer. Thankfully, she doesn't have it.

He paused, sliding a glance at me on the couch.

"She spent a lot of time researching you, pulling your records from all over the military and the VA so I could help you. Did you know that?"

I was beginning to feel like a major shithead. But Pat saved me.

"Randy, I get that attitude. It's always that way with the hardcore soldiers, you special ops types. You guys have a hard time with the civilian world. You think it doesn't run as perfectly as the military. No standards. People can dress like they want. Eat like they want. Act like they want. It's called freedom." He paused again, staring. "You're not a soldier anymore, Randy. You may learn to adjust, to love life outside the military. You'll think about what I said?"

I knew I was hard on people. I mean, they usually deserved it. "Yeah, I will."

Pat opened my file.

"Randy, listen. I've studied Dr. Berlin's notes. You were a mess. I don't know what that cat therapy was, but *something* worked for you down in Mexico. You're doing well. There's still some treatment left, but you did the heavy lifting before we started."

"I'm supposed to bury my dead, whatever the fuck that means," I said, but I'd thought about it and knew what it meant.

"I agree with Ferd. And I understand. You don't want to apologize to her because she's hurt your feelings. Yeah, guys like you *do* get hurt emotionally. She cheated on you, not once, but several times. The betrayal!

"But Ferd's not asking you to say you're sorry because *she* cheated on you. That's *her* cross to bear. He's suggesting you apologize for throwing her into that wall. Maybe other things you haven't told me about. That's *yours* to bear."

He was looking into my eyes. "I know what's important to you. Your boys. And that woman from down south. You can do something about your boys. Her? I don't know what to tell you there."

He loved pausing to let me ponder his words.

"You don't need to tell me anything, Pat," I said. "I was raised on *make shit happen*. I was a pest and kept pushing her for her address. She wouldn't give it to me, said I'd rush down to her. She was right. I would have. I would have gone anywhere, as long as it's where she was. She said I wasn't ready, I needed this time. She was right about that, too.

"I'm in love with the woman, Pat. But I'm okay with being patient, letting it play out without me pushing everything and everyone to do what I want. So, we write nice emails to each other."

"Sounds like a good plan," he said. "But I think you're probably settled down enough to where you could handle a relationship. And maybe we can talk more about that decision to go to Mexico when we meet next month."

As I walked out, Darcy was assembling a file. A photo of a vet was on one side. Darcy saw me looking and shut the file. "Sorry," she said. "We have to protect the privacy of our veterans."

"Pat said you did a lot of work finding my background, getting reports from the VA."

"Well," she said. "Pat's great. He needs to know all he can about you."

"I wanted to thank you," I said. "That was a really nice thing to do. It has helped me. *A lot*."

Her eyes got wet. She nodded her head. I think she said, "You're welcome."

Matilda was awake and came to me as I opened the gate to her enclosure. It was five in the morning. I came at this time every day to sit in a chair at the edge of her pool. It was my thinking spot. She sat by me, bumping my leg as I drank coffee. I heard purring, then licking sounds.

Why didn't I get out? It would never get any better than Firdos Square.

Because the Army meant more to me than my family?

No, I loved them.

Because I believed the God and country bullshit?

I did, but that wasn't it.

I looked deeper.

I loved the missions, the patrols, the constant edge, the danger. I loved scanning, picking up the rhythm of a war zone. I was an adrenaline junkie, the warrior, the badass. I loved being in charge, the biggest shit-kicker in the world.

I fell in love with how good I was at killing.

There was no PTSD back then. In war, paranoia and being on edge made sense. They kept me alive.

It was never enough.

Then came the grim realization of what I loved most of all.

Matilda was on her side, catching the early sunlight on her fur. She was a different cat now, relaxed and alert. She lifted her head. She squinted and looked at me.

"Girl. I need one more favor." I sat on the ground next to her and rubbed her favorite spot behind her ears.

Her ears went up, studying me.

"I need your help."

It was three in the morning when we pulled up to the al-Qaeda safe house. Inside were between seven to fifteen terrorists, mostly low- to mid-level. Our mission was to clear it before they moved to their next temporary home. We were moving fast, with a green light to kill anything inside.

A few scattered rounds came from the second-story window. Then the house opened up, AKs firing from four upstairs windows, an RPG on the roof taking out one of our Humvees. We moved along the walls lining the dirt street.

I was first in, killing two with a burst from my M4. Other Rangers cleared the kitchen as I ran up the stairs. The first door was shut. I kicked it in. There was only a bed. Then I saw the AK barrel pointed to the door. It moved, raised slightly. I emptied the magazine, thirty rounds, and moved off from the doorway. I thought I heard cries, but I wasn't sure. I emptied a second magazine, watching the dirty blankets jumping, sending pieces of cotton to float. I backed out of the room, jammed in a third magazine, came back in and moved to the bed.

Sergeant Anderson and Corporal Mendoza ran in and moved to my side. The three of us screamed at the bed. The barrel was still there, pointed at the door.

I flipped the bed. That's when I saw the two kids and the woman.

They were all blood. The woman's arm was laying across the stock of the AK. Her head was pulp. She wore a hijab and a dress. Otherwise, I wouldn't have known her gender. The kids were on their sides behind her, their arms covering their faces. The little girl, about three, had the top of her head blown off. She wore no head covering. The boy was facing away from the door. It looked like somebody had taken a shovel to his abdomen. I saw his intestines.

He looked to be about two.

Outside this room, I heard screaming and shots. In here, the silence was broken when Anderson said, "Fuck Randy. You wasted some kids."

The regimental command looked into it. Colonel Cox flew in from Baghdad to deliver the findings.

He sat tall behind his desk, whitewalls down the side of his head. "We've interviewed the witnesses who were there," he said. "Anderson, Mendoza, seven others, even two of the al-Qaeda prisoners. The killings of the woman and the two children were in accordance with the Rules of Engagement, Sergeant First Class Andrews. Upon seeing a rifle barrel protruding from under the bed, the ROE mandated that you defend yourself. This *was* a lawful killing. The board that investigated found you had no other options, that you did what you were trained to do."

He softened his tone. "Randy. What the fuck else were you *supposed* to do? Lift the bed first to see who was pointing that rifle at you? If it had been a bad guy, maybe one of the guys who tried to kill you from the window *in that room*, we wouldn't be having this discussion. You'd be dead."

He stood, walked over, and put his hand on my shoulder. "You didn't have a choice. You did the right thing, Randy."

"No, sir. I did what the ROE said to do. My youngest, Danny, is about the same age as that little boy."

A chaplain came by my room that evening. He ignored the bottle of Jack Daniels and my drunkenness. "You want to talk, Sergeant Andrews?"

I looked at the cross on his shoulder. "Not really, Chaplain."

He didn't seem to hear me. "Bad things happen in war, sergeant. Sometimes we do everything right and they still happen. You hear the term, 'shit happens?'"

"This wasn't shit, Chaps. I wasted a woman and two kids."

"We pray on it, then we put it down. You're going to have to find a way to do that, Sergeant Andrews."

Friends and more commanders told me—and more chaplains—that I did what I had to do, that it wasn't my fault even though I was the one who emptied sixty rounds into that bed.

None of that made any difference. I never told Sara.

I should have.

Eventually, I quit thinking about it so much. Then I quit thinking about it at all.

Until two tours later when I washed the blood of my two best friends from the Humvee.

Matilda was staring in my eyes. Killing those three under the bed wasn't something I could change. But there was something I could.

I stood and hooked Matilda's leash to her collar. "Time for our walk, Mattie." The sun was rising. I'd been sitting with her for over an hour.

We swung by my cabin so the dogs could join us. A three-mile trail headed into the forest, then along the edge of the meadow to the east. The dogs were off leash, running crazy. They always did at the start.

Matilda moved with a lazy cat saunter that said *I don't have a care in the world.*

The four of us loved it up here.

The dogs were running circles around Matilda, taunting, wanting to know why their friend who ran and chased them in her enclosure wasn't doing it now.

A bull and several cow elk were on a rise in the distance. We were downwind. Oblivious to our presence, they were munching on grass along the north side of the meadow. I wished I had a good camera. Pictures like these would look nice on the empty walls of my cabin.

I took the photo of Athena and me from my shirt pocket. It was always there. I read her message.

The dogs were still acting the fools, running up to Matilda, trying to entice her into a game of chase. The elk moved back into the trees. We had the meadow to ourselves.

I had to do something.

I undid Matilda's heavy leather collar and took it off, then moved away from her.

She looked first at the open field, then at the dogs. Then at me. Her leash and collar were in my hand. "Are you serious?" her look said. She began sauntering toward the dogs. They kept running at her, dodging closer and closer, then darting away. At some point she understood she was free.

She bolted, ran after the Labrador, knocking Sandy down. She was up to thirty miles per hour at one point. Matilda ran in huge circles, full speed, opening up her leg muscles for the first time, like the performance car that finally has been let out on the track.

I sucked in air, held my breath. She leaped as she ran. All four of her legs were airborne most of the time, a cougar flying low over the grass. I felt what I sometimes did when the clouds opened and a ray of light descended; that there was a reason for everything, even the bad shit, even the things we couldn't understand.

They ran like frenzied happy animals. At one time the three were half a mile off. Finally, they stopped a hundred feet away, worn out from the mad dashes. Matilda looked north to the edge of the clearing where the elk had been. I think I was holding my breath.

This was the moment, the head shot, gambling on a bond. If she took off, Ferd couldn't provide cover. He'd have to fire me. He didn't even want me taking Matilda on her walks, but tolerated it because I had good control over her.

She sniffed, continued to look north, then turned and loped toward me. She slowed to walking speed twenty feet away and eased her way over with her cat saunter. She brushed her neck on my leg as I put the collar on her.

"You came back," I said.

She looked up at me with her big eyes.

We walked home.

My legs were a little shaky. Matilda would nap most of the morning.

I'd call Sara.

CHAPTER 36

Ferd sat across from me at my kitchen table. The paper between us was blank.

"How many times we need to go over this? Figure out what you want to say to Sara. Write it down. Read it to her."

He tapped his pen on the table. His forehead had more wrinkles from him scrunching it, trying to look stern, but it was an act. He'd been ecstatic since I'd caved and said I'd call Sara.

"It will keep you from getting off track, from attacking. Just say 'I'm sorry for hurting you that day.' Don't add a bunch of crap about cheating and badmouthing you to your boys."

I tapped the pen on the paper.

"This isn't that difficult, you know, apologizing for hurting her," he said. "You did."

I rolled the pen back and forth. Ferd reached over, grabbed it and the paper.

"Here, let me write it for you." He had the pen in his hand and moved it as if he was writing but he didn't touch it to the paper. "*I'm fucking sorry.*"

"Fuck you," I said.

"I think you're delaying, brother, because you don't want to do this."

"You're right. I don't want to do this," I said. "But I am." I took the paper, wrote, "*I'm fucking sorry,*" then stood. "I'm ready."

I turned to Ferd at the door to my bedroom. "I'm calling her from in here—*after* you leave. I'll swing by in a few hours, tell you how it went."

I shut the door behind me. Ferd's voice came through the wooden door. "Remember, this is for you, Randy. For *you*. And remember something good about her. Think of that before you talk." He'd said that four times.

The front door shut. I sat on my bed and called Sara before I could ponder my actions.

Her landline went to voicemail. As I was leaving a message, I got a call back.

I answered. "Yeah?"

"*You* called me, Randy."

"I did, I know."

"So, what's this about?" Her voice had *the edge*, the one that stiffened my back. When I heard it, I became defensive or argumentative, depending on my mood. It spoke of exhaustion, weariness, caused by me. We argued when it crept into her voice. The image of some naked asshole sweating over Sara in *my* bed flashed. I thought about hanging up.

I looked at the paper, wishing I'd have written more before calling.

"*Think of something good about her before you open your mouth.*" That was the fifth time I'd heard Ferd say that, this time in *my* voice in *my* head. *That will keep this from getting derailed. Sara can't be all bad, Randy.*

I heard breathing. Then a huff. Then a second huff. "You're wasting my time," the huffs said.

I felt my anger bubbling. Then I paused, remembered something. The memory came, something my anger hadn't obliterated.

I was on the quad at Santiago High School in Fullerton, my first day at my new high school. I was a senior. Three months earlier, my father had died. Three days earlier, the man who killed him cried at having to serve thirty days in jail.

I wanted to be anywhere but *this* place. My high school in Bonners Ferry had a hundred and eighty-three students. I knew everyone. Santiago High School had more than 4,000. No mountains, just concrete and asphalt and city for untold miles into the horizon.

Kids stared. I wanted to blend in, but my clothes were wrong. My red and black lumberjack shirt was one of a kind in the ninety-degree Southern California heat. I was a freak.

The campus guide was the size of the Idaho roadmap my dad kept in his glovebox. Wind blew it in my face when I opened it. The sun was hot, burning my neck. I was sweating under that wool shirt. The cement was bright, so I kept my eyes narrowed. My class schedule was simple, but I'd read it three times, and nothing registered. It was September 1990.

I heard a soft voice. It was so feminine, an angel's—that thought actually went through my head—and I turned to look at the divine. The sun was behind the source. I was blinded.

"Hi there. You're new?" She laughed. The wind was sticking the map to my face and my chest. She pulled it away from my head and I put it by my side. "Ohhhh yeah, you're new all right, aren't you? First day?" She laughed harder, but with no meanness.

I was squinting and holding the map over my head to block the sun. I looked stupid. She walked to my side and the sun was no longer behind her.

She cannot be talking to me.

I saw all of her in three seconds. I was unable to make words. Her hair was blond and long and waving about in the wind. She swept it away from her face and I saw her nails. They were pink on tanned skin. Her eyes were blue, the color of the sky on nice days in Bonners Ferry. I had seen girls like this in the Sears catalog. Her face was long, lean, like an athlete. She smiled and giggled as my lips moved silently. I saw her white teeth.

Girls here all dressed the same—faded jeans, white sneakers, bright pastel shirts. In the quad, the open square between buildings, it was a sea of pink, sky blue, and orange all moving about with somewhere to go.

This girl stood out, but not like I did. She wore a gingham blue and white dress that ended just below her knees. I was too scared to look in her face. I would never look at her breasts, so I focused on her neck. It was tanned and perfect.

She was your California dream girl dressed for *Little House on the Prairie*. We were both sixteen.

I mumbled, "Hi."

"You look lost," she said. "Do you need some help finding something? A class?" She paused, adding, "Anything?" Her eyes were big. She was the most beautiful thing I'd ever seen.

She tilted her head and winked. My mouth must have dropped. *This girl is flirting? With me?*

"My name is John," I said, "but I go by Randy. Yeah, I'm not sure where the room . . . room B224 is. Is it in the B Building?"

She laughed harder. I didn't get the joke until that night in bed.

"Well, John-who-goes-by-Randy, I know where the B Building is," she said. "If you ask my name, I'll take you to your class. You just need to ask and off we go."

I didn't say anything. My mouth was still open.

"Okay, then. I'm Sara. Can I walk you to your class?"

I nodded. She took my hand.

We were holding hands! I felt heat spreading from my hand, then to my head and my chest, then down to my groin. She asked me where I was from. Sara had never been to Idaho. She had cousins in Colorado, and she loved the high mountains. She loved snow but it never snowed here. Our birthdays were both in November, only four days apart.

I looked at her brown lace-up boots and the eighteen inches of leg that showed beneath the hem of her dress. Her muscles moved under her skin.

We found my class. Inside my head, I screamed. *Get her number!*

Somehow, I asked. I was late for class, but I didn't care. I was in love with Sara Christine Kessler.

"Call me." She wrote her telephone number on a piece of paper and gave it to me. "Bye," she said as she walked off, backward at first, giving me a wave.

That night I dreamed of her face and her legs and the muscles of her calves. I couldn't sleep. In my replays, I said witty, cool things as we walked the quad. I saved her from danger and fought those who would dare insult her.

I told myself I would die to protect her. That never changed, even after we didn't love each other anymore.

Sara and I were together that year. Her father had died of a heart attack three years before at age forty-four. My mother suggested after a few months that perhaps we should slow down, that we were so young, but we couldn't.

We married on my eighteenth birthday. Two weeks later, I left for basic training.

"Randy!" The Sara of the present broke in on my thoughts.

"I'm here," I said.

"What is it?" She spoke in her *get to the point* tone. I first began to hear it over the phone on my third tour to Iraq. Sara was remarrying in a few months. Maybe her soon-to-be husband heard a different voice, the one I heard on the quad that day.

"Sara, I had some things I wanted to tell you. I should have said them to you a long time ago."

She cleared her throat. "Go screw yourself."

Maybe I *had* married the wrong woman, as Athena said. But, for so many years, loving her had made sense.

"I wanted to thank you for all you did for me in high school.

Remember that day we met? You introduced yourself. You were so nice to me. It was tough then, with my father just dying and all and moving to the big city. Orange County was so different. You got me through that senior year. I'm sorry how things turned out between us."

Silence. *Get it all out, Randy.*

"And I wanted to say . . . *I am sorry* I hurt you that night. I'm sorry I was never home. I should have thought more about that."

Her throat cleared again, but it sounded different. She might have been blowing her nose.

"It must have been hard on you," I added.

I did not think I could ever say what I'd just said. But I heard the words in my voice and knew they were true. The Army had worn us out.

She loved you. Remember the things she whispered at night?

And I remembered then why I'd loved her so much. She couldn't be happy with what she became—angry, dishonest, and unfaithful. Not the girl who walked me to class and made me fall in love with her.

She sniffled.

"That wasn't you that night, Randy. I saw your eyes. You said strange things. You asked me why I didn't have a helmet on."

Sara was wrong. It *was* me that hurt her. I signed up for all the shit, had wanted the grit and the pain and the unvarnished hell of war. It made me feel so alive.

But she was right, too. In saying it wasn't me. As badly as she wounded me, she was the mother of my sons. In my right mind, never would I have hurt her.

"I was scared of you," she said.

When I came out of that weird blur, Sara's face was a few inches from mine. I remember the mole above her lip, the one she was always getting removed. I had my palm on her face, covering her mouth. She wasn't just scared. She was terrified of me. I saw the volleyball-sized dent in the drywall that hadn't been there before I kicked in the door.

From my side vision, I could see John standing in his bedroom doorway. He was seventeen. He'd seen everything.

I lost all strength then. I sat on the couch until the police came.

"I am so sorry for that, Sara." I heard sniffling sounds on the line. "Why did you introduce yourself to me that first day of our senior year?" Twice I thought she was ready to talk. Then she did and, again, I heard the voice from the quad.

"You looked lost . . . and I thought you were cute . . . so cute," she said. "But I don't know. I'd never done that before. I just wanted to, Randy."

I started to say, "I'm glad you did," but stopped. Instead, I said, "It's nice up here. Quiet. I think I needed that."

We talked a bit more. I told her that I didn't have flashbacks anymore, that I knew how to deal with the things that caused them. "I want to see John and Danny. I go to the local VA. My therapist thinks I'm doing pretty well. He'll write me a letter. I'll send it to you."

She was quiet. I wished I'd written down some notes on how to end this conversation.

"Thank you for hearing me out, Sara. Congratulations on your marriage. I hope it goes well."

"Thanks, Randy," she said. "Thank you."

I wanted more. I wanted her to say, "I'm sorry, too," to shoulder some of the blame for the death of our marriage. But she was silent.

"Well, you take care of yourself," I said. "Give my love to the boys. I'll send Danny another package in a few days. I will keep working on John. And I'll send you that letter. Bye."

I left the bedroom and sat on the couch in my living room. Except for the scratching sounds Cleopatra made playing with her ball, it was quiet. The blinds were drawn, the room dark.

I didn't need to hate Sara anymore.

I understood it now.

She fell in love with a man whose first love was killing.

Later, I would walk over to Ferd's and thank him.

CHAPTER 37

Dear Ms. Andrews:

Over the past eight months, I have met with your former husband, John Randall ("Randy") Andrews III, twenty-one times for therapy. I have diagnosed Mr. Andrews with post-traumatic stress disorder ("PTSD"), in remission. Mr. Andrews has asked that I write a letter addressing his response to treatment. I will also be sending a letter directly to the Orange County Superior Court in support of his request for unsupervised visitation with the minor child Daniel Andrews.

PTSD is the mind's response to witnessing traumatic events. Randy witnessed countless traumatic incidents during his military service. Randy's treatment involved reliving the witnessed incidents. This treatment is not a cure. PTSD is never "cured" because no treatment can erase memories. Treatment can, however, reduce or eliminate the extent to which those memories bring about distress and anxiety. Treatment can also eliminate unhealthy behaviors focused on avoiding or preventing the distressing memories, i.e., self-medicating with alcohol and drugs.

It is my professional opinion that, while Randy still suffers from PTSD, he has regained control. He is functioning well and has learned mechanisms to prevent symptoms or flashbacks to traumatic events. His PTSD does not interfere with his life. He is working at a job he loves and suffering no adverse symptoms. He no longer uses alcohol as a "coping mechanism."

> *In my professional opinion, Mr. Andrews does not present as a danger to his children, or anyone for that matter. I strongly recommend he once again enjoy regular unsupervised visitation with his son.*
>
> *If you need further information, I can be reached at the telephone number on this letter. Thank you.*
> *Sincerely,*
> *Patrick MacAfee*
> *PhD, Clinical Psychologist*
> *Veterans Administration, Flagstaff Region*

"Thanks Pat."

"It is my pleasure, Randy. You know, I didn't say all that because I like you," he said. "Or so you could see your sons. It's all true. You *are* doing well. But you need to remember: the wolf is always at the door. We don't need to see each other as much anymore. Maybe every three months."

He put his pad down. Then placed the pen on top of it deliberately, a man with a point to make.

"I do have a question, though. Why'd you go to Mexico? You told me about watching *The Shawshank Redemption.* Call it a gut feeling. There's something else, isn't there?"

"It turned out to be a good idea. I didn't know it was when I was in that motel in Orange County, drunk. I got lucky."

"There's more, though. Isn't there?"

I thought back fifteen months. Stuck on the freeway, seeing how fuckin' crazy I looked in the reflection of that cop's shades. The divorce. John's letter. *The Shawshank Redemption* on the television.

And what pushed me over the edge.

"It was the four smokestacks pumping out that shit," I said.

He looked interested but didn't react.

"They were still pumping out that shit."

"What's the significance of the smokestacks?" he asked.

"I knew the area, had been on patrols there two dozen times. I was looking at those smokestacks when the IED detonated, the one that killed my friends."

"You mean Darnell and Vince? You've talked about seeing them die. I know you loved them."

He stopped talking for a moment and just looked at me, one brow slightly elevated. "We've never really explored that, you know. You go so far, then you shut down. But I'm still not sure why you thought the answer was in Mexico."

"ISIS took Samarra. Iraqi defense forces, the ones the US trained, cut and ran. Twenty-one years and everything I was told was important is given to thugs? Ground my buddies died protecting gets handed to ISIS? Without a *fight*?" I shook my head. "What a privilege to fight for *your country*. Turns out, I never did. I just killed a bunch of people in shitholes halfway around the world. And that fuckin' Iraqi army we trained walks off, leaving their equipment? Pathetic. I don't understand those fuckin' Iraqis. What the fuck were we doing over there, *liberating* them? We should have left Saddam in there. At least he kept the lid on the place."

"You're not answering my question," Pat said, unrelenting. "Why'd you go to Mexico?"

I stared, silently, feeling the rage build up.

"Because I woke up with a fuckin' .45 in my hand. Mine. Loaded, bullet in the chamber, safety off. I got up to puke and I was carrying it. *I found it in my fuckin' hand.*"

Pat's eyes held mine steadily. I couldn't tell what he was thinking.

"I don't remember getting it out of my footlocker," I insisted, reeling with the memory. "I don't remember loading the goddamned thing. I don't remember *any* of it. Scared the shit out of me. I took my two nines and the .45 and left them with a gun dealer. Went to Mexico, a place they don't let people have guns, at least, none I could get ahold of."

I thought of Athena's complaint that Americans sent guns south to the cartels.

"Stupid, I know. There's a lot of ways to kill yourself without guns. All I can say is it seemed like a good idea at the time. I got lucky. Mexico *was* a good idea."

Pat was studying me as if searching for words, but not finding any.

"I knew that *Shawshank Redemption* story was bullshit," he said.

"Wasn't *all* bullshit. It did come on. But I wasn't like the guy in the movie, starting a new life. I went south so I couldn't kill myself."

I trailed off for a moment, suddenly realizing the weight of what I had just told him.

"You still gonna send out that letter?"

He looked surprised. "Why wouldn't I? I wasn't taking notes."

He picked up his pad and put it in a file. "Well. You're not suicidal now. I'll get out those letters today. I'll even send them express. We need to get you reconnected with your boys."

I thanked him. We set up an appointment three months out. I was walking to the door when he said, "I don't think you got lucky. I think maybe you made your own luck."

I didn't. What was the chance of running into two unofficial therapists at a sleazy nightclub in Mexico?

CHAPTER 38

Three weeks later, the court modified my visitation so I could spend unsupervised time with Danny. I didn't need the court to visit John. He was nineteen now. It was up to him.

A week later I was on a school visit, explaining to a six-year-old with no front teeth why we couldn't remove Matilda's collar and set her free in the forest. My cell phone vibrated. I let it ring out.

"That would be a bad thing for me to do. Matilda has a nice home at Big Cat Rescue. She doesn't have the skills to survive in the wild. And she told me she doesn't want that."

The kids laughed. They didn't know it was true, in a manner of speaking.

Sara had left a message. *Call me,* it said, and I did.

"The boys want to come visit you," she said.

"The boys?"

"Yeah, your boys. Remember. Your sons?" She laughed. I hadn't heard her laugh in a decade. "Well, John is a little reluctant, but I've talked him into it. Danny, no problem there. He wants to come see you.

"You and John need time, but he'll come around. He's doing a project for his major. He called it, 'Last of the Wild: Through the Eyes of a Predator.' It's all he talks about, photographing endangered species. I told him you're the best person to help him get the photographs he needs. He says you're not. I told him you would show him you were."

I had pieced together that John was a photography major at the

University of Arizona, but not much else about his life. His last email said, "Stop bothering me."

This was huge.

I couldn't talk, a knot having suddenly lodged in my throat.

"Randy, may I suggest something? You know about the wedding. It's October 15. Ryan and I are leaving on a honeymoon for a week after that. Maybe you can schedule this then."

That was only a month off. I didn't know what to say.

"Where you live is nice," she said. "The boys can meet your cougar." Sara thought we could also visit the Grand Canyon for two or three days.

"Or Idaho. I know the country."

"I was thinking of him taking photos of the tigers and lions at that rescue you live at. And your cat. What's her name? Melissa?"

"Matilda. He could go to a zoo for that. A backpacking trip into the Idaho Rockies would get him a ton of photos."

"You don't think something a little less, uh, ambitious? Look, why don't you drive down to Phoenix and have pizza with John? Set up your trip from there."

"In Idaho I could get him to his photographs. I could meet him at the airport. Can you talk John into Idaho, Sara?" Somehow, I knew. It had to be Idaho.

I was mapping this out when I thought of the mountain caribou head on the wall in the basement of my parents' home. They were as endangered as it gets.

"I don't think it's a good idea to take them on a backpacking trip," she said. "Go a little slower with them, particularly John. He's angry. He wants to be a wildlife photographer. He's not a hunter, but he picked up your love of the outdoors. He's a lot like you, you know. Tough, brave, loyal, headstrong."

She's trying to say something nice.

"Thank you, Sara."

She paused, then continued. "You have John's email and phone number. He promised me you're not blocked anymore. Danny wants you to email him. Okay? I'll talk to John about Idaho. He'll be here for the wedding. You have to talk to him, Randy, listen to what he wants. If it works, Danny can fly to Idaho with him."

"I hope you have a fun honeymoon."

"Thanks. Randy, if you need anything, any help, let me know. I hope this works for you."

Despite his promise to remove the block, I still couldn't contact him by phone. We did talk by email. His words were serious, businesslike, but at least we were communicating.

He surprised me, agreeing to a backpacking trip to Idaho.

"Anything would be better than sitting around that zoo you live at," he wrote. The packing list I sent was "controlling," he wrote.

"Just pack it, John. I know the mountains up there. I know what you need," I wrote.

A month later, I left Williams at three in the morning to meet my sons at the airport in Spokane, Washington. Ferd would taking care of Matilda, Buddy, Sandy and Cleopatra in my absence. I drove around the Grand Canyon, then north through Utah, then into Idaho, north into Montana then west, again into Idaho. Twenty hours, stopping only for stretch breaks and gas.

I would spend the night in Sandpoint, Idaho. The airport in Spokane was another seventy-five miles. My sons would arrive in two days.

I needed to check out the terrain to get my boys close to those caribou.

The deputy game warden at the Forest Service Office in

Sandpoint could have been Darnell's brother. Same chiseled features. He didn't have Darnell's outgoing personality, though. He left me standing by the counter while he filled in the blanks on a form. When he did look up, he didn't speak.

I asked where I could find the caribou herd. He studied me like I was a poacher. "I just want to get my sons some photos."

"You know, that's wilderness out there. People are always getting in trouble, getting lost, dying." He went back to filling in the blocks on his report.

"I know." He flipped the page on his report. "I'm looking for where the herd was last seen." I frowned, then said, with sarcasm, "I guess you're too busy filling out that paperwork to answer my question."

He looked up fast, speaking just as briskly.

"You won't see those caribou. That herd is only fourteen animals. We don't give out information on where they are." He stood, took a file out of a cabinet, then went back to his report. His movements said he worked out a lot. He took pride in his uniform.

"I saw them once. With my dad. Around '85. The herd numbered over sixty then." He wasn't listening. "He was the district ranger. He had that office back there."

My father would take my mom, Becky, and me into his office. Photos of us sat on his desk. This deputy was around my dad's age when he died.

He looked up—another sudden move—as my last few sentences sunk in.

"When?"

"1980 to 1989."

He got friendly. "What's your name?"

"John Randall Andrews. Randy. That was my father's name, too."

He walked to the counter and put out his hand. "Greg. Nice to meet you. Thanks for stopping by. Hey. Can I show you something? Come here."

It was on the wall outside the door of the office in back. A plaque with my father's photo. It read:

> *John Randall Andrews, II*
> *Ranger, Sandpoint Ranger District*
> *EOW: June 3, 1989*

"I never met your dad, Randy. That was before my time. People say good things about him."

My father was smiling and didn't look so huge. Greg stepped back, giving me space. I studied the plaque again, committing the photo and verbiage to memory.

I can't believe I never brought my sons up here.

"Chad Garrison still work for the Forest Service?"

"No. Chad retired four, five years ago. He's living somewhere near Palm Springs. He retired out of the Coeur d'Alene office. He was the district ranger after your dad. Chad was sick of the cold."

The deputy, Greg, smiled, and I once again thought of how he really did remind me of Darnell.

"Hey, sorry if I was a little rude before," he said. "I thought you were another flatlander out to shoot a caribou. Let me show you something."

He walked to a map on the wall. "I was up there two weeks ago. I didn't see the herd, but I saw fresh tracks. It was here."

He had his finger on Border Mountain.

That night at the hotel in Sandpoint, I wrote Athena.

> Athena:
>
> I have good news. Tomorrow afternoon, I am picking up John and Danny at the airport in Spokane. We are going to Northern Idaho for four days backpacking. I will do my best to get John close enough to photograph some endangered species.

He is taking pictures for a college project.

I haven't been back to Idaho in 25 years. This country is home to me. It feels like I never left. I never told you much about the years before my dad died. I was sixteen when he was shot by a hunter.

I don't think you've seen mountains like these. These are the Rocky Mountains, the backbone of North America. With wolves and grizzly bears and . . . COUGARS TOO. Looking out the window, I wonder, why didn't I bring my boys here sooner? I am afraid all I am doing now is playing catch-up, doing what I should have done years ago.

Today I was driving across Idaho. Some of the taller mountains have snow. They are so beautiful. I feel so small. Remember you said palm trees made you feel free? I feel that way in these mountains. Sometimes I look at them and know that everything has a purpose, and there is a God, even for guys who've done what I have.

You were right. I wasn't ready back then. I do love you.
Randy

Her response came in minutes.
Randy:

There is a purpose to everything. Remember the time you said you could make the world you wanted. I was wrong when I said you couldn't. I believe we can. I believe you will.

I am doing fine, living in Quepos, Costa Rica. Remember I showed you the pictures? The ocean is calm and clean, not like the rough, dirty water along Rosarito Beach.

I am saying prayers for you. I am asking for your guardian angel to come and help your sons see what a good man and father you are.

Love, Athena

Two days later, the boys arrived at five. I was waiting just outside the security area at the Spokane airport. I saw them before they saw me. It had been almost two years.

John looked more like me than I remembered, an inch taller and a little leaner, but he had my build. He walked with his chest puffed out and his shoulders back, exuding an air of confidence. Same cleft chin. Same eyes and strong gaze. So serious. I still saw the little boy sitting on the couch with me watching war movies. He was pulling a Nikon carry-on bag.

Danny was a step back, shuffling his feet fast to keep up with his brother. He had Sara's blond hair and long face. He was laughing like a kid on vacation. He threw his head back and it reminded me of the way Sara once laughed.

"John. Danny."

They stopped. It looked like Danny was ready to say, "Dad," but John put his hand on his shoulder. Both said, "Hello."

John's tone said this would be tougher than I thought. I didn't try to hug them.

"How was your flight?"

"Okay," John said.

"It was a direct flight?"

John rolled his eyes. "You don't know?"

"No, I do. I was just asking."

"Then you don't need to ask."

Danny was wheeling a carry-on bag. I watched him push it back and forth.

"You both have luggage?" John nodded. "Let's go get it."

John's expression suggested he was going to a funeral or something equally unpleasant.

"How's your photography coming, John?"

"You mean my major? My college major?"

"Yeah. I do."

"Oh," he said.

His back was stiff, as if his spine was fused from his head to his butt.

"How's school, Danny?

"S'okay."

"You like your teachers?"

"They're okay."

After a few more tries I ran out of questions. We watched the circling luggage until John walked over and took two bags riding side by side on the belt. John said, "Here," sliding one to Danny.

"I'm parked out front. Hey, you have to see my truck. It was my dad's." I heard only the wheels of their luggage. They made scraping noises on the asphalt of the parking lot.

I said I would put the luggage in the bed, but John beat me to it. He threw Danny's two pieces on the truck. Then he heaved up his suitcase. I put the three into the toolbox I'd installed a week before this trip.

"So, what do you think of the truck?" Danny liked it. He was running his hand on the paint. "And if it rains?" John said. "That toolbox doesn't look waterproof."

"Don't worry. It is," I said. "I have plastic just in case. Danny, why don't you sit in the middle? Guys, I rode in this truck with my dad. I'd sit where you are, John. Are you two hungry? I already have our rooms. You want to stop? Your mom said you'd like pizza."

Silence. It was tight with three of us in the cab.

I saw the lights of our hotel a mile off. "Okay. We'll stop here," I said, pulling into the parking lot of Antonio's Pizzeria and shutting off the engine. I started to get out.

"We just had pizza," Danny said. John was smiling and nodding. "Mom took us for lunch on the way to the airport."

"So what would you like, Danny?"

I thought he wouldn't answer. "Mexican."

"Okay. I saw a place."

Over dinner at The Matador, I spread a map out on the table.

"Here's where we are. This is where the caribou herd was last seen. Do you know much about them, John? There aren't many left."

John answered, releasing a floodgate of sarcasm. "The mountain caribou, also known as the woodland caribou, is the most endangered species in the lower forty-eight states. They number a dozen. The only remaining herd inhabits the panhandle of Idaho.

"They are known as the *gray ghosts* because they are never seen," he finished, turning stony eyes on me. "And you think *you* can get me to a spot where I can photograph these animals, these gray ghosts?"

"I'll do my best."

"When's the last time you were in these woods? Forty years?"

"I spoke with a ranger today. He said there are fourteen."

"Well, you and he must know something the New York Times doesn't," John said. "The article said there are twelve."

Though he wasn't making pleasant conversation easy, I was determined to try.

"Last of the Wild: Through the Eyes of a Predator? How did you pick the name?"

"Humans have decimated our wild places," he said. "The predator I am referring to is us."

"You want to tell me what type of project this is? Are you publishing an article?"

"Not really," he said, giving me a fuck-off smile, then laughing. John looked at Danny, who began laughing with him.

This would be a long five days, trying to find gray ghosts that wander over 500,000 acres with these two.

That night, I prayed on my knees by the side of the hotel bed.

"Give me a fuckin' break with my boys, Lord. Something. Please."

I figured He would at least listen, if only to hear what the hell I had to say. It had been a long time since we'd talked.

CHAPTER 39

During the two-hour drive from Spokane, only I spoke. I parked at the end of the Forest Service road halfway up Border Mountain.

These two never had carried a ruck. It took half an hour to redistribute the weight in their packs. A few times, I wanted to ask John, "Did you actually *read* my packing list?" Fortunately, I had brought extras of everything and added them to his pack. Danny's had everything on the list, plus a Ziploc bag of candy bars that wasn't.

Our three packs were lined up on the tailgate.

"We need to talk about bears, guys."

My dad's Henry .45-70 was in the gun safe in my cabin. Sara talked me into leaving it at home. "John hates guns. It'll make this harder if you bring it, Randy." She emailed articles that said bear spray was more effective than a bullet in deterring a grizzly attack.

A spray bottle for a grizzly? I didn't believe the articles. Most people would freeze, did not have the wherewithal to kill a charging bear with a firearm, the articles said.

I did. But I wanted a relationship with my sons more than with any firearm. So I had a can of bear spray in a holster on my hip.

"There's bears up here. Black bears aren't much of a risk. Grizzly bears are. We do not want to surprise them. They will avoid us, but we need to make noise out here so they know we are coming.

"If you don't want to talk, John," I continued, looking at him, "sing, whistle . . . whatever. I have bear spray."

I patted the canister on my hip.

John gave me another this-guy-is-an-idiot look. This was too important.

"John. You've never done anything like this. So, please, lose the attitude and listen. I was brought up in these mountains. If you want to feel the pucker factor, you just face off with a grizzly. They are six . . . maybe eight hundred pounds. Nothing on earth is more dangerous than a mother with cubs. They are aggressive. *They will kill you.* You got that?"

I had made my point with John, but I didn't like Danny's expression. In getting John's attention, I'd scared the crap out of both of them.

"We talk going up the hill. We let bears know we're coming. If we see one, we avoid it. If one approaches, we stop, group up. We raise our arms so we look bigger. And this is the most important thing . . . we do not run. Running triggers their predatory instinct to chase and kill. A grizzly can do forty miles per hour. You can't outrun them. You got that?"

Their faces said they did.

"If they do come after you, you drop and play dead. You got that. Drop and play dead."

"Okay, that's over. Let's have some fun, gentlemen. We're getting John up close and personal with some endangered species."

We were moving up the trail my dad and I took in 1983.

I remembered it differently. More views over open country to the mountains, more green meadows. I think my memory added grandeur. The trail was overgrown, ferns thick along each side. At times, it felt like hiking through the jungle. Walking two paces ahead of my sons, I did all the talking.

Walking side by side, both had the same slumped shoulders, heads down, and feet shuffling. They moved as if weighed down, even though

John's pack was only twenty-five pounds, and Danny's fifteen.

"I hiked this trail in '83, headed just where we're going. Somewhere around there, at least."

"Hmmm." I think that came from John.

They looked away when I looked back.

"I was with my dad on my first hunting trip. I was ten. I snuck the makings of s'mores along. Remember, we used to make them, John. When my dad found them in my backpack, we drove back down the mountain. He chewed my ass out all the way down and all the way back up the mountain."

"That must be where he gets it," John muttered, just loud enough for me to hear.

"Then we hiked up this trail," I said. "We didn't say anything. I was too scared to talk."

I heard whispering but couldn't make out words. I pointed out animal signs along the trail. Several times deer tracks crossed the trail. In a meadow the muddy ground was chewed up, filled with tracks. Some blood. "This is elk rutting season, guys. Bull elk are up here fighting for the cows. They go crazy."

"See that tree, how the bark is rubbed off? A bear did that, scratching his ass. A black bear. But we don't need to worry about them."

Their expressions said they were worried, anyway.

At our stop for the night, I wouldn't let them have a fire.

"It scares the animals."

So, we sat in the dark, eating lukewarm rehydrated dehydrated beef stew heated over a portable burner.

"I'll get you to your photographs, John. I don't know anything about taking pictures. You're the hunter. It will be your call how to take the shots. We'll see elk. I will try for the caribou."

"I'm a *photographer*," John corrected me.

I quit making small talk.

I'd made them leave their phones in the truck. There was no signal up here, but it was more than that. I didn't want them doing what teens do, looking at them all the time. Under the full moon, I could see their faces. John kept checking his empty back pocket, then wincing.

My father and I sat in silence the first night of that hunt. We were probably camped near this place.

I had high expectations for this trip, saw it playing out differently. I did not think it would be this bad.

But they had agreed to come. "I love you two," I said.

John looked at Danny, shook his head. Neither said anything.

"And . . . I'm sorry for what I did. Hurting your mother that day. Things were bad for me then."

I didn't think John and Danny knew anything about PTSD or flashbacks. They didn't know much about me either, only that I hurt their mom. My apology sounded hollow. I'd forgotten how to talk to them.

In the moonlight and silence, I could see anger on John's face. I think part of it was at himself. I had reminded him that he'd done nothing to protect his mother.

Maybe I should have listened to Sara and done something less ambitious.

"How's school, Danny?"

"Okay," he said. The two were across from me, their legs crossed, knees touching.

"You like your teachers?" I asked.

He didn't answer. John did. "You asked him that. You don't know much about him, do you, Randy?"

My right ear was ringing.

"I'm trying here, John."

And my son, who had my name and looked so much like me, yelled.

"You're trying? *Now* you're fucking trying? There were a lot of years I wanted you to try, Randy. Where the fuck were you?" He got louder.

I followed Sara's advice and let him vent.

"All those years you were off killing people. Always leaving, then after a while you came back, but you weren't *there* anymore. All those things Mom took us to—alone—because you were off defending your country."

His gaze heated. "What did it get you, Randy? Fucking answer me that! Now you want us to come up here to relive some goddamn turkey hunt you went on when you were ten. How in hell did you think you could do that?

"I don't know why the fuck I agreed to this. Mom pushed me. Remember her, that lady you shoved into the wall? She thought it was a good idea.

"You know something? You want to fuckin' *know* something? I was actually proud of you for a long time. I'm not now. You haven't changed."

John was burning out, his voice half its earlier volume. He looked ready to cry. "Now we can't even have a fire because it scares the animals, the ones you say I'm hunting with this camera."

He kicked at the ground in front of him, again looking over at me. "Is *that* why you think we came on this with you? To *take pictures*? You want to know what you are? You're a fucking idiot."

Danny was writing in the dirt with a stick. I heard movement in the distance, a small animal John's rant hadn't scared off. He broke the silence. His voice had a bite.

"I heard you talking with your buddies in the backyard, drinking beer . . . heard the things you joked about. Seeing people blown up, wasting some motherfucker, punching some asshole's ticket? Really funny shit, Randy. How many tickets did you punch?"

"We were just blowing off steam, John," I said. "I saw a lot of shit. It's hard to leave it over there."

"No shit. You brought it home. I guess bringing it home was okay?"

"No, it wasn't."

John was trying to be stoic, but his tears wouldn't let him.

"Yeah. I did a lot of shit wrong, John. I love you. Both of you. You know that, don't you?"

John looked at the dirt between us, the place a campfire was supposed to be.

He was right. My father earned the right to make me sit in the dark without a fire, to take away my rifle for sneaking s'mores on a hunting trip. I hadn't. My boys were strangers.

Danny spoke. "I took your article to class for Veterans Day, Dad."

John glared at him.

"What did you take to school?" I asked.

"The newspaper article about you and the cougar. I took three articles to school. You were in all the papers, all over the internet, on the TV. It was about all the medals you have, all the things you did in war and how you saved the cougar by stealing her from a bar in Mexico and bringing her back to the US."

I started laughing. Danny laughed, too. If I had been sitting next to him, I would have hugged him.

"Well, all I can say is it seemed like a good idea at the time."

John laughed, but there was no humor in it. Selling John on the idea I was not an asshole would be near impossible. I needed a miracle. An owl hooted in a tree across the meadow.

"My teacher said you were a hero because you saved the mountain lion."

"Your dad's a fool, Danny," I responded.

Danny and I started laughing.

"If you want it, and if your school says yes, I can bring that mountain lion I saved to your school. Her name is Matilda. I also have two dogs and a raccoon. We travel as a team."

Danny and I talked while John stared at the ground. Danny wanted me to come to his school. He liked having a dad who'd been a soldier, but I was afraid I was only an exciting stranger to him.

I couldn't fix all of the damage, but there was something I could fix right now.

"Gentlemen, we need a fire," I decided. "Let's find some wood and kindling and get one going. I'm about to freeze my ass off."

My dad was a hero.

I know now what heroes look like. It's a therapist in his 70s who's dying yet keeps showing up to help veterans. A ballsy young lawyer who volunteers to defend a man she'd never met. A Vietnam vet who builds a sanctuary for big cats because he doesn't like how they are being treated. It's a woman with a scar, who goes on living and finding and bringing out the best in those around her after enduring the worst thing imaginable.

CHAPTER 40

The next morning, we reassembled our packs and started on the trail. We were headed to the peak of Border Mountain, another four miles.

The sky was blue and clean, no clouds. The trail cut through old-growth cedars. It had rained lightly the night before and drying grass scented the air. Birds chirped. Squirrels ran on the rough bark of the trees, hiding on the far side and then running around to watch us after we passed.

We were headed to the meadow just shy of the ridge where I killed my turkey. I was going by memory. It had been more than twenty-five years since I had walked this ground.

John hadn't said a word all morning. But at least he wasn't trying to shut his brother down. Danny and I talked. With him, it was getting easier. I would look for things and point them out. Then I'd search for something else.

"That's deer scat." I stopped, pointing to seven piles of crap under some fern fronds.

There were four more piles in the dirt just up the trail.

"What's scat?" Danny asked.

"He means deer shit, you dumb shit." John laughed, sharp and mocking.

Danny turned and tried to give a fierce look to his brother. He'd need to work on that look for it to have any bite. "Shut up, John," he said.

I was treading lightly, but I was still their dad. "John." I looked at him. "Your brother's not a dumb shit. Don't call him that."

He shook his head, then let out a breath. I think my sudden rapport with Danny bothered him. I could tell John was ready with a retort, so I spoke.

"Yeah, you're right, John. It's deer shit. You know why that's important?" I sounded like a professor teaching class. "You can tell they were left on different days. See that? Some are drier. They're returning to eat the grass in this meadow. They stay near the edge of the clearing so they can duck into the woods if they detect a predator. If I was hunting, I would set up just inside the tree line over there about two hours before dawn."

"So you could kill them?" John's voice had a sarcastic, self-satisfied ring, like he was unveiling some hidden truth. "Right? Right?"

He wanted me to engage. I took a breath. "No, I'd just take their pictures. I don't kill animals anymore. I may get myself a nice camera, like you. I'll come up and take picture. I forgot how much I love it out here." I paused, took in our position. "The wind's kicking up."

I was looking for a place to take a break when we walked into a large meadow. The wind was blowing directly in our faces. Weather changed fast up here. Clouds were coming from the west and raindrops began stinging my face. Thunder cracked in the distance and echoed. The air felt heavy and wet. Above there was only a cloud ceiling. It looked like I could hit it with a rock.

The wind increased to about thirty miles per hour. Storms were rough in these mountains. It looked like one was coming.

The clouds dropped more. Just ahead, the trail went into dense forest. Ferns took over. Danny said raindrops were stinging his face. John lagged ten feet behind. "Oh, great. Fuckin' rain," he said.

Then I felt it.

Something was wrong. That tingling feeling hit the hairs on my neck. This wasn't PTSD. I hadn't felt this way since my last tour. I was off-kilter, as if the air pressure suddenly dropped. The birds and the squirrels disappeared even before the rain started.

It wasn't the rhythm that was off. Only humans did that to the wild places.

We were in danger. If I had a rifle I would have taken it off safe.

"Halt!" I said in a whisper, spitting the words so my boys could hear over the wind. I held up my fist. They stopped. I was on instinct. It all made sense again. I knew where the danger was, but not what it was. We were not welcome up ahead on the trail.

"Back up. Slow. Don't turn, quiet," I said. We began walking backward. "Stay together." John had moved up by me and my left palm was on his chest. My right was on Danny's.

Wolves? A mountain lion?

The wind smelled of wet grass, strong, like an entire lawn cut and stuffed in a bag and held under my nose.

My father knew everything about surviving up here. "Animals smell like what they eat, Randy." Then I knew what quieted the forest. One animal had a diet of mainly grass and roots. I also sensed it did not know we were here, and that any encounter would be a surprise.

A thirty mile-per-hour of rainy wind pelted our faces.

John said, "What is—"

"Quiet," I whispered. "Both of you. Back up softly. I'll tell you in a minute what's going on."

With a grimace I tried to convey this was no time for a discussion. Danny didn't worry me. His eyes were huge, and he was breathing fast. But John had that teen *you're a dumbshit* expression he had been wearing since we started this hike. He wasn't afraid.

I was.

After another twenty steps, I said, "We are going to head back down the trail. Slowly. Silent. You two stay ahead of me."

I had a bowie knife. On our way up, John saw it on my hip. "Who do you think you are, Crocodile Dundee?" he mocked. I undid the clasp.

I spoke, enunciating. "We will stay in a group. I will stay in front of you two. No fast movements. *Do . . . not . . . run.* Do not say a word. Why aren't you guys moving?"

"What is it?" John wasn't whispering. He was facing me, but at least he was moving backward.

"I'll tell you after."

"What is it?" he asked again. He rolled his eyes, muttering under his breath. I couldn't hear the words, but I could guess what they were.

I didn't answer. Just a little farther, and John could forever think I had overreacted.

He stopped. I pushed him lightly, but his feet were stuck to the ground. He stared at me angrily, his lips twitching.

"John, move!"

I was as stern as I could be in a whisper. I pushed him again, but he was planted.

Not now, John, please . . . not now.

"John, it's a grizzly. This is fall. They are very dangerous now. We may have walked into something we do not want to approach. Now, would you *please* keep moving?" I looked into his eyes.

John spoke. "You said we should make noise, not be silent. Remember you said that? *Now* we're supposed to be quiet?"

"I know. I did. Right now I think it's best we stay quiet and avoid the bear."

I longed for my father's rifle. The bear spray was useless. Only John, Danny and I would be blinded if I used it in this wind.

"You can't know all this shit," John said. He threw my hand off his chest, then stood, his face fierce like some crazy tribal mask. "This is fucking bullshit, do you know that?" He was yelling. "This whole trip is such fucking bullshit. Deer shit and grizzly bears. You're so full of shit!" He was screaming. "I don't know why I came. There isn't a fucking thing ahead of us." He stared, his jaw tight, the anger frozen on his face.

The rain had stopped but the wind picked up even more and the silence ended. I turned to look up ahead where the trail entered the forest.

The brush in the thicket began to shake. There was crashing, a sound of ferns and plants being crushed, stomped and broken. It was loud, an angry sound, paws slamming into the ground. It came from an animal that didn't give a shit about noise. He owned this forest.

The grizzly broke through the fern thicket and headed toward us, head down, at thirty miles per hour.

It was a huge male that would kill us if we ran. "Stay put," was all I said.

Thirty-five feet up the trail he lifted his front paws, slamming them into the ground. The stop was abrupt, and he slid a few feet. He stared, his massive head moving from side to side like a pendulum. He weighed maybe eight hundred fifty pounds, as large as grizzlies get up here.

He was huffing. Water droplets hung on the end of his golden hairs. He made a clacking noise with his teeth, closing and opening his jaw, the sound of an ax hitting cement. He must have some prize—a dead elk or deer—ahead.

His eyes were locked on us, daring us to look at him.

I whispered without turning my head. "Do exactly as I say. Do not run. Do not look into his eyes. Look at the ground. Keep your arms out. We will keep walking backward. Slow. No fast movements. He's got something . . . food, probably. I don't think he will hurt us. We need to show him we are no threat."

We continued to back up. Danny began sniffling, then he whimpered.

"Quiet Danny, don't cry. Stay in a bunch behind me."

There was only the smell of wet grass.

I lied to my sons because I didn't want them to run. This bear was close to killing us. If I had my dad's .45-70, I would have flattened him when he charged from the thicket. He was stamping his feet. His ears were back, streamlining his head for the charge. Every two seconds, geysers puffed from his nostrils.

If he charged, I would fight him and he would kill me—but not before I plunged the knife into that thick hide of his four or five times. Maybe I could hurt him enough for my sons to live.

We moved back another ten feet. Then another ten. Only fifty feet separated us.

He lowered his head. The geysers stopped; he stamped his feet once more, then roared and charged.

A brown, hairy shape the size of a Volkswagen charged with its massive head down. He came to an abrupt halt twenty feet away, his feet sliding in the dirt. I saw his claws.

Bluff charge.

The only thing I could think of doing was to try to get inside his head, to feel his rhythm. His breaths were loud, and the wet-grass smell was overwhelming.

The trail moved next to a river. I thought of the map and remembered. My father and I swam near here. The water was deep and slow. There were cliffs along the river's edge. It was only forty feet off the trail. If I gave them a head start, the bear wouldn't follow them into the water.

Maybe I *could* die at Firdos Square, after all.

"John, listen," I said over my shoulder. "You are to get your brother down the trail. Keep backing up together. I am going to stand here. If he attacks, I will fight him. The two of you drop your packs and run to your left. There's a steep slope and a river. Fifty feet. Jump into it. It is deep and slow here. The river goes southwest to the highway. The trail runs along the river for two miles. The bear won't follow you there."

Splitting up is almost always a bad idea with a grizzly. This time it wasn't. I felt it.

I turned and looked at John one last time as I handed him the keys to the truck. I saw it, then; he once more was the boy who wore my uniform, the one I watched war movies with on Saturday mornings.

He was *my son*, my father's grandson. John Randall Andrews IV.

And that was enough.

"Do it. Please." I looked at the bear. Behind me, I heard them moving.

The bear had grown bigger. The hump on his back shook fast like tremors, wet golden hair shooting water droplets. He was dogging me. I wished I'd told my sons I loved them.

I spoke gently, a monotone loud enough for the bear to hear over the wind. "I'm not letting you hurt my boys."

Time had slowed for the bear and me. John and Danny still were moving back, and the bear still hadn't moved. The grizzly was probably twenty. An old warrior. I now could see he was missing one ear. One shoulder was all scar tissue.

Last time counts for all. I looked into his eyes.

My chest tightened. The air was bad, but that was only part of it. It was fear rising, closing off my throat. I opened my window to listen. Hamm's right arm jutted from the window of the Humvee, his thumbs-up gesture a big fuck you to Sergeant First Class Promotable Andrews. I knew then how much he hated me.

He moved that hand up and down as the left tires brushed the curb. The thumb stayed pointed to the sky. Above it all in the distance, those four smokestacks spewed that shit I was breathing.

Then it all disappeared.

Everything exploded. Six blasts in a line, a daisy chain that took out Hamm's entire platoon and one of the SUVs. I watched the shock waves, speed of sound, rocking palms, the air blast alone knocking down mud walls. Huge mounds rising from the dirt. One of the blasts was directly under Hamm's Humvee, launching 6,500 pounds of metal and flesh thirty feet into the air.

The vehicle flipped, landing on its roof. Then the second round of explosions hit directly underneath the Humvee. It rose again, but I couldn't see how much. Everything was dirt and fire and black smoke.

I rubbed my hand on my neck; it was bloody, sliced open. Deep, but nothing major. Blood oozed from my right ear. I couldn't hear out of it. Even with earplugs, the blast blew out my eardrum.

Then I saw the man on the cell phone in the third-floor window of a building a hundred meters from the road. I ordered our .50 cal and the SAWs to lay down suppressive fire as we ran into the destruction. I didn't wait for the lieutenant to give the order.

I screamed into the radio. "First platoon, out, now! Gunners, I need suppressive fire on those buildings to the right. Sir, Pearce, call in a medivac. Medivac, medivac. Twenty-one down."

I pulled the number from my ass. I needed those birds. Pearce was outside his Humvee. He looked dazed.

I moved to what remained of second platoon. Hamm's Humvee took the worst. I looked in, prayed somebody would be alive. Five guys had been inside. I saw an arm. It was big, must have been Vince's. Our two medics took one look at Hamm's vehicle and moved to the next.

I heard gunfire, AK 47, from the three-story building. *Ambush.* They were moving into the street.

I don't remember all I did. I did not take cover. I gathered first platoon. I ran into gunfire. Insane, I wanted to die. Twelve of us cleared the street and ran to that building, moving floor to floor, room to room. The insurgents split up. It was easy to kill them, piecemeal.

Nineteen insurgents were cleared. All except one was dead.

I found him on the third floor, looking out a window to the street. I emptied a magazine into the room. Thirty rounds. He was on the floor, mouthing something, reaching his hand to me. He had four, maybe more, bullet holes in his chest. I was alone with him. I kicked his AK-47 across the room. He was all blood. It came from his lips. Had I been a medic, I would have written this guy off.

The cell phone was on the floor by the window. This motherfucker was the one. My finger was on the trigger, the lever on auto. Ready for the satisfaction, the release, wanting to see the bullets make the fucker hop. We stared at each other for ten seconds. I saw his eyes in my sights. His corneas were gray.

I lowered the barrel.

Lieutenant Pearce ran into the room.

"Andrews, Sergeant Andrews!" he said. "Thank God." He let out a long breath of air, put his hand on my shoulder and started crying.

I patted his shoulder. I felt close to him. I'm not sure why.

"Good job, LT."

"Thanks for calling that halt, sergeant."

Maybe I couldn't finish off the guy on the floor. But I damned sure wasn't helping him.

Pearce still looked dazed.

"Lieutenant Pearce. You're the senior officer. You need to account for your troops. And I'm not sure we've killed everyone we need to. And you need to get those birds in safely without an RPG taking them out."

Pearce was twenty-two. His tears made lines in the dust on his cheeks.

"That's what officers do, sir. Take charge."

Pearce's face had a glow, as if he was looking at a saint descended to earth. All I did was survive. My friends took my place in line in that convoy. I felt blood running out my ear. I didn't feel the pain.

Second platoon was all casualties. The lead Humvee was a total loss, all killed—Hamm, my two best friends, the gunner and the driver. Four died in the second Humvee. Two each in the third and fourth Humvees.

Pearce put me in for a Silver Star. The citation read, *First Sergeant John Randall Andrews, III. without regard for his personal safety, demonstrated unparalleled courage and composure under relentless enemy fire, rallying the survivors of a massive blast from an Improvised Explosive Device and leading an assault into a fortified enemy position, killing nineteen enemy combatants, thereby saving the lives of the surviving soldiers of first platoon and six civilian contractors.*

When I got home I was awarded the medal, along with two Purple Hearts for the shrapnel wound to my face and neck and the hearing loss.

Colonel Cox ordered me to attend the ceremony. The medals stayed at the bottom of my footlocker, then moved to the bottom of the tool locker on my truck. I'm not sure why I never threw them away.

That motherfucker on the floor actually survived.

Why couldn't I let this one go? I didn't kill my friends. It was those insurgents. They put a bomb by the road. And Hamm. He drove right into the blast.

But I knew.

Hamm's arm shot from the window. His thumb rose to the sky and started waving up and down. Then I saw the flash, huge, a hundred feet across, then everything disappeared into smoke.

And I was glad, fuckin' happy, that I was alive — that it was my friends and not me who'd been blown up.

Vince and Darnell would have died for me. That's what I couldn't forgive myself for.

Staring into that bear's eyes, I thought of Athena's message on the photo: *Sometimes the hardest person to forgive is yourself.*

And I understood. It never had been my fault.

I forgave myself.

The wind stopped and the rain went down to a light drizzle. I felt sun on my right cheek. The bear and I still faced off. If I was going to use the spray, the time was now.

I put my hand on the canister but didn't take it out. The geysers were still blowing out his nostrils, but they'd slowed to every seven or eight seconds. He wasn't stamping his feet anymore, either.

I am not sure what convinced him, but he turned and ran back up the trail like he remembered something he'd forgotten.

I walked to my sons. They were seventy-five feet down the hill, all big eyes and jerky movements. They'd seen it all.

"Let's keep moving away from him," I said. "He could come back, but I don't think he will." We walked down the way we'd come, into the forest, then into a second meadow. I couldn't smell wet grass anymore. The rain stopped. A bird sang in one of the cedars. Then dozens of birds were singing. A squirrel ran around a tree to our left.

I was never happier to see a squirrel.

"This is enough," I said, a hundred meters down the trail. I was looking at their backs. "Turn around. Let me look at you two." I put my hand on Danny's shoulder. Then I put my other hand on John's. "Good job, guys. One screwup and he would have charged. I saw grizzlies as a boy. Never like that."

Both of them looked at me, their mouths open, silent. I thought again of how Lieutenant Pearce had looked at me that day.

Danny burst into tears and put his arms around me. I pulled John to us and he started crying, too. I hugged them and said I was so proud they were my sons, that if we had made one wrong move we would all be dead.

We all laughed. It was exhilarating. I laughed this way with my Rangers after we wiped out those Republican Guard. This was better.

I pulled the map from my pocket. A large flat area was ahead on the trail in the direction the bear moved. I thought it might be a meadow but was relying on old memories. There were sheer cliffs on one side of the meadow that no bear could climb. I spread the map on a rock.

"How good is your zoom lens, John? I mean, how far out can you get a close-up shot?'

"Three hundred yards."

"Can I show you something on the map? See this big flat area? It's a guess, but I think the bear is around here." I pointed directly ahead. "Now, see all these lines bunched up on the east side? That's a straight drop. Those cliffs are about a half-mile northeast. We can circle around this bear downwind, so he can't smell us. I'll get you to within a hundred yards and that grizzly won't be able to do a goddamned thing about it."

"We're not going home?" John asked.

"Hell, no. You're a *photographer*. You got a mission. I said I'd get you to the pictures. And he's the only bear on this mountain."

John looked unconvinced.

"If you were him, would you share it? We'll avoid him."

We headed back up the trail and then moved cross-country, circling to the east of the meadow where I was guessing the bear went.

We flanked him, staying downwind. "Careful, the cliff is up ahead." It was a sheer granite drop of eighty feet. We looked into the meadow and there he was, a football field away.

"There's your shot, John. Now, be really quiet and don't let him see you. He can't get up this cliff, but I don't want to tempt him to try."

The grizzly was devouring what was left of a cow elk, ripping the flesh and jerking his head to the sky while he gulped the meat. I doubt he'd killed it. It probably had been wounded by a hunter and ran off to die.

The grizzly picked up on something and stood on his back legs, head to the sky, nine feet tall, sniffing. Then he went back to his elk. If he was smelling us, he must have known we didn't want raw elk meat.

John's camera clicked as he took his photographs, two shots a second. He was at the edge of the cliff, as close as he could get without falling over.

I was thankful Sara talked me out of bringing my .45-70, after all.

CHAPTER 41

It had been thirty-two years since I'd braced my Henry on these boulders.

My memory was mostly accurate. Drilling that turkey through the head *was* a tough shot from sixty yards with iron sights. But the crack of that bullet firing didn't echo over Border Mountain and into Canada and west to the mountains of Washington State. It was only a .22. Washington was twenty miles away.

I found what I thought was the spot where my father and I had camped, the place he made me remove my jacket and keep my mouth shut to teach me about the rhythm of a place.

Nothing changed up here. The mountains stayed the same.

John Randall Andrews II would have been disappointed at our huge fire. I told my sons about the hunting and camping trips my father and I took up here. I should have brought the makings of s'mores.

Everything was funny around that fire. I told stories. "Once, I cried because I lost a candy bar. I snuck it out of the mess hall. That was against the rules of Ranger school. It was swamp phase in Florida, the middle of winter and around eleven at night. I was under a fern sitting in cold mud under a bush. Life sucked bad. Then it started to rain. I reached into my pocket because I was going to eat that bar. But the bar was gone. Just the paper was there. The water had dissolved it."

I watched John and Danny as they stared into the fire.

"I'd been up thirty hours. I started to cry. One of my buddies walked up, sloshing in the mud, asked me what the hell I was crying about. I told him. So he reached into his pocket and pulls out a candy bar. His was dry. He gave me half. 'How did you do it, how did you keep it dry?' I asked him. 'It's called a plastic bag, dumbass.'"

We camped for three days in that spot. I spent time with my boys and actually tried to teach them some things about these mountains. John took great photos of deer and elk—even a turkey hen—with that huge zoom lens.

He actually called me *Dad* a few times.

CHAPTER 42

"Keep it down, boys." Our coats hung from a cedar. It was around forty degrees.

The sky was clear but, to the west, clouds were headed our way. They were taking their time.

"Do you feel the air? The air pressure? Rain is coming." I was whispering.

And John asked, "How do you know all this stuff?"

"I spent the first sixteen years of my life up here. We're heading out to a few places today before our hike back to the truck. Now, let's listen. The animals move to the rhythm of the forest. So we'll be quiet, perfectly quiet. This may take a while."

I watched a minor miracle unfold; John and Danny actually shut up and quit making noise.

I understand why my father did not want a fire. All I smelled was burned wood. The wind was beginning to pick up, bringing clouds from the west.

After ten minutes, I began to hear birds and squirrels. One squirrel ran into our camp and scampered in short bursts of three feet. One of his bursts took him over John's shoes. He looked up, made an *Oh, shit, that's a human!* expression and bolted up a tree.

After a few more minutes of silence, I saw my boys look toward the meadow at the same time. Whatever was there, I couldn't hear it.

Then I did. It was movement in the trees on the north side of the meadow. Brush was cracking and there were the rustling and crashing sounds of large animals moving through thick forest.

Clouds were coming in just over the treetops. The wind was cool and moist and hitting our faces, blowing the sounds to us. The crashes were growing louder.

Elk, I thought. A bull with his harem. This spot was beautiful. John would get great photos. The crashes got louder, and I saw brush moving at the edge of the woods.

I sucked in air.

A caribou bull, six hundred pounds, sauntered from the brush into the field. His antlers pointed to the sky and then curved inward. He looked in all directions, then looked back to where he emerged into the meadow. Another caribou joined him, then another, until a herd of fourteen, including two juvenile caribou, stood together in the meadow.

All of the adults had antlers. Most of the herd began eating the long grass. The two juveniles stayed with their mothers. Some of the animals had their noses raised in the air.

They were a half-mile off. For great shots, John had to get within three hundred yards.

I tried to keep excitement from my voice. "You need to film this. Nobody gets to film this. Let's move out. Really slow and quiet."

The caribou were relaxed as we moved toward the meadow. It took us half an hour to cut the distance in half. I handed the binoculars to John.

"You see the two large boulders on the south side of the meadow?" I asked him. "If you can make it there, you'll be sixty yards from the herd, downwind. These animals spook easily. Danny, you and I will watch the herd from here. Only John's going on. You brother needs to be quieter than he's ever been."

John smiled as I squeezed his shoulder. "You got this."

I was so scared they would spook and John wouldn't get his photos. I needn't have worried. Though he wasn't a killer, he was a hunter, fully focused on his target and moving silently. Danny and I watched him for the ten minutes he took to set up behind the boulders and point his camera at the herd.

The herd stayed, eating the grass, heads pointing north to the summit of the mountain. The clouds had dropped and were skimming the treetops. The green of the cedars and the white of the clouds formed a beautiful backdrop for the animals.

All the times with my father and I had never seen these animals. They truly were the gray ghosts of these mountains.

John was behind those rocks for fifteen minutes. He took more than seven hundred photographs. Then he stepped out from behind the rocks, his camera facing the herd. The animals turned their heads, all of them, then they galloped as a group into the trees. Danny and I walked over. John was leaning against one of the boulders. I put my hand on his shoulder.

"You did it," I said.

John couldn't stand in one place. "I did. I did!" Over and over he whispered those words.

"Hey, we don't need to whisper anymore," I reminded him, smiling. "Well done."

John had found the magic in this meadow. He kept looking at his photos on the back of the camera. He showed them to us. I could see they were magnificent, *National Geographic* quality.

The faces of the caribou filled the entire screen. The best shot was the one of the herd staring and ready to bolt when he walked from behind the boulders.

"*We* did it," he said.

"You're right, John, we did it."

"Can I get a picture of the three of us?" John asked.

He put his camera on the rocks and set the timer. I was in the middle, my arms around my boys. I heard ten clicks from his camera.

This is a fucking miracle.

I cleared my throat to yell what I felt. "Yessss! We did it!" We kept screaming those words, scaring everything on that mountain. We yelled louder, jubilant.

And this time I think our yells really did make it down the north slope of Border Mountain and into Canada—maybe even all the way to Washington State.

CHAPTER 43

It was the best day, and we didn't kill anything.

The General Store in Good Grief was still in business. My boys didn't like beef sticks. "You know, Dad, there's no meat in those things," John said. "They're just scraps of skin and organs and bones left on the floors of slaughterhouses. They gather that junk up and put it in a membrane to make into that weird shape. You shouldn't eat them."

When we got back into the car, we had Cokes and beef sticks and potato chips.

"You know," I said, "I read a magazine article that quoted all these big nutrition experts. You'd get more nutrition from eating the bag than you would from those potato chips."

We laughed.

It was a great fall day in Northern Idaho. The clouds up the mountain didn't follow us down. Here it was only blue skies.

Parked outside the store, I went through my old iPod. "We need some tunes for our ride."

I had replaced the cassette player and the old speakers. The new set of Bose were even Bluetooth capable.

"Gentlemen, I'd like to introduce you to Ms. Laura Branigan. You're going to like this." I cleared my throat, ready to sing again with Laura.

I put on "Gloria" as I pulled onto US 95 and cranked up the volume. Laura rocked the cab of the truck. She was as good in 2015 as she'd been thirty-one years before. I floored it. I wanted that turkey hunt. I wanted to drive with my boys like a bat out of hell.

But it wasn't 1983.

My sons didn't know Laura Branigan. She hadn't had a hit since I was twelve. She'd been dead for eleven years.

John and Danny didn't know Patty Smyth and Scandal either.

"That song sucks," John said. "I'd shut it off if it came on the radio. Can we listen to some *good* music?"

They were united on this. Danny nodded his head in vigorous agreement.

I pulled over.

"Go ahead. Look on my iPod. I have hundreds of songs on there."

"He still uses an iPod." John said, looking at his brother. Both were smiling.

"Do you have anything from this millennium, Dad?" Danny said. I saw Darnell holding this same iPod, asking the same question.

"You know, you can keep songs on your cell phone," John added. "Or stream it." They continued to scroll through the music, passing the iPod back and forth and laughing.

"Here's something newer," John said. "'I'm Not Dead.' You and mom got me this album."

Only one album on that iPod was recorded after 2000. The blood left my face and my head got light and cool. Adrenaline kicked in. I felt sweat on my forehead that hadn't been there a moment before.

"Pink's not bad," John said. He jerked his head fast and looked into my eyes. "Dad. What's wrong? Dad, you okay?"

Darnell, Vince and I had danced like crazy men to that song. I thought on that. I made the fear pass. I felt my vision clear, and my heart slowed. The smile just came. That shit had no power anymore because I wouldn't let it.

I started laughing. John's eyes narrowed. He searched my face. "I'm just happy," I said, then added, too low for anyone but me to hear. "So fuckin' happy."

My boys laughed with me. They joined me, the three of us laughing a wild laugh that filled the cab and spilled out the open windows. It was powerful and said fuck the pain, fuck the guilt, fuck the PTSD. Embrace the craziness that began the day I met a cougar in a bar in Mexico.

"Just thinking of some good friends, that's all," I said. "Play Pink. She's gorgeous."

Darnell had said Sara looked like Pink. I hadn't seen it then, but I did now. Both blond and sharp, put-together looks. Both had long faces, squared off at the chin and forehead.

"She looks like your mother, just not so pretty. You know that?"

Pink's voice came from the speakers as I pulled back onto US 95, joining the Canadians heading south. "John, Danny, let's show these goddamned Canadians how we do business in the U . . . S . . . of A."

I punched the accelerator. Danny squealed.

I pushed that fire-engine red Ford F1 harder than my father ever did. The odometer rose to ninety-seven —as fast as that old truck could go.

We knew the words.

We hit ninety-nine.

We flew, screaming the words to "Who Knew," trying to drown out Pink.

You were wrong, Athena. A burned-out soldier with PTSD and a Mexican stripper can live happily ever after with their pet mountain lion.

Then it happened. The highway took a slight down slope. We hit one hundred miles per hour.

An old couple in a sedan with Alberta plates stared a hole through me as we blew by at forty-five miles per hour over the posted speed limit.

They saw a middle-aged guy with a beef stick hanging from his mouth, screaming like a kid.

They must have thought he was stone-cold crazy.

They would be wrong.

CHAPTER 44

"I love you, Dad."

John and Danny both said that as we parted at the airport. "I love you guys, too. Oh, and maybe we ought not mention to your mom meeting that grizzly bear on the trail? Just tell her we never got any closer than that cliff where John took his pictures."

I missed my animals down south.

My plan was to drive without stopping along the way, but I ran out of energy fifty miles south of Salt Lake City and rented a room at a Holiday Inn in American Fork, Utah.

I hadn't checked my emails since dropping off my boys.

There was one from Athena with the heading, *How did it go with your sons?*

> *Randy:*
>
> *I believe good things happened in those mountains. Somehow I know God answered my prayer and sent your guardian angel. Please let me know how it went with your sons.*
>
> *I love you.*
> *Athena*

I answered. My heading read, *Your prayers worked!!!!!*

> *Athena:*
>
> *The Good Lord did send me a guardian angel. He was 850 pounds with shaggy brown fur and four-inch claws. I am ready*

to fall asleep. I'll tell you about him sometime. I got John to some great photographs. John is going to send them to me. My sons are planning on visiting me at Christmas. I am so happy.
I love you always. Randy.

Two weeks later, I was decorating my cabin with John's photographs. My twenty favorites were now mounted on metal. In the center of the display, my boys and I stood on Border Mountain. On another wall, I mounted my three Silver Stars.

Athena had sent another email a few days ago. I hadn't responded yet.

> Randy:
> I got the photos you sent me. Amazing. It is so pretty up there. I am so happy for you. Sometimes things work out the way they should. You sound so good.
> I was considering opening a small restaurant in Quepos. That was my plan, wasn't it?
> But I want to see those mountains you talk about. I want to hear about your big guardian angel with fur and big claws. Do you really have a photo of him? It's not that bear in the photographs you sent me, is it? Why are you holding out on me? I like the photos you sent of Matilda but I want to see her in person.
> I want to see you!
> I love you.
> Athena
> El Arado Restaurant
> Puntarena Province, Quepos, Costa Rica
> 506-2519-9366 (You have to dial 011 first, then the number)

This is everything I wanted.

So why wasn't I firing off a response? Or calling her?

I went to Matilda, put on her collar, and walked her into my cabin. I opened a beer and sat on the couch. The dogs and Cleopatra were happy to see her. Matilda lay on her side and tried to groom, but the dogs kept falling over her to start a wrestling match.

"Athena wants to see me, you guys. She wants to see you, Matilda. She hasn't met you three, but she'll love you, too." Then I read her email out loud.

On the beach after Athena and I made love, I had watched her looking over the ocean. She thought I was asleep. The moon was reflected in her eyes. It felt as if I could see inside of her. She was so strong. I felt her pain and she understood mine. But there was so much more to her than that. Her laugh, her kindness, her curiosity and, yes, even her stubbornness. She was a remarkable person.

Matilda walked over to get her neck scratched. The other three joined in, pushing their necks into my hands. I only had two hands. "What do you guys think?" I asked. "She thinks I'm ready." They continued to jam in closer.

"You know, this cabin is pretty big, but all five of us are crammed into the corner of the couch." Cleopatra walked up my pants. "Damnit, Cleo," I said as her claws bit into my skin. She sat by me on the couch.

Athena had sent another email. "Listen, guys," then I read it aloud.

> *Randy:*
>
> *I can book a flight into Los Angeles International Airport. It arrives November 22 at 1:00 pm.*
>
> *If you do not want me to come, I understand. It has been a long time. Please answer.*
>
> *I love you.*
>
> *Athena*

She was arriving in nine days? I read the email three times.

I stopped breathing for a moment. I was excited and, for some reason, scared.

Scared to see her? Of fucking this up? Because what I wanted was now happening? I wasn't entirely sure.

I looked at the four faces in a semicircle around me: Matilda's, big and round with pointed ears; the two dogs, with flat snouts and floppy ears; then a small, pointed bandit face. They all were still, mouths tight, serious and waiting.

"What do you guys want?" They kept staring.

"We'll go on our walk in an hour."

But that wasn't it. It wasn't food, either. Somehow, I knew they wouldn't budge until I understood.

When I was a boy, I was always bringing home stray dogs and promising to take care of them. "Randy," my father said, "you're good at finding dogs, but you forget to feed them. Your mother does your job. These animals depend on you. You are responsible for them. You need to do better."

I looked at the faces of my pack and understood.

"Right. She's going to have to come here. I will never, ever, leave you guys behind."

Two calls to make before I responded to Athena.

"Raquel? It's Randy. I want to come by and see you and the kids."

She cried, then said, "Randy, Randy. When?"

In my picture of her, she hadn't aged. Dark skin and black hair to her shoulders. Her nose a bit too large, making her sexy. She had always been so good to my family.

We talked for ten minutes and set up a time for a visit. Two of Vince's kids were living on their own, but Raquel would make sure they came over. And I would tell them what a brave man their father was, and how he was my friend, and how much he loved his family.

And it would all be true. What I knew of his failings, I would take to my grave.

Then I made the second call.

"Mrs. Bradford," I said. "This is Randy. Randy Andrews. I brought Darnell home." We both started crying. Then she started laughing, said she was so happy I'd called. "I was hoping I could come by and visit next week," I said. She said I could come whenever I wanted. "Just give me a day's notice, Randy, so I can get the family over."

And I saw her again in my mind's eye—gray hair, late 60s by now. I was struck at Darnell's funeral how much he had looked like his mother.

"I loved Darnell, Mrs. Bradford. He was a real hero."

Then I dialed a number in Costa Rica—011 first.

AUTHOR'S NOTE

When I began writing this novel, the mountain caribou of Northern Idaho was the most endangered animal in the lower forty-eight states.

When Randy took his sons into the mountains of Northern Idaho in the fall of 2015, the Idaho/South Selkirk herd of mountain caribou numbered twelve animals. My estimate of fourteen animals was optimism.

Today, the animal is extinct in the continental United States. Once numbering in the thousands, this unique subspecies fell victim to habitat destruction, disease and predators. The last remaining American mountain caribou was captured in a net and taken by helicopter to a twenty-acre enclosure near Revelstock, British Columbia. It lives there today.

John's photographs would be the last taken of the herd.

Interestingly, a cougar killed the second-to-last remaining caribou.

www.ingramcontent.com/pod-product-compliance
Lightning Source LLC
LaVergne TN
LVHW091706070526
838199LV00050B/2292